I0614308

DAY ZERO
CREED MOOR

This is a work of fiction. Names, characters, places, and incidents are either the product of the author's imagination or are used fictitiously. Any resemblance to actual persons—living, dead or undead—events, and locales is entirely coincidental.

Library of Congress Control Number: 2018905616

ISBN 978-0-9914702-4-2
10 9 8 7 6 5 4 3 2 1

Edited by Judith Swain
Covers by Terry Fogarty

www.DayZeroBook.com

To the real Jude, the love of my life.
May your faith in me never diminish,
may your reflexes remain lightning quick,
and may your aim forever be true.

Acknowledgements

It is imperative to thank those who have supported and provided a measure of inspiration and drive as I wrote this book.

To Frank, a creative force in his own right, who is always a fount of knowledge for all zombie, comics, horror, and Family Feud. Keep making those films, friend!

To my fellow authors who made me realize that I could push myself even more than I thought I ever could—especially to the amazing Adrienne Lector whose friendship, work ethics and success with her Green Fields zompoc series is something I aspire to.

To my friends at Starbucks who are not just baristas serving me much needed coffee. Fernando is a beacon of goodwill. Erica and Andy put a smile on my face. Theresa is the avid reader who devours my advanced copies and challenges me to reflect upon my characters and story and defend them—all in an effort to craft a better story.

Last, and certainly not least, to my editor and partner, Judy, who supports me in all things. She may be the Day Zero series editor, but she is also an irreplaceable collaborator for the story and for my life.

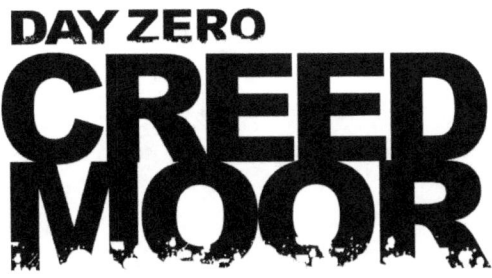

DAY ZERO
CREED MOOR

Written by Charles Ingersoll

Edited by Judith Swain

Terms

Bulkhead
A Naval and Marines term, meaning wall.

Exfil (also exfiltration or Extraction)
The process of removing targets out of a hostile environment and taken to a secured location.

Frontline
In military terminology, frontline is the position closest to the area of conflict of personnel and equipment.

Fuselage
The main body of the plane which holds the passengers and cargo.

Helo
Military slang for helicopter.

LZ
Military slang for landing zone.

Merc
Slang for mercenary. Someone who carries out combat missions but aren't part of an official organization, like the military, or CIA and are usually not motivated by justice or an allegiance.

Rack
Military slang for a bed or bunk.

Wetwork
Assassination, or a job that is likely to include killing someone.

Table of Contents

PROLOGUE

Reunions   3

DAY ZERO: CREEDMOOR

Chop, Chop   13
Freight   16
The Not-So-Great Escape   22
Vague Introductions   27
Remember When?   34
Getting Up In The World   37
Promotions   42
Bitter Rivalries   48
Foolproof   50
Heavy Heart   56
Costume Change   58
Ascent   63
Ramping Up   67
Altitude Adjustment   74
Voices Carry   80
Into the Breach   83
Check, Please   90
By Appointment Only   96
Razor's Edge   99
Incoming   104
Half-Court   107
Testing The Limits   115
Up, Up And Away   119
Branching Out   122
Any Crash You Can Walk Away From   129
Fast Friends   134
He Said, She Said   146
Ward of the State   152

Hard Landing	159
Stick Figures	162
Solace Before Daybreak	166
Huddle	168
Girl, Interrupted	176
Lemon Law	182
Laundry Day	194
The Sound of Silence	197
Ships, Rivers and Things Dreamt	199
Three Part Harmony	204
Bring Out Your Dead	208
Dirty Laundry	211
Under New Management	215
This Way, If You Please	219
All the World is a Stage	222
A Numbers Game	227
Lock and Load	230
Building Blocks	233
Joe Cocker Songs	236
The Mouth of Madness	239
Climbing the Stairway to Heaven	242
Deep Guano	244
Great Unwashed	249
Who Let The Dogs Out?	255
When the Bough Breaks	258
Fork In The Road	265
He Who Laughs Last	272
Pearly Gates	277
Bus Stop	280
Black Friday Rush	284
Remember the Alamo	289
Rinse Cycle	297
Simple Request	303
Put a Cork in It	306
Taking Stock	313
Every Tom, Dick, and Harry	315

Floating in the Ocean   317
Two Men, A Duffle and a Machine Gun   325
In Through the Out Door   335
Rubber Fetish   339
Sitting in Judgement   345
Going to the Chapel   351
Short Staffed   355
Council Counsel   363
Call to Arms   367
Refills   371
Exit, Stage Left   373

WHAT YOU NEED TO KNOW TO SURVIVE

Coming in 2019   383
Other Books by Charles Ingersoll   385
About the Author   387
Learn more and be social   389

PROLOGUE

CREEDMOOR

1

Reunions

+74 Days – 2249 hours

The intersection at Institute Road had Tuckerman to the left and Harvard to the right. The United Congregational Church—where I had saved Deb from the FRACs—stood quiet on the next corner. The massive concrete monolith of the Worcester Memorial Auditorium took up the entire block ahead to our right. The street map of the area was clear in my mind.

A few more steps and the Worcester Art Museum would be behind us.

"John."

Sean and the rest of our group would be ahead. Even Alex and the rest of the museum residents could be there as well.

"John," Jude repeated. "A light just flicked on."

She nodded up the block toward Salisbury Street and the entrances to the museum courtyard and the delivery bay.

A faint glow lit up the corner of the Renaissance Court atrium building. The street between the light and us was littered with piles of garbage.

Holly growled.

"It's not a fire," Jude said.

"And it's not light from the museum."

"Something new? Should we check it out?"

"Better to rule out more problems."

I drew up the Glock and stepped onto the sidewalk.

Jude, with Holly in her arms, followed at arm's reach.

We walked quickly up to the handicap parking lot along the courtyard fence, staying quiet and keeping low.

Thank you.

The children sang in unison from inside the walls.

You should have bugged out.

Bob echoed a warning from nowhere and everywhere, not making a physical appearance but leaving his words in his dreadful, dripping spectral voice.

We moved back to the sidewalk through an incline of dried bushes and mulch.

"Christ," Jude whispered.

The large lumps in the street were not garbage.

Amid the backpacks and shopping bags of supplies and food the bodies of the museum residents lay bleeding out in the street.

I moved closer.

Jude stared from the sidewalk, her face half buried in Holly's fur.

Double tap shot to the chest. And a single shot to the forehead.

The same was true with the next former museum resident.

My stomach turned.

The Benelli lay on the asphalt.

Percy stared at me from his side, his finger still on the trigger.

This may be your fault.

Bob pointed out something I already knew. Every member of Percy's party—all the people I told to leave for their own safety—lay in the street in their own blood.

They were all shot military style.

Make sure they don't get back up.

There were so many faces.

Most of their eyes were open.

Looking at me.

Blaming me.

Rightfully so, I would think.

"...lights." Jude said.

"What?"

"There's movement in the lights."

Shadows danced from beyond the corner of the atrium wall.

"Sergeant John Walken," boomed a voice through a megaphone.

"What the fuck?" Jude and I said in unison.

"I suggest you come forward to the front of the museum," the voice ordered, echoing off the walls of the building.

"You and your friend," the voice asked politely. "And the canine, if you please."

"Do we run?"

Motion came from our high 10 o'clock.

Snipers on the atrium roof

I looked at Jude and Holly.

Run, the little girl said.

"No," I shook my head, weary and defeated. "No more."

I walked toward the voice, careful not to disturb the bodies or the rivulets of blood in the street.

Jude and Holly followed, more slowly.

"Good," the amplified voice coaxed. "Very good."

When we reached the driveway, several red laser sights clicked to life. They trained on my bare chest. A couple found their way to Jude's forehead and one even to Holly's chest.

"Keep coming," the voice ordered. "Hands up, if you please."

"Very polite," Jude sneered.

My Glock went into its holster and my hands went to the top of my head. Jude did the best she could to comply.

We rounded the corner of the building. The searchlights from three HumVees bathed the area in white, blinding us.

When my eyes adjusted, I found Bowers and the others.

On the top step of the museum entrance, in front of the revolving door and its flanking single doors, were the remaining members of our group. All were in a kneeling position with their legs crossed at the ankles and their fingers interlaced on top of their bowed heads. Tears streamed down Summer and April's

5

faces. Melissa muttered something indecipherable. Victoria simply stared at the pavement. Only Bowers glared straight at the firing squad that stood on the driveway in front of them.

"I need you," I whispered. "Now."

Two mercenaries in black tactical gear peeled away from the vehicles, intercepted us, and escorted us to the bottom of the steps.

My muscles tensed.

"Please no drama, Sergeant," the voice anticipated. "The others will not fare as well as you, in any event."

One of the two mercs pulled out my Glock and pocketed it.

"I may kill you with that," I warned.

He scoffed at my comment as they both moved back to the row of Humvees.

"Should have run," Jude told me.

I looked at the snipers on the roof.

"Wouldn't have mattered."

"Young lady and puppy," the voice behind the searchlights ordered. "Please join your friends on the steps."

Jude held Holly tight while the dog growled. She stood defiantly until one of the soldiers put a M4 barrel to the back of her neck.

"Ok. Ok."

She climbed the steps and knelt down next to Summer.

"What do you want?" I yelled.

"I thought that was obvious," the voice answered. "We've come for our property."

"What are you talking about?" I asked.

"You are truly dense sometimes, Sergeant."

"Now," I whispered.

"The fact that you –" the voice was cut short.

Boom.

The large ornate metal doors to the museum vibrated.

Boom. Boom.

A dent appeared in the middle of the metal.

Glass broke from farther away.

A chorus of mews and growls could be heard.

The mercenaries trained their weapons and laser sights onto the bank of three separate doors.

"Now," I repeated.

Boom. Boom. Boom!

The doors rattled.

The mercs backed up a few steps for a better angle, clicking off the safety on their rifles. It put Bowers, Jude and the others in the crossfire.

The growling and banging stopped.

It was quiet for a moment before a soldier screamed from the opposite side of the parking lot. His gun discharged into the air. The little girl with the pigtails and strobing furry boots leapt up and bit into the soldier's exposed neck, ripping out skin, muscle and his carotid artery in one tear.

The other soldiers turned their guns to the little girl.

Thank you.

Thank you.

I tackled the closest guard.

His back broke as I slammed into his spine.

We both fell into another solder, taking him out at the back of the knees. I drove an elbow into his throat, crushing it.

More children appeared from around the corner. The soldiers opened fire. Practiced marksmanship dropped many of the small walkers with a single headshot each.

Still they came.

April panicked and screamed. She raced down the steps, straight into the crossfire. A bullet tore into her neck. She gurgled and slammed to the pavement.

"No!" Jude yelled.

"Stay put!" I yelled back.

Two of the mercenaries rushed to April's side, one of them clamping his meaty hands around the side of her neck to provide compression to her wound.

I grabbed a discarded M4 and fired at the backs of the three other mercenaries still holding their weapons on my people. They staggered but did not go down, two of them turning toward me.

Body armor.

I shot two of them in the head. That put them down.

The others continued to fire at the children.

A familiar pop and a pain in my thigh. I went down.

The children dragged down two more mercenaries to the grass.

Good.

More screams.

Victoria screamed. A stray teenage boy clamped his teeth onto her arm. It was the bully.

No! I yelled at it with my mind.

The bully stopped and turned back to stalk the soldiers. His head exploded as it was taken down by one of the rooftop snipers.

I pivoted and shot the offending sniper in the head. Another two shots took out the other one. The second sniper slumped dead against the parapet.

Victoria screamed again, holding her bitten and bleeding arm. She stood up and nodded at me.

No!

She shrieked and lunged at the closest soldier. The merc turned smoothly and shot her in the heart. She skidded to a stop on the bottom step.

I shot the soldier through the ear.

Bowers and Jude covered Summer and Holly.

Melissa searched wildly for the closest weapon.

"Enough!" the megaphone voice yelled. "Finish this nonsense, please, my dear."

A whoosh.

An explosion and a wave of heat rushed at my back.

RPG.

Another whoosh and whistle.

Another explosion of heat and flames. The new smell of burning rotten flesh. The children were ablaze, screaming in my head.

I turned toward the vehicles and shot out two of the searchlights. I pivoted to take out a third.

A fist came out of the light.

Pain.

Fog.

I arched back, sweeping my leg.

It connected with nothing.

Another fist connected to my temple.

I rolled out and onto my numb legs.

They didn't support me.

I fell to my side.

"John!" Someone called out with concern.

All I saw were shapes and silhouettes in the remaining lights.

Two slender forms wavered closer to me.

One moved right.

The double-click of a pump-action shotgun.

A barrel pressed against my temple.

"Douse the floods, please," the now unamplified voice commanded.

The remaining searchlight darkened, the space lit only by the Humvees' headlights.

The slender black form sharpened but was still dark. He wore a suit with a stark white dress shirt and a narrow black silk tie. He wore polished black wingtip dress shoes, even here in the field.

He crouched down, pulling up the creases of his dress pants.

The Gaunt Man examined me, making tsk-tsk sounds.

"My," an all too real version of my personal specter said,

"aren't you are a sad sight to behold? At any rate, it is good to have you found again."

"Let's clean up," he said to the others as he stood up.

I dove at the Gaunt Man.

A powerful fist to the back of my neck drove my face to the asphalt before I halved the distance to him.

Coming up on my hands, I spit out blood.

The Gaunt Man continued to walk back to the Humvees, paying me no mind.

I just registered the movement of the soldier to my right before a kick caught me in my midsection, flipping me onto my back. A boot quickly pressed square on my chest before I could roll away, the shotgun aimed at my face.

"Move and I clean up like the man said," a soft voice warned from behind the barrel.

The remaining searchlight came back to life, illuminating the dark raven hair and tan Latina skin of the familiar Marine standing over me.

"Rosalita?" I whispered in disbelief.

"Not anymore," she answered.

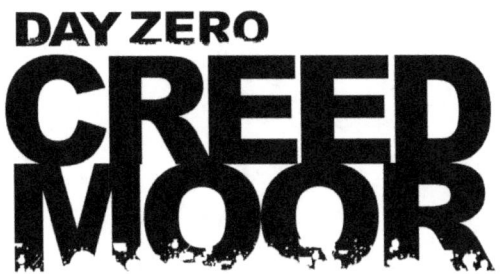

1

Chop, Chop

+76 Days – Night

The rhythmic chop of rotors was coupled with a dim world covered in dark gauze. There were distant murmurs I couldn't make out, my senses isolated with the dead headset over my ears. Iron shackles and chains bound my wrists to the steel deck. A blindfold covered my eyes. I didn't know exactly how much time had passed since the museum. At least two days, I would have guessed.

After the museum, I had been pushed into the back seat of a HumVee, Alvarez with her sidearm to my neck. Jude and the others had been taken away in their own truck. The real Man in the Black Suit had made a hasty exit as his private armored vehicle veered away while we made our way to the top of a parking garage roof-turned-helipad. Two Chinook helicopters had been warmed up, waiting. Even Bob, my trusty spectral companion, had opted out. Maybe he had realized he was irrelevant since I had run into the real deal on the steps of the Worcester Art Museum. That had left me with Alvarez and a team of mercenaries with itchy trigger fingers.

I was alone.

Before being blindfolded, I had caught a glimpse of the others being herded up the rear ramp of one of the Chinooks. Since, apparently, I was special, I had been loaded as the lone prisoner into the second impressive and massive transport helicopter. Not knowing how long we would be in-flight I had sat back against the fuselage and opted for sleep. The chop of the Chinook's blades through the air and the vibration of the helicopter's shell were comforting, in spite of the confinement and my flayed and punctured body.

Like the old days.

The days before the walking dead started to outnumber the living. The days when mission objectives were straightforward. The days where the hot desert sands and the gagging salt gulf air were the worst complaints. Back when I understood who the enemy was.

"It's all different now," a familiar female voice crackled through my now live headset.

I said nothing. I had the right to remain silent.

"*We* are different now," she continued.

I swallowed but kept my mouth shut.

"You're different, too," she said. "I can feel it."

My mind perked up, but I forced my body to stay relaxed.

The dead woman I had known as USMC Corporal Rosalita Alvarez moved toward me, her boots thumping hollowly on the steel deck. Even under my blindfold I could still feel the aura of her presence and the beat of her heart.

"I can definitely feel it coming off you." Alvarez wavered in front of me for a moment before sitting down on the bench across from me.

"What?" I asked, curiosity finally getting the better of me.

"The hum? The strange sensations running across your skin? Feeling the difference between the living and the dead?"

Yes, I felt it. It was impossible not to. The itch across the back of my neck whenever FRACs were close felt like angry bees buzzing under the surface.

"You know what I'm talking about," she confirmed for me.

My brain couldn't come to terms with her voice. The voice of a Marine and a woman I had failed to save from a mission that had quickly gone sideways. A woman I had loved once. I had seen her die.

"I died, you know," Alvarez said, as if plucking the thoughts directly from my brain. "Or maybe you didn't know. I saw you in the medic tent. I thought you died, too."

"No," I replied quietly. I wasn't sure which point I was responding to. Yes, I had thought she had died in that medic tent in the desert. That seemed like eons ago; before sharing a world with the undead.

We hit a pocket of air that made the transport shudder. The shock banged into my ruined back, the glass still embedded in the muscle and flayed skin. I hissed out air.

"You will heal, Marine. We both know that you will. Quit being a pussy," she teased. "But we do need to get those shards out soon. Before your body starts healing over them. I'm sure they'll take care of it when we land."

"Who?"

"The doctors at Roanoke & Raleigh."

2

Freight

+76 Days – Night

I rubbed the blindfold against the bulkhead. When I tilted my head back, I could see out from under the gauze and through the porthole to the landscape below. A swatch of dark blue gray water cut through the ashen and flame-filled landscape, one side with low industrial buildings and older suburbia while high-rise apartments and corporate offices rose out of the granite bedrock on the other. The cityscape, while dark and solemn against an even darker sky, was still instantly recognizable. We had flown to Manhattan, New York; the Big Apple of the Empire State.

Oh, how giants have fallen. Bob's voice echoed through my headset, rattling around my head more so than coming through the comms.

The pilots smoothly landed the Chinook atop a tall oval-shaped mirror-skinned building, the tallest of the dozens of Midtown skyscrapers creating urban canyons of concrete, steel and glass. From the air, the building's cross-section had looked like a stretched-out football with its points snipped.

The smell of oily smoke filled the cabin and my nostrils as the rear ramp hummed open and pitched to the deck. Someone came toward me, accompanied by the sound of jingling keys. He removed my shackles and blindfold, freeing me from both my tether to the deck and my veil of sensory deprivation. Two other mercenaries in black tactical uniforms arrived. They pulled me roughly to my feet and led me toward the rear of the helo. Once at the ramp, another soldier shackled my hands and feet to a chain that he wrapped around my waist.

"Taking enough precautions?" I asked him as he checked his

handiwork. "You afraid I'm going to hurl myself off the roof?"

"Following orders," he replied openly. "You understand."

"I guess I do," I admitted, testing the restraints anyway.

He moved aside and pointed me forward. Four pairs of boots stamped hollowly on the ramp until we touched down onto the surface of the helipad, the chains forcing me to take small hurried steps.

"Inside," Alvarez ordered as she caught up to us from the cabin, pushing me forward toward a set of steps and a roof access stairwell.

Another pair of mercenaries in black tactical gear—like those men already assigned to my security detail—drew their AR-15s up and followed us. R&R was not fooling around with how they armed their soldiers. These ARs were Connecticut made Colt LE6920 SOCOM IIs, considered by some to be the standard and preferred primary weapon of operators around the world.

One of the mercenaries trotted out of formation to open a door leading into a glass-walled lobby. Alvarez ushered me in with the rest of her squad drafting in behind us. There was no sign of Jude or the others. No indignant yells from Melissa. Not one bark from Holly. Sean and Jude would have never given our captors the satisfaction of verbal defiance, but I also didn't see any spilled blood or bruised faces.

We approached an elevator at the back of the lobby. Alvarez stepped forward and swiped a card across a security access reader. A bell chimed and the brushed steel doors slid open.

"After you," I offered with mock chivalry.

Maybe, not so mock?

"No, thanks." Alvarez pushed me inside with another show of her surprising strength. "Although you were always such the gentleman."

The mercs filed in behind the two of us, the barrels of their guns angled toward the floor in order for all of us to fit. The doors shut us into closed quarters with a limited range of motion. I was still shackled. Alvarez was still a wild card.

"Stand down, Marine," Alvarez said suddenly.

"What?"

Ding.

She leaned in closer. "I feel you tensing up. Don't be stupid. You'd lose. You're in chains in a confined space. This would be the worst place for you to make a move."

Ding.

My shoulders relaxed, but I continued to glare at her.

"Good boy," she complimented. "We may reunite you with your friends sooner than originally scheduled if you keep up this good behavior. We need that 'can do' attitude."

Ding.

We continued the rest of the ride in silence, all of us listening to the faint piped-in music and the chimes of the elevator as we descended. The guards started shifting from foot to foot, tightening their grips on their weapons. Alvarez, on the other hand, stayed loose and calm. She rested her right hand on the left breast pocket of her tach vest, away from her sidearm.

The elevator slowed before coming a smooth stop, denoted by a series of chimes and a metallic female voice announcing that we had arrived at 'P3'. The doors opened to reveal gray concrete and quick darkness beyond the glow of the elevator. A smell of death hung in the stale air. Low moans came from somewhere in the dark a long way off. The mercenaries did not move outside the car.

"Christ," Alvarez whined, "you're all pathetic. Move out of the way."

The mercenaries shuffled around the perimeter of the car until they were standing on either side of me. Alvarez stepped out into the parking garage, disappearing into the black.

"Come on," her bodiless voice called back.

One of the mercs poked me in the ribs, showing at least the

smallest measure of bravado. I gave him a sideways glance before stepping out of the elevator. The doors closed behind me, leaving the guards with soft white light and me in the dark.

A tap on my left shoulder.

"Made you look," she chuckled.

"You want to do something about these?" I asked, lifting up the chains and cuffs in a gesture close to prayer.

"Sorry. Those stay on for the time being," she replied. "Doctor's orders."

"You enjoying this?"

Alvarez didn't respond. Instead, she gestured me toward one of several medical curtain dividers illuminated by freestanding worklights. All around the garage—between the medical bays—were rows of stacked wooden crates labeled with oversized barcodes, the Roanoke & Raleigh corporate logo, and an abbreviated description.

"Straight ahead, please."

I did as I was instructed.

Walking between the crates, I read a variety of labels.

AK47.

M4.

9MM.

50CAL.

FLAK.

PLAST C4.

Lots of that last one and no shortage of the others. There were dozens more crates with dozens of different labels that were too hidden in shadows to read. The faint outline of crates stretched out for as far as I could see, stacked far beyond the sporadic pools of light. Small red letters marked EXIT floated at different intervals in the distance.

"Don't get any ideas, John," Alvarez warned.

I walked between two of the medical bay curtains. There was a smell of new death here to mix with the older rot that I recognized when the elevator doors had opened. The bay was well lit and lined with medical monitors, three glass front metal cabinets filled with medical equipment, and two rows of adjustable hospital beds.

Ah, memories.

You're always around when I don't want you.

Feels like you've died all over again, right? Bob said, ignoring my comment.

Shut it, Bob. Now is not the time.

When is it ever the time?

"Sit down," Alvarez ordered, appraising me with a tilt of her head.

I picked the closest bed. The faintest of stains dotted the sheets, the result of several heavily bleached cycles in the wash. "I thought I was going to get the best medical treatment."

"I guess the doctors are busy elsewhere," Alvarez speculated.

"No matter. I'll give you the best care. Then maybe I'll get a break and finally get a reward for my efforts."

She unlocked one of the cabinets and pulled out a deep stainless steel tray with several small handled forceps, rolls of medical gauze and adhesive tape. She circled behind me, placing her supplies on the bed.

"This is going to hurt," she advised, cutting through what remained of my stiff bloody clothes and dropping the rags on the bed beside me. She left the restraints on my wrists and ankles, but did gently pull the impromptu field dressing from my back. The clinking of metal on metal was replaced by the sensation of hot razor-edged spikes being pulled from my back. "A lot."

I hissed with pain.

"Take it like a man," Alvarez said. "We all have to deal with shit we don't want to."

Clink.

More digging into my flayed flesh.

Clink.

Clink.

"Christ, you did take on quite a bit of shrapnel, Sergeant."

"War is hell." I conceded with a sharp exhale.

3

The Not-So-Great Escape

+76 Days – unknown

An obscene amount of glass had piled up in the tray, along with more than a few twisted pieces of metal and large wood splinters. Once she completed the evacuation of my back, Alvarez had covered the area with a stinging salve, a shaped bandage, and a few more explicit remarks concerning my manhood.

I was tired. Maybe it was from the salve. Maybe I was finally coming down from the adrenaline rush or blood loss—or a combination of all three. In any event, my body needed to shut down at some point.

With me still in chains, we took the elevator to the next sublevel—P4. I shuffled along in front of her as she guided me with gentle pushes until arriving at a corridor with several doors.

Alvarez used her key card to access one of the rooms and pushed me inside. She unlocked my shackles and pulled away the looped chains, tossing them outside the small room. I thought about moving against her since she was alone, but a warm haziness was coursing through me.

Before I knew it, Alvarez stepped back into the corridor and closed the door. I was alone in a three-meter square windowless concrete walled room. A single LED light glared down at me from the middle of the low ceiling, now dimmed to its lowest setting. I sat down on the cot. It must have been brought in especially for me since the space was not designed for occupancy. Three waist-high gray steel storage units sat against the other wall, lined with several thin drawers.

My groggy mind was torn between thoughts of what had happened to Alvarez since the deserts of Pakistan and what R&R

was doing with Jude and the others. Alvarez had become something more, willingly embedding herself in the same military corporation that had a hand in altering her genetics. The real question was how the others were being treated.

You know they are in the building. And alive.

I was not alone. Unfortunately, it was the wrong company at the wrong time.

Bless reunions, dear John.

I sighed and looked up at the pale thin man in his retro black suit with its crisp white dress shirt and skinny black tie. His chalky skin pulsed in the dim room, casting a faint glow.

"Our reunion?" I asked.

You and me? No. No. I'm always going to be around. Bob said with a shake of the head. *I am referring to your long-lost girlfriend.*

"Did you know about Alvarez, Gaunt Man?"

What? Gaunt Man? I thought we had grown past those formal titles?

"Fine," I conceded. "Did you know about Alvarez... Bob?"

Bob beamed, showing his brilliant white teeth. Finally, he waved his hands and spoke. *No. I did not know about her.*

"I thought you knew everything?"

He shrugged his bony shoulders. *Apparently, she was outside my scope of knowledge.*

"That's your story?"

It is the best I have, I am afraid.

"That's pretty weak, Bob."

And so are you. You need to rest.

"I need to get to my people," I replied, feeling the weariness in my bones.

And how do you propose to do that?

The locks to the storage room door clicked.

"Like this."

The door opened and I rushed it. A guard swung his AR-15 toward me as I drove a shoulder into his gut. I pushed him into the corridor's opposite concrete wall, hearing a crack and a pained exhale. His rifle clanked off the ground. I grabbed for it as the guard slumped down the wall with his arms hugging his waist.

A boot heel connected to my temple.

My vision flashed.

My knees buckled.

I lost my grip on the weapon, hearing it slide away.

"Cut the shit, John," Alvarez ordered, looming over me. "We don't have time for this."

I looked past her into the storage room that doubled as my jail cell. Bob, my flaky and annoying ghostly companion simply shook his head.

Don't judge me, Bob. You weren't any help.

"Hey, Marine?" Alvarez asked. "Do you want this food or what?"

I looked at the covered hospital-style tray and smelled something that reminded me of Thanksgiving... turkey and gravy. I didn't say anything, but Alvarez smiled at me all the same. She grabbed me painfully around the bicep and half-led, half-dragged me back into the storage room. She deposited the covered tray on top of the storage cabinet.

"Don't worry about Victors," she confided in a whisper, the scent of vanilla coming off her hair. "He's been a bit of work to train. Hopefully, your outburst will make him realize that he needs to get his shit together."

She chuckled, her warm breath hitting my neck and ear. It raised a flash of goose bumps on my neck, a much better feeling than the ache I got when the undead were closing in.

Isn't she one of the undead now?

Like me? Not unless R&R killed her a second time.

I am fairly certain that Diggs was not affiliated with Roanoke & Raleigh.

That's what I'm saying.

Alvarez backed out of the room. Victors was still on the floor, holding his arms to his chest and taking in ragged breaths. She turned to him as she closed the door. The deadbolts engaged.

Yes, two deadbolts on a solid steel door.

"Get up, shit heel" I heard Alvarez say in a sweet tone to Victors.

Sweet tone? I assume that you are being sarcastic.

Maybe. She always had a hard way about her.

And that appeals to you?

Makes it easier.

Relationships. Certainly, nothing easy about them.

I sighed my agreement and pulled off the cover on the food tray. I was rewarded with a thick paper plate with slices of turkey breast smothered with a light brown, spiced gravy. It even came with two pieces of wheat toast with pats of butter.

I hope the food does not have the same problems as the eggs at the museum.

I didn't care. It was the best thing I had tasted in the last several days. It only took me a couple minutes to devour the white meat and use the toast to sop up every drop of gravy. I washed it down with a swig from one of the bottled waters I realized had been lined up against the wall.

In spite of my belly's contentment, the satisfying knitting feeling in my back, and the warm wash of sleepiness behind my eyes, curiosity forced me to open the storage cabinet drawers. Each was filled with flat blueprints. Licking my thumb, I started to leaf through the drawings, if for no other reason than to quell the Gaunt Man's voice in my head until notoriously elusive sleep actually arrived. At the very least, it would serve as a distraction to keep me from scratching my back against the wall to relieve the itch that I knew should be left alone.

4

Vague Introductions

+78 Days – unknown

"Your cooperation would be greatly appreciated, John," Alvarez advised, digging her fingers into my bicep again. She led me through a service corridor to a different bank of elevators than the one we used upon my arrival. "I know it's been a couple days since I last saw you and I don't want you to forget your manners."

"A couple days," I mumbled, reeling at the fact that I had been left so long by myself.

You were not alone. You had me.

Alvarez leaned in. "You haven't forgotten that we also have your friends, right?"

"Why do you think I attacked your man?" I glared at her. She held her eyes on mine, not looking away. When I realized she was prepared to dig in for a staring contest, I relented and asked a different question. "How's Victors doing?"

She didn't respond but her vise-like grip remained around my arm. The brushed steel doors slid open after a quiet chime announced the car's arrival. The interior was deeper than a typical office elevator, with oak trim and a set of doors on the opposite end. Alvarez directed me inside and pressed me against the sidewall with one hand while she entered a pass code and the button for the desired floor with the other. Once the elevator chimed again and the doors slid closed, she released me.

Damn, she was strong.

"Nice shirt," Alvarez said with a smirk. "Seems appropriate."

I wore an undersized black T-shirt with a Kiss licensed Detroit Rock City tour graphic on the front. One of Alvarez's men had tossed in a stack of shirts not long after my attack on Victors.

"I see the back is healing, too," she added. "No bleed through?"

"Not through this shirt, at least."

"Good. I don't need you bleeding all over the place."

"Gee, thanks. You're all heart."

"Hey, I need you at 100%."

"Why's that?"

Alvarez opened her mouth but the elevator rolled to a smooth stop and the doors opened onto a carpeted lobby with a semi-circular brushed aluminum reception desk. The plush burgundy worked well with the earth-tone wall colors and wall mounts. Behind the un-manned lacquered cherry desk were heavy chrome panels bolted to the wall at different depths, creating a set of floating plates. Thick raised san serif letters spelled out Roanoke & Raleigh across them.

Alvarez prodded me right of the reception desk, guiding me through a curved corridor with a bank of offices on the outer wall and larger conference rooms on the interior. A hulking older grizzled veteran with a scar across the bridge of his nose and a fresh out of Basic mercenary stepped out from one of the offices. They fell in line behind us as Alvarez opened a black glass door on our left and waved me inside. The others moved to either side of the door without coming inside.

The conference room was at least fifteen meters deep by five meters at its widest, with curved sidewalls framed with floor to ceiling blackened glass. A second door was opposite from where we entered. The near end of the conference room boasted a huge white board with a motorized retractable projector screen halfway covering it. The far end had an array of four inset flat screen monitors with slowly bouncing and colliding colored balls.

An elongated oval high gloss cherry table filled the center of the space with high back leather upholstered chairs around it. The table was covered with an assortment of fruit, muffins, and two silver roll top chafers steaming with what smelled liked sausage and eggs. There might even be melted cheese in those eggs, making them more akin to omelets.

My stomach growled.

"Sit."

I walked toward the food, Alvarez shadowing me from the other side of the table. Picking a chair near the monitors and the hot food, I pulled it out and sat down. The padding and lumbar support felt great on my back, almost as if my skin and muscles had not been ripped open with shards of glass, shotgun pellets and broad swords less than a week ago.

"Comfy?"

"Peachy," I replied, less interested in her words than in the food spread out before me.

"Don't touch anything."

I tapped my fingers in my lap.

Alvarez stood at parade rest in front of the monitors. The balls bounced off where the contour of her shadow hit the screen instead of continuing to the edges.

Alvarez's earbud buzzed to life.

"Why-bee-are," came over the open channel in perfect digitized clarity to my heightened hearing.

"Acknowledged. Out." Alvarez responded to her raised wrist. One of the monitor balls ricocheted off the tip of her elbow as she returned her arm to her side.

With a bang of the door, the mercenary War Horse and his Spring Chicken partner entered the room with a fluid movement and their ARs drawn like they were clearing the room of suspected insurgents. They separated and circled the room, passing Alvarez at the same time as they moved in opposite directions around the perimeter. Alvarez slightly rolled her eyes, making sure that her men didn't notice. The maneuver was excessive and pointless in a secured room in the center of an already locked down building, but it had been amusing to watch.

Maybe they are trying to impress the boss.

Or, maybe, they are afraid of the boss.

War Horse and Spring Chicken regrouped at either side of the now open door, their weapons lowered but their bodies tense. I was now flanked with Alvarez at the head of the conference room and the mercs at the door. The other door, still closed, was not covered.

"Stay put, Marine," she ordered, quickly coming around and pressing her hands into my shoulders. She pushed me deeper into my chair. "I don't need any black marks on my watch while the boss is around."

I continued to contemplate making a break for the door.

"Don't make me hurt you, Sergeant," she said, leaning close enough to feel her breath on my neck as she continued to feel my muscles tense. "It won't go well if you do. For you or the others."

I exhaled and rolled my shoulders, trying to relax.

"Good boy. Here he comes."

A black silhouette slid across the panes of dark windows. The mercenaries straightened to attention. The Gaunt Man came into the room, more solid and less illuminant than I was used to. He still wore the same black suit, crisp white dress shirt, narrow black tie and shiny, black wing tip shoes that I had become familiar with.

"Don't get up. Don't get up," he said, patting down the formality with a wave of his hands.

Alvarez firmly kept her fingers on my shoulders.

This Gaunt Man's voice was different now. It had less reverberation and echo. His words didn't cut into my head with surgical precision; didn't mix up the dormant hornet's nest that now permanently resided inside my skull, currently slumbering under a cloud of smoke. He made his way around the other side of the conference table toward the monitors. He stopped for a moment to the left of the screens before walking across to the other side, the balls on the screens deflecting off his shadow. The balls behind him drifted off his back like a smoking contrail.

"I never get tired of that," he commented to himself with a smile. He turned and walked across the front of the monitors again, stopping at the center of the four. The balls disintegrated into black, the bold silver logo for Roanoke & Raleigh replacing them in the center of each screen.

"Sergeant Jonathon Nathanial Walken," he began, "I am thrilled to see you again. It has been much too long."

"We met?"

"Quiet," Alvarez ordered.

"That's quite alright, Ms. Alvarez. Sergeant Walken is welcome to ask anything of us he wishes."

Alvarez let go of my shoulder and stepped back from my chair.

"Yes, Sergeant," the man who would be Bob said, "we have met before. In the desert before you were discharged. You may remember me from the medical tent where we found you and the Corporal after that disastrous showing at that mud heap village in Afghanistan last year. Horrible intel on that mission. Should have been scrubbed before it was ever considered a go. Regardless, though, we do have you and Ms. Alvarez as a result."

"You were the one who put the needle in my neck?"

"Ah," he clapped his hands together. "You do remember!"

"I didn't catch your name."

"I do not recall offering it."

"Are you offering it now?"

"When the time is right. It is a 'need to know' sort of thing."

"So I'll call you Dick."

He clenched his teeth, his cheeks flexing. "I would prefer you did not."

"Ok, Dick."

The newly named Dick clenched his fists until the knuckles turned white. He suddenly released and splayed his fingers, putting on a wide smile. "At any rate, we will not be in company long, I am afraid."

"And why is that?"

"We have a job for you."

"Didn't realize I was a contract employee of Roanoke & Raleigh."

"More like indentured servitude if you have to put a proper label on it," Dick said. "You are more property than an employee."

"Because you put some shit in my neck?"

Alvarez stepped closer to my chair, looming behind me.

"Yes," Dick agreed, looking between the corporal and me. "Exactly because of that. We have use of your skills, but will write you off if we need to. For the greater good, you see. In the end, I believe you will make the correct choice."

"And why is that?"

"Because you want answers," he mused as he approached the chafers to help himself to a plate of scrambled eggs and two sausage patties. "And because if you don't we'll be sure that you will suffer something worse than death."

"And what's worse than death?"

He held the plate from the bottom and shoveled a fork full of eggs into his mouth. He chewed it quickly and swallowed it down hard. He wolfed down another bite of eggs and half a sausage patty.

"What's worse than death?" He reiterated my question as he pointed the fork with the remainder of the sausage patty at me. "I know you don't fear death. You are death. That fact is proofed by the body count you have amassed in your path. You never racked up as high as a death rate in your entire career as a Marine."

"So, what's worse?"

"Simply put?" He shrugged. "The death of all of those people you hold close to your heart. We have plenty to choose from so we can prolong the agony for as long as we need to until you come to your own epiphany. Do you think we really needed to patch up the young woman? It was a shame, though, that we lost the other one at the museum."

"You mean Victoria?" I asked, hammering home the fact that the woman had a name.

He went back to eating the sausage and eggs on his plate, walking around the conference table as he did so. His heartbeat was steady and slow, with a faint odd cadence to it. The pulses of the mercenaries were slightly more rapid, but steady. I couldn't feel any rhythmic vibrations from Alvarez but did sense a general darkened murmuring aura sweating off her.

"What say you?" he asked, setting the plate and the fork on the conference table before grabbing an apple from the bowl of fruit. "Would you prefer to help pay off your debt?"

I thought of Summer, a young life that would never have a real sense of innocence or normalcy again. She had already been plagued with so much death. Sergeant Sean Bowers and his quest for a redemption cut short. April and Melissa, having suffered loss, facing a uncertain future because of me.

Jude…

I pushed the thoughts away. I wouldn't give Dick the satisfaction of thinking he could manipulate me through my friends. "Go fuck yourself," I said, instead, through gritted teeth.

"Well," Dick said with an understanding nod and a slight furrow in his brow. He put the apple back in favor of more sausages. "I will let you think more about your answer. In the meanwhile, I have to tell you that I am famished."

5

Remember When?

+78 Days – morning

Dick hadn't explained the plan in more detail after my refusal. I wasn't offered breakfast as a consolation prize. Alvarez had returned me to my concrete bunker of a prison cell without another word, the only sound being the slide of the deadbolts behind me.

I slid down the wall opposite the door and stared at it. After a few minutes, the solitary LED light started to flicker and tick. Another minute passed before it went dark altogether. I sat in the darkness amid the cabinets, cot, water bottles and floor plans, still able to make out vague shapes in the dark sealed room.

"Figures."

It does, does it not?

"Dick is a bigger prick than you are."

I will take that as a compliment.

"You can take it any way you'd like."

Aren't you curious why you are here?

"And you know all?"

I know enough.

"To be dangerous."

That is one way to see it.

Bob materialized into a bright form, mirroring me by taking up residence on the floor against the locked door. He looked solemn, almost earnest.

"So?"

It is amazing how poor your memory is, John.

"And what should I know?"

Do you not remember your last mission?

"Of course." I did remember. Botched from the jump, the

mission had been about securing and eliminating a high-value insurgent target in the arid craggy terrain on the Afghan border. The intel had been incomplete. Shitty, actually. The enemy's military strength had been underestimated. I had lost my entire team that night.

Except Alvarez.

"Apparently." But she had died. I had carried her out of the hot zone with a barely drivable Russian-made transport. I had airlifted her back to command where she ended up on a gurney with her life seeping out of her body.

Always with a flair for the dramatic. You saw her bloody on a gurney. You did not see her die.

"No," I admitted, "I didn't see her die"

Her wide-open eyes staring off into space and her chest failing to rise to bring in breath seemed like a good indication of her death, in my opinion. Why would I think she had survived after all that?

You survived.

"But I wasn't dying in that medical tent."

Yes, you died on Rainier Island when Diggs got the jump on you.

Yes, I did die that day at the hands of a childish handyman-turned-sociopath. Diggs was an island local who had discovered that injecting the living with the brackish blood of the undead was more fascinating than pulling the wings off of flies or dunking bags of cats into the Atlantic Ocean. A man who, after the FRACs started to appear, decided to experiment on island residents. Shit, why would anyone suspect that people hadn't abandoned the island to search for their loved ones on the mainland? Turning them and letting them loose once they turned into undead walkers was more fun for him. It satisfied his morbid curiosity… and his psychotic urges. Several days had passed before the mystery of how FRACs possibly could have been sighted inside a secure perimeter had been solved.

Diggs had killed me with his injection of necrotic black goo. He had changed me. Something that would never have been approved by the scientists of Roanoke & Raleigh. At least, I didn't think so. R&R couldn't know what Diggs did to me. The real Man in the Black Suit, now several floors above me, had been there at the medical tent that day after the mission failed to inject me in the throat. What did the mix of both doses do to me that R&R wasn't aware of?

R&R had injected Alvarez, saving her life. But at what cost?

Don't forget after.

"After?" I asked. "After what?"

Vague recognition swept through my brain. The Man in the Black Suit had visited me at the military hospital after they airlifted me out of the desert to a U.S. military base in Germany. I had thought that had all been a bad dream.

Like Bob.

No. He was there. He was not a figment of your imagination.

"Not a figment like you."

For the record, sir, I am as real as you are.

"You do realize how crazy you sound, right?" I asked.

No crazier than you. You are talking to someone only you can see, are you not?

36

6

Getting Up In The World

+79 Days – unknown

The deadbolts to the cell slid back and the door opened. Alvarez stood in the doorway, her hands on her curvy hips. Behind her, a quartet of mercenaries stood two to each side of her with their weapons drawn. Three of the forefingers relaxed against the trigger guards while a fourth—Victors again—pressed a finger with a little too much pressure on the trigger of his AR.

I tensed.

Alvarez sighed.

With impressively quick reflexes, the former corporal grabbed the barrel of Victors' weapon. She pushed the stock into his shoulder and him into the wall with it. She released the barrel and continued her elbow into the center of his face. Victors' nose cracked loudly and burst into a splatter of red. His eyes rolled up into white and his legs gave out. He slid to the floor in a heap, unconscious, Alvarez grabbing the stock of the AR before it hit the floor.

The other three soldiers of fortune had barely reacted by the time Alvarez turned back to me with the rifle in her hand.

"Thanks for the heads up, John," Alvarez admitted. "He was always so twitchy. I don't think there was hope for him."

"I didn't say anything."

"You didn't have to. You should have realized that by now. We are simpatico, Marine." Then she looked at me with a cocked head. I wasn't sure if she was mocking me or gazing at me with a measure of genuine concern.

"What?"

"I don't know, John." She shrugged. "Maybe you really don't

37

have a clue what's going on with you these days."

"I'm not sure anyone knows what's going on these days."

"That's not too far from the truth."

I moved a step forward.

The three remaining soldiers backed up a step with their weapons still up. They were quick to react to me, but none of them had helped their fallen comrade.

Thud... thud.

Each of their heartbeats were elevated but still controlled. Victors, on the other hand, had no heartbeat. I felt his body temperature increasing and his core aura darkening.

"Don't worry about him," Alvarez assured me. "He probably won't turn."

"Doesn't he have to be bit?"

"Is that how you think the world works? Geez, John, have you been on an island somewhere?"

"Are we going somewhere? Or are you just here to air out my cell?"

"Oh shit! I almost forgot." Alvarez winked and smiled as she slapped a palm to her forehead. "The boss wants to see you."

"Am I going to get something else to eat?"

"Sorry about that before. He can be a little eccentric."

"Are the others getting food and water, at least?"

"Who? Your girlfriend, the kids, the grunt, and the bitches? You mean those people?"

"Are they at least being treated okay?" I asked with a sigh.

"For now," she admitted. "We have only been giving you the special treatment and the deluxe accommodation."

"Wonderful."

"Quit your whining. You have more than handled it."

"We going?" I asked curtly, realizing the isolation and scarce rations were an attempt to make me more pliable. I barely slept these days. I wondered what my limits for not eating and drinking were. The worst part of all this scheduled deprivation was having to listen to Bob most of the time.

"Sure, Sergeant. Come on." She relented a little bit. "You've always been so sensitive. Must be because of your childhood."

She knew more about my upbringing than anyone else. Probably the only one left who knew anything about my personal life before the Corps. There had been more than one occasion in the barracks where we had shared a cot and exposed parts of our past... parts of ourselves.

I walked through the doorway and headed in the direction Alvarez pointed me behind two of the mercenaries. Alvarez and the remaining guard closed ranks behind me. Victors was left behind dead in a pool of his own blood. We headed to the bank of elevators where the doors were already open. The two forward guards moved aside. I stepped to the rear of the car with Alvarez and the others filing in behind me. Not bothering to turn around, I stared at the closed doors at the other end of the car.

A button was clicked behind me, lighting up the number 48 on the duplicate panel to my right. The cab lifted smoothly and quickly, a bell chiming as we passed each floor.

I could take the mercenaries. The closed quarters of the elevator car would work in my favor. Rifles were difficult to draw up with so many people. By the tenth floor, I had figured out how to disarm and immobilize the troops. That left Alvarez with her superior strength and newly-honed skills.

Ding.

I needed something quick and lethal.

Ding.

If she was anything like me, she wouldn't be easy to take down without going for a killing blow right from the get-go.

Ding.

We slowed just as smoothly as we had accelerated, a double chime announcing our arrival to the forty-eighth floor. The doors slid open to reveal War Horse and Spring Chicken standing in the lobby.

No one moved.

Thump... thump.

The noise in my ears, or maybe inside my head, quickened.

Thump, thump.

Weapons from the corridor rose ever so slightly.

"Jesus Christ," Alvarez said with a groan. "John, get your ass off the elevator, please."

"If I don't?"

"Then you will end up in the lobby anyway," she said, "but with a dislocated knee and a limp."

"Fine," I replied, already regretting not taking action instead of trying to think myself around it. A chime sounded and the doors started to close. I threw an arm up and the doors halted and retracted.

Like magic!

Bob was never too far away, even if he decided to stay hidden inside my mind. I stepped a meter out into the lobby and stopped. The soldiers in the elevator had to squeeze past me, brushing against me. I couldn't help but smile as I did all I could to be an inconvenience. The third guard purposefully bumped me with his shoulder, not amused.

A hand slapped against the back of my skull. Hard. My head rocked forward.

"Enough, John," she hissed as she leaned in to whisper to me, not amused by my antics. "I can't have you in the field acting like an incompetent idiot."

"In the field?"

"I don't want to spoil the surprise," Alvarez said as she put on a sweet smile. "I'll let the boss fill you in on the details. He tried to tell you the last time you had a chance to speak."

That smile brought back too many memories that I didn't want to acknowledge. However rational my mind wanted to be about seeing her, Alvarez stirred up something in my heart that my brain couldn't circumvent and think logically around.

You are letting yourself be manipulated.

She must be redeemable. R&R can't have their claws that deep into her. She was a good Marine. She was a good person.

I would not be so sure.

7

Promotions

+79 Days – morning

I was escorted to the same conference room as before, facing disappointment. There was no food on the table. In fact, there was nothing on the lacquered cherry surface at all. The monitors were dark save the R&R corporate logo suspended in the middle of each screen.

"Have a seat," Alvarez ordered.

I complied by sitting in the same conference chair. Leaning back, I could hear the chair springs creak quietly with just the right amount of lumbar support. Fortunately, the gashes and punctures in my back had healed over completely. The body was an amazing engine for self-repair. My body just happened to be turned up to eleven—although that hadn't made the itching any less annoying.

Alvarez, War Horse and Spring Chicken moved to three of the four corners of the room. They stood at attention, not acknowledging me or each other. The room took on a decidedly oppressive feeling with the stoic stares and tight lips.

Finally, a slight crackle and a murmur brought Alvarez's finger up to her right ear. She whispered something into her wrist, Secret Service style. Just like last time. "Suit in twenty."

The other sentries stood straighter and taller, their senses on high alert and their fingers pressed tighter against the trigger guards of their weapons. Spring Chicken glanced at his rifle nervously. I think he needed to remind himself whether his AR's safety was flipped on or off.

Seconds later, fuzzy outlines moved in a processional across the tinted glass wall. The door swung in and a new man in black tactical gear stepped inside the room to hold it open.

Dick, the Man in the Black Suit walked in. He strode with purpose to the front of the conference room, stopping in front of the monitors. He didn't acknowledge my presence or glance at me. Instead, he seemed pre-occupied with other matters as he stared at the doorway with his hands clasped in front of him.

Movement at the door caught my attention. As Jude entered, our eyes locked. Hers widened with something close to surprise and relief. She looked good. Her wounds had been tended to and she was decked out in a clean pair of skinny jeans and a peasant top. While all that was new about her, Jude still wore her well-worn cowboy boots and her silver rings. The nervous Spring Chicken directed her to the chair opposite me.

"Thank you," she said to him as she took her seat. When she saw my face, she gave me a slight smile and a shrug. "Never hurts to have manners."

Bowers' arrival into the room was not as cordial. Sporting a bruised jaw and one darkened and bloodshot eye, the Sergeant shuffled in with his hands at his waist in zip tie restraints. Small drops of blood were splattered on the shoulder of his shirt. He had not been offered new clothes.

Or, maybe, he had refused.

Bowers definitely didn't look to be in an agreeable mood. He looked up from the floor and locked eyes with me. I wasn't sure what I saw there. Defiance? Hatred? Both were great qualities to harness in a fight, but both came at a cost as they artificially fueled bravery and clouded actions with recklessness and impulsiveness.

War Horse took Bowers by the arm and steered him into a chair at the other end of the table. Bowers twisted his arm out of his grip with a venomous look. War Horse smiled at him and made a quick lunge that made Bower cringe. He slumped smaller in the chair and remained quiet, his eyes focused on his lap.

Summer came in next, holding hands with April. The older girl sported gauze and medical tape around her neck where she had taken the bullet from the museum skirmish. They both looked well. Melissa followed them with one hand on each of them. She walked behind them as a shield against the two trailing soldiers on their detail.

The last of us.

Each of them survivors.

April had lost her boyfriend Lenny when her professed soulmate shielded her from the hulking knight of a mad king. Melissa had lost both her father and her sister—Summer's mother—to the undead. Jude hadn't spoken much about her family, other than to allude to having a hand in putting them down once they'd turned. I'd lost men and women, both in fields of battle around the globe and here stateside. Bowers may have lost the most. I didn't know what family he had left, or where they may be holed up if they were alive, but he carried the heavy burden of knowing he had a part in pillaging and plundering down the east coast, resulting in the cold-blooded murder of more people than he probably had ever mentioned.

"You okay?" I asked Jude, leaning forward and keeping my voice low. "Where's the mutt?"

She nodded and pointed her index finger down on the table.

We were all here. Somewhere.

"Why are we here?" Bowers boomed, piercing the heavy silent tension in the room with heavy animosity.

"Sergeant," Dick began, as if on cue, "I will not keep you waiting." He spread out his arms as if he was a minister officiating a wedding. The monitors behind him popped to life. Each showed a quadrant of an overgrown and fenced-in complex of early 20th Century industrial-looking buildings. The aerial shot was a live feed from a high-altitude reconnaissance drone, the video in high resolution with the time stamp ticking away in the corner of the lower right monitor.

"Welcome to the Creedmoor Psychiatric Center. Fifty

buildings on over three hundred acres," Dick boasted, although I was fairly sure neither he nor R&R had a hand in erecting any of the structures.

The aerial feed changed as the drone adjusted its angle in its counter-clockwise circuit over the facility's perimeter. At its current height, the drone's camera caught a breathtaking sight that made all of us gasp. A four-lane road bordered the campus. Against some sort of barrier—most likely a fence—was stacked a swarming mass of bodies. The mob of undead illustrated the perimeter in perfect relief as they swarmed against one side. A few dots wandered around inside the perimeter too; slowly moving around a horseshoe shaped drive that led to a larger building with a main central area and major wings extending out from it on each side. Two smaller annexes jutted out perpendicular from them.

Looks like a comb.

Can you please keep quiet, ghost?

I prefer Bob, please.

Fine.

Bob sat in the chair at the other end of the conference room next to the unimpressed and seething Bowers. The near twin to the Man in the Black Suit, Bob leaned back in his chair before pitching it upright and spinning it around in a slow circle. After three rotations he faced forward again, slapping his palms on the table to stop and steady himself. His antics did nothing to break Bowers' anger.

Dick cleared his throat.

"I do require your full attention, Sergeant Walken."

"Keep talking," I replied without taking my eyes off Bob. "I can hear you."

Dick and Bob shrugged at the same time.

"This center was home to several notable residents over the years," Dick lectured, "including Woody Guthrie and Lou Reed. I imagine the young women at the table have no idea who those people were. Very popular and influential to the music industry in their day."

"Is there a point coming?" I shifted to look at the corporate bureaucrat in front of the still-panning aerial surveillance feed.

"I am coming to that, sir," Dick said through a gritted smile.

"I hope so," I said with a wave of my hand to the room. "Because this is getting old."

"Very well," Dick acknowledged, his face flushing to a pale pink for a moment before it disappeared again. "To business."

He paced, patting Alvarez on her arm and nodding as he passed. As he reached the end of the conference table, Dick stopped and put his hands on the back of the chair where Bob was sitting. Bob looked over his shoulder at his more substantive twin.

"There is a man at this facility," Dick began again, "who must be exfiltrated from the property and brought here." He pointed to the monitors. The panels flickered away from the continuing aerial feed to a still photograph of a young man with a slight build, long brown hair and a tight well-trimmed beard. The target looked like a young folk singer.

Maybe one of the musicians that he seems to like so much.

"You have men for this, Dick," I said, continuing to annoy him with my pet name. "Why do you need me?"

"Yes, I have men at my disposal. But I require someone with your specific skill set, Sergeant Walken."

"You have Alvarez here," I pointed to my former Marine sniper spotter.

"She is only one woman. The operation requires more than one special operator."

"And why should I help you?"

"One, because it is in your nature," Dick said, extending his forefinger as he counted. "Two, because it would be in your best interest…"

Alvarez stepped forward, pulling something from her vest.

46

Before I could react, she pulled aside Jude's head with her bicep and pressed a pressure power injector to Jude's neck.

"What the…" was all Jude got out.

Hiss. Click.

I lunged across the table at Alvarez. She slid Jude and her chair out of the way. Her fist connected to my face.

Crack.

Summer screamed.

Alvarez's elbow struck the back of my neck, the force crashing me against the table.

"Fuckers!" Bowers yelled as he kicked back his chair.

War Horse tackled him.

Melissa huddled over a distraught Summer and April. Curses and cries sounded out from around the room. Jude held her neck where a thin rivulet of blood had started to fall. Alvarez pinned me with her full weight on my shoulders. I tried to shake out from under Alvarez's hold, but couldn't.

Dick came around the table and squatted down in front of me so that our eyes were at the same level. He made sure that his dress pants pleats were adjusted to his liking before he continued to count the reasons why I would be helping him on this operation. "And, three, because Ms. Sawyer has forty-eight hours before the injected micro-capsule detonates."

8

Bitter Rivalries

+79 Days – morning
47:15:23

Dick had quickly left the conference room after listing his compelling reasons why I would help him on this mission. After that, all hell had broken loose.

My vision was glazed under shades of red.

I hurled Spring Chicken against the glass wall on the side of the conference room. His momentum rattled the transparent material without breaking it. He slid down the wall to the carpet in a heap.

"Stand down," War Horse ordered, his AR pointed at me and his finger squeezing against the trigger. I spun around and hurled a chair at him, catching him broadside and sending him to the carpet. As he struggled to get untangled, Bowers rushed over and delivered a two-fisted axe handle to his jaw, his hands still bound. Warhorse stopped trying to get out from under the office furniture as he slipped into semi-consciousness.

Melissa huddled with the girls in the corner by the closed door. Jude sat in her chair and held her neck, her eyes still wide with disbelief.

"You serious about this, Sergeant?" Alvarez asked, stepping in front of my sightline.

"Try me," I hissed, my anger needing an outlet ever since Dick had left the room.

"Okay." She pistoned out her arms, her palms slamming into my chest.

I sailed into the shatterproof transparent wall. It also shuddered, but held, against my impact. Landing on my feet, I launched myself at her. She caught me mid-air with her elbow under my armpit, hurling me headlong over the table and into the opposite wall where I crashed into the just-reviving Spring Chicken.

Alvarez pounced on me, both hands grabbing the back of my shirt and pulling me off her R&R merc flunky. She swung me around like a ragdoll, throwing me on the table again. This time I landed on my back. She leapt over the table like it was a 2nd graders' desk, wrapping my neck in the crook of her arm as she slid me to the edge of the table where she leaned against it.

"Stop, Walken" she whispered in my ear. "It's not hopeless."

Alvarez had never called me by my last name unless we were intimate. This display was rough but it was far from a close encounter. It was enough to bring the world—or at least this confined room—back into some semblance of order.

"The node in your girlfriend's neck is not irreversible," she assured me. "The boss just wants your co-operation. He's on a clock for some reason."

I relaxed a bit more.

"I'm going to let you up," Alvarez told me. "Let me fill you in on the op. It's in and out."

Even in Alvarez's viselike grip, I could see the monitors and the drone's continued circular flight pattern over the Creedmoor compound and the swarm of FRACs trying to get in. "You better have an ironclad plan," I promised, "or heads will roll."

"Trust me, John." She smiled thinly. "It'll be a cake walk."

Never trust a woman who asks you to trust her.

9

Foolproof

+79 Days – morning
47:13:09

"You okay?" I asked Jude.

She looked up at me and pulled her hand away from her neck. While she had dried blood on her fingers and palm, there was no new seeping evidence. "I guess."

Alvarez went to a credenza in the corner, took a linen napkin from a small stack and poured water from a pitcher onto it. She brought it over and held it out to Jude. While she gave Alvarez a seething look, Jude still took the cloth and start wiping her hands clean. Once done, she turned the napkin inside out and started the process again on her neck.

"I'm sorry," Alvarez offered.

"Your apology doesn't mean shit though, does it?" Jude retorted. "Like asking for forgiveness instead of permission."

Alvarez helped up the groggy Spring Chicken and pointed him and the rest of the security detail out of the room. Once the door clicked closed, it was all of us alone with her. Bowers moved over to Melissa and the girls. April was weepy, while Summer simply looked on at our conversation with grim curiosity. She seemed to be adjusting well to a new world of violence and death. Bowers put a hand on her arm.

"I'm okay, Sean," Summer assured him.

Probably because of all of the videogames these kids are subjected to these days. Well, used to be subjected to. Before the power went out. Definitely won't be playing online anytime soon.

Melissa looked at me from where she had corralled the girls. She had a venom in her posture and a glare in her eyes that seemed destructive, both to herself and to anyone in the immediate vicinity. Like Bowers, both had an anger that needed an outlet.

That woman just has hate in her heart. Atari Asteroids and Pac-Man do not do that to a person.

While I had my own opinion about the reduced sensitivity to violence of teens in our culture, I tabled the discussion with my phantom friend to focus on the operation at hand. "Fine. Let's get down to it."

Alvarez nodded and walked over to the monitors. She touched the lower corner of the bottom left screen with her palm. The area under her hand pulsed three times. All of the monitors lit up with a static satellite image of the Creedmoor Psychiatric Center. Based on the technology we had already seen from Roanoke and Raleigh in this conference room alone, I was starting to realized just how far their reach extended.

"The plan is simple," Alvarez started. A sine wave pulsed to match her voice, cordoned to the same area of the screen where she had pressed her hand.

"I'm sure it is," Sergeant Sean Bowers snorted, licking the drying blood on his split lip. "Everything's been so easy and well thought out so far."

"The target's name is Xavier Alexander Westsmith," Alvarez continued, ignoring Sean's comment. "Based on our tasked satellite and the drone recon, we know he is currently in the Creedmoor compound where he has been since the beginning of the outbreak."

"Why does he have his own surveillance?" I asked.

"Not important," Alvarez replied. "What is important is that Westsmith is holed up in the Inpatient Services Building."

"That's a lot of floors to cover," Sean added.

"It is," Alvarez agreed. "Which is why we will have a ten-man team with boots on the ground."

"How're we getting there?" I asked.

"CH-47 Chinook," Alvarez smiled. "Same way you came in. We lift off from the roof and land inside the compound. We acquire the target and transport him back."

"And why do you need us, again?" I asked in a different way from my first inquiry to Dick. "This seems very cut and dry. 'In and out', like you said."

"You know there's always risk," Alvarez said. "We have mitigated all the risk we could, but there have been a few incursions of infected onto the property that makes simple extraction a bit more tenuous."

"Why not have this Westsmith guy meet you at an LZ for a quick exfil?" Sean asked smartly.

"We have no way to get word to him," Alvarez said.

"How about the mics from the Chinook?" I added as an option.

"That would call attention to our arrival," Alvarez countered. "And we won't be in any better position if he doesn't respond."

Sean smirked. "A twin-engine, tandem rotor helicopter doesn't draw attention all by itself."

"So," I read back to Alvarez, "we inbound onto the property, search for Westsmith floor by floor in this high-rise, exfil him safely to the chopper, and back here for debrief, correct?"

"Correct," Alvarez agreed.

"And what about me?" Jude nearly screamed, spitting out the words. "What the fuck did you put in me?"

"The micro-capsule embedded in your neck has a 48-hour limit," Alvarez replied, not quite meeting Jude's glare. "After that, it releases a measured medi-dose into your blood stream."

"Of what?" I demanded.

"The same thing that we were injected with," she replied, locking eyes onto mine. "Just at a more concentrated and developed dose. R&R has come a long way since the Middle East."

"Fucking bitch!" Jude glared at Alvarez, starting to pace along the side of the conference room.

I didn't know what to say to her. I didn't want to think that Jude could end up like me. Not a fate I would ever want for her.

Certainly, an unfortunate outcome if it were to come to that.

Bob hadn't moved from the chair at the end of the conference table, his fingers intertwined.

"Why?" I demanded.

"Simple," Alvarez answered. "You apparently have a special skill that none of us have, me included. The boss wanted your compliance and this was the way he deemed best to get it."

"And after we complete the op?"

"We neutralize the capsule." Alvarez slapped her hands together. "Easy, peazy."

"And how do I know she's safe in the meantime?"

"Oh, that's the easy part."

"How's that?"

"She will be in the field with us."

"Are you shitting me?" Sean exclaimed.

"Don't worry, Sergeant Bowers," Alvarez added. "You'll be there with her in the field to ensure her safety."

"Let me get this right, Alvarez," I confirmed. "Sergeant Bowers, Ms. Sawyer, you and I, and six of your men are on mission."

"No," Alvarez corrected, "Me, you, Sergeant Bowers, Ms. Sawyer, and five R&R operators will be in the field."

"And who's the last member of the detail?"

Alvarez answered, "Ms. Russell."

"Now you *are* shitting me," Melissa chimed in as she threw her hands up.

"Why not just put Summer and April in the field, too?" Sean barked.

"That would be stupid, Sergeant." Alvarez shook her head. "They are to stay here in quarters. As an added incentive for you to stay on task."

"You want to put amateurs in the field and not expect distractions?" I asked.

"Hey," Jude and Melissa said together with a lace of indignation.

"That's not what I meant," I apologized.

"Having your own people in the field provides familiarity," Alvarez said. "You've all already seen shit and gotten through it together. You're all capable. I assumed you'd be happier having your people in sightline versus worrying about their accommodations."

On that point, Alvarez did make some sense. In some twisted way, it was the best solution to the shittiest of problems. Dick had all but guaranteed our cooperation. Jude was on a clock. The op was on a clock. April and Summer were the carrots in case all else failed in the field.

Dick was thorough and ruthless in his mechanisms.

A man after my own heart.

Fuck you very much, Bob.

I am here to serve.

"How far is it?" I asked.

"Forty-five minutes?" Sean offered.

"By car, maybe," April added. "Without rush hour, traffic and accidents."

"What is it?" Sean calculated. "Eighteen... twenty miles?"

"Sixteen miles," Alvarez corrected. "Remember, we are not driving."

"You from New York, Sean?" April asked.

"Born and bred," he replied with the slightest welling of pride.

"Enough speculation and bonding," Alvarez cut in. "Sergeant Walken and I will continue our briefing. Sergeant Bowers, Ms. Sawyer and Ms. Russell will be taken for outfitting. The younger Miss Russell and young Ms. Arden will– "

"Arden?" Sean asked.

"That's me, Sean," April said with a raise of her hand.

"Really, people? I may have to reconsider you being a tight-knit group." Alvarez shook her head. "Ms. Arden and Miss Russell will be escorted back to their quarters. We will be wheels up in ninety minutes."

As if on cue, four fresh soldiers arrived.

"Please," Alvarez asked politely.

"Go ahead," I prompted. "It'll be alright."

The others slowly stood up and filed out, all looking at Alvarez and me with a mix of bewilderment, dread and shock. They returned to being fuzzy silhouettes behind the glass walls before they disappeared from view altogether.

Alvarez and I were in the conference room alone—almost. She and the candid satellite image of Xavier Alexander Westfield stared at me from one end of the room, while Bob stared at me from the other end.

Another grand adventure begins.

10

Heavy Heart

+79 Days – late morning
46:57:32

"We transport by Chinook onto the property by 2000 hours, sweep the buildings until we find Westsmith, and return him here." I recited. "That's the whole plan?"

"That's the whole plan," Alvarez confirmed.

"Cut and dry?" I asked.

"Yes," she smiled.

"Ops are never that easy," I reminded her. "Or have you been with R&R so long that you've forgotten?"

"I haven't forgotten." She swallowed hard. "I'm just a bit tougher these days."

"I would say so," I agreed with a nod and a flex of my still sore neck.

"Come on. You act as though you don't have the same miracle running through your veins."

"I didn't ask for this miracle," I replied, almost choking on the last word. "I was happy being a Marine."

"Well, you aren't in the Corps anymore, are you? You're probably better off. They say that most of the world's armed forces didn't survive the initial wave of the plague."

"Well." I grimaced. "Your boss would know, wouldn't he?"

"We all know, John. Why are you being so obtuse?"

"Why are you?"

Alvarez clenched her jaw. She did the same with her fists at her side.

I shifted my weight.

I could hear, or maybe feel, her rapid heart rate. Her arteries expanded with the increased pressure.

Thump, thump... thump, thump...

Breathing in small even measures, I felt my own heart rate.

Thumm, thump... thumm, thump...

I continued to listen to her heart.

Thump, thump, thump, thump...

I continued to keep mine at a steady rhythm.

Thumm, thump... thumm, thump...

Thump, thump, thumm, thump...

Thumm... thump... thumm... thump...

Thumm, thump, thumm, thump...

I flexed the fingers on my right hand.

Thumm... thump... thumm... thump...

Thumm... thump... thumm... thump...

Alvarez exhaled and relaxed, flexing and splaying her fingers. I was just happy that Alvarez was no longer in a combative mood. That was something.

"Let's just get this op over and behind us, John," she finally commented as her eyes narrowed on me. "I have more important things I would like to focus on."

11

Costume Change

+79 Days – 1900 hours
46:21:54

"This is a half-assed bullshit plan, John," Sean advised as he lay on a bed with the crook of his elbow over his eyes

Of that, Sean was absolutely right. Jude—our Ms. Sawyer—nodded her agreement from the edge of her own cot. I watched Melissa pace the length of the pristine barracks, catching a sideways glance from her as she passed where I leaned against the wall. It was easy to be a little jealous of their spacious accommodations after the time I spent cooped up in my concrete cube prison.

At least you had reading material.

There were six beds in the barracks, three on each long wall. I wasn't sure if the term barracks applied since we were not on a military base or with other branch service personnel. Two beds were empty, April and Summer having already been assigned and confined to other quarters.

"Better not hurt them." Melissa seethed as she passed me again. "Either of them."

"They have each other, Melissa," Jude offered. "And Holly."

"That's small comfort, Jude," Melissa replied.

"I know."

"What 'I know' is that this is all bullshit, John," Sean repeated.

"I know," I finally replied. "The plan is flimsy."

"And the confinement," Sean said as he counted with his right hand. "And the extortion! And Jude having a time bomb in her neck!"

"What the fuck did they put in me, John?" Jude asked, her

voice breaking a little bit. "What did they do to you?"

They all looked at me expectantly.

"R&R made me a lab rat before I was discharged from the Corps," I said, choosing my words carefully. "Alvarez and me, both. We both got stuck with whatever serum or virus they have been working on for probably the last fifty or sixty years."

"And what is this stuff supposed to do?" Jude asked.

I wasn't sure what to tell them. Dick's injection had taken my voice away, drummed me out of the Corps, and made me start seeing hallucinations. What Dick tried to do didn't seem to have done anything worse than shackle me to the Gaunt Man. It was Digg's lethal injection that gave me the strength, senses, and stealth.

"I think," Sean offered, "that the FRACs don't see him."

"Yeah, right," Melissa interjected.

"They don't react to John like they do the rest of us," Sean continued. "Remember the minivans and the battery?"

"They attacked him," Jude reminded Sean. "I remember that much."

Sean shrugged. He didn't say any more, but he had been paying attention that day. Sean didn't mention that I had tapped the minivan with the blade to catch the walkers' attention that day. I'm sure his assumptions were further confirmed when we had dispatched the FRACs in the construction site pit. Going against the walkers kept providing examples of how I was different from everyone else.

Except Alvarez.

"I heal faster," I finally admitted, hoping to spin the conversation. "I'm a bit stronger, too."

"Summer and April wouldn't stop going on about how you threw that guy across the corridor at the museum," Melissa said.

"Makes sense that Alvarez is able to toss you around," Jude added. "And we're supposed to work with that bitch?"

"She was always a bitch," I admitted, "but she was a good Marine once."

"Wait." Sean cut in. "She's the one from your team?"

I nodded.

"Thought you said she died?"

"I thought she did. Apparently, R&R took better care of her than I was led to believe."

Better care, John? I'm pretty sure that is an understatement.

A bell chimed twice through a hidden speaker system. I looked at my Cobra watch that Alvarez had been kind enough to return to me after the briefing. The face was marred and the edges of the housing were scratched. The timepiece had seen a lot more battle since we had returned stateside than it had ever endured in any of the hotspots I had dropped into around the globe.

"Thirty minutes to wheels up," I told them, knowing the chimes signified an alert to get ready. "Let's suit up."

"This plan *is* shit, John," Jude said. "Sean is totally right about that."

"We don't have much choice at the moment, do we?"

"Maybe," Jude warned me, "but if something happens to those girls, this place is coming down hard."

"I'm with you, Jude," Sean added. He was midway through changing into black tactical cargo pants, stripped down to his boxer briefs. We watched as he hopped on one foot before finally getting both legs situated and the pants pulled up.

Melissa and Jude were more demure as they sat on their cots to change with their backs to us. I turned away out of respect. Sean was shrugging into his compression shirt, too distracted to notice.

I quickly stripped down to my underwear and pulled on the black cargo pants before putting on my own black compression shirt. It had a different and thicker feel to it, more like stretchy scales than a Spandex/cotton blend.

"Christ almighty," Jude exclaimed as my head was caught in

the collar.

"What?" I heard Bowers ask. I finally got the shirt around my neck. Bowers' eyes darted to Jude before chivalry got the better of him again. He snapped his neck back around toward me. "Jesus, John!"

"What?"

"Your back," Jude pointed out. "The scars."

Jude had come out of the museum with me but hadn't seen my back in ruins. Even though my clothes had been in tatters and my back had been covered in blood, she had not realized just how deep the flaying had been. While Alvarez had stitched the gashes and punctures in a professional manner and I had almost healed over completely, I knew that my flesh was a crisscross of angry and gnarled skin.

"I guess the blood threw off just how much abuse you'd taken," Jude conceded, almost reading my thoughts. "You have so many scars. But it looks like they were from a long time ago."

"Like the man said," Sean said. "he's a fast healer."

"Plus, R&R has some good doctors. They used some kind of stem cell biotech salve," I replied, finishing with a lie. I don't know why, but I wanted to minimize how much of a freak I was because of what Roanoke & Raleigh had subjected me to.

Sean continued, "Your body has all the earmarks of being to the battlefields of hell and back."

"Like Audrey Murphy." Melissa joined the conversation, looking surprisingly menacing in her black tactical gear.

"Damn, Melissa," Sean whistled. "You need to go with John on his next jaunt to hell. Keep him safe."

"We're already in hell, Sean," Melissa reminded him as she pulled down one twisted sleeve. "The faster we get this Westsmith guy, the quicker we can deal with getting Summer and April back."

"And Holly," Jude added.

"Can't ever forget the mutt," Sean muttered.

"You know you love that mutt, Sean."

"I'll never admit to that. Not in a million years."

12

Ascent

+79 Days – 1920 hours
46:01:14

We sat in silence on the cots, each of us fully dressed in the black tactical gear that R&R had provided us. The lace-up combat boots were comfortable, but still new. I worried that they weren't broken in enough for fieldwork. Alvarez had said that the weapons and Kevlar would be distributed on the roof. We still had ten minutes.

Bob decided to make an appearance, also dressed in matching tactical black. He looked ridiculous and completely emaciated under his compression shirt.

We are already cutting things short. Tick tock.

Agreed.

A truly shoddy bit of work we have to contend with.

Also agreed.

Was Alvarez ever that sharp a strategist?

A lock clicked and the sliding doors opened at the other end of the barracks. Bob disappeared as Alvarez stepped into the room outfitted in the same gear as us. Additionally, she wore a light tactical vest. It was modified with articulated armored sections that resembled something like what motorcycle riders wore to protect themselves at high speeds. Even the backside of the vest looked like layered resin vertebrae. She was loaded to bear with a Glock 19 and a tactical knife in the vest, plus two more handguns— Berettas—strapped to each thigh. The wardrobe was completed with military-issue boots and a dark adjustable ball cap that let her ponytailed raven hair flow out the back.

"Let's go, people," Alvarez ordered enthusiastically. "Daylight is burning."

It is not even daytime anymore.

It's a figure of speech, Bob.

We all stood up.

Alvarez snapped her boot heels together and spun a sharp about face, striding out of the dorm at a healthy clip.

"I guess we are in Road Warrior country, now," Sean mumbled so only we could hear it. He shrugged and saluted a bird at the corporal's receding back. I put a hand over his persistent middle finger, shook my head at him, and led him and the rest of my people after Alvarez.

I was lucky they followed me at all.

Jude and Melissa brought up the middle while Sean covered the rear. We navigated the corridor where Alvarez had gone, one turn to the left finding her and a bank of elevators waiting for us.

"You all look so cute," Alvarez teased. "Almost like real soldiers of fortune."

"Let's stay on point," I said firmly. "We're already dangerously close to starting this operation late."

The elevator doors opened, already half filled with three R&R mercenaries I had not seen before. They were dressed the same as Alvarez but with different complements of weapons.

"After you, Sergeant," Alvarez waved me toward the lift.

I stepped into the car, the R&R soldiers backing to either side to make room for us. We turned around as Alvarez followed us in and faced us. The doors closed behind her.

She pressed the H button without taking her eyes off mine.

The elevator chimed as it started its smooth ascent.

Strangely, there was no music playing in the car. Had music played when we were brought in? I could have sworn I had heard music on one of the trips up to see Dick. A facility as upscale as R&R should surely spring for some traveling music.

Everyone stared at the digital display as the floor numbers

flashed on its screen. Alvarez and I stared at each other. The tension was thick enough to cut with her tactical knife. She put one hand on its handle while she settled her palm on one of the Beretta's at her hip. When my eyes met hers again, she winked. A smile crept to her lips, as if to tell me that she welcomed another chance to prove she was more than a match for me. I wanted to take that knife and prove her wrong.

You've done a bang-up job so far, haven't you? Zero for three, I believe.

Jude, partially hidden from Alvarez's line of sight, put a hand to the small of my back. The tension subsided and the crimson I hadn't noticed creeping into my vision receded back to the far corners of my periphery.

"Good boy," Alvarez smiled wider.

Just as the urge to slam Alvarez against the wall started to rise again, the elevator came to a stop and the doors opened behind her. She stepped backward into a concrete and cinder block vestibule with sliding glass doors ten meters behind her on the opposite wall. Beyond the glass doors was the Chinook with its two-man crew going through their pre-flight check.

To our right was a stainless steel prep counter with tactical vests and a variety of weapons. The three mercs led the others to the table and started sizing tactical vests for each of them. The weapons consisted of Advanced Colt Carbine-Monolithic M4s and standard Beretta M9s. The ACC-M M4s were decked out with a vertical foregrips with laser sights built in. The M4 was the standard for the United States military, even though it had gone through its ups and down in terms of popularity. The others shrugged into their gear. Each checked that their straps were tight and that their weapons were holstered and quickly accessible.

Alvarez pulled me aside to the end of the table and reached into a plastic bin. She pulled out some familiar friends. She handed my shoulder holster to me. I quickly slipped it on. Once I had the holster comfortably in place, she handed me my tactical knife which was sheathed in its scabbard. Finally, she handed me my Glock. "I had to pull some strings. I know your attachment to this thing."

I hefted the lighter than usual Glock before holstering it.

"Thanks," I said. Alvarez must have realized that I would notice the difference in weight in a weapon I had used for so many years. I guess we would find out soon enough.

13

Ramping Up

+79 Days – 1930 hours
45:51:48

The Chinook lifted off the pad and tilted eastward.

The three R&R mercenaries sat in the jump seats opposite us, their backs against the fuselage and their eyes on us. Alvarez didn't bother with the stares, returning to old familiar habits with her eyes closed and a headset over her ears.

There were two M240 7.62mm fully automatic machine guns mounted between us and the cockpit, a belt of high-caliber rounds laced into them from a series of ammunition cases strapped to the bulkhead. Those were effective weapons systems.

At least we got introductions before we started carpooling.

Bob had not materialized on the flight, but was always rattling around in my head somewhere.

The man next to Alvarez, name patched Damon, chomped down incessantly on a wad of bubble gum like a cow chewing its cud. He had piercing sharp dark eyes and brown hair pulled back in what the Millennials called a man bun. He was clean-shaven and young, his life as a soldier of fortune barely begun.

A man named Heinz sat next to him, a hulking crew cut blond with a massive jaw and blue eyes. It may have been very stereotypical, but this European mercenary possessed all the earmarks of the Fuhrer's master race. He stared straight through me, never blinking.

The last member of Alvarez's team was an Asian woman named Lee. She was small with a muscular build, her body pitched forward and her arms wrapped tight around the shorter M4 rifle. I guess the ARs were only for office work. She had a severe downturned mouth, black framed wraparound glasses magnifying her almond-shaped dark eyes.

Sean covered the headset's mic and leaned in to be heard over the whine of the motors and the slap of the twin blades. "Quite the motley crew. And, I ain't talking about us, either."

I nodded, smiling in the slightest.

From my left, Jude patted me on the leg. I turned her way.

"This is going to work, right?" Jude asked, my headset picking up her words into the mic. Her eyes searching mine for answers as her other hand rubbed her neck.

"No worries," I assured her. As if supporting my statement, the lights in the cabin changed from white to red. "Heck, we're halfway there already."

Alvarez opened her eyes and cupped the headset tighter to her ears. "Alright," she barked. "Off-load in five. Check and inspect."

She and her team checked their weapons and patted their tactical vest pockets, giving Alvarez the thumbs up when finished.

I grabbed my Glock from its holster and pulled back the slide. Letting it click back into place, I then released the magazine into my free palm. Holding it up closer to the red light, I frowned. It was just as I had expected.

"Sean," I ordered. "Show me your magazine."

"Sir, yes sir," he teased, releasing the magazine from the modified M4 and holding it up to the light for my inspection.

"Thanks," I said.

"No problem." He frowned with the same realization as my confirmation.

"Any chance," I asked Alvarez, "that we're going to get actual ammunition for this operation?"

"I didn't want you thinking of blasting your way out of here to freedom," she admitted, holding up an olive camo nylon duffle.

"You think I would leave my people behind?"

"Left me behind, didn't you?"

"You know that's not true."

"Isn't it?" Alvarez asked. "I didn't see you anywhere around after we got out of that shit show in the desert. But R&R has been attached to me at the hip ever since."

"That's a –," I began.

Alvarez whipped up a finger to halt my words, listening to something that only her headset picked up. She got to her feet. "Saved by the LZ."

Taking off the headset and hanging it on a hook above her jump seat, she moved to the back of the cabin and slapped an oversized red button. Motors whined as the rear ramp dropped open. The slap of the rotor blades became deafening even with the headsets, coupled with the whistle of wind and the swirling of dust.

Alvarez held on to one of the straps by the opening as the Chinook swung around the building and fired up its searchlights. A huge tan and orange building loomed outside. It looked to be sixteen stories in height, taking up a massive amount of real estate on an otherwise wooded and grassy property.

"That's Building 40... Inpatient Services," Alvarez yelled over the roar of the helicopter. "We're going in on the roof."

I pointed to another headset above her head.

From the aerials I had studied back in the conference room, Building 40 was a long rectangular building with a slight jutting wing at the central hub. Two additional lower story wings midway down the front face bisected the building into quarters. At the ends were two exterior stairwells separated from the main building by bridges at each floor. The brick façade was a solid grid of windows except at the stairwells and the mechanical housing on the roofs. The upper floors were dotted with black sooty scars around broken windows.

"Fire broke out on the top three floors," Alvarez warned once she donned the new headset. She strapped the ammo duffle we needed to her back, "so we're not touching down. At all. We're jumping down on the southern roof."

"You shitting me?" Melissa yelled back. "We ain't trained for that. I ain't, anyway."

"Gotta start sometime, sweetheart," Lee commented with a grin, adjusting her glasses and checking her rifle one last time.

Damon and Heinz smirked as they filed toward the rear of the cabin behind her.

"What th–?"

"It'll be okay," I interrupted Melissa, closing in almost nose-to-nose to her. I turned my eyes to Jude and Sean, who both looked like Melissa sounded. "Trust me… and in yourselves. Clear?"

They looked back at me and each slowly nodded their tentative resolve in the suddenly green cast of the cabin.

"Green means go, people," Alvarez yelled. "We are a go. Lee, ladies first."

"O-M-G, Alvarez. Thanks for being a doll." Lee shot her a wink. She shuffled forward toward the edge of the ramp and a very dark exterior except where the Chinook's searchlights and running lights cast their beams. Alvarez waved her on and patted her on the back. Lee jumped off the edge and out of sight.

"Go!" Alvarez waved the others forward. Damon gave us a six-shooter salute, trotted to the edge, and dropped off the ramp. Heinz followed three seconds later without a single look back.

"Let's go, John," Alvarez ordered, her free hand resting on the grip of her Beretta. "I'll be the last one off this bird."

I patted Sean on the chest and nodded him toward the rear of the craft. He swallowed and huffed several times before he started moving. I followed him to the edge.

Outside, the gravel roof wavered between one to two meters below the edge of the Chinook's ramp. The pilots kept the helicopter steady, even with the crosswinds and the wash from the rotors. Alvarez's team was deployed in a loose perimeter with their weapons drawn.

"Just drop and let your knees give way," I instructed him, "Tuck into a roll if you pitch forward too much. Don't try to brake yourself with your hands."

"Sure," Sean said with no confidence.

"Ooh rah," I reassured him.

"Ooh rah, Sergeant," he smiled weakly.

"Then let's do this," I added. "I'll be down in a minute."

Sean nodded and jumped without giving himself any time to think more about it. He landed and pitched forward. He threw out one hand in front of him before remembering my instructions and rolling through it. He recovered quickly and moved away toward Lee.

"Melissa," I called.

She shook her head but Jude wrapped her hands around her shoulders, whispered something in her ear, and walked Melissa forward to the ramp.

"You both got this," I told them.

"Please, I have brothers," Jude added. Her face fell for a moment as she heard her own words. She no longer had any living brothers.

Melissa grabbed the canvas hanger straps as far as she could to the ramp.

"Let's go, ladies," Alvarez yelled. "Christ, it's like I'm waiting on a dinner date."

Jude shot her a look since that's all she could do without a full magazine for her sidearm. Alvarez was definitely trying too hard to command with bravado. It was out of character for the Marine Corporal I once knew.

Like a tandem skydiving instructor, Jude rocked Melissa back and forth. When the helicopter dipped toward the roof she pushed Melissa out, jumping off next to her. The drop was only a meter but they landed in a tangled heap. Jude helped Melissa to her feet, giving me thumbs-up before they hurried away to Sean's position.

"Like old times, huh," Alvarez smiled.

"Something like that," I replied, a twinge of regret around my heart as I thought back to the outcome from the last time we exited a helicopter on a poorly planned op. "How about that ammo?"

"When we get gravel under our feet, Marine. After you."

I trotted down the ramp and stepped to the edge. The Chinook suddenly dipped its nose and lifted the ramp up and away from the roofline. I launched myself into the air, flailing my arms for balance. The roof sped toward me from five meters away. My boots crunched into the gravel, my ankles and knees taking all of the shock of the impact. I turned and watched the Chinook try to reposition in the sudden strong updraft. It shimmied for several seconds before leveling out, Alvarez's silhouette hanging on to the strap with the green glow of the cabin behind her. I stepped back to the others, all of us watching the shimmying transport.

"The wind's not dying down," Damon yelled, his finger to his earbud comm.

"She'd better figure it out," Heinz grumbled in a surprisingly and decidedly British accent. "We don't have time for this shite. Stupid US Marines."

"Oh my god," Lee commented. "Give her a second, will ya?

As predicted, the wind did not relent. The helicopter continued to pitch and yaw in the updraft as it tried to get back into position over the roof. Alvarez was holding onto the strap with both hands in order to keep from being buffeted against the fuselage.

The bird made it close to the building again, several meters above the edge of the roofline. Alvarez's outline disappeared from the ramp. She backed up for a moment before running and leaping into the air out of a perfectly good aircraft.

"Christ," Damon blurted out.

Alvarez flapped her arms like she was a fledgling bird, her body pitching forward with her dive toward the roof.

"Not gonna make it," Heinz bet. "Not gonna make it. Christ."

It was 50/50 odds, at best.

I raced toward the edge as she flailed out of sight.

Melissa yelled out.

The Chinook pitched away.

I skidded to the edge of the parapet, gravel kicking up from my boots. More gravel crunched as the others came up behind me. The woods, asphalt drives and Long Island's arteries of parkways and expressways hugged the landscape, serving as silent monochromatic monoliths in the full moon. It was a long way down.

"Are you just gonna stand there?" a voice asked.

Alvarez stood on a small roof a couple meters below us to our left. It was one of the external security stairwells.

Lee started. "Oh my–"

"God," Alvarez interrupted her. "Save the Millennial slang for later after we get inside."

"You need help up?" Damon asked.

"Nope." Alvarez shook her head, pointing to the smaller separated roof under her feet. "This is our way in."

14

Altitude Adjustment

+79 Days – 2020 hours
45:01:11

After everyone was lowered into the stairwell annex causeway, we convened at our first locked door to the hospital wing. It was quite the tight fit between the hospital and the separated stairwell.

"Tell me again why we landed on the roof instead of the lawn," Damon wondered aloud.

"Easier to do floor-to-floor searches going down then up," I answered.

"Give the man a cigar," Alvarez chimed in.

"We bothering with these three top floors since there was so much fire damage?" Damon asked.

"Before we do anything," I added, "I want those magazines."

"Since you asked so nice," Alvarez said, swinging the duffle off her back and into my hands. "Just remember that we got plenty of insurance."

"I haven't forgotten," I said as I opened the duffle and handed out full magazines to my team for both the M4s and Berettas. We loaded our weapons and filled as many pockets as possible. "Glock magazines?"

"Smaller pocket on the side," Heinz advised.

I fished out several magazines, loading the Glock and filling my tactical vest pockets. Once done, I zipped up the duffle and shouldered the bag. "What's the plan, Alvarez?"

"We start clearing the wards two floors down."

"How do we even know Westsmith is still here?" I asked.

"Lee?" Alvarez ordered. "Fill the man in."

"We have had a dedicated heat signature on Westsmith for

several weeks," Lee said with pride, pushing up her glasses. "We lost that signal a few days ago, but we still have subdermal tracker operational."

"So he could be dead," I said, wondering why the thermal profile would have dropped off the scanners.

"No. The tracker operates off the electrical impulses on the body. If he died, it would be dead, too." Lee pulled out a handheld device that looked like a cross between a radar gun and a Beretta with a silencer attachment. It was made from a black composite material and sported a three-inch heads-up digital display.

"More R&R tech, I imagine," I speculated.

"Only the best," Lee responded cheerfully, unaware of my sarcasm.

"Is that a suppressor?" Sean asked, pointing to the perforated metal cylinder at the end of the device.

"Uh, no." Lee shook her head. "It's a sensor array."

"See?" Alvarez beamed. "Easy, peasy."

"Is there a reason to keep this information to yourself?" I asked Alvarez.

"Need to know basis," she replied plainly.

It was a shitty answer, but one I had heard from the command structure more times than I cared to remember. Compartmentalized data typically led to failed missions. Alvarez should have remembered that from our last op together.

"Can that thing ping the altitude of the signal?" I asked Lee, wondering what else Alvarez deemed classifiable under the Need to Know column.

"Uh," Lee mulled the idea over for a few seconds. "Uh, yeah… yeah, I think we can do that."

Sean and Melissa shrugged their shoulders and rolled their eyes at Lee while Jude and Heinz nodded in understanding. Damon and Alvarez simply stared at me as Lee played with the settings on the gun.

"We go floor to floor," I advised, "checking the signal strength on each floor. Once we get a high signal we go down a couple floors to verify where the signal is strongest. Then we breach those floors. Saves time and breaching rounds. Understand?"

Heinz continued to nod. "That's a bloody proper and smart plan. Otherwise, we're going to spend a lot of breaching rounds and floor sweeps."

"Agreed," Damon concurred.

Alvarez said nothing, but nodded her consent.

"Okay," Lee said. "We're recalibrated."

"Good," I said, anxiety spreading with every minute we stood still. "Let's get to work."

Damon grabbed the fire door handle and swung it open as Lee turned up the sound on the device. We filed into the stairwell with Lee in the lead and Damon closely behind her, his rifle up over her shoulder. The rest of us spread out over a full flight of stairs.

The device pulsed, making a series of diminishing pulsing pings at five-second intervals. The sounds echoed throughout the stairwell, leaving hollow remnants behind until they were covered by the next wave. We remained focused and quiet as we descended, the pings becoming louder and more insistent.

Something else became insistent. A low-grade itch started at the center of my shoulder blades and slowly worked its way up my neck until it nestled into the base of my skull.

The device pinged.

Echoes reverberated off the walls.

Faint hisses.

Another ping.

More echoes.

A moan.

Heinz tapped Damon on the shoulder and squeezed between him and the rail, both of their tactical light beams bouncing off the walls as they switched positions.

"On your left, luv," Heinz advised, passing Lee to take point. "We got more than Westfield in the proximity."

"I hear it," she replied. "Sounds like it's coming from everywhere."

It did sound like the moans were coming from all around us. That would be impossible, though, since we had started at the top floor.

Therefore...

Therefore, Bob, all of the undead are below us. The first-floor stairwell door was probably left open.

Always with the very astute observations, young man.

Heinz and Lee pulled away from the rest of the team, circling past the next landing. Damon went back up the stairs to cover our flank, taking position above Sean and Melissa.

"You know we got this covered, right?" Sean asked, his M4 at full draw and pointed to the landing above him.

"Just doin' my job, man," Damon assured him with a pop of his bubblegum. "It's what I do."

"Me, too," Sean concurred.

In between the strengthening echoes of the homing signal, the gurgling moans got louder. Lee adjusted the signal sensitivity dial and kept going while Heinz kept the tactical light beam shining the way in front of her.

Alvarez halted me at the eleventh floor while Lee and Heinz could be seen passing the landing a full flight below us.

"Your senses tingling yet, John?" she asked.

"What?"

"Come on." Alvarez rolled her eyes. "Don't screw with me."

The itch between my shoulders carved a deep groove to the base of my skull, insistent but faint. Regardless of what intel Alvarez thought she knew, I wasn't going to be the one to confirm anything for her. It was need to know. "Not sure what to tell you."

Alvarez shined her own tactical light at my face. The beam

was blinding but I made sure not to wince, even though my pupils had shrunk to pinpricks.

"I know," she insisted.

"I'm sure you think you do. I'm sure Dick has me all figured out, huh? Now get that light out of my face so we can work."

The moans continued.

She frowned and redirected her light down the shaft. "There's something flitting around down there."

Damon piped in. "I think we got that much figured out. Why do you think I'm up here with Bowers?"

That got both him and Sean smiling.

"Just keep your eyes open, Damon," Alvarez said, her voice an annoyed hiss.

"Yes, ma'am. Lady, ma'am. I still got the flank all buttoned up."

Alvarez gritted her teeth, her jawline setting into a strong angle. She shook her head and descended to the next landing and looked over Lee's shoulder at the homing device.

"What the hell?" Jude whispered to me once she felt that Alvarez was out of earshot. "What have they gotten us into?"

"Ditto that shit," Melissa whispered as she joined in the conversation.

"We find this guy and get him back to Manhattan," I answered as positively as possible, knowing full well that I wouldn't believe my words either. "It's straightforward… especially with the tech R&R is putting up."

"Tell that to the FRACs wailing downstairs," Melissa griped, tapping her rifle nervously. "Christ. Walkers in closed spaces."

"Melissa," I said.

"What?" she snapped back.

"Take a few deep breaths," I coached. "We'll get through this. Focus on your breathing and keep your wits about you."

"Easy," Melissa said, breathing in, "for you to say."

Jude and Melissa, in unison, exhaled heavily.

I might have, too.

"Like yoga," Jude added.

"Something like that." I smiled at Jude's comparison. "Plus, we have plenty of firepower and a stretch limousine waiting to whisk us back to the city when we're done."

The three of us breathed in unison for several seconds. When Melissa's fingers stopped shaking, I pressed my hands against her arms. "Remember, there's a little girl in the city that needs her aunt."

Melissa squared her shoulders and a simmering anger crept back into her cheeks. "I don't want to think what that asshole could be doing with Summer."

"They're safe," Jude offered. "I know it."

"Let's do this thing," Melissa said with a strengthened resolve. "We got places to go, and corporate asses to kick."

"Ooh rah, ladies?"

"Ooh rah, Sergeant," Melissa replied.

"Ooh rah, John," Jude confirmed.

"Ooh rah," Sean said as he passed us on the landing. "Alvarez was right... you guys are so cute."

Sean smiled with a nod and moved down to the next landing, leaving Damon above us on our flank and our 8-man team spread out over three flights.

Ooh rah, Sergeant.

Make that an odd nine.

Without a doubt, definitely an odd nine.

15

Voices Carry

+79 Days – 2037 hours
44:44:39

Five flights later the clicks from Lee's scanner pinged loud enough to drown out the moans from the undead. Heinz stalked the steps below Lee, hunting for walkers.

"We don't have much more to go," Alvarez noted as she looked at the screen of the device in Lee's hands, tapping her vest breast pocket absently as she did so.

We had tightened up our column between floors.

"Keep going?" Lee asked for confirmation.

"Wait—" Alvarez started.

"Keep going," I replied over her. "If the signal strength drops on the next floor, we come back up and breach on the sixth floor."

"Roger that, Sergeant," Lee replied. She held the homing gun at full draw and headed off in pursuit of Heinz and of a stronger, stabilized signal.

Alvarez glared at me with her piercing dark eyes.

The itch in my neck had intensified along with the signal from Lee's device. I rolled my shoulders and neck to keep them loose, knowing that this ache would only go away with distance or death.

You checking out of the program, Marine?

Not my death, Bob.

Oh. So, the poor people who didn't choose their lot in life...

Life?

Do not be melodramatic, John. You know what I mean.

So why aren't our friends coming up to meet us?

Your guess is as good as mine.

I know you have more than a guess.

Maybe you just need to do some of your own reconnaissance work for a change.

I didn't answer Bob.

He was right.

"Bowers," I called back.

"Yeah, Sergeant," he replied.

"Keep an eye out," I advised. "And on our team."

"Ooh—" Sean started.

"I ain't helpless, John," Melissa interrupted.

"We got this," Jude added. "No worries."

The three of them grouped together on the landing with Damon behind and above them by half a flight. I shined my light to the landing below and descended to catch up with Lee, Heinz and Alvarez. As I turned at the switchback mid-flight landing, I nearly bumped into Alvarez as they came back up.

"He's on the sixth," Alvarez alerted. "We go in on the sixth."

"About bloody time, too," Heinz grumbled.

"At least we were going down the whole time," Lee added, spinning in a silver lining.

"That's what she said," Sean said with a grin.

He was met with rolling eyes and what I could have sworn was a human groan to mark the death of good comedy. Sean shrugged and kept grinning anyway.

"Right." Heinz continued to grumble. He passed me on his way back up to the others, already checking his Benelli for the breaching round.

"Time to get dirty," Alvarez smiled. "Ooh rah."

"Ooh rah," I added, with little enthusiasm.

Lee smiled at me as she climbed the stairs after the others. "Just like you said, Sergeant."

The buzz in my neck was constant, a pulsing ache that never seemed to fully go away these days. I swept the tactical light around the next landing and the stairs below it. The beam penetrated another flight before it gave up to the darkness. A low mewing crept up from the blackness, followed by a metallic tapping. Grabbing the railing I could feel the reverberation through the metal tubing traveling up from below.

"Sergeant," Heinz called down. "We're a go up here."

Leaving so soon? I thought I heard, but it was so fleeting and seemed to come from everywhere except from inside my head.

"Waiting on you, mate," Heinz called out again, his insistence revealing his own eagerness to get out of the stairwell and into the shit.

I waited a moment longer. The voices and reverberation from the pipe railing had stopped. Only the darkness remained.

16

Into the Breach

+79 Days – 2049 hours

44:32:01

We stood on the bridge between the stairwell and the door to the Inpatient Care facility, all of us crowded on the narrow open causeway of concrete and steel. The night pressed around us and several stories swirled below us, the railings not doing much to make us feel secure.

Heinz held the Benelli to the door latch and the frame, the muzzle adapter against the metal. He tightened his fingers on the weapon's pistol grip.

"You may all want to take a step back, yeah," Heinz advised.

I swept a hand to move Jude, Melissa and Bowers toward the stairwell door. Damon stepped toward the hinge side of the door with his M4 at quarter draw. Alvarez and Lee stood between Heinz and us, their Berettas at the ready.

"Do it," she ordered, reaching forward and tapping Heinz on the shoulder. Alvarez was not a leader. She had been an extraordinary spotter for me and a tenacious operator, but she had never exhibited the natural abilities to be a field commander. Leadership could be trained with the right amount of practical experience, but I feared she still was too green. R&R made her a commander because of her new genetics, not her strategic acumen. I was happy to let her lead, as long as she made the right calls.

BANG!

Heinz snapped his head around to look past us to the stairwell fire door. He had not fired a shot. Another bang rattled the steel behind us. We swung our weapons up toward it and what pressed in from the other side. Multiple thumps came through the hollow metal. We backed up a step toward Alvarez's team, my shoulders suddenly afire with pain. Eight of us stood on a narrow bridge, caught between a locked door and an unknown number of FRACs in the stairwell.

BANG!

The door buckled and puffs of powdering mortar dropped to the floor of the bridge. Two fingers found their way through the gap in the door and started to pull the metal inward, the moans and snarls now louder. The door wouldn't hold them for long. If Heinz breached the door the FRACs would follow. We couldn't guarantee that we would have a quick way to barricade them or that there weren't dozens of FRACs waiting for us deeper inside the hospital.

"Get behind me," I ordered as I stepped toward the door.

"You're going to be in the crossfire, mate," Heinz advised.

"They get through and it's only going to take a few seconds before we're fucked," I shot back. "We don't have the room to fend them off."

"We could drop down–"

I cut off Damon's idea by kicking in the stairwell door. The stench billowing out threatened to close up my throat. The putrid smell made my eyes water. As the first of the FRACs lunged past me, I pulled it down by the shoulder and wrapped my arm around its neck. It slapped at my legs until I lifted it off the ground.

Snap.

Its neck now broken, the FRAC crumbled to the floor.

Dozens of mangled hands reached out from the dim interior of the stairwell. A quick punch to the face sent blood splatters into the air and another of the undead to its knees. I pulled the tactical knife, its blade finding the base of an orderly's brain through an upward jab through the throat. Swinging to the left, I found the ear canal of another Creedmoor employee. My weight against the door slammed it shut behind me, casting me into darkness.

"John!" The hollow steel between us served to muffle Jude's yell.

The FRACs, hearing Jude's voice, clamored at the door behind me. They didn't sense me—for all intents and purposes I was invisible to them. I would never be sure whether it was a result of Dick's serum or Diggs follow-up concoction.

"John!" Jude called out again. The FRACs reacted with louder groans and scratching at the door with more fervor.

With my vision adjusting, the walkers lit up in startling crimson detail. I thrust my blade into the base of one of the FRACs neck as he continued to slap at the door. He gurgled as he collapsed. He looked like someone who had come to visit a patient at a very inopportune time. I grabbed one of the walkers by the back of the head and drove it into the steel frame. The slaps of the undead were drowned out as I repeatedly slammed the FRAC's face into steel until its skull was a shattered bloody mess.

A woman's arm—a too-thin patient in hospital-issued pajamas—got caught up under my armpit. A male patient grabbed at my other shoulder. Two street-clothed walkers continued to wiggle their fingers through the gap of the ruined door.

Stop, I thought at them.

The FRACs at the door pushed their bodies against it but stopped trying to bend back the metal. The two walkers tangled up in my arms pressed me against the bodies at the door, their grips uncommonly strong while their skin and muscle were sloughing from their frames.

Fucking stop! I thought.

The two patient FRACs did not stop. The male patient had wrapped his arms around mine. I couldn't use my tactical knife. I tried to swing my arms to drive them together but they held me fast against the now still door walkers.

Goddammit!

The woman moaned into my face, her breath exhaling a sour

metallic stench. They both snarled at me, chattering their blackened teeth as they attempted to sink them into me. While they could have bit into my covered forearms, both were obsessed with getting to the hot bare flesh on my neck.

Why are they sensing me? Were they just reacting to me being in their way? Was it because I was holding them at bay? Are they just reacting to my grip? I wasn't going to test any theories by letting go and seeing what developed.

The female snapped at my face.

They were too strong to shrug off.

Or maybe I was too weak.

The FRACsy twins lunged at me at the same time, their mouths agape and their dark teeth glistening. My elbows were close to buckling. The female's drool dripped onto my arm, beading off my shirt. A wet copper taste touched my lips as blood splattered across my cheek. The woman fell to the floor.

I turned to my larger captive, only to see his head explode through an exit hole in his right ear. He tipped away from me, staggering to the rail and pitching right over it. The clangs of a soft body bouncing off metallic rails filled the space until he landed with a thud several stories below.

Damon came up the stairs from the lower floor, his M4 drawn and the night vision scope operational. "You set, Sergeant?"

I didn't get a chance to reply because the walkers at the door reacted to Damon's voice, turning around and reaching out for him. I buried the tactical knife blade into the closest one's septum. Damon squeezed off a shot that pierced the other walker's temple and sprayed gore all over the painted concrete walls. Both walkers slumped to their knees before they fell over on their sides, leaving me with nothing to lean against except cold wet metal.

"Sorry, Sergeant," Damon apologized. "I thought you were just propping up their dead bodies."

I nodded in appreciation of Damon's handiwork.

He reciprocated with a huge pop of bubble gum.

Sliding the bodies out of the way with my leg, I knocked on the door four times. "We're coming out."

"Okay," Alvarez's muffled voice replied.

I opened the door, still hitting the leg of one of the walkers.

"Jesus Christ," Sean said with a whistle to boot. "How many were there? You got enough blood on ya for quite a few."

"Seven," Damon added. "I caught another three coming up from four." He squeezed past me to rejoin Heinz at the door.

"What was that stunt all about?" I asked.

Damon shrugged while he chewed his gum. "Got your back, Sergeant. Simple as that. It's what I do."

Damon didn't come across as a killer. He was young, not seasoned in combat experience but versed in disciplined training.

"Thank you," Jude said to Damon on my behalf.

Sean nodded, too, but he averted his eyes as his face took on a forlorn quality. "Bullshit move, Walken."

"Thanks, Damon," I spoke up for myself, putting Sean's comment aside. "But you were reckless. I would never have okayed what you did. Too many risks."

"But it's okay for you?" Sean asked, almost under his breath. Of course, we all stood on a narrow causeway where even a whisper would be heard.

"It's different." I explained without explaining anything.

"Doubtful," Sean replied.

I wish he could understand that I couldn't in good conscience put their lives in any more danger than they already were. This was my shit show, not theirs. They didn't ask for any of this. How did I explain that I was better equipped to take on the undead?

Damon did have to save you from the patients who attacked you.

Yeah... there was that wrinkle. More to figure out.

"At any rate," I amended to Damon, "thank you for the assist."

Alvarez examined her close-cut nails—perfect for field work—and looked up when silence settled between us. "We good? Can we get back to work? Or do you boys want to hug?"

Damon stepped back to the stairwell and peeked inside.

Aside from the smell, there was no movement or sound welling up from below.

"Clear on this side," he confirmed.

"Alright," Alvarez declared. "Heinz, let's get back at it."

"Bloody right," Heinz replied, shooing us back.

We moved as a group toward the stairwell door, Damon still glancing at the broken door for any possible surprises. Heinz checked our distance and nodded. He reset the barrel of the Benelli against the door lock. After taking one more look at us over his shoulder, he squeezed the trigger of the shotgun.

BLAM!

The crumbling of brick and the implosion of metal followed the loud blast. Heinz backed off the smoking shotgun muzzle, put a gloved finger into the new opening and pulled.

Nothing.

"Damn," Heinz said with surprise. "I guess we need another go."

"Then go," Alvarez ordered.

Heinz squatted in front of where the blast ripped open the metal and shined his tactical light inside, moving the beam around the edges.

"Alright," he commented, standing up and pressing the shotgun muzzle at a different angle toward the frame inside the opening. "In three... two... one."

Another blast and flash.

This time a huge gash tore open the frame around the latch and the door swung open a few inches.

"Unlocked, mates," Heinz smiled, pulling the door open toward us. "Welcome to Creedmoor."

"Damon, hold it open," Alvarez ordered. "Lee, on point."

Lee nodded and moved to the front, turning up the sound on her tracker. She rolled her shoulders and took a deep breath, taking out her penlight. Since the scanner did not have a built-in tactical light, she held it over the penlight in a well-practiced Harries Hold. She shined the light around the immediate black interior before entering. Heinz followed quickly behind her with his weapon drawn, swinging out wide right to flank Lee and have a clear line of sight. Alvarez and Damon entered, leaving me to step up and hold the door.

"Clear," Alvarez whispered, waving us in.

Sean rushed to take point of our group with Jude and Melissa filing in behind him. I took one last look at the mangled stairwell door and the stunningly dark empty night. No dogs barked. No cicadas chirped, except those that had taken up permanent residence in my skull. Clouds covered the sky, obscuring the stars in the heavens and the moon hanging precariously in its orbit. I looked at the spit and blood on my hands and arms, wondering if I had lost a war that I didn't know was being waged.

Ahead of me was a gaping hole leading into a monument to madness. I took one more moment to take in the fresh air and a vague sense of freedom before balling my fists and stepping over the threshold to be swallowed by the dark and unknown depth of Building #40.

17

Check, Please

+79 Days – 2057 hours
44:24:32

Swirling murals were painted on the walls. Padded chairs were scattered around the room. The ward was otherwise silent, the sharp lines of walls and corridors negating any sense of calm that the paintings and feng shui may have had on its patients in its heyday.

A nurses' station—or maybe a security checkpoint—was to our immediate right. A phone receiver sat on the counter instead of nestled in its cradle. Sean looked at it under the beam of his light.

"Can't not do it," he said, walking over to the station and lifting the receiver to his ear. "Nothing."

"Did you think anything different would happen?" Jude asked. "Dork."

"Had to try." Sean shrugged, putting the receiver back on the counter.

"You going to hang that up?" Melissa shook her head.

Sean put his hands up, mouthed the word 'Sorry' and placed the receiver gently back on the cradle. He hiked up the strap of his M4 and moved past Melissa and Jude with a wink.

"It's confirmed," Jude whispered in a strained voice to Melissa. "He's a dork."

"Was that ever in dispute?" Sean called back. He seemed to have already moved on from our little disagreement on the causeway.

"Never," Melissa confirmed. She and Jude exchanged nervous smiles. The mirth faded quickly from Jude's face as her hand returned to her neck.

A soft whistle from farther down the center corridor caught our attention. Sean waved us up, his own eyes glued to the gloom deeper in the ward.

"What's up?" I asked, my Glock up and its tactical light trying to pierce the veil of the new mystery.

"I don't hear the others," Sean advised. "They went ahead."

I took point and led Jude and the others past a series of patient rooms, complete with mesh glass security windows and deadbolt locks. We came to an intersection through a set of steel doors that were swung open toward us. To the left was a common area with a motley collection of couches, oversized chairs, and end tables. To our right was another set of security doors–

Reminds me of a certain museum I once visited.

–that were also wide open, this time swung open into a second corridor. Beams of light bounced off the walls toward the far end, the sound of Lee's tracker faint but detectable. We passed several closed white doors, one side of the hallway a mirror of the other.

Finally, we heard voices.

"Oh my god," Lee insisted. "I'm telling you the signal is strongest inside."

"Fuck," Alvarez exclaimed. "This won't do."

"We still bringing him in, yeah?" Heinz asked.

"What's the problem?" I asked, approaching the group as they clustered around the last door to the left.

"Doesn't look good." Damon shined his light through the dirty mesh window.

I nudged him away and looked into the room. Between the smears and drips on the other side of the glass I could see a huddle of people at the far-left corner of a padded cell. The room was clearly meant to isolate and protect patients from themselves and others. On the floor under the crowd protruded a pair of feet. The others stomped through a sticky mess of blood.

"See?" Damon commented. "Doesn't look good."

"What's the problem, Lee?" I asked again, ignoring Damon.

"The signal's strongest in that room," Lee replied. "Otherwise the tracker would have to be suspended in midair on the other side of the outer wall. So, that's unlikely."

"So? Go in."

"I have no idea what's going on in there," Alvarez rationalized. "I don't need to let out any crazies."

I looked back into the square five-meter room and shined my light off the wall to the crowd's right. They did not react to the light, continuing to huddle in the corner. Trying to elicit a response, I tapped on the glass. No reaction. There was no worsening of the itch in my neck. I tried the door. It turned freely.

"I guess we're going in," I said. "I'll take care of it."

"I'll come, too," Sean offered.

"Stay close to the door," I ordered. "It's too cramped in there and I need you all out here to keep them from getting out."

Sean stepped back as I pushed open the door. It swung in and bounced silently off the padded wall. I held it open with my foot and waited. Still no reaction.

"Damon."

"Sergeant?"

"Keep this door covered."

"Yes, Sergeant," he replied.

"Hey," I called out and received no reaction. I brought the Glock up to a full draw and flanked the crowd from the right side. I closed the distance to three meters and whistled. Still... no reaction. Maybe a small shift in positions. It was hard to tell, even with my enhanced vision and the swaying beams of several tactical lights besides my own.

I stepped up to a woman with long blond hair, wearing a pajama top and bottom adorned with tiny SpongeBob SquarePants and Patrick figures chasing after elusive jellyfish with butterfly nets. I tapped her on the shoulder. She spun around and howled.

One eye was missing. Part of her cheek flapped from her cheekbone. She gurgled and spat out blackened saliva.

"Shit" Damon yelled in surprise, slamming closed the door and my route to escape.

SpongeBob SquareFRAC lunged at me.

I drove the grip of the Glock into her forehead.

Her skull cracked and her remaining cloudy eye rolled up to see what I had done to her.

"Let me in there." I heard Sean yell at Damon.

"Hell, no," Damon yelled back.

Another patient turned around and moaned at me. No advanced warning. No itch. This FRAC, in sweatpants and a too small shirt that advised 'Grace wins' attacked me. I had no invisibility from the undead.

This one was not Westsmith.

I pulled my knife, sidestepped and planted the blade up to the hilt into Grace FRAC's ear. I gripped the knife handle tight as he fell, letting gravity slide him off the blade. He thudded to the floor.

The other two upright FRACS flailed at me. Neither matched the photo of Westsmith. One caught a blade under the soft tissue of his dangling jawbone. The other caught a bullet from the business end of the Glock. He snapped back, his brain matter spraying onto the wall. The gun's report was muffled within the acoustically suppressed space.

I flung the FRAC off the end of my blade toward where Damon stared through the window, the walker's body slamming against the door. All that was left was the man whose legs and feet had been under the mob of FRACs. He was dressed in a dark suit with a blue shirt and a whimsical tie featuring Bugs Bunny and other Looney Toons characters. With graying hair and an Abraham Lincoln style beard, he was also not Westsmith. This man had not been dead for long. In fact, we may have just missed his expiration

A scuffle and shoving match was escalating in the corridor. I dragged the body away from the door and opened it. Damon nearly fell into me. Alvarez had a Beretta in each hand, one pointed at Sean and one pointed at Melissa. Both had their rifles at half draw, their arms and fingers tense. Heinz was backing his commander's play but only at half draw.

I pushed Damon upright again.

"Lee?" I asked.

"What?" she replied, her own sidearm swinging between Melissa and Sean. It had replaced the tracker she usually held. The best way to defuse this situation was to ignore it.

"You busy?" I asked. "I cleared the room. You can trace the signal now from inside."

"Ok," she said almost as a question as she moved away from the drama in the corridor, fumbling between her sidearm and the tracking device.

She approached me at the door and peeked inside.

"It's clear, I promise."

"Ok," she said cautiously, her shoulders hunched and her feet still not stepping across the threshold into the room.

With one last look at me, she swallowed and flanked right against the wall, swinging the business end of the tracker left. The signal was definitely louder and stronger where the gray-haired man lay, the pulse almost a continuous tone whenever she pointed the device directly at the body.

Sounds like the sound of a flatline on a heart monitor.

"Now what?" Lee asked. "That's not him."

I knelt down, careful not to drop a knee into the congealed pool of blood around him.

"How big?"

"What do you mean?"

"How big is the tracker?" I said pointedly, a little irritated at handholding Lee through the conversation.

"Oh. Roughly the size of a Tylenol capsule."

I checked the man's outer and inner jacket pockets. Wallet, magnetic ID card, eighty-two cents in change, cough drop, lint.

No tracker.

I curled my hand and reached into the man's left pants pocket. Keys. More loose change and something else. A tin of Altoids mints. I took it out and shook it before holding it in front of Lee's device. The pulse was a loud single buzz. Opening the lid, I saw three mints, two orange pills and one tiny poly-composite clear capsule with microelectronics and a blue flashing tip connected to a homemade contraption with wires and a flat watch battery.

I held it up for Lee and the others at the door to see.

"Definitely not Westsmith," Melissa grumbled.

"Easy peasy, huh?" Sean asked Alvarez sarcastically.

18

By Appointment Only

+79 Days – 2115 hours
44:07:57

We were definitely still two distinct groups.

Alvarez and her team stood around a coffee table in the patient common room back at the intersection. They talked in low voices about what to do next. Damon rolled his shoulders to work out kinks in his neck while Lee continued to fiddle with a tracking device that was now of little use. Heinz stood off to one end of the table looking across the commons area toward the wing where we had found the tracking device. Alvarez had her palms resting on the grips of the guns on her hips, waiting for all of the opinions to be voiced.

The rest of us sat on a sectional couch in another corner of the room, watching the drama as it unfolded. Jude rubbed at her neck. Melissa's fingers kept drifting to the trigger of her rifle, its barrel pointed in the general direction of Alvarez. Sean kept releasing his Beretta's magazine and clicking it closed again.

"What's the odds on this mission, John?" Sean asked, not stopping his nervous distraction.

"What he said." Jude showed restraint by keeping her weapon holstered. "We're wasting time."

Yes, John. What are we to do?

I didn't know.

Come now. You are an adept operator. Surely you are not going to let these amateurs run the mission.

I stood up.

"John?" Jude asked.

I didn't say a word but went over to Alvarez and the others.

"...could sweep the rest of the building," Damon offered.

"We don't have that kind of time," Alvarez replied.

I stood next to Lee.

"We're in the middle of something here," Alvarez warned.

"Give me the tracker," I said to Lee, my hand out.

Lee fumbled around her vest pockets until she rooted out the Altoids tin. She handed it over.

"We don't have time for this," Alvarez warned.

"No, we don't," I retorted.

I opened the tin and picked out the tracking capsule. It was a wonder of miniaturized electronics, complete with a long-life biometric battery and sophisticated coiled antennae. The blood on its surface was still tacky to the touch. The wirework and battery a nifty way to keep the tracker powered outside the body.

I put the capsule and rigging back into the tin and tossed it back at an unprepared Lee. She fumbled with the tin as I walked away from the group. I walked out of the visitor commons area. My team followed me, leaving the somewhat bewildered mercenaries behind.

The padded room's door was still open and letting out the stench of death and spilt viscera into the corridor. I went inside, not worried of any surprises. The others stopped at the doorway.

Bob was waiting for me inside.

Hey there, friend.

Hey. Is this one going to come back?

No. His lights are out.

Damn.

Sorry. Mind melding is not on today's menu.

Was worth a shot.

I checked his pockets again, locating the swipe card and his set of keys. In the inside breast pocket of his jacket I found several business cards denoting his status of doctor and his office on the third floor.

Clicking on the tactical light, I lifted his well-manicured and soft hands. His blue cotton shirt cuffs were crisp and professionally pressed. But the shirt was marred by droplets of blood. I blotted a finger into one and pulled it away to reveal more tackiness.

"What's up, mate?" Heinz asked as he arrived.

I lifted my smeared finger.

"It's still red and wet," I revealed. "The tracker wasn't taken out too long ago."

"And?" Heinz asked. Alvarez, Damon and Lee crowded around him at the doorframe.

"Does Westsmith have any blood conditions, Alvarez?" I asked.

"Why?"

"Does he or not?"

"No," she finally admitted. "He was in perfect health."

"Based on the air temp in here and the wetness of the blood, the tracker was taken out within the hour."

"That doesn't help us find Westsmith," Damon chimed in.

"Well," I said, "I would assume a doctor wouldn't do an extraction surgery in the hallways."

"So?" Alvarez asked.

Did you actually ever like this girl?

Yes. I did.

"So," I replied to Alvarez, holding up the keys and business card, "it's time to make an office visit."

19

Razor's Edge

+79 Days – 2137 hours
43:45:16

We used the central stairs to make our way down to the third floor. We didn't encounter any problems along the way, a surprise after dealing with the undead in the exterior stairwells. The third floor was laid out the same as the sixth floor, minus the doors separating the commons areas from the secure wards. I didn't feel any aches or itches in my neck and shoulders. The lack of sensation was somehow more disconcerting than its constant dull annoyance.

Maybe there are not any friends here.

I looked at the backs of Alvarez and Damon as they walked point, clearing open offices and rattling the knobs of locked doors. While we all had the same objective, I couldn't really count them as friends.

How can we be lovers if we can't be friends?

A Michael Bolton reference? Really, Bob?

I celebrate his entire catalog.

My phantom was like one of the Bobs from the *Office Space* movie, wasn't he? I shook my head anyway, surprised at the depths of Bob's continued pop culture references.

Crash!

We all spun around to the rear of our column. All beams and barrels were focused on the noise. Lee had her hands up in the air, a metal inbox tray at her feet with papers still sliding across the tile floor away from it.

"Sorry," she whispered, as if the break in silence could be recaptured by her low-voiced apology.

"Smooth move, Ex-Lax," Sean said. "You may want to keep it down before all of the undead hone in on us."

"They don't have sonar, luv," Heinz interjected. "No worries."

"But," I advised, "they're still attracted to noise."

Heinz glared at me for a moment, but just a moment before he hiked up the strap to his rifle and brushed past me toward Alvarez.

Yep, definitely are going to be BFFs.

"Sorry, Sergeant," Lee whispered again, already on her knees corralling the escaping papers and putting them into a stack in the inbox still on the floor.

"Come on, Lee," I ordered. "Leave it."

She grabbed several more papers in the immediate vicinity and dumped them into the inbox before abandoning the recovery project altogether. Jude reached out a hand to help her to her feet. Melissa and Sean covered their flank, watchful for any other movement.

There may be hope for that one.

A whistle came from ahead of us.

"Enough," Alvarez hissed from the darkness. "Everyone come up."

We did as we were instructed, forming a tight group in front of a nondescript wood door with a long rectangular inset of frosted glass.

"This is the one, John," Alvarez said, shining her tactical light on the door number. "Do the honors."

I nodded and pulled my Glock.

Damon reached out for the doorknob. He did a silent countdown with the fingers on his other hand, nodded, turned the knob, and swung open the door. I stepped forward, the gun barrel leading the way into an empty waiting room with a receptionist pass-thru and a door on the left side. I opened the second door to an interior office. All I found was an empty reception desk and filing shelves. I turned left down a short hall. Closed doors were on my left, right and straight ahead. The left side door opened into a personal office. It was empty. Door number two revealed a combination supply and coat closet. I stepped back into the hallway for door number three. It was locked so I pressed my ear against the wood grain. Nothing.

Another dead end, John.

This *was* another fucking dead end.

I detached the tactical light before holstering the Glock. Stepping back to the doctor's office, I shined the light around. Everything was organized and positioned in symmetrical lines. Nobody was hiding behind the desk. I stepped back out to the hallway.

Tick. Tock.

Would we ever find Westsmith this way? I thought I had a clever idea with the business card, but we could spend days just clearing this building—let alone the entire compound. How long would Dick remain a man of his word if we came back empty-handed? How terrible would the girls' existence be if the clock ran out?

Keep moving, Marine.

Christ, I needed to get my head twisted on right. Focus on the mission in front of me. Worry about Jude and the girls later. Compartmentalize that shit.

"Status, John," Alvarez said from the reception desk.

"Dead end," I fumed.

"We need to regroup," she replied.

"We need to," I insisted, "find this guy. Now."

"I know," she replied.

"No, you don't," I yelled. "YOU AREN'T ON A DEADLINE!"

"Screw you and your bitch," Alvarez yelled back. "You aren't the only one dealing with pressure."

I moved forward.

Alvarez brought up her tactical knife.

Really?

"Really?" I asked.

I grabbed her knife-wielding wrist, slamming it against the wall and breaking her hold on its hilt. The knife dropped and embedded into the receptionist's desktop. Alvarez punched me in the jaw with her free hand. I dropped to one knee, my grip still on her wrist. Pistoning my legs up and pulling her wrist down, I head butted her under the jaw. Her head snapped back.

My vision went red.

I let go of her wrist and drove into her gut under the ribcage, smashing her into the doorframe between the reception desk and the waiting room. An elbow drove between my shoulder blades. I punched her in the kidney, still pinning her into the doorframe.

I might actually win this round.

A sharp pain in my back.

I released her and stepped away.

Fuck.

Her tactical knife was no longer stuck in the reception desk. It was sticking out of my shoulder.

Double fuck.

"STOP THIS SHITE!" Heinz yelled from the hallway, trying to wrestle control of the situation. "NOW!"

The bitch had stabbed me.

She was partially doubled over, her arm across her belly.

"Stop, John," Alvarez panted, stepping back into the waiting room.

"You both need to get your personal shite squared away," Heinz warned. "What the bloody 'ell?"

Stabbed in the back. Seems appropriate.

I reached over my shoulder and grabbed the knife handle.

"Christ," Damon said.

Pulling out the blade, I pointed it at Alvarez. My blood dripped from its tip and glistened from its edges. "You fucking stabbed me?"

Alvarez moved to her right.

A soft click.

Heinz and Damon stood in the doorway with their weapons trained on my team, blocking them from entering the doctor's suite. I could just make out Lee's wide-eyed face from between Jude and Melissa's shoulders.

I flipped the knife in the air, my blood spraying out from it as it spun. I grabbed the handle and threw it at Alvarez. It whizzed past her face and embedded into the drywall behind her.

"You dropped something," I said with a growl.

"Jesus, you two," Heinz commented. "Get a room."

"Yes," a new voice said from behind me. "A room may be appropriate."

I spun around, pulling my Glock.

The owner of the new voice pressed the palm of one hand into the end of the barrel. "No need for that, my friend. I assume you are here for me."

The man stepped back, raising his hands to shoulder height. He squinted against the beams of several tactical lights, his long brown hair doing little to shield his eyes from the spotlights on him. His beard was disheveled and uneven, giving him a look less like a hipster and more akin to Jesus returning from the desert.

"Xavier Alexander Westsmith," Alvarez announced with her retrieved knife in hand. "I'm Rosalita Alvarez and we're here to rescue you."

Westsmith appraised each of us, stopping to give Alvarez's knifepoint and my wet shoulder longer consideration.

"You are here to retrieve me," he finally conceded. "Of that I have no doubt."

20

Incoming

+79 Days – 2149 hours
43:33:56

"Mr. Westsmith," Alvarez advised in the less cramped confines of the corridor, "we have an airlift ready to extract you back to Manhattan."

"The city?" Westsmith asked. "Isn't that more overrun than here in Queens?"

"We have a quarantined area mid island," Heinz added. "Hard defensive perimeters."

"Sounds lovely," Westsmith replied, straightening the cuffs of his light blue button-down dress shirt. It was still pretty crisp and clean for being months into the apocalypse.

Except that blood stain on his forearm.

Can't all be pristine.

We may have to Shout it out.

Bob, you're retarded.

Maybe.

At least we could get out of this crazy house and get back to the city. Get back to Roanoke and Raleigh. Get my people back. Get that ticking death bomb out of Jude's neck.

"We just need to get to the lawn so the transport can touch down," Alvarez advised Westsmith. "Then we're wheels up and back to safety within the hour."

"That certainly *is* a good plan," Westsmith agreed. "Very well thought out."

Westsmith must be a little crazy if he thought this extraction was well thought out. It was only by sheer luck that we had found him.

Or, maybe, he found us.

"End justifies the means, I guess," Sean murmured to me where Alvarez and her team couldn't hear us, echoing my sentiments. "If you hadn't thought to come down here, we would still be in a world of shit. Still can't believe that she stabbed you."

"I wasn't expecting that," I agreed, a thin layer of anger still underlying my words. "But I'll live."

"Still a dick move," Sean asserted.

"That it certainly was."

Jude and Melissa stood a few meters off, just inside the glow of the tactical lights. They held hands, Jude nodding and smiling weakly at Melissa's comments. Lee stood farther away, her M4 trained into the darkness.

"At least," I said with a nod, "this will be over with soon."

"And with plenty of time to spare," Sean added.

Heinz came over to us. "We're heading down in three minutes. Chinook is inbound."

"Roger that," Sean replied with a half-assed salute.

"You're an asshole," Heinz mused. "I like that about you."

"Ready to serve." Sean smiled.

"Sean, go tell the others," I ordered.

Sean pivoted toward Jude's group. Heinz glanced at me before returning to Lee and Damon. Alvarez stood farther down the corridor with Westsmith. His chin pitched toward his chest and his shoulders slumped while Alvarez talked to him. She stood rod straight next to him, one hand resting on the grip of her pistol and the other with its thumb hooked into her waistband.

I stood alone, halfway between all of them. The corridor was quiet. The buzzing in my neck was quiet. Even Bob was being silent. Small blessings.

Suddenly, the faintest of static broke the silence. Alvarez pressed her ear bud into her ear. She replied into her throat mic. "Roger, that." She gave us a triumphant grin. "Chinook is one minute out. Downstairs. Now."

Alvarez put a hand on Westsmith and steered him toward the stairwell. Damon, Heinz and Lee led the way with Alvarez and the prize Westsmith in tow close behind.

"I guess we're on our own," Sean muttered as we were left alone in the third-floor corridor.

"We better hurry then," Jude said, pushing past us. "Come on, boys."

Melissa bumped into me with purpose. "Yes... boys... let's get back to whatever passes for civilization these days."

"Can't argue with that, Boss," Sean agreed.

I took one more look at the corridor. With the team and the tactical lights gone, the corridor was dim and devoid of life. Lines of moonlight cast through the tall windows, allowing dust to dance and swirl through them. It was unfortunate that these storied walls would only ever hold decay and restless spirits from now on.

I tapped the door frame and descended once again.

21

Half-Court

+79 Days – 2201 hours
43:21:01

The stairwell led out into a central lobby.

Nothing stirred.

Not even a mouse.

Alvarez's team had fanned out across the marble interior by the time we set feet on the marble floors. She had her considerable grip on Westsmith's shoulder, both guiding him in the right direction and keeping him from running off. He winced in discomfort from where her fingers dug into him.

We moved slowly as a group to the main entrance. It was blocked off with office furniture and cabinets. Sean, Heinz, and I holstered our weapons and pulled away enough of it for Heinz to squeeze through to the doors. Other than a turn lock, there was nothing else to impede our exit.

Probably the reason for the IKEA store stacked against the entrance.

Heinz opened the door a crack and slipped out to the porch. He checked both sides of the drive and sidewalk before waving us out. Sean stepped through next and held the door for the rest of us. Heinz crouched down on one knee, his rifle to his shoulder as he slowly pivoted at the waist continuously for two hundred degrees while we made our way outside. We took up kneeling positions in a semi-circular deployment under the awning. Alvarez and Westsmith were the last to join us.

A warm breeze puffed against my face from the west, bringing with it both the scent of decay and flowers.

Smells like potpourri.

The increasing thump of the Chinook's rotors drowned out any of the silence that the night was hoping to cling to.

Alvarez put her hand to her ear again. "What do you mean? Shit!"

"What's the problem?" Heinz asked.

"No clear LZ."

I stood and moved to Heinz's position closer to the driveway. Dozens of trees landscaped the lawn to our right, close to the expressway. Lamp posts lining the drive would be problematic for the Chinook's rotors at slower speeds. The parking lot would have been a good landing zone except for all the abandoned cars littering the asphalt in a haphazard fashion. "Why didn't someone scout a clear LZ?" I ground out, more to myself.

"We could move some of the cars," Damon offered to anyone who would listen.

"It would take too long," Heinz replied. "The bird's attracting enough attention as it is."

My mind went back to the drone surveillance video footage. A return to the roof was impractical. The parking lot and lawn on this side of the facility was difficult at best, even if the pilots hovered in a Pinnacle maneuver to get us all aboard. There was a bigger lawn with younger trees on the southwest side of the property. There was a tennis court, additional parking, and–.

"What about the basketball court?" Lee asked. "It's pretty close."

"It wouldn't work," I countered with a shake of my head. "Assuming the court size is standard at twenty-nine meters. The Chinook is over thirty meters with the rotors."

"What about the ball fields on the other side of the road?" Sean asked.

I don't think anyone else heard him.

"We'll chance it," Alvarez said as she started walking to the southwest corner of the facility. She raised her hand to her throat mic. "Come in to the south. Basketball court. We're heading there now."

She listened to her earpiece.

"I don't care," she replied. "Just do it."

The pilots had probably told her the same thing that I had. She had always been hard headed. I guess some things never change.

"It's a bad play, Alvarez," I told her. Why the fuck didn't she scout out a better landing zone? I would have hoped that they had reviewed the aerials way more than the few minutes I had.

"We'll risk it," she shot back. "We need to get into the air."

Alvarez hurried away with Westsmith still in her clutches.

Jude, Melissa and Sean remained by my side.

"Landing there is a shitty idea," Sean admitted.

"We're already committed," is all I could reply. "We don't have a way to contact the pilots anyway."

We moved toward the corner of the building. Damon and Alvarez were on point, Westsmith between them. The ache between my shoulders made it painfully obvious that we were going to face another problem way before we considered boarding the Chinook.

A tall security fence with razor wire coiled along its top surrounded the recreation yard. The basketball court was set off to the far right, a gazebo and a handsomely paved raised patio in the middle of a lawn between us and the LZ.

Unfortunately—

Unfortunately, as my buzzing brain confirmed, the courtyard was teeming with FRACs. Some pressed against the fence while others wandered throughout the yard. We closed in on the chained gate. Many of the walkers at the fence migrated to the entrance, their moans growing louder. One even tried to bite through the chain link to get at us.

"Christ, luvs," Heinz stated.

Alvarez ignored him and talked into her mic. "Of course, I see them. I'm not blind. We'll clear them while you move into position to set down."

There was more static through her earbud.

"Do as you're told," she ordered the pilots through the comms, her hand back on Westsmith's bicep. "Move. Now!"

However bad this idea was, we were committed to seeing it through. Westsmith had to be returned to R&R. That was the most important objective.

"Heinz," I said.

"Aye," he replied.

"Blow that lock," I ordered him, pointing at a chained gate entry. "Everyone else, stay in a tight formation. Clean headshots. We fan out once we deal with the congestion on the perimeter. Let's move."

I got nods from Heinz and Damon. The others gave me a mix of wide eyes and grim resolution. Heinz pumped the shotgun, touched the barrel to the padlock, and squeezed the trigger. The weapon flashed and sparks accompanied the tearing apart of the lock and chain. The whole thing, plus some of the gate frame itself, fell to the asphalt. It was overkill, but effective.

The gate swung open. Three FRACs staggered over to meet us, attracted by the noise. Each received a shot to the temple from my Glock as a reward for their hospitality. Heinz, Sean and I swept inside the perimeter, moving right along the fence line to take on the curious undead amassed against the chain links. Alvarez, with Westsmith and the others, pressed forward toward center court.

"Go, mate." Heinz tapped my shoulder.

FRACs turned toward our movement and the sound of weapons fire. Heinz and I stood shoulder-to-shoulder, placing practiced shots into the undead crowd. The FRACs bunched up at the fence spread out in a wide line, the walkers on the periphery of the herd lumbering at a faster pace around their undead companions. Some veered off in Alvarez's direction, finding her an easier target. FRACs staggered around the tables and benches, effectively collapsing our rear flank. Jude and the others slowed down their pursuit with sporadic headshots, but we were close to being pinned against the fence between two herds of walkers.

"They're driving us back to the gate, mate," Heinz declared.

My answer was a quick succession of headshots. Four walkers returned to being dead, their bodies thumping to the lawn. The remaining FRACs, in their hunger to get to us, snapped their teeth at each other. Like some other predatory animals, they wanted the food to themselves. Did FRACs subscribe to the notion of survival of the fittest? They struggled to get over their fallen comrades, the newly dead slowing down their pursuit of us warm bodies.

Never leaving a man behind was a concept that the Marines hammered into us. Of course, terrorist snipers around the world took advantage of that fact by maiming soldiers to draw out their enemies. Listening to a screaming member of my team and being able to do nothing about it would go against my personal and professional code of conduct. The undead didn't concern themselves with fallen comrades. Probably why we'll always lose to the undead in the end.

"John," Sean called out. "You busy?"

A female Hispanic FRAC—wearing green hospital scrubs, one slipper, and a trustee swipe card on a lanyard—lunged at me.

Fuck! They can see me, too?

I punched her square in the nose.

Her face crumbled and snapped back from the impact. Her long black hair swept forward to cover her face, slower to get the message that her body had suddenly changed direction. She careened into the path of three hospital patients, impeding their forward progress just as they were going to lunge at me.

Why can they see me?

Sean crossed behind me and shot another patient in the side of the head. Heinz drove his shotgun's tailstock into the forehead of the in-patient to my right.

The herd swarmed us.

Stop, I commanded them.

Most of the FRACs kept coming, manically pressing forward as they tried to untangle themselves from the patio furniture and fallen bodies.

I pulled my tactical knife.

Stop, I thought harder. A couple of them stopped and stared blankly at the moon. Most responded with louder hissing, and outstretched digits intent on clawing at our flesh. It wasn't working. Apparently, my command over the undead was waning. And, some of them could sense me.

I thrust a blade into the eye socket of an overweight black man in soiled and bloody white pajamas. He gurgled, his dead weight falling against my knife. I sidestepped and pulled the knife down. Fat Albert FRAC hurled to the grass beside me.

Two other patients grabbed at my sleeves. I backed up and swung my arms together. The grip of the Glock crushed one skull. The blade of the tactical knife drove in to the hilt in the ear of the other. The force slammed their heads together, shattering their skulls into something closer to pulp. Blood spattered onto my face from the impact. I shot the next undead patient through the septum immediately behind them.

"Bloody good work." Heinz stepped closer to my right, taking out two FRACs with blasts from his Benelli. "Just keep your head in the game."

I brought up the Glock and fired three times. Two of the patients crashed into a patio set, coming to rest on the stone surface to bleed out whatever dark fluids had pumped through their bodies. The third of the group, a short white woman with dirty blonde hair, pursued me with a bullet graze across the edge of her temple. Black pus oozed from the wound while a guttural scream gurgled from her gaping black-gummed mouth.

I wiped the sweat from my eyes with the back of my hand. Lining up another shot, I pressed my finger against the trigger. The side of her head exploded. I tilted the Glock and looked at the non-smoking barrel.

"Need to be quicker than that, sweetheart," Jude said, bumping into my left side with a grin. "Having fun yet?"

"A blast," I replied, actually dishing out a kill shot of my own on one of the couple dozen remaining FRACs.

Jude continued to fire, each squeeze of the trigger resulting in a clean headshot and one less walker. With every muzzle flash, her grin was visible and her eyes lit up. We traded shots as we racked up our kill count working in tandem.

That is one way to deal with the stress of the situation.

At least the target practice was keeping her mind distracted from the capsule in her neck. Small favors. Gunfire from our left reminded me that Sean and Heinz were continuing with their own wetwork. Melissa trotted over on our flank, keeping her weapons trained on the interior of the courtyard. Alvarez, Damon and Lee, from the raised position of the gazebo, fired on a few of the stragglers who had finally shuffled over to them. Westsmith was on his knees with his hands over his head in the middle of the gunfighters.

The buzzing at the base of my skull subsided a little more with the killing of each walker. It wasn't quelled entirely as there were still twenty or so FRACs to dispatch. Several rounds later—and ten more dead walkers—brought the pain in my head down to a cloudy dull ache instead of the impalement of a hot dagger.

With the courtyard mostly cleared, I could make out the others' individual heartbeats. All were strong and thrumming from surges of adrenaline. Another booming pulse quickly drowned out the engines of life.

Thwap... thWAP... THWAP...

Beams from powerful searchlights lit up the recreation yard, casting the courtyard into an illuminated center stage. The beat of the Chinook's rotors was a concussive force as the transport hovered above us, the wash from its rotors tipping over anything that wasn't secured.

Alvarez had moved from the gazebo to the perimeter of the fence, leaving her teammates and prize for a better vantage point to guide in our multi-ton whirling ride home.

22

Testing The Limits
+79 Days – 2218 hours
43:04:59

The increased pressure of the wash from the Chinook's twin rotors pushed everything from the court, sweeping it all away as if by invisible hands. The transport rotated slowly as the pilots tried to get the best entry angle without getting the blades clipped.

Heinz and I joined the rest of Alvarez's team in the gazebo, crowded with the cowering Westsmith under its roof for cover from the remaining FRACS and the Chinook's dust storm. Heinz drew up his weapon and took down two walkers who were being buffeted into the fence by the Chinook's down draft. Sean stepped out from cover next to a concrete garbage can and drove a blade into a walker's ear. The patient dropped to the grass, cured of her mental illnesses for good. Alvarez stood at the edge of the basketball court trying to guide the Chinook down.

"She looks like a crazy person, flapping her arms around like that," Sean yelled in an effort to be heard over the Chinook.

"Aye." Heinz joined the conversation. "She is a might looney, that one."

The Chinook tilted five degrees to starboard, the pilots keeping its nose up. It was a precarious descent, the painted tips of the blades inches away from the light posts. The transport swayed hard to port. Sparks burst off one of the lights as the whirling blade shattered the glass dome.

"Shit!" Damon declared.

The pilots over compensated the controls, the Chinook sliding dangerously in our direction. We realized we were still too close to the LZ if the Chinook rolled and crashed, scrambling down the opposite steps of the gazebo.

The last of the rec yard FRACs snarled at us from the grass. Melissa and Heinz swung their weapons into the top of two of the walkers, their heads caving in to the nostrils, their faces crushed into visceral wedge shapes.

Sean flitted past me, his knife raised over his head. He sailed into a FRAC's loving embrace, sinking the blade into her face as she wrapped her arms around him. Her teeth were inches from Sean's neck as she clawed at his armored back with fingers torn down to bloody bone. Her fingers ripped across the sleeve of his shirt as Sean's blade sunk deeper into her cheek. Luckily, the scaled material of the compression shirt did not tear, holding up to the FRAC's abuse.

I kicked a small man in the chest, driving him off his feet into the much larger woman behind him. They collapsed together with the man on top. Melissa stepped forward and shot them both in the face with a double hail of shot from her M4.

Damon added another two to the list of the dead.

Lee surprised me with a near decapitating roundhouse kick to a teenage boy, his head hanging on his shoulders with a few remaining sinews of muscle. He staggered a couple meters before giving up and collapsing on the gazebo steps. It was only then that the head came fully away from its neck.

Jude shot another walker in the back of the head as it tried to get at the prone Westsmith still curled up on the planks of the gazebo. A FRAC growled at her. She spun right and drove the barrel of her pistol into his mouth and pulled the trigger. The muzzle flash was muted as the back of his neck and lower skull exploded in a spray of brains, bone fragments and oozing black blood.

Sean's words about how crazy Alvarez looked guiding in the Chinook echoed in my head. Testing a theory, I stepped slowly toward the last two FRACs. Both walkers had wandered in from outside the recreation yard. They were dressed in ragged puffy jackets and torn jeans, although the jeans could have been purchased that way. Their boxers were on full display, their pants defying gravity as they clung to their emaciated hips.

"What're you doing?" Jude yelled out over the roar of the Chinook's motors as I holstered my weapons.

I waved her off. I had to know. When the walkers closed within three meters, I willed them to stop and look at the pretty helicopter. They took another two steps toward me.

Shit! They weren't listening to me anymore.

Stop and look at the flying thing, please.

They stopped and craned their necks over their shoulders to watch the Chinook finally touch down on the asphalt of the basketball court. It bounced a couple times as the blades' downdraft to the ground continued to want to lift the transport back into the air. The pilots slowed the rotors to compensate. The Chinook's full weight settled onto the landing gear, thousands of pounds compressing onto the floating pistons, torque arms, and the tires. The rotor blades were still dangerous as the pilots didn't slow the motors enough to allow the human eye to differentiate the individual blades.

The walkers stared at the Chinook, then started to lumber toward it and its still spinning rotor blades.

Stop.

They did.

With the GangstaFRACs lined up side-by-side, I drew the Glock and shot the closest in the side of the head. His skull had become so brittle that the bullet retained its shape as it tumbled through his head. It exploded out the far side and went through the second thug's temple.

The first stumbled into the second. The baggy jeans finally gave way, dropping to their knees before they dropped dead in a heap. The yard was clear and the Chinook was ready to transport us out of this shit show.

"You are a bloody crazy motherfucker, Sergeant," Heinz said, patting me on the back. "You sure you don't need to be checked out, too?"

Why? Because I'm crazy? I thought those words instead of saying them. I could be wrong but I think that people who had mental deficiencies in life could still sense me in death. It was the patients who had been immune to my commands.

"Yeah," Jude agreed, her lips tight and the corners of her mouth downturned. "He's certifiable, alright."

There was no glint in her eyes now.

"Maybe a 72-hour evaluation wouldn't be a bad idea," Damon added, wanting to get in on the joke as he chewed on his flavorless gum.

Alvarez approached, dragging a sullen Westsmith by the arm. "You ready to get aboard?" She smiled, puffing out her chest and patting her tech vest breast pocket.

"I want to get this shit out of my neck, if you don't mind."

"Bloody fine work, boss," Heinz commented. "I'm with Ms. Sawyer. I'd like to get out of this muck post haste."

"You heard the ladies." Alvarez beamed. "Our taxi awaits."

23

Up, Up And Away

+79 Days – 2240 hours
42:42:13

Being back inside the humming Chinook never felt so good.

Alvarez pushed Westsmith to the jumpseat left of the cockpit and harnessed him in. His eyes were glazed over and his skin pale, his shoulders slumped.

As my people strapped in, Sean leaned in to my left and whispered, "Weird he's so shocky after being out here for so long. You think he lost too much blood from cutting out the tracker?"

"He didn't seem like it." I shook my head. "Not unless that doctor was a hack."

Alvarez and her team strapped into the seats opposite us. Lee and Heinz closed their eyes and leaned back with the hopes of some rack time before the eventual debrief back at R&R. Damon tinkered with the sights of his M4.

The Chinook's motors revved up. Very quickly, the transport lifted off.

"Told you." Alvarez looked at me and smiled.

"Told me what?" I asked.

"Easy, peasy."

"Not based on that clusterfuck I was a part of down there."

Her smile faded. "Why are you being an asshole? We got the job done."

"This is Afghanistan all over again," I advised. "Thank God no one was hurt or killed. Plenty of opportunities for that to have happened."

"Name one," she snarled.

"Shitty recon on landing zones," I said with one thumb in the air. "Wasn't like those cars in the parking lot had been driven over for a tailgate party within the last 24 hours."

I added my forefinger. "There was no contingency plan beyond using the tracker gun to find Westsmith. Tech we were left in the dark about."

"We found him, didn't we?" Alvarez said in her defense.

"John gave you that lead," Sean shot back.

"Your team had to step up while you obsessed with getting the Chinook touched down in shitty conditions," I reprimanded Alvarez, adding my middle finger to the others. "Especially with better LZs available."

"The rec yard *was* infested with those things," Heinz said, his eyes still closed.

"You know the lawn on the east side of the property is wide open with just scruff bushes and saplings, right?" I asked her. "I'm sure the pilots were telling you the same thing, right?"

"We would have had to dispatch more walkers," Alvarez replied after several seconds, the confidence draining out of her voice. "The mission's done and we can return to some normalcy. That's what's important."

"It's a good thing that your Dick of a boss roped us into this thing," Jude said with a hand on her neck. "You would have been screwed otherwise. You needed all hands out there."

"She's right. A real Marine wouldn't have fucked up that bad," I taunted Alvarez, dropping my thumb and forefinger in favor of highlighting my middle finger.

Alvarez looked down and clicked her harness release. She launched herself at me. The Chinook suddenly tilted hard to port, lowering her trajectory toward the deck. I kicked her in the neck, whipping up my leg and snapping my ankle at the last second into her throat. She landed hard on my legs, her hands moving to her throat. She dropped to her knees. I shrugged off my harness and grabbed her by the pull handle of her tactical vest, dragging her back into her jumpseat.

"I'm tired of this bullshit," I said as I strapped her in. "We're even for the knife you put in my back. Let's just get this done."

She glared up at me, one hand still to her throat.

A gunshot reverberated through the fuselage. Everyone snapped to attention with their hands reaching for their sidearms. Except for Westsmith. His jumpseat was empty and his harness loose.

A muzzle flash from a second gunshot came from the cockpit.

The Chinook dove hard, its nose at a forty-five-degree downward angle. I was lifted off my feet and hurled toward the front of the cabin. I covered my face as I bounced off the ceiling. Spinning, I failed to grab the cargo netting a second before impact.

24

Branching Out

+80 Days – unknown

..**

I opened my eyes to darkness and a deep ringing in my ears. There was pain. Always pain.

Seems like you came back this time with something extra, Bob the Gaunt Man said as he loomed over me.

My back was pressed against the cockpit's instrument panel. The pilots' arms dangled down at me, their bodies still harnessed into their seats. The pilot had the hilt of a tactical knife in his shoulder. His sidearm was missing. One of the bullets from its magazine had found its way into his temple. Another bullet was lodged into his co-pilot's forehead. Blood dripped forward off the pilot's nose, his green eyes staring at me.

I don't think they will be returning any time soon.

I looked back at Bob.

He was poking his finger on something jutting toward him from the instrument console. It didn't look like a part of the Chinook. It looked more organic. Bob plucked a bloody leaf off of it. My side reverberated in sharp distress.

A branch jutted out from my side.

How did the leaves stay on?

"Don't know," I mumbled in disbelief. "Nature is a hoot."

Nature is an amazing system, isn't it?

I grabbed the branch, my right hand directly on the left side of my abdomen. I tried to snap the branch, only succeeding in sending shooting pain into my gut.

"Fuck," I spat out. A hot tear streamed from my cheek back into my hairline. I wrapped my fingers around the branch that seemed more like a tree trunk. Trying again to bend it, I was met with another grueling, twisting pain in my belly.

"Not going to work," I said to myself as much as I said it to Bob who was still tapping on the tip of the branch. "Do you mind not doing that, please?"

Bob put his hands up in surrender as he leaned on the back of the pilot's seat.

Sorry, John.

"Help?" I croaked.

Where were the others? Were they okay? Did they leave me to die?

Maybe they are dead?

Then I would know, wouldn't I?

The Gaunt Man shrugged. *You are losing blood. Maybe you are not in your right mind.*

I squeezed the branch in frustration.

Damnit!

Crack.

An indentation had appeared in the bark under my grip.

"Well," I said with a painful swallow, "that's one way to do it." I repositioned my hands closer to my body and squeezed again. The pain was bearable this time. I added pressure to my grip and waited for that satisfy–

CRACK.

The branch had a decidedly smaller diameter where my hands had been. It was cracked and compressed, but not broken. The pilot stared at me, a bloody rivulet draining from the hole in his forehead.

No pain, no gain, Johnny.

"Christ," I said. "This is going to fucking hurt."

Bracing myself and taking in a deep breath, I slammed my right fist into the branch above the compressed area. I gritted my teeth as pain rippled through my gut. Spittle escaped from my lips as more tears streamed down my face.

I punched the tree again.

It took on a decidedly extreme angle, sappy sinews of wood still keeping the young tree branch flexible enough to withstand my blows. This wasn't working, either.

The co-pilot stared at my failures.

I reached for my knife. It was gone. No, actually it was wedged in the console on the other side of the co-pilot's seat. I felt for my Glock. Thankfully, it was still in the holster. It had been taken from me too many times in the last several weeks as it was.

Unlike me, the pilot was resting peacefully, his eyes closed and his lips upturned slightly. I reached out with my fingertips. The cockpit was designed so that pilots wouldn't have to stretch to reach any of the instruments. I was now part of the console. Unfortunately, as part of the panel, I wasn't meant to reach the top of the pilot's shoulder.

Definitely a flaw in the design schematics, I think.

I grabbed the pilot's arm and pulled him down as much as the harness would allow. I was able to slip his shoulder down toward me enough to grab the hilt of the tactical knife embedded in his chest. I pulled it out, a slick of blood running down the blade. The pilot's wound, now unplugged, was free to drain at its leisure.

This airman had a special taste in knives. It was a full tang model, with a line cutter hook at the base of the double-edged blade and top serrations on the spine. Bless you.

I flipped the knife around with my right and started sawing through the underside of the bent branch. With every stroke, the branch vibrated and sent searing pain radiating out from my belly.

From somewhere came a low mewing noise. Ignoring it, I focused on sawing through the branch. The sound persisted, gaining strength with every back stroke. It was only then that I realized the noise was coming from my own throat. I gritted my teeth in an effort to silence it.

Finally, the branch snapped off and left me with just the

bloody stump jutting from my side. I sheathed the borrowed knife in my scabbard and tossed the branch away.

Sweat beaded on my forehead. It was hard to catch my breath.

There wasn't any movement or sound from the rear of the craft. From my position, I could see down the center the main cabin, the cockpit bulkheads blocking my sightline to the jumpseats where the others had been strapped in. All I could make out was the toes of limp combat boots.

My shoulders were screaming in dull pain, but it wasn't from the familiar throb of the undead. I tried to hear the others' heartbeats but the ringing in my ears overpowered any other sounds.

Or... they are dead.

I didn't believe that. I couldn't believe that.

They are not here to assist you now, though, are they?

True. I was alone.

There was no way for me to get enough purchase or leverage on the instrument panel to lift myself off it. I was like a turtle on its back, with the added dilemma of a tent stake hammered through the shell into the ground.

A gaping hole in my abdomen was altogether different from being flayed. My enhanced healing wouldn't be able to close up the wounds nearly quick enough to keep me from bleeding out. I had to get off the stump and then get something packed into the wound immediately. Strapped to the rear bulkhead of the cockpit, behind the co-pilot who continued to stare at me with mild interest, was a first aid kit. If there was gauze, medical tape and a staple gun in there... if the wound tract was between the oblique muscles... I might have a chance.

One thing at a time.

First, get off this stump.

Then, worry about dying. Again.

I reached up and grabbed the base of the pilot's harness. I

wrapped my fingers around the nylon like a bull rider would wrap the leather strap around his hand. My slick bloody fingers kept slipping off the harness of the co-pilot. Finally, I was able to wrap my fingers around the nylon there, too.

Ready? Bob asked from between my legs.

"Get the fuck out of there, Bob." I muttered. "I'm not giving birth."

I like the view.

"Asshole," I said, fighting the swirling darkness forcing its way in from the edges of my vision. I took a deep breath, exhaled sharply, and pulled.

The pain was blinding.

My biceps and the muscles in my shoulders burned like heated railroad spikes that had been hammered into my body, threatening me with a fatigue that I wasn't prepared for. I couldn't succumb to it. Not now.

There was a sudden rough sliding sensation in my midsection, more excruciating spikes dragging against my innards. Something felt like it was uncurling from inside my stomach. I inched closer to the dead pilots. The stump disappeared into my belly, replaced by a bubbling of blood.

My biceps were on fire.

A heart thudded wildly in my ears.

The cockpit became dimmer.

I screamed as I pulled as hard as I could.

There was a sticky sucking release before I found myself free.

I rolled left onto the instrument panel, my hands pressed against the window. Lifting myself up as quickly as I dared, I pressed my right hand into the exit wound and stood up.

The cockpit swam around me. Bloody hand prints glistened on the glass. Were we still in the air? I braced myself against the back of the co-pilot's seat, reaching up at the blurry white blob with the red emblem on it. My vision tunneled to a pinprick of light and the white box retreated to miles away. I stretched out my arm, even with the cockpit pitching about.

My fingers finally bumped into hard plastic. I blindly ripped it off the bulkhead and fell hard against the rear of the co-pilot's seat. Lying there with the first aid kit on my chest, I panted and clumsily used my slick fingers in an attempt to open it. My fingers slipped off the latches, too weak to pry the lid open.

Slow down. Focus.

I tried again, putting all my dim vision toward the single latch above the handle. My fingers slipped again. I pressed the box against my chest with my left forearm. Using my thumb, I wedged it under the latch and pushed up. The first aid kit opened, its contents spilling all over the instrument panel behind me.

A strange little whimper of frustration and desperation escaped my lips as the gauze was now out of reach. Still held inside the plastic case by fitted clips were three thick clear plastic syringes filled with what looked like aspirin. Jackpot! You may be a dick in my book, Mr. R&R, but I had to appreciate what Roanoke and Raleigh stocked their transports with. The clotting foam was some advanced military medical tech.

I grabbed one of the oversized syringes. The tip had a multiport delivery system. I pressed the tip into the exit wound and pressed the plunger. The white pellets dumped into the bloody tract, instantly expanding and turning a foamy bloody red as they hit the air and my insides.

The bubbly fluid slowed and then stopped within fifteen seconds. I felt around for the second of the three syringes, grabbing it and turning it around in my left hand. I jammed the syringe into the entry wound in my back and injected the high-tech expanding medical foam into what I was sure was a gaping ruined hole.

Within less than a minute, I was no longer bleeding out from either wound. I stayed on my side, trying to recover my breath. The interior of the cockpit swam around me in an abstract Salvador

Dali way.

The seats were distorted.

The pilots were a strange surreal shape.

Like funhouse mirrors.

I rolled to my right.

The stump stared back from beside me.

The bark had peeled away in spots. The stump was ragged and uneven. A small curling branch forked off from the main shoot, just as bloody as the rest.

I think you found the snake from your belly.

"You may be right, Bob." I thought I said it out loud, although Bob could hear me regardless of whether I spoke the words.

Aren't I always right?

Not even half the time, my friend.

Well. I never.

You'll get over it, Bob. Now, give me a minute.

I needed to get this mess wrapped up so I could tend to the others.

And hunt down the mysterious Mr. Westsmith.

He's the least of my problems.

He's the biggest problem. Do not forget what is in store for the lovely Ms. Sawyer if Mr. Westsmith is not found and returned to the Man in the Black Suit.

One thing at a time.

First, let me get my feet under me.

Then, Jude… and the others.

Then, Westsmi–

25

Any Crash You Can Walk Away From

+80 Days – unknown

..**

"... that stuff off the deck!"

Insects biting into my skin.

Floating in flashing tendrils.

"… get that light down here…"

More sharp jabs.

More blinding sparks.

"… hurry up…"

Uncomfortable tightness.

Dull pain.

Better pain than before. Lighter pain. I opened my eyes. Sean's tactical light blinded me. I was in the spotlight again. Or, at least, my belly was.

"…where were you?" I whispered. "…why didn't you come…"

Lee hunched over my naked midsection, ignoring my questions as she focused on binding my waist with heavy gauze and clips from a handheld device. A staple gun? She pressed her fingers against the material in several spots on and around the wounds.

"Take it easy, Sergeant. What's the pain threshold? One to ten."

I swallowed and tried to think about numbers and how they translated into degrees of discomfort. Shouldn't it be on a 100-scale?

But this one goes to 11.

My belly hurt but it didn't seem to be too bothersome, even

with her poking and prodding.

"Three," I croaked.

"Three?" she asked with a bit of disbelief, a blotch darkening on her cheek. "I don't know what the hell went on here between you and this bloody stump, but you did good with the expanders. Really good."

I nodded.

"I sutured your muscle tissue and dermis. You're wrapped, but still leaking a bit. So, no sudden movements, okay? The expanders will dissolve as you heal so you won't have to be re-opened to get any of it out."

I tried to sit up. 'Where is every–"

"And, finally," Lee said, with her hand on my chest to keep me in a prone position against the back of the co-pilot's seat, "we need to get you into a waist compressor, just in case."

"And it will whittle down that pudgy midsection into that hourglass figure you always wanted," Sean chimed in with a weak smile, fresh blood on his already split lip. "Welcome back, boss."

We locked eyes.

"The others?" I asked, my eyes trying to blink away the fuzzy spots in the middle of my vision. "Where?"

"Accounted for," Sean said, flashing his light at the gauze, "and in much better shape than you from the looks of things."

"Jude?" I asked, although it came out as more of a demand. Had she abandon me? Had she thought I was going to die and couldn't bear to stand witness during my last moments?

"She's banged up, but good," Sean assured me. "She went with the others after Westsmith."

"Westsmith?"

"In the fucking wind for a second time. Can't believe that shit he pulled." Sean shook his head, looking at the dead pilots. "Alvarez cursed up a storm. He could be anywhere now with the jump he's got on us."

"And the walkers on the property are starting to take an unhealthy interest in the crash," Lee added, still pressing her fingers into my muscles. "We need to move out. This transport is just a hunk of junk now, anyway." She moved her probing hands from my stomach to give the Chinook instrument panel a loving pat.

"Am I going to make it?" I asked her.

"Sure."

"You don't sound too sure."

"On your feet so I can cinch you up," Lee ordered, ignoring my comment. "Umm, put a shirt on first."

I wasn't sure, but I could have sworn that Lee's eyes had darted across my bare chest in a less than professional way. Sean handed her a black rubber waist cincher and tossed me a clean scaled compression shirt. I shrugged into it.

"Where's my gun?"

"I got the Glock and your gear, John," Sean said. "Needed it out of the way so Lee could do her work. Did you know she has three degrees and a doctorate?"

"I'm not surprised," I replied, pulling my shirt down over my waist with a fair amount of nausea and the strange sensation of my sides twisting and threatening to tear.

"Good boy," Lee said with a blush. "Now put your arms up."

I did as the doctor ordered. She fitted the rubber device around my waist and proceeded to fasten the hook and eye closures as tight as she deemed fit. It hurt. She tightened the series of straps that were on the side away from the wound. Those adjustments hurt even more. Once she was done adjusting my truss and straightened up, the pain slowly subsided.

"Go ahead and get this man his gear," she announced with a mix of admiration of her work—and, I think, a bit of admiration for my body. "Lookin' good."

"Ma'am," Sean acknowledged her embarrassment with a

snicker, while handing my tactical vest and weapon back to me. "Yes, ma'am."

I shrugged into the tach vest and shoulder holster. I retrieved my knife from the other side of the still dangling co-pilot.

"Very Road Warrior-esque, John," Sean commented.

"Umm…very," Lee added with an outright grin.

I grabbed at the seats and the bulkhead to pull myself up toward the main cabin.

"Careful, John." Sean braced his legs against one of the rear jumpseats and reached out a hand to help me up. Lee was behind me, her hands braced to give me a push on my backside, if necessary.

I am sure she would find helping you out of the Chinook very necessary.

This was neither the time nor the place for such thoughts, Bob. She saved my life. That was a debt not easily repaid. We needed to stay on our mission objective.

I climbed out the side hatch and gingerly lowered myself to the grass. The pain wasn't minimal but it was manageable. I stepped away from the transport. The Chinook had come to a crumpling end with its nose deep into the earth. The branches from a grove of five trees had impaled the transport's metal skin in several places.

Sean crunched boots down to dirt, his tactical light piercing the night from over my shoulder. My eyes adjusted fine to the intermittent moonlight, even if the rest of my body was slower to catch up.

Lee hopped down to join Sean and me.

"Where's Jude and Melissa?" I asked.

"Over there." Sean pointed to a series of buildings. Their architecture was more turn of the century—the 1900s, not the 2000s—than the more modern, but still dated, medical high-rise Building 40 we had just exited. Its dark shape loomed above us from across a surface street.

"We didn't get too far," I muttered.

"That's Union Turnpike," Sean recited. "The rest of the compound is here on this side of the road."

Recalling the aerial video from Dick's drones, I knew we were still on the Creedmoor property. There were dozens of buildings on this side of the road, separated from the surrounding roads by a tall wrought iron, spike topped fence. At least we were safe from any FRACS beyond the perimeter.

For now.

"Lee," I said, "you're with us."

"Uh, duh," she replied sarcastically. "I ain't staying here by myself." She raised her M4 and took point, winking at me as she headed toward the closest group of Creedmoor buildings.

"She's ready to go," Sean surmised.

"Better not keep her waiting," I replied, still worried about ripping open my wounds.

I took one more look at the downed Chinook. It was a shame. She was an excellent flying machine, with plenty of firepower left in her if she ever managed to get airborne again. I patted the landing strut that couldn't quite stretch down far enough to touch the ground.

"Walken!" Sean called out. "Take your own advice. Come on."

John, why did the Chinook cross the road?

I ignored Bob and turned to follow Sean, the pain in my side shifting around with the twist of my oblique muscles. It was still manageable. Let's hope it stayed that way. At least the stab wound from Alvarez was a dull distant ache in comparison.

Give up? Because a maniacal bearded man shot the pilots!

Westsmith had to be found and we needed to a way back to the R&R citadel. Our time was running out.

26

Fast Friends

+80 Days – 0201 hours
39:12:01

"Faith Chapel." Sean nodded toward a building that looked like a church, a single spire rising out from the front façade directly over the entrance. To our right was an empty expanse of asphalt—a parking lot—designated for another group of buildings adjoining it.

"Oh my God," Lee commented. "There's a good LZ we could have used."

"It's a lot farther away. It wouldn't have mattered though, would it?" Sean retorted. "The pilots would still be just as dead."

"I guess," Lee agreed in a smaller than usual voice.

"That's the Lifeline Center ahead of us." Sean pointed out. "It's for autistic kids. I'm not sure about these others."

We crouched next to an abandoned sedan in the middle of the parking lot. Sean flashed his tactical light three times toward a long building at the end of the asphalt.

"Come on," Sean whispered, a frown on his face.

"What's the problem?" I asked.

"Nothing. Jude and Melissa were supposed to swing around to the end of the parking lot."

"Why did they leave the transport?" I asked, still finding that I was annoyed at Jude for leaving me alone. She had every right to go after Westsmith. She had more reason than anyone to want him in custody.

"I told you," Sean replied. "They went after Westsmith. Wasn't like Lee was letting them get close to you while she worked on you."

"Damn right," Lee chimed in. "I need elbow room."

I took a breath, trying to understand why I was pissed that Jude had left me in the cockpit. Jude wanted that thing out of her neck, asap. I did, too. Everyone on my team was after the same objectives. Get Westsmith to R&R so we could get the rest of our people back, get that damned device out of Jude's neck, and move on with our people as if this had been just a bad dream.

Sean repeated his signal. Then he tried for a third time.

"Let's just go," Lee said impatiently.

"There!" Sean pointed to the left edge of the two-story brick structure ahead of us.

Three lights winked back at us again where Sean was pointing.

"Like a lighthouse guiding us home," Lee mused.

We double-timed it toward the edge of the building. The stitch work Lee had administered was holding, although I held my wound as a precaution. We were halfway to the building when we caught darting movement from our right. Our weapons and the beams of our tactical lights swung around.

Just beyond the cone of our lights, over a dozen pair of amber or green dots shined back at us, floating low to the ground. Some of the pairs winked in and out of existence, while the rest held steady. A single low mewing started. It was quickly joined by several others of similar tone.

"What the hell?" Lee muttered.

One pair of glinting green rushed toward us. Our sights zeroed in on it. My finger went to the trigger of the Glock. Lee tensed up next to me. The dots leapt forward into the pool of our lights. A thinning calico cat sat down on its haunches and proceeded to lick its left forepaw, now uncaring of our proximity—as cats are known for.

That was why I liked dogs.

The other dots came into the light. All of them had seen better days, but they weren't lean enough to look like strays. Someone was still feeding them. Or, at least, they had been cared for up until very recently. With the fall of the world, it was easy enough to pick clean any remaining shred of food scraps without being shooed away with the broom of an angry shop keep or homeowner.

"Jesus," Sean said with a chuckle. "I thought we were going to be overrun by tiny FRACs."

"Poor babies," Lee lamented, obviously a feline fan.

I'd take Holly over a bunch of pussies any day.

Once we accounted for Green Eyes and every other grooming, quarrelling, and darting cat on the lawn, we looked back in the direction of where we were heading. Three winks from a tactical light came back to us from the shadows of the building ahead.

"Race you," Sean jokily challenged us. He jogged ahead, moving quickly to the corner of the building. He looked back with a grin at Lee and me a moment before he was completely enveloped in the structure's shadow. The smile was erased with a fist to his throat.

"Gak," was all he uttered as he fell to his knees. He dropped his weapon as his hands instinctively went up to his neck. The light from his rifle winked out as it was obscured in the dry yellowed tall grass.

The depth of the shadows along the wall lightened to a dark gray. Jude and Melissa were not there. But their weapons and tactical vests were. One man held Jude's sidearm on me as I rounded the corner, her vest draped over his shoulders. He hadn't bothered to tighten the straps. His partner held Heinz's Benelli against Sean's temple. Melissa must have scooped it up to go after Westsmith. She had always coveted that weapon. I guess her ownership of the shotgun had been short-lived.

I brought up my Glock.

"Nah," the scraggily haired and bearded shotgun man declared, pressing the barrel harder into Sean's skin. "Nah."

The darker-skinned man with Jude's Beretta waved it between

me and Lee, his eyes wide and his finger twitchy on the trigger. "Don't do nothing!"

"Where are the women you took that gear from?" I demanded, Sean still trying to recover. Better to have their attention on me.

"Whatcha worry about them for?" The black man with Jude's Beretta replied. "They're okay." He shifted from foot to foot, the barrel of the gun swinging from Lee to me with each step. He towered over Lee.

"Guns," the Shotgun Messiah ordered.

Tiny Dancer swayed back and forth.

Sean flexed his fingers. I blinked back at him.

"Come on," Tiny Dancer said with a twitch. "Guns. Like the man said. Or this guy gets it."

"Okay," I said. "Okay. We got you."

"Better." Tiny Dancer nodded, still working very hard on keeping his rhythm. White wires trailed from earbuds to an inside pocket under the tactical vest.

"Lee," I said, putting my hands palms up and away from the grip of my still-holstered Glock.

"Yeah?" she asked, her voice not carrying very far.

"Please hand over your sidearm to the gentleman. Make sure the screen is dark so the battery doesn't die."

"Umm." She sounded puzzled. "Ok."

"What screen?" Shotgun Messiah craned his neck to see what wonderful weaponry we had for him. "Nah."

"Let's you see infrared," Sean croaked, adding a hard swallow at the end to push down the pain.

Shotgun Messiah and Tiny Dancer shot each other a look. Tiny Dancer's eyes narrowed with suspicion while Shotgun Messiah expressed his lack of understanding with slumped shoulders and dull eyes.

"You can see people in the dark with it," Lee chimed in, slowly pulling out the piece of R&R tech. She held up the gun at the bottom of the grip with just her thumb and forefinger. "You can see the heat coming off people. See?"

Tiny Dancer stepped forward to get a better look. Lee was still half a meter behind me and to my right. Shotgun Messiah stepped to his left in an attempt to see the gun, my body blocking his view. The barrel of the Benelli lifting away from Sean's skin but still dangerously close to inflicting a mortal wound. Sean continued to keep his hands raised, flexing his fingers.

"Wha iz et?" Shotgun Messiah said.

I didn't move.

Lee moved forward one more step, the gun held out in front of her. Shotgun Messiah took another step away from Sean. Tiny Dancer reached out for the gun with his free hand. Lee handed it over.

"That's a big screen," Tiny Dancer said, turning the gun over in his hand. "Does this turn it on?"

Messiah stepped closer to see what Dancer was looking at. "Flip the switch. I wanna see."

"Good enough?" I asked. Dancer was to my three o'clock. Messiah stood directly in front of me, pointing to the tracking device with his free forefinger.

"Nah." Messiah shook his head. "Show me."

"Ok," I agreed, stepping between them and pointing to a switch on the top of the grip. "Just flip the switch there."

Dancer flipped the switch. Nothing happened.

"You doin' it wrong," Messiah shouted, slapping Dancer on the arm. "Gimme."

"No," Dancer shouted back, squaring his shoulders to block Messiah. "Stop!"

"You almost have it right," Sean interjected positively, his voice still raspy.

"Maybe the batteries did go dead," Lee offered.

"Flip it back," I said. "All the way."

Dancer held the side of the gun close to his face, turning away from Messiah. He flipped the switch back. He flipped it forward again. He pushed the switch with his thumb as far as it would go.

"Nah." Messiah looked over his shoulder, trying to reach around Dancer's arm to help.

"Stop!" Dancer wrapped his arms around the gun. "You're gonna break it!"

"Let me show you," I said calmly.

They both looked at my outstretched hand. They looked at each other, Dancer now cradling the tracking device in his arms like a toddler's security teddy bear.

"Na–" Messiah exhaled as Sean tackled him, pinning the Benelli-wielding arm to his side. They brushed past Dancer as they ended up on the grass.

Lee kicked Dancer in the side of the face. It caught him unaware as he had been staring slack-jawed at his friend in the grass. As his arms flailed, I stepped in and plucked both guns out of his hands.

"Hey!" Dancer muttered.

I handed the tracking gun back to Lee and pointed Jude's Beretta at Tiny Dancer. The double-click of a round being pumped into the Benelli's breach told me all I needed to know.

"Secured here, John," Sean announced, holding the shotgun on the kneeling Messiah.

"Good work, Sergeant," I replied. "Lee?"

"Good," she answered."

"Nice," Sean replied.

"You." I pointed to Dancer with the end of the Glock. "On your knees."

He raised his hands and dropped his eyes to the ground as he complied with my order. His lip quivered a bit and his eyes started to well up with tears.

"I'm sorry," he pleaded. "I just work here. Me and Harry,

both."

"Dwayne!" Dancer's partner hissed, slapping a hand over his mouth as soon as the words left his lips.

"Where are the women?" I asked. "That's all we want to know."

"Secret," Dwayne muttered to the barrel end of Jude's Beretta.

"Ain't supposed to tell," the scraggily Harry added. "Nah."

I pushed Jude's sidearm closer to Dwayne's face.

"I can keep a secret, Dwayne," I promised. "All we want is our friends back. Then we're gone."

"Promise?" Harry asked with a hint of hope from the end of Sean's shotgun barrel. He dug into his pants pocket.

"Easy," Sean said. "Easy there, friend."

"Nah." Harry, the former Shotgun Messiah, held up a pack of baby wipes. He dug a wipe out of the pack and started to wipe his hands with it. He jammed the pack back into his pocket.

"We just want to be back with our friends," Lee spoke up. "I'm sure you know what that's like."

"We have friends," Dwayne replied, starting to rock back and forth on his knees. "Good friends."

"Dwayne is my best friend," Harry confided. "Nah."

"We're glad you're such good friends," Lee said with a sweet smile. She walked forward and put a hand on the barrel of the Beretta, pushing it down. "Friends are very hard to come by these days, you know?"

"Definitely hard to come by," Dwayne admitted.

"Can you take us to our friends?" Lee asked.

Dwayne nodded his head to keep in rhythm with the rocking of his body. I slipped Jude's Beretta into the back of my waistband. Sean rested the barrel of the shotgun in the crook of his elbow and extended a hand to Harry. The bearded unkempt man took the offer, Sean bracing and backing up a step to get him to his feet. Sean still held the gun in his direction, just in case Harry was under the impression that he had already been forgiven for the shot to his throat.

"Thanks," Harry said, his eyes averted to the right.

"No problem," Sean said with a hard swallow.

"Oh my God." Lee clapped her hands. "This is fantastic. Great." She let that comment sink in for what seemed like a ten count. "So, how about taking us to our friends? Can we do that, Dwayne?"

"Uh huh." He nodded, slowly getting to his feet. He gestured toward one of two institutional dormitories. "They're over there."

There were no slivers of light peeking from the edges of any of the drawn curtains. No shadowy movement flitting from behind the glass. The building was decidedly dark.

Decidedly looming and ominous, you mean.

"Doesn't look too inviting," Sean said, echoing my own sentiment.

"Nah," Harry said, either in agreement or to refute Sean's comment. It was very difficult to say.

"It's fine, Harry," Dwayne replied. "We'll take you to meet your friends. They're safe. We have lots of friends over there."

Sounded like Dwayne was offering us a veiled threat.

"Then why did you take their stuff," I asked.

"Keep us safe," Harry interjected. "Now we safe, too."

"I thought you had lots of friends?" Lee asked.

"We do," Dwayne said. "But lots of termites, too."

"Termites?" Lee asked.

"They get inside from outside," Harry whispered, looking over his shoulder across the compound. "Make my skin bumpy. Nah."

"Oh," Lee voiced her understanding. "You mean those people outside the fences?"

"Nah. Not people. Termites."

Well... I think that statement is a bit presumptive.

You'll get over it, Bob.

"They're on the outside," I said. "Doesn't the fence keep them out?"

"Most times," Dwayne answered. "Real people get in, too. We lose a few of our own once in a while. People always want what someone else has."

"Real people," Harry added, pulling at the vest he had taken to wear. "So, we need safe."

"Makes perfect sense," Sean said with a shrug that only I saw. "Can you take us to our friends?"

"Sure." Harry's eyes lit up as he trotted toward a brown grass and brick paved common space. "Come on." He was apparently unconcerned about our weapons or about the events of the past few minutes.

Dwayne was a bit more cautious as he walked ahead of us with his hands still raised to waist level. "I guess we're going now."

We crossed the street in slow pursuit of the strange duo, keeping them a few meters ahead of us. Dwayne caught up to Harry and hooked an elbow through his friend's arm, slowing down his pace. Harry dropped his head and slumped his shoulders, but nodded some unspoken understanding between them even as his enthusiasm dampened.

The courtyard path led to a circular roundabout with a raised circle of grass and a single oak tree at its center. Wood benches lined the path facing the tree, five other walkways branching out like the spokes on a wagon wheel. The grounds were filled with mature trees on each patch of grass except the section beyond the lone raised tree. The trees there were underdeveloped and scraggily in size and shape, stunted and deformed.

Harry pulled Dwayne to a bench to the right of our path. They were still arm in arm as they sat, Harry's legs dangling under the seat. He pointed his toes in an effort to scrape them on the pavers. He dug out another baby wipe and scrubbed his already clean hands.

"We can't stay long," Dwayne advised him. "And put those away. You only got two packs left."

"We don't get any time outside to just sit." Harry pouted, putting his wipes away without wasting a second one.

"I know." Dwayne nodded. "You know the rules."

Harry's lower lip jutted out and his shoulders dropped again.

"What's the hold up?" Sean asked me in a whisper.

"Don't know," I replied. "Let's give 'em a minute."

"We ain't got time for this, John."

I nodded to Sean before speaking up. "Harry, we need to go."

"Nah. I know," Harry said in agreement. The *nah* seemed to have different meanings depending on its context.

Dwayne stood from the bench and pulled at Harry. "Come on."

"Ok, Dwayne," Harry said, but was reluctant to leave the bench. He furrowed his brow and slid his hand across the backrest and the seat as if they were old friends. Finally, once his forehead smoothed out again, Harry touched his feet to solid ground again.

"Thank you," Harry said to his friend.

"Welcome," Dwayne replied. "Now let's get them to their friends so we can get back to ours."

"Ok." Harry smiled.

"Where to," I prodded.

Dwayne pointed to the pathway left of the patch with the unsettling grove of trees. It led directly to the center entrance of the building.

"It was the Wellness and Recovery Center," Sean said.

"For what?" Lee asked.

Sean said no more, raising the Benelli to a full draw and swinging it at something under a shadowy copse of trees. "Thought I heard something."

Dwayne and Harry crossed 5th Street—according to the sign— to a large covered porch. They climbed six steps to a set of heavy double doors recessed into an ornate rectangular opening.

Like being on Easy Street.

The façade was flat, with a series of triple paned windows on each floor of the three-story structure. Each pane was completely painted over in black. I remembered from the aerial videos that the dormitory wings ran perpendicular to the face of the entrance. Each dorm was three stories and had two-story bay-shaped outcroppings with windows on each face. Some had air conditioners in them instead of glass. It was all very early 20th century institutional architecture.

"Cute couple," Lee commented.

"As long as we get going," Sean added.

"And where the hell are the others?" I asked. We needed to find Jude and Melissa. Hopefully, Alvarez's team would hunt down Westsmith again and we could get back to Manhattan sooner than later.

Harry and Dwayne looked at each other before slapping on the metal door three times in unison. They paused before adding two more. Two faint taps came back from inside.

Sean raised Heinz's Benelli—Melissa's Benelli now—and pointed it at the door. Lee held her M4 at half draw, her finger ready on the trigger guard as she surveyed the grounds we had just walked through. I thought to draw my Glock but stayed my hand. There was something about these two that gave me a measure of comfort, even here at the end of the world. There was a tingling at the base of my neck, but it lacked any bite or sharpness. It was just a mild directionless ache.

The sounds of chains rattling through metal came from the other side of the doors. I thought I heard an unintelligible voice but couldn't be sure if it was real or not. The right door slowly opened, just enough for a shadowed face and dark eye to peer through. The faintest of light flickered from behind her. "Yes?"

"Come on, Sally," Dwayne said. "We brought more friends."

The eye darted from Dwayne to each of us.

"I don't know you," she said, her wild hairdo of wavy black and white pressing into the opening between the doors.

"I know them," Dwayne said, starting to dance from foot to foot again. "They're okay people."

"Nah," Harry added. "Didn't kill us."

The door opening seemed to narrow.

"Come on, Sally," Dwayne insisted. "They're the same friends as the others."

Sally's one visible eye widened. She backed up and swung open the door, partially hiding behind it. The interior was darker than the porch, the candlelight inside much weaker than the moonlight we had been afforded up to now.

"Come on in," Harry said, heading inside the darkness over the threshold. Dwayne followed closely behind. Sally continued to peer at us from the edge of the door.

"Well?" Sally and Lee asked at the same time.

Sean looked at me with the slightest of nods, his finger tapping on the Benelli's trigger guard. I led by example, stepping through the door and into the dark unknown with our new friends. Sean and Lee followed me over the threshold, for better or for worse.

27

He Said, She Said

+80 Days – 0238 hours

38:35:01

The vestibule was dark save the flickers of lit candles on the floor, surprisingly narrow compared to the grandness of the portico and doors. Sally closed the door behind us with a soft click. The soft click was followed by a loud click as she threw the deadbolt. As a last precaution, she slid a chain back into place between the door and frame.

A chain seems out of place in an institution such as this one.

The entrance was darker now, the moonlight cut off by the door. Sally pressed her back against the door, her gun coming up from behind her. I spun and swiped it out of her hand before it came up to half draw. Three faint clinks came from somewhere on the landing of an open stairwell, the sound of hammers being pulled back. Using my momentum, I grabbed Sally by the shoulder and slid her around in front of me, her own gun now at the side of her neck.

Two armed men in dirty and ragged clothes trained their weapons on us from the first landing of the open cutback stairwell. One had a black finish Winchester 30-30. The other held onto what looked like a Smith & Wesson 36-1 Chief's Special double action revolver. Lee and Sean split and slid to the walls of the vestibule, both partially hidden by cast iron radiators as they brought their weapons up to firing positions. Dwayne and Harry stood at the base of the steps with their hands up. Dwayne shifted from one foot to the other while Harry had his hands over his ears, his eyes closed, and his lips in a thin tight line.

Looks lik–

"Don't even finish that thought," I told Bob in too loud a response.

The two gunmen kept their guns trained on me, assuming that I was talking to them.

"We were vouched for," Sean called out.

"And?" The man with the Remington asked.

"And we thought that friends were taken at their word," Lee said. "We were promised that we could see our friends and that they were safe."

"Not our call," Remington called out.

"Not their call, either," Smith & Wesson said, waving his pistol barrel toward Dwayne and Harry. The pair sat down on the third step. They had returned to having their arms intertwined at the elbow, huddled close and rocking together. They looked like children playing grown-up dress-up with the tactical vests still over their shoulders.

"Move," I whispered in Sally's ear. I pushed her forward with my hand firmly on her shoulder and the barrel of her Ruger LCP to her neck. I passed Lee and Sean, still in low defensive positions with their weapons locked onto the stairwell gunmen with Sally still shielding me.

"Go to your sidearm, Sean" I advised.

He slung the Benelli and drew his Beretta. "Thanks. Better."

Lee kept the sights of her M4 trained on the guards.

I moved the shorter stocky Sally to the bottom landing, Dwayne and Harry sitting to our right. "Where are our friends? That's all we want. This standoff is unnecessary."

"Maybe," Remington replied. "Maybe not."

"So, if none of you can make decisions, who's calling the shots?" I asked, moving Sally forward one more step for a better look at the gunmen's faces. "Get the boss here to make the call before someone gets killed."

"Christ," Sean muttered. "I thought walking away from a

helicopter crash was going to be the highlight of this op."

"Oh my God," Lee replied. "Right?"

"Get the boss," I yelled at the gunmen. "Now!"

They looked at each other, both shaking their heads and shrugging their shoulders.

"Harry," I said in a softer voice. He squinted his eyes tighter and covered his ears.

"Dwayne," I said again, more firmly and with more bass.

"What?"

"We need the person who makes the decisions. Can we put an end to this?"

"Uh...."

"Pretty please?" Lee asked.

"With fucking sugar on top," Sally added, her body trembling a little bit under my grip.

Dwayne puffed out his chest a bit and the thinnest of smiles crept to his lips at Lee and Sally's added incentive. "Ok. Come on, Harry." They pulled themselves up from the steps and disappeared down a hallway to the right.

"They better come back," Sally muttered.

"It will be fine, Sally," I assured her.

"You don't have a gun to your neck, do you?"

"No," I agreed, "but I do have two barrels zeroed on me from an elevated position."

"And I'm still between them and you, aren't I? And they ain't the calmest of the bunch, neither."

"It'll be okay," I promised her. "You have my word."

"Words ain't worth much these days."

The gunmen shifted their positions and stretched their necks, apparently the weapons getting heavy in their arms. Isometrics can be a bitch if you don't train for it.

And it helps if you're enhanced.

Yeah. That helps, too.

Smith & Wesson switched from a two-handed to a one-handed grip, shaking out his free arm while his gun hand dropped considerably as a result.

"Get that gun up, fool," Remington scolded his partner.

Smith & Wesson raised the revolver too quickly. A shot rang out. A chunk of tile shattered high on the wall, debris raining down on Sean's head. I pivoted Sally behind me.

The Remington discharged. The top of my right arm erupted in sharp pain. Blood trickled from my bicep, the bullet grazing my muscle below the shoulder joint.

I raised Sally's Ruger. Smith & Wesson retreated to the rear of the landing, leaving the weapon's sights only able to center on Remington's chest.

My pulse quickened.

Red crept into the periphery of my vision.

More pressure on the Ruger's trigger.

Sean steadied his sidearm. Lee did the same with her M4. Both had their fingers squeezing on the trigger.

"Stop!" A booming voice echoed off the walls.

I froze.

Remington lowered his rifle, his shoulders still tense and his forefinger still adding too much pressure to the trigger. Luckily, I don't think it had dawned on him that he had to eject the spent brass and load another round before he would be able to fire again. Smith & Wesson slumped to the rear wall of the landing, still shaking from his unscheduled weapons discharge.

Dwayne and Harry peeked into the entry from the side corridor. They moved aside as another figure came into view. Dressed in a flowing robe with a deep hood, this new person walked silently across the tile floor without a sound. The hem whisked across the floor, barely disturbing the dirt or debris there. The boss's hands were covered in black leather gloves, the left clicking the end of a two-meter black finish hardwood bo staff off the tiles with each step.

"Enough," the boss said in a deep bass voice. "Thank you, Dwayne."

"And me?" Harry asked.

"Of course," the voice under the hood confirmed melodically. "You, too." Harry's eyes lit up as brightly as his grin was wide. Several molars were missing, but he didn't seem to mind.

"Peter. Darwin. Leave now."

The gunmen from the stairs ascended quickly to the second floor without a complaint or word of discussion or opposition.

"Sally," the voice under the hood said.

Sally quickly reappeared from behind me. She approached the robed figure who leaned down to whisper something to her. Sally whispered something back. The hood nodded.

"Sally's gun, please."

The voice's words held a demand around it that I wasn't going to refuse. Plus, we all had our own weapons if it came down to us having to still fight our way out. I turned the Ruger around in my grip and handed it back to Sally by the barrel. She took it and nodded slightly. Turning back to the hooded boss, she whispered one more thing before exiting down the side hallway past where Dwayne and Harry stood. The pair looked at us for a final moment before turning to follow her. Harry gave us a final wave before disappearing with the others.

The boss's face was obscured by the staff and the shadows, shrouded with a scarf and curly hair that kept everything but the eyes hidden. The wood of the staff squeaked against the leather of the wringing gloved hands. I sensed tensing muscles a second before the staff was tossed at me. I easily caught it with my left hand. It had good balance.

"Good reflexes," complimented the same low melodic voice.

The gloved hands reached up and swept back the hood. Long brown curls were let loose to fall down past the shoulders. Next, the scarf was pulled away from the face to nestle in the folds of the robe's cowl. The gloves swept the hair away behind the ears.

"I apologize for the guards," the boss said in a decidedly softer voice, with now visible delicate and soft facial features. "My name is Alisha. Welcome to Creedmoor."

28

Ward of the State

+80 Days – 0300 hours
38:13:22

"You're the one in charge?" Sean asked, a lilt in his voice that sounded just a little like he thought that women shouldn't be left in charge of things at the end of the world. Of course, I knew that he didn't think that, especially after he had followed a male military officer and a blazing trail of destruction down the east coast.

"It would seem so," she answered. "Now let's get your friend's arm looked at before he bleeds all over my nice tile floor."

"What about our friends?" I asked.

"First things first," Alisha insisted. She led us back through the corridor she had emerged from. Harry and Dwayne, who had not run off too far after being dismissed, hurried along ahead of her. While making somewhat of a theatrical entrance, Alisha had quickly quelled our standoff with Peter and Darwin.

"I'm glad we're dealing with her," Sean said to Lee, then added a louder comment for me. "John, you okay?"

"I'll live," I responded, glancing at the blood on my sleeve and the red of the gash. "It's clotting up, at least."

"Dude." Lee slapped Sean on the arm with a measure of disbelief. "He had a tree branch through him a half hour ago. What's a matter with you?"

"For one, ouch," Sean replied. "Second, John has seen worse."

"Worse than a branch?" Lee asked in disbelief.

"Branches and bullet grazes in the same night does rank up there on the list," I admitted.

"Don't forget the knife in the back," Sean reminded me.

"Oh my God! What could possibly be worse than impalement

by a branch?"

"Near incineration from an RPG," I said.

"Being stabbed and shot several times in a museum," Sean added.

"Crucifixion."

"Trapped in a burning building."

"Shit!" Lee shook her head. "What's a tree branch through your side against all that? Damn!"

"Sally said," Alisha's voice rose above ours with authority in the tight hallway, "that you used her as a shield against my men, but then pulled her behind you when the shooting started. Is that true?"

"Yes," I replied.

"Why?" Alisha asked.

"Why what?"

"Why did you use her as a shield, then pull her out of harm's way at your own peril?"

"We just want our friends back," I said. "We aren't looking for a fight that we can avoid. Unfortunately, it seemed that your men didn't see it that way."

"Some of my people can be a little... overzealous these days when meeting strangers."

"A little?" Lee commented.

"We've had problems with outsiders. It's put us a bit on edge."

"People are attacking you?" Lee asked.

"One moment," Alisha said without answering Lee, holding up her staff to halt us. The corridor turned left and ended at a mesh glass door. Alisha pulled out a ring of keys and quickly selected one that slipped easily into the lock. The deadbolt clicked open and she went inside. We followed her into a larger square lobby with a similar glass door on the opposite side. Alisha walked around us and used the same key to lock the door behind us once we had filed into the lobby.

"Where did Dwayne and Harry disappear to?" Lee asked.

"Dwayne has his own set of keys," Alisha replied. "He's a trustee. I assure you, people do not evaporate into thin air. This way."

She pointed to a solid six-panel door to our left. This door did not have a working deadbolt but did have a 2x6 piece of lumber with one end wedged between the underside of the doorknob and the other end braced into a notch that had been hacked out of the floorboards.

"What's with all of the barriers?" I asked.

"It is for the safety of the people in our care," Alisha replied, setting the plank against the wall. "I assure you that all's well with your friends."

I heard a faint rub between the skin of Sean's palm and the composite of the shotgun's grip as he tightened up his grip.

"This way," Alisha repeated, walking through the now open door. The three of us stood at the threshold a moment longer, watching the robed leader with the bo staff walk to the other end of a five-meter corridor. She waited without turning back to us or addressing us.

"Eyes up," I turned and whispered to Lee and Sean. "Be smart."

We walked through the door in single file and started through the corridor.

"Close that door, please," Alisha asked.

As Lee was the last of us to enter the hallway, she did as our host instructed. The door clicked softly as it closed behind us. Alisha's robed figure filled the space. Once we met her, she stepped to the left. The corridor opened into a wide and deep space, lined with hospital beds and metal nightstands beside them with a wooden chair.

The smell of decay and excrement assaulted us.

Dozens of stringy haired FRACS shuffled around the ward.

Sean swung up the Benelli.

Lee did the same with her M4.

Nothing stirred at the base of my neck.

I raised my arms to bar them from doing anything rash.

"Ba... ba... ba... ba...," one of the FRACs recited over and over, tapping his dull face with his gnarled fist in rhythm with his mantra.

"Be smart," I reminded Lee and Sean, breathing through my mouth.

A male, dressed in only feces-stained striped pajama bottoms, made slow circles around a support column with his hands tight around the neck of a threadbare one button-eyed teddy bear.

A female rushed at us, clucking like a chicken. She had a huge grin, in spite of a dirty face and wild, stringy hair. Her bathrobe was flapped open, revealing a ragged T-shirt and a little bit more than was suitable for casual observation. She suddenly turned away, happy to wander toward another group in order to cluck at them.

"What the fuck?" Sean demanded.

Alisha stepped in front of us again. "My apologies. I guess we have become so used to the patients that we sometimes fail to realize that they can be a bit off-putting at first sight."

"And that smell," Lee said with a hand over her nose and mouth.

"Does it smell?" Alisha asked. "The brain is great at making your senses blind to unpleasant stimuli."

"These are all patients?" I asked.

"Most are," Alisha said. "I imagine that getting loved ones discharged from long-term psychiatric care was not high on the family's list of to-do's when the shit hit the fan."

"Christ," I muttered. "All these people."

The woman who had rushed us wandered from group to group, clucking at them until they got too agitated by her chicken noises.

One went so far as to clap at her face, stomp his foot and make slurring shooing noises.

"Karen!" Alisha shouted. "You leave Edison alone. Go roost."

Karen frowned and kicked back her left foot three times before hopping up on a nearby bed. She grabbed a pillow from behind her, wrapped her arms around, and buried her face into it to scream.

"Definitely not a chicken scream," Sean commented. "Can chickens scream?"

"You might be confusing it with *Silence of the Lambs*," Lee joked, her voice a bit strained.

"Maybe," Sean replied with an exaggerated shrug of the shoulders.

Tell me about the lambs, Clarisse.

Bob appeared in the aisle of the ward amid the beds and patients. He stood ruler-straight with a smile and his hands clasped behind his back.

You're definitely in your element, Bob.

Oh, yes. These are my people.

"Exactly," I said out loud to Bob, "they're crazy."

"They are not crazy," Alisha said with a hint of defensiveness. "These folks have deficiencies, addictions, or mental defects."

"I didn't mean to offend," I apologized, glaring at the smiling Bob.

"Sorry," Alisha said. "I guess I will always be a bit sensitive about outsiders labeling my people."

"How do you care for all of these people?" I asked the logistics questions. "Keep them fed?"

"We had a fresh non-perishables delivery the morning of the news. No water delivery this last time, but we have plenty stockpiled. The driver abandoned the truck when he realized what was going on outside with the termites. We were lucky enough to take advantage of what was left in the trailer. Which was quite a bit."

"Termites," a tall lanky young man with a buzz cut came over to whisper to us. "Gonna tell Maria."

He shuffled off, apparently to tell Maria.

"Ritchie is great," Alisha told us. "Something that more people should aspire to."

"Amen to that," Sean agreed.

"John!" a familiar voice called out from the other end of the ward.

Jude and Melissa emerged from a throng of Creedmoor residents, Ritchie holding Jude's hand as he smiled and dragged her toward us.

"I guess Ritchie found Maria," Sean said with amusement.

"Hi Maria." I smiled to Jude as they arrived. "Happy to meet new friends."

"Thanks, friend," Jude replied, giving Ritchie a pat on the shoulder and a kiss on the cheek. He let out a squeal, balling his fists up and shaking his arms around as he laughed. He ended by telling us that he was going to tell Maria and hurried away.

"A shame for him," Alisha told us. "I think his family would have come for him had they been able to."

"He's a sweetie," Melissa admitted.

"You going soft, lady?" Sean asked in disbelief.

"No," Melissa shot back. "Give me back my gun. Now."

Sean frowned and pouted out his lower lip before handing over the Benelli.

"How did they get your gear away from you to begin with?" I asked.

"Stupid trade," Melissa griped. "So they could be safe while they went back out to get you."

"I'm glad you're up and around. Lee said she could fix you up at the transport," Jude said before frowning. "Except now you have another gunshot wound. Damnit, John!"

"That's not John's fault," Alisha cut in, bringing a roll of gauze she retrieved from a glass cabinet. "My men got overexcited and decided that John was a proper target for their precious ammunition."

While Melissa enjoyed the return of her beloved shotgun, Jude gave me a look that included a raised eyebrow, a piercing glare and slightly downturned lips.

"You can't survive like this forever, John," Jude said, taking the gauze from Alisha and starting the wrapping process around my bicep. She never took her eyes off mine as she wrapped and pulled it tight.

"I know," I replied.

"What do ya mean?" Lee said. "Sounds like the sergeant survives pretty much anything. What's a bullet graze going to do to slow him down?"

Alisha stepped in and cut the gauze with a pair of scissors, then handed Jude a roll of black duct tape to keep the dressing in place. "This will be more sturdy than medical tape, I think."

Once Jude had wrapped around the gauze twice, Alisha cut that, too. She returned her medical supplies to the cabinet.

"Now that you've been reunited with your friends," Alisha speculated, "I wonder what the council will want to do with you?"

29

Hard Landing

+80 Days – 0317 hours
37:56:21

"What did you mean back there, Alisha?" I asked as we followed her upstairs.

"What do you mean?"

"Your comment about what to do with us?"

"Ah," Alisha said with recognition. "Yes, the council will want a say in what to do with you."

"We just wanted our friends back so we can get back to the city," I said. "We don't have time to waste."

"And we're waiting on a couple others," Sean commented.

Alisha stopped at the top landing, spun around and struck her staff soundly on the marble. Her voice lowered and resounded with more bass. "More of you? Now there are more of you?"

We stopped on the steps between her and the middle landing, spaced out along the rails.

"We never misrepresented ourselves, Alisha," Jude spoke up. "I told you we had others with us."

Her eyes darted between us.

We stared back at her.

Her hands squeezed the staff, a twitch pulling at the corner of her mouth.

Good thing you still have your weapons.

Bob stood beside Alisha, peering at her from a sideways angle.

She's seems a bit stressed. Maybe she needs some anti-depressants? A Zoloft? Maybe an Ativan?

Alisha looked toward Bob, who tensed up. My breath froze in my chest.

159

Then she looked down on us again. "Who else?"

"Well," Jude said. "We came in with another woman. She is the head of our group. Plus, she has two other men with her."

"We're tasked with finding another man to take back with us," Lee added. "We found him, but he took off after the crash."

"Yes," Alisha agreed. "You weren't unnoticed with that monstrosity flapping about above the grounds. I would be surprised if you haven't drawn even more termites to us. Or worse."

"The sooner we regroup," I offered, "the sooner we can leave you to your rounds."

"I don't believe you appreciate just how disruptive your presence here has been to us," Alisha said. "You have agitated many of the residents. I agree that it will be better when you depart."

"Just need to find the rest of our team," Lee declared. "And the man we are after."

"And who is this man who is so important to you?"

"His name is Westsmith," Lee confirmed. "He was holed up on the grounds in Building 40."

"Inpatient Services building?" Alisha said to herself. "And the rest of your people are still looking for him?"

"Bastard managed to bring down that annoying helicopter you mentioned all by himself," Sean said with a grimace.

"If he is a thin man with a beard and longish hair, then we have dealt with him before. We've had our pantry stores raided a few times." Alisha nodded slowly. Her hands loosened on the midsection of the staff, still tapping it slowly on the marble. The twitch had softened to an occasional tick, replaced by a slight upturn at the corners of her mouth. "Very well, then. I will speak to the council on your behalf. I'm sure they will be agreeable to letting you depart as soon as you are done. In fact, I believe we may be able to help speed up the process."

"What's up with this council of yours?" I asked. "I thought that you were in charge here,"

"Me?" Alisha said with a snort. "Hardly. I only administer to the residents. They seem to appreciate me."

"It seems that they do," Jude added.

"Just structure... routine," Alisha corrected. "I'm who they know... who they're familiar with."

She continued to tap the staff on the stone.

"So, what's next?" I asked.

"Hopefully we can find your friends," Alisha offered. "Save you some of that time you keep on about."

"I'm not sure your men are trained for this kind of work," I replied.

"That may be true," Alisha agreed, three others joining her on the landing, "but we know Creedmoor more intimately than any of you. I'm sure your drones don't see the tunnel systems. And, as you can see, we have resources."

How did she know about the drones?

"Don't be so surprised," Alisha said with a chuckle. "Those things have been buzzing around this place for months. They aren't that difficult to spot."

I looked at Alisha's men. They had hardened looks in their appraising eyes, their jaws set and their lips thin. They didn't look like residents.

"We would be most appreciative, Alisha." I thanked her, wondering just how much she really knew.

"That's settled, then," Alisha said. "I will have you returned to the Fourth Ward until your friends are found and returned. There is bottled water for you in the cabinet."

30

Stick Figures

+80 Days – 0427 hours

36:46:16

I sat on a spare cot that Alisha's men had pulled out for us, watching the team and the residents in the ward. Ritchie ran over to Jude and gave her an awkward and lanky long-armed hug. Afterward, he giggled with a hand over his mouth.

"You good?" Jude asked, her hand on his cheek.

"Stop," he squealed with delight. "I'm gonna tell Maria." He ran off to tell Karen the Chicken Lady all about Jude's audacity to return his affection.

Melissa sat cross-legged on the bed next to me, her hands on the Benelli in her lap. She said nothing, but the heat from her glare was evident. She hated to just be still.

Jude wandered around the ward, following Ritchie and keeping a casual eye on him. She stopped to check on the other residents, touching some on the arm for positive reinforcement and leaving others alone aside from a few soothing words.

Sean had left his weapons on the cot with me, sitting on a separate bed several meters away with a young girl. She sported haphazard blond pigtails and was dressed in jeans and a plain red T-shirt. She swung her legs out straight from the bed and held them there, stretching out her toes and revealing the dirty soles of her calloused feet. He spoke to her in whispered tones. She replied with the slightest of nods, tightening her arms around a small pillow in a stained and yellowing pillowcase with a puffy fabric smiley face sewn on one side.

The ward was a strange dichotomy, both orderly and dilapidated. The beds and nightstands were lined up with military barracks precision. What cheapened the effect of the well-positioned furniture was the overall condition of the ward. The freshest paint on the beds was applied years ago, brushed on over already peeling undercoats. Thick layers of dust clung to the corners where dingy and worn tiles met scuffed graying baseboards. Several dead flies lay on the wood window sills, their wings wide and their legs pointed in the air.

Lee was in the corner on the other side of the medicine cabinet with her hands on her hips and her head cocked to one side. She was concentrating on a dry-erase board full of pictures and nonsensical sayings and phrases. She seemed fascinated.

We had allowed ourselves to be locked in on the ward floor. It was for the safety of the residents, Alisha had said. We told her we understood. I was comforted enough by the fact that my Glock was in its holster. At least, for the time being.

A resident from the other side of the dormitory shuffled toward me with a twisted leg that forced his foot almost sideways. He walked on the edge of it, his body contorted side to side like a metronome with every step. He seemed oblivious of his physical plight as he stopped in front of me. His tongue poked into his cheek, a thin string of saliva escaping his parted lips and his eyes focused on a point well beyond my left shoulder. After a full minute of silence from him that even caught Melissa's attention away from her brooding, I asked, "How can I help you, young man?"

His head tilted forward and his striking cobalt blue eyes slowly focused on me. "You one of them?"

I glanced at Melissa with her shotgun and then at Lee still staring at the whiteboard. "Yeah, we're just visiting."

"No!" he shouted at me.

"No?" I asked. "It's ok. We'll go soon."

"You one of them," he said with more conviction, pointing a nail-bitten finger at me. "Them."

"Ok." I assured him, gesturing him to calm done.

"Them," he repeated. His accusing finger plunged back into his sweat jacket pouch, meeting the other hand already hidden there. They rolled over each other, lumping and stretching out the fabric with their antics. "One... them."

I had no idea what he was referring to, or how to calm him down.

His tongue returned to his cheek and his eyes dulled a bit as something caught his attention high on the wall. He pivoted around and craned his neck toward the ceiling. His eyes darted around as if he were following the path of a butterfly navigating around the lights hanging from the ceiling. "Bye," he muttered, and then shuffled away.

"What the fuck?" Melissa commented. "That one was an odd duck."

"A little bit," I replied.

That odd duck seemed to have your number.

About what?

About you being one of them.

Bob appeared next to Lee at the whiteboard. Her lips were still moving as she read the tiny scrawls that had been written there. He stepped up next to her and pointed to something in the center of the board. The medicine cabinet was blocking what he pointing to.

I looked around the ward. Jude, Sean and all of the residents were at least six beds away. "Melissa, watch the weapons." I walked over to where Lee stood with a furrowed brow and a cocked head. As I cleared the corner of the medicine cabinet, the entire dry-erase board was visible. Someone had written *termite* in alternating blue and green in tiny block letters around the outside edges. The word Alisha used to describe the FRACs. There was an odd arrangement of single eyes with lashes in all shapes, sizes, and colors. Dozens of phrases were scrawled on the board in haphazard directions fighting for my attention, but at its center was what Bob was pointing his bony finger at.

A black stick figure man was drawn with red pointed teeth, green slits for eyes, and red scribbled across the torso, arms, and legs to give the body more substance.

He knows you are one of them.

31

Solace Before Daybreak

+80 Days – 0629 hours
34:44:31

Karen muttered a low clucking from behind the pillow on her bed. The other residents were still fast asleep, some deep enough for ragged snores even in the early morning. Sunlight broke along the parapet of the building's next closest wing to the east. The wood-framed windows were tall and narrow, built with a heavy sense for turn-of-the-century institutional aesthetics. Some of the panes of glass were wavy, warping the light as it crawled into the ward. With sleep still an elusive and long-off lover, I stared at the rundown ward. The coats of paint did nothing to gloss over the deterioration of the layers ready to slough off. The trim looked fresh, but the fissures and cracks were always just under that thin veneer ready to be exposed.

Like makeup on a pig.

How did he know, Bob?

How did who know what?

The kid from yesterday. How did he know I was one of them?

About being a termite? Maybe he was just speculating.

I don't think he speculates about too much of anything.

That's an unkind thing to say.

Some of his brain is shut down while the rest is free to take in all the stimuli around him. Dots get connected. Theories voiced. An out-of-the-box thinker.

Wonderful. It's just something else to deal with. Don't we have enough to contend with? Westsmith and the missing Alvarez and her team. Jude's life on a timer. April and Summer under house arrest as bargaining chips. Holly was probably oblivious to it all, taking advantage of a charmed life.

Sean slept in one of the far beds with the young pigtailed girl, her hands wrapped around his arm that he hugged her with. It was an interesting relationship, as the little girl hadn't let him leave for his own bunk at all during the night.

Jude and Melissa shared the bed next to my cot, both snoring lightly. Jude was spooning with Melissa, and Melissa was spooning with her Benelli. Matches made in heaven. Jude had finally been able to tear herself away from Ritchie, the last kiss from her lips to his forehead sending him running and giggling to his bed where he put the covers over his head. He had still threatened to tell Maria about his opposition to Jude and her stolen kiss, but sleep had finally quelled his lamentations on the topic.

Lee had managed to pry herself away from the white dry-erase board far enough to curl up on the vacant bed next to it. Even in slumber, her closed eyes were facing the board.

Let's hope she doesn't see what that young man saw.

We can only hope.

32

Huddle

+80 Days – 0701 hours
34:12:19

Melissa sat up on her bed with her back against the headboard. She was alone as Jude had left her after waking. She hugged her Benelli with one arm and fanned herself with a medical chart clipboard with the other. She stared out the partially opened window opposite her bunk. Yellowing and rusting steel bars were mounted on the outside brick to keep us inside. Good for keeping the undead outside, too.

"You good?" I asked.

Her eyes slowly drifted toward me. "You better get me back to my niece."

"We'll get there," I replied.

"Oh, yeah? How much time does Jude have left?"

I opened my mouth to say something—I wasn't sure I knew what it was that was going to come out—but Melissa didn't give me a chance to sound out a single syllable.

"I didn't ask for this shit," she said in a clipped and curt monotone, each word a sentence unto itself. "I know you didn't ask for this either, John, but you better step up to get us out of here. This sitting around is going to kill us. Literally."

I closed my mouth and nodded, restraining myself from uttering any stupid comment. Melissa was right about Alvarez. The Marine had not shown much in the way of leadership. Up to now, she had been flustered and reckless. The secondary landing zone in the recreation yard for the Chinook was a testament to that. We had expended too much ammo and effort in the yard while there were better LZs readily available. Alvarez had put us in harm's way. The rest of us dispatched the walkers without injury, but it had still been an unnecessary risk.

History is written by the victors.

There won't be anything to write if we don't get back to R&R in time. Our exciting exploits will fall on deaf ears if we're all martyred for this covert cause.

Bob, now materialized, wandered away from Melissa and me with his hands behind his back. He ventured deeper into the ward like a general assessing the condition of his soldiers in an Army infirmary. I followed, hoping for a distraction from Melissa's glaring eyes and the streaming sun's rays washing through the windows.

These people are the lucky ones.

"I don't know about that."

I do.

We walked down the center aisle of the ward, his arms outstretched and elongating beyond what was considered humanly possible, his fingers not quite touching the metal footboards of the beds on either side. Some of the beds were empty, their occupants crowded at the far end of the ward where a commotion of pressing bodies was taking place.

"What's happening?" I asked, rushing over to where Sean, Lee and Jude were trying to pry their way into the crowd of restless residents.

Jude looked over her shoulder. "Thank God!"

"What?"

"I don't know," she said with a shrug, still trying to get an arm between the clucking Karen and a large Hispanic man whose rolls of fat stretched his green scrubs to their breaking point. "Ritchie is in the middle of... whatever this is."

Well. Is this not another fine mess.

"You think you can get in there, John?" Sean asked, struggling to wedge himself between two other patients.

I tested the idea by picking up a patient under the armpits. The fabric was damp and pungent. He went rigid as a board, arching his entire body back and throwing off my balance enough to stagger me back a few steps. I turned around and set him down on the floor away from the rabble, his body still stiff and his hands curled up into gnarled fists.

I turned back to the crowd. There were still over twenty patients crowded into a tight circle.

"Damn." Sean's face was a bright red. "These kids don't know their own strength."

"No, they don't." I pulled at the arms of two more patients.

They are not hindered by the perceived limits of the human body.

"Don't hurt them, John," Jude pleaded.

"Trying," I replied with a grunt. I pushed a hand between two bodies and used my strength as gently as I could to wedge myself into the crowd up to the shoulder. Using the fingers of my other hand, I pushed against one of the residents with as much force as I thought I could get away with.

Like Moses parting the Red Sea.

I was now part of the crowd.

I am sure that is a strange feeling.

"What's that?"

Being part of the crowd.

"Hilarious."

"You good, John?" Sean asked.

I nodded. "Just trying to get through."

My arms were pressed between several bodies. I had no leverage to push forward, my feet lifting off the tile floor.

A wonderful plan. How is it going in there?

"Fuck you."

"What?" Lee inquired.

"Nothing," I replied.

Bob, you're a pain in my ass.

I do what I can.

I was stuck.

Suddenly, there was a metallic banging that rang in a continuous rhythm. The congestion of bodies loosened, the acrid sweaty skin no longer pressed against me. My heels returned to the floor as the crowd dispersed and shuffled away in the direction of the noise.

"Bed, now!" Melissa stood in the aisle on the other side of the ward, a dented metal cafeteria tray in each hand. "Move it!"

The patients complied, each returning to the familiar surroundings of their own beds. Karen hopped onto her mattress to roost on squatted legs, lazily flapping her arms. The young man who had recognized my unusual condition stared at me with folded arms from a metal chair next to his nightstand. The heavy Hispanic man was on his knees with his head resting on the mattress and his hands stretched out across the bed.

"You're welcome," Melissa said sarcastically, tossing the trays to a service cart and returning to her own bed. "Idiots."

She talking about the residents or us?

Probably just you, Bob.

Jude, Sean and Lee surrounded the last remaining resident from the scrum. Ritchie's head was bowed and his hands were rummaging inside the pockets of a pair of blue jeans.

Jude went over and knelt down next to him. "You okay, kiddo?"

Ritchie shook his head.

Jude felt along his arms, shoulders and torso. Ritchie jerked away from her touch. His hands were still burrowing in the pockets of the jeans.

"No," Ritchie voiced.

"He okay?" Lee asked.

"He seems to be," Jude answered. "Not sure why he's saying

no."

Jude went to check his hands.

He pulled away again, taking the jeans with him.

"No."

"Looks like he's okay," Sean said. "As long as you don't take away those pants."

"Leave him to his pockets," I said. "He's quiet and content."

Jude patted Ritchie on the back and stood.

"Telling Maria," Ritchie mumbled to her, apparently keeping a running list of all the transgressions that Jude had committed.

"You tell it all to her, sweetie," Jude agreed. "And enjoy those pockets."

"Well," Sean said as we closed ranks, "that was fun."

"At least it was a distraction," Jude said, rubbing her neck. "How long are we going to wait for Alisha to find Alvarez and the others?"

"Not much longer," I replied, Melissa's words echoing through my brain.

"They can cover way more ground than we can," Sean argued.

"Maybe," I said, "but we're on the clock. And we still need to get back to the city."

"How long would it take?" Jude asked Lee.

"Not sure," Lee replied. "I wasn't anticipating walking back."

"Doesn't Alvarez have ears on?" I asked Lee.

"Get R&R to send in another Chinook," Sean exclaimed. "Or deploy another armored column like he did at the museum. That should be an easy request, right?"

"We won't know until Alvarez gets back," Lee said with a shake of her head. "Her comm is on a private scrambled frequency so we're in the dark until then."

"What a shit storm." Sean shook his head. "R&R is a military contractor, right? Shouldn't they be better at operations than this? No offense, Lee."

Lee glared at Sean for a second before shrugging the comment off and putting a smile on her face. "Hey, I'm just the tech and med support. No skin off me."

"This op seems way more personal to Dick than just a typical exfil," I speculated. "Any reasons why?"

"He was very tight-lipped about the whole thing," Lee admitted. "He was hot on your trail. And, then, once he had you, he started jonesing to get Westsmith."

Dick must have had his sights on Westsmith for some time. The tracking device implanted under his skin was proof of that. There was something more specific about Westsmith that prompted the rushed operation.

Dick did put you first.

So?

Maybe Dick needed you before he could greenlight this operation.

"… little desperate and un-organized, if you ask me," Sean said, pulling me back into the conversation. "Even Wallace never went into an operation without mapping out a dozen contingencies first."

"He was an efficient and organized killer," I agreed.

Sean looked down at his feet.

"Sean, he was a good leader with solid plans and some genuine charisma," I said, trying to convince him that the burden of the events leading him to Rainier Island did not rest entirely on his shoulders. In fact, Sean was one of the few who showed any of the island residents kindness back then. "Soldiers are trained to follow a chain of command."

"Doesn't change the decisions I made," Sean said, "or the consequences."

"I know," I said. "Better than you know."

Definitely better than he knows. You are a very complex creature.

That's one way to look at what I was.

"It's not easy to peel away from a direct chain of command," I said. "We defer to our superiors because we expect them to have a firmer grasp of the big picture."

"Maybe." Sean's voice drifted off.

"So." Jude cut in to get the conversation back on track. "We moving this expedition along or what?"

"It's after ten," I said after consulting my Cobra watch. "We wait until lunch. After that, we make our own calls."

"What about Westsmith?" Lee asked.

"Unfortunately," I said, "Westsmith is not as important as Jude, April or Summer."

"And Holly," Jude reminded me.

"Can't forget Holly," Sean muttered good-naturedly. "You love that mutt better than the rest of us."

"Of course, I do," Jude said. "She's much more agreeable than you two heathens. The females are the better of the species, as we all know."

"Oh my God," Lee said. "Preach on, sister."

"Crap." Sean counted silently on both hands, ending up with four splayed finders on one hand and all fingers open on the other. "Even when Alvarez returns, we are dead even guys to girls… unless you count Westsmith."

"I wouldn't count Westsmith," Jude advised. "Unless you want a murderer on your roster."

I'm fairly certain all of you are murderers at this point.

I wanted to dispute Bob's comment, but I couldn't come up with a truly valid argument to contradict him. We had all killed—both the living and the undead. I guess it was all a matter of degrees. In my case, I guess the killing of FRACs would be considered murder in the third degree.

Wallace.

Diggs.

Duke.

Roy.

Those were not pre-mediated killings, but they had been willful.

Were they satisfying kills?

I ignored Bob, trying to focus on the actual conversation in front of me.

"... fifteen miles to the city," Sean said. "Five hours if we don't have any obstacles."

"You know that won't be the case," Jude said. "We can't even get off the grounds without running into a sea of FRACs as soon as we step outside the gates. Remember the streak of black from the aerial...?"

Were they satisfying, John? Killing Roy for what he had done to Jude? Killing Wallace for what he had done to Donovan? Killing Diggs for what he had done to Lucy?

"Fine!" I shouted. "Yes!"

The others looked at me with cocked heads. My Creedmoor accuser continued to stare at me from his metal chair. I worked my mouth but nothing came out.

That was all I wanted to hear. It is just truth. Nothing more, nothing less.

"Sorry," I finally whispered, finding it difficult to swallow with my burning throat and a dry mouth. I walked away from them, knowing that their eyes were following me with a shade of concern and confusion.

And, maybe, a little fear.

Oh, I'm sure fear was always there just under the surface somewhere.

33

Girl, Interrupted

+80 Days – 1106 hours
30:07:19

Karen had stopped clucking long enough to let Jude know that lunch was coming at noon. She was surprisingly pleasant and articulate when she wasn't busy clucking. As the top of the hour drew near, the residents of the fourth ward slowly shuffled their way to the door. Since the food was coming in, I intended to make sure that we found our way out—whether Alvarez and the rest of her team showed up or not. At 11:45, I positioned the others on either side of the door, mindful to keep them away from the whiteboard and the undead stick figure at its center.

Bob, on the other hand, was looking at the board intently. *Termite,* he said with a chuckle. *Very clever.*

"When the door opens and the food comes in," I said, "we go."

"Isn't this the same plan as the museum?" Sean asked.

"Just without the pooch to run interference," Melissa corrected.

"We were told we weren't prisoners," Jude reminded us. "And we do have our weapons."

"Even though we're behind a locked door?" Melissa asked. "Sounds like being prisoners to me."

"I don't want another standoff," I said. "Just want to be out there operating instead of in here waiting."

"Waiting around does suck," Sean agreed.

BAM!

The door burst open, catching us off-guard.

"Jesus!" Lee said in surprise.

"Move it," Dwayne shouted. "Move it."

Dwayne and Harry carried Damon between them, Dwayne at the armpits and Harry at the knees. They rushed him to the bed next to the dry-erase board and dumped him on the mattress, the mercenary groaning and holding his arm over the left side of his ribcage. Dwayne rushed to the medical supplies cabinet.

Alisha hurried in, Alvarez and Heinz behind her. I almost didn't recognize her without her signature robes. Her bo staff was in hand but she quickly handed it off to Harry in order to better work on Damon.

"Save him," Alvarez ordered, Damon writhing in agony. "Save Damon."

Lee rushed over to Damon to triage the situation.

"They have him," I said, pointing to the crowd of people administering to Damon's injuries. Any more of us around him would just be a hindrance. Harry stood to the side with Alisha's staff in his hands. "What happened?"

Alvarez stared at Damon.

"What happened?" I repeated.

"What happened, mate," Heinz spoke up, "is that Westsmith is one slippery fucker and snared us into a bloody fracking ambush."

"What did he do?" Lee asked from her place at Damon's side.

"Once we finally picked up his scent, he led us on a merry chase through the basement of the dorms across the way." He tossed a thumb back toward the entrance of the ward. "He just stood there on the other end of the corridor and let us sprint on after him. Once we got halfway across the boiler room, he steps aside and a bloody contingent of walkers poured in from all around us."

He sat down hard on the cot I had occupied overnight, the blood becoming more evident as it dripped off his clothes and onto the sheets. "No ammo left, boys," he announced. "Went hand-to-teeth just to get out of there."

"And Westsmith?" I asked.

"Still in the wind, but I suspect he's close," Heinz reported. "He had plenty of time to ghost off the property before now but, for some bloody reason, he chose to stay local."

"And Damon?" Jude asked.

"We were almost out of the thick," Heinz told us. "Got close to where we saw Westsmith. A walker lunged out and took a chunk out of his midsection." Heinz ran his hand down his face, pausing his fingers over his mouth as his eyes welled up.

"Jesus, Mary and Joseph," Melissa whispered.

I hadn't taken her as a religious woman.

Other than to scowl at God for her miseries.

Does Damon have a chance?

You know he doesn't. He is already...

"...feverish," Alisha said. "I don't think we can do anything for him except to stop the bleeding and make him comfortable."

"Christ," Alvarez finally spoke up, her hand on the collar of her tactical vest. "This is such a clusterfuck."

"Now what?" I asked her.

"What?" Alvarez looked confused.

And scared.

"What's the plan?" I asked.

"I... I don't know." She shrugged. "It's all sideways. We're going to lose him."

I looked at Damon gritting his teeth on the bed as Alisha and Lee quickly stitched closed the pulsing tear of skin and muscle. Looking back at Alvarez, I saw her gritting her teeth, too.

"I...," she started, choking on the rest of her thought.

"We have no transport," I assessed. "We're down a man. Westsmith is more resourceful than expected. Our ammo reserves are almost gone. And I want that thing out of Jude's neck."

Alvarez looked up at me. "Don't worry about that."

"Yeah? Why not?"

"Just don't worry. I have that covered if it comes to it."

"That doesn't comfort me."

"Help me get this op back on track," she said. "Get Westsmith and get us pointed back to the city. If we run out of time for Ms. Sawyer before we get back to R&R, I'll be able to deactivate the capsule."

I grabbed her tactical vest and lifted her close to my face. "You're able to stop this thing in her neck? And now you tell me?"

"Had to guarantee your cooperation," Alvarez answered. "It was the only way."

"Your boss already has hostages." My words spit back at her. "What else did you need as incentive?"

"My boss," she answered with searching eyes, "needed to guarantee that you would stay on mission."

"So, Dick thought that threatening to detonate a bomb in Jude's neck would do the trick?"

"Yes," she said with a sigh. "He knew. I knew it. And you know it and why."

While Lee, Alisha and her inexperienced assistant nurse Dwayne worked, I realized that the others had crowded around Alvarez and me. Heinz had his hand on the hilt on his knife. He didn't try to bluff his way through this standoff with an empty rifle.

Sean stood on the other side of Damon's bed, his M4 raised to half draw. Melissa wasn't messing around. She had the Benelli already set against her shoulder with her finger on the trigger.

Ironically, it wasn't gender that divided our team as Sean had feared. We had returned to *us versus them*. Things like this always came down to a matter of trust. I used to trust Alvarez with my life. That was no longer the case.

"Enough," Jude shouted from deeper in the ward. Her arms were outstretched with Ritchie, Karen and the other residents crowding behind her. "What the hell is wrong with all of you?"

My tactical knife was in my hand.

I hadn't realized I had done it.

I guess you are ready to take on all comers.

"Put your weapons away," Jude ordered. "Now."

I hefted the finely balanced blade for a moment before returning it to its scabbard. Heinz holstered his own knife. Sean slung his rifle. Melissa returned to assigned bed, her hand never leaving the stock of the Benelli.

Harry held onto Alisha's bo staff with it held out on open palms like an offering. His eyes were wide with the worry that he was the only person in the ward still wielding a weapon. He started shifting his weight from foot to foot.

"Fear not, Harold," Alisha spoke softly. "These fine people are getting their emotions under control. It will be okay."

Harry's shuffling slowed down but didn't stop completely.

Jude was now consoling Ritchie. His arms were at his side but he was letting her hug him. Karen alternately nuzzled and pecked at Jude's arm with her nose as if it were a beak. Jude spoke quietly to them in a slow soothing voice.

See. They feel more than the rest of us. Just as I said.

"Just as you said," I repeated.

"What did you say?" Alvarez inquired.

"Nothing."

"I've done all I can do to keep him comfortable," Alisha announced. "He's stitched up and the wound has started clotting."

"Thank you," I said, knowing that her ministrations wouldn't make any difference for Damon. Once the infection caught hold in his bloodstream, it was only a matter of time before he succumbed to it.

"Yes," Alvarez added. "Thank you."

"It won't be long," Alisha advised. She handed off the bloodied instruments and gauze to Dwayne. "You need to watch him, keep compresses on his forehead and neck, and prepare."

"Prepare?" Alvarez asked.

Alisha looked at the former Marine corporal with a measure of amazement. "Haven't you had to deal with a termite before?"

"What do you mean?" Alvarez asked with more confusion.

"John," Alisha asked me, "am I to assume that your friend has never dealt with a victim of a termite?"

"She lives in an ivory tower," I replied. "She hasn't dealt much with the dead."

Alisha returned her attentions to R&R's team leader.

You should be the team leader, John. The head cheese... the big kahuna...

I'm sure Dick doesn't see me as anything better than an indentured servant, I thought to Bob. I will keep my affiliations to that of the United States Marine Corps.

"My dear," Alisha said. "Your friend has a termite bite. However the transfer works, your man is showing signs of the virus. It's only a matter of time before fever and death. Then he will be a termite."

"Then we will put him down once he comes back," I confirmed. "We'll take care of it, Alisha."

"Be sure of it." Alisha nodded. "I will have Dwayne and Harry change your man's bedding. There is no reason to lie in one's own waste. We will burn the sheets and disinfect the area."

Not sure that will stop the spread of the infection.

"Thanks," was all that I could say.

34

Lemon Law

+80 Days – 1225 hours
28:48:45

Noon came and went and we still found ourselves in the ward.

Dwayne and Harry left and came back with an armful of fresh linens. When they were finished, Heinz and Sean carried Damon back to the bed. The crimson-stained sheets were stuffed into a garbage bag. Lunch came and went. Damon's bandages were checked. Once Dwayne and Harry had finished their chores and left with their pushcart filled with dirty dishes and bloody linens, we were alone again with just our thoughts and a ward full of patients. The smell of melted processed cheese slices and bleach swam through the air.

A strange silence descended on the ward. It wasn't that the room was devoid of sound. On the contrary, Karen still clucked like a chicken. Ritchie continued to wave his hands in front of him and murmured his negative opinions on matters of the day. Sean's little girlfriend tapped the metal pipe of her headboard with the tip of the handle of a wooden paintbrush. As each of Damon's periodic groans broke through the heavy air, the rest of the residents of the ward shrank further into themselves.

Melissa had gone back to staring at her shotgun. Lee and Heinz sat vigil in metal chairs on each side of Damon's bed. Jude and Sean had returned to corralling and entertaining the other residents, trying to keep their attentions away from the man who would soon be dead.

"Will either of them be able to do it?" I asked.

"Heinz will be able to do it," Alvarez replied. "I don't know if Lee would be up for it."

"How about you?"

"I don't know," she said with a shrug. "I guess you were right."

"About what?"

"Ivory towers," she said with a sarcastic smirk. "I'll have you know I've put down plenty of deadheads, Walken. But I haven't had to put down someone I know. Or had to watch it happen."

"Seriously?"

"R&R took me straight in from Afghanistan after that last mission. Quarantined me for a few months once I got Stateside. Took a lot of blood and studied me. Started a training regimen a few months ago before putting me into the field a few weeks ago."

"Doing what?"

"What else? Looking for you!"

"Why?"

"How should I know? Boss was obsessed with you. With the one that got away." She air-quoted the last four words, accompanied by an eye roll.

"That's right," I acknowledged. "Dick thinks of me as R&R property."

"We're all R&R property," Alvarez agreed. "They got their claws in everything. More than anyone probably knows."

"Well," I pondered, "they're now the proud owners of a world that has gone to shit. I guess they bought a lemon."

"Pretty sure that they were a key part of making the world what it is."

"That's what I had pieced together too," I admitted. "Not that it matters much."

"How did you find any of that out?"

"I knew a guy who knew a guy." Felix Laraby, with his blood and brain matter dripping off the sidewall of his dining room, sprang to the front of my mind. That, and a rear garage wall that fluttered with copies of loose sheets of documents and photographs hanging from nails and pushpins.

"You usually do, don't you?" Alvarez said with a grim smile. "Always finding yourself smack in the middle of things."

"It's a gift." A gift and a curse. Why can't I just find a quiet corner of the world to settle down? Someplace for me and my own? Why does every step I take end up with lives in the balance and death swarming around me?

"The world really that bad?"

"Yes," I answered, still baffled that Alvarez had been kept off-grid so completely. "Couldn't you see the streets from the R&R building?"

"I usually was in quarters or training when I wasn't deployed. We would get an op, drop into a hot zone looking for you, run recon, then ghost when we came up empty," she admitted. "The museum was our fifth stop."

"Where else did you look?"

"The base where you landed stateside and a stretch of road south of it. The island. A housing development. A construction site."

"The island?"

"Looked like you left your mark there, for sure. Whole buildings razed to the ground."

"Did you have boots on the ground?" I swallowed.

"No. They were pretty well fortified and armed. We reconned for three days with the high-altitude drone surveillance. Facial recognition got no hits. We moved on after the techs using the directional mics heard someone lamenting about losing you to the road." She gazed at me with her piercing eyes. I couldn't figure out if it was admiration or resentment. "Sounded like you were well-respected."

"And here we are," I said. "In the field hunting down someone who's killed two men, downed a Chinook transport in the process, and ambushed your team with a third life hanging in the balance."

"And?" she asked, waiting for the follow-up question.

"Was it worth it?"

"Was what worth it?"

"Hunting me down in Worcester," I answered. "Both sides lost people at the museum. Innocent people were killed. And here we are, losing more men as we sit in the remnants of a psychiatric ward." I swallowed hard as I remembered the museum residents.

"I'm just doing my job."

"Death is a dirty job," I said. "What about all those people you and your team massacred at the museum? All the people you left like garbage in the streets?"

"Fuck you," Alvarez said with a glare. "You're the last one who should be lecturing me about me about death. Christ, how many people have you left in your goddamn wake since you set foot back on American soil?"

"Too many," I admitted. "I just want to be left alone."

"Then maybe you should make yourself harder to find."

"Like your man Westsmith?"

"We'll get him."

"I'm sure," I replied sarcastically. "But how many more are going to die before you track him down and get him back to your master?"

"More than likely, you'll survive. You seem to have that knack." She glanced down at my side where the tree branch had gone through me. "Impaled by a tree. Bullet graze. Knife to the back."

Survive like a cockroach. Bob's voice chimed in from the dark recesses of my skull.

"Still can't believe you did that," I muttered, my body having totally forgotten about any pain from the stabbing. Even the bullet graze had reduced itself to a dull ache. Only the sharp pain in my abdomen reminded me that I might still be mortal.

"We better get back to R&R before anything happens to Jude."

185

"I told you," Alvarez said, rubbing the vest breast pocket of her tactical vest absently, "Ms. Sawyer is in good hands. I can take care of her if it gets close to detonation."

"How?"

"Like I said... I have it under control."

"You better."

Alvarez opened her mouth to say something else, but her thoughts forming into words were interrupted by Damon's sudden violent thrashing.

Heinz and Lee sprang up to restrain him, their metal chairs tipping over behind them. The muscles in Heinz's neck stood out as he wrestled with Damon's flailing arms and arching back. Lee pressed her weight on his shoulders and hugged his head.

Melissa passed us with her shotgun at the ready.

I realized I had my hand on the grip of my Glock, although I hadn't yet drawn it from its holster. I grabbed Melissa before she brought the shotgun barrel up into a full draw.

"Don't," I whispered to her.

"Let go, John," she replied. "Why haven't we put him down yet?"

"We don't need you blasting away in the ward," I warned. "When the time comes, we use our knives."

Melissa tore her wrist out of my casual grip and walked back to her bed. I stared at her until she dropped her eyes to her lap.

Pulling my hand away from my holstered Glock, I felt a definite change in the air. The residents cast off a sour energy of simple, naïve, and superstitious fear... of monsters under the bed or from the recesses of a closet. Some muttered unintelligible nonsense. A few of them rocked on their beds with their arms hugging their knees. Others pulled the covers over their heads, even with the heat of the midday. Jude and Sean did their best to soothe them.

Damon stopped convulsing just as quickly as he started, his

breathing evening out after several more ragged exhales. Heinz lifted his weight slowly off of his teammate, raising his hands and backing away. Lee continued to hug Damon, whispering positive words in his ear as she pressed her cheek into his.

"We need to put him down," Melissa insisted from her bed. "Now."

"You try and I'll put you down," Alvarez warned her.

Melissa looked at her with a distorted look of disgust. "If only I was afraid of you. You may be strong, but you're still a useless bitch."

Jude, Sean and Ritchie stood a few meters away, watching how this new developing drama was unfolding. The little girl who had taken a shine to Sean sat on the bed next to them, her legs swinging through the rails of the footboard with her arms hugging the low top frame. She still held the paintbrush between her fingers.

Jude waved me over. Melissa got up from her bed and paced a few meters behind me. Ritchie shook his head at me as I joined him and the others. The little girl stared at me from the top of her folded arms, her head buried up to her nose. Sean looked over my shoulder at Alvarez's team hovering around Damon.

"Melissa is right," Jude finally said in a low voice.

I searched her face. "I know."

"Alvarez is going to get us all killed," Sean added. "Christ, there's an entire baseball field on the other side of the street we could have landed that transport. We didn't need to land on a basketball court full of FRACs."

"We need to look forward, Sean," I advised. "We can't keep looking back at the choice of landing zones."

"Wouldn't have mattered anyway," Jude muttered. "Would it?"

"Not with Westsmith butchering pilots at the drop of a hat." I shook my head.

"In fucking midair, mind you," Sean exclaimed. "How'd he figure he'd survive?"

"Maybe he's crazy," Jude said. "Maybe that's why he's at Creedmoor."

"But why does R&R want him so bad?" Sean asked. "It's a lot of hardware and manpower to bring back one man."

"And don't forget the tracker under his skin," Jude said.

"You gotta take command of this shit show," Melissa said. "Otherwise we're screwed. Who knows what's happening to my niece. Jude doesn't stand a chance if we don't start moving. And if you aren't going to lead, I will."

"Agreed," Sean added.

Jude nodded slightly, but didn't say the words.

I looked over at Alvarez and her team as they hovered over the fading and feverish Damon. This shit had gone on for long enough.

Yes. You have been a good little soldier so far.

"Soldier?" I muttered.

My apologies. You have been a good little Marine. Corpsmen are all so sensitive.

"What'd you say, John?" Sean asked.

"Nothing," I responded. "You're right. We need to make a chan–"

Damon screamed.

His back arched again, lifting him off the bed. Only his shoulders and shins still had contact with the bed sheets. Heinz put his full weight on Damon's chest in an attempt to keep him from hurting himself further.

The itch began between my shoulder blades.

Hmmmm.

Bob the Gaunt Man stood at the head of the bed, bent at the waist in order to get his face close to that of the dying man. He inhaled deeply and slowly shook his head. Damon continued to fight against Heinz's weight, his body still rigid off the bed.

188

"Christ!" Heinz shouted, his tendons straining in his neck. "How did he get so bloody strong?"

Tiny daggers impaled the muscles in my neck. Something else burrowed deep under the skin, clawing itself up over each vertebra and sniffing for the gray matter inside my skull.

Damon's body went slack.

The pain in my head did not.

So very close now.

Heinz lifted himself off Damon's body but kept his hands on Damon's chest in case of another seizure. Lee kept her hands on her dying teammate's shoulder, tears running down her cheek. Alvarez stood back from the bed with one hand cupped over her mouth and the other on her chest, her back nearly touching the dry erase board and the monsters drawn in the center of it.

Termites. Fitting.

"Quiet, Bob," I muttered.

The itch increased.

"Quit talking to yourself," Melissa said, brushing between Sean and me to get closer to Damon. She chambered a round in the Benelli with a loud click.

"Whoa!" Lee threw her hands across Damon to protect him from Melissa.

Damon twisted toward Lee, his arms flailing around her.

He bit into her throat.

Shit!

I pulled my Glock.

Quiet wasn't going to get the job done now.

Lee's scream was blood curdling.

Heinz backed away, wide-eyed.

Melissa shouldered the shotgun, moving right for a better angle.

Alvarez backed into the marker board, rattling it.

Lee tried to pull herself away from Damon's gaping mouth.

His fingers dug into her shoulders. His teeth ripped out a mouthful of bloody flesh from her throat.

I lined up my shot.

"No!" Alvarez pleaded. "John, no!"

More screaming. Not just from Lee.

My vision went red. The sheets, Lee and Damon were covered with Lee's blood.

"Colors!" Ritchie pointed out.

The little girl, who was so fond of Sergeant Bowers, screamed. Karen let out a series of strained clucks. Sean and Jude stepped back to keep them and the other residents away.

BLAM!

The residents recoiled, dropping and cowering close to the floor. Jude tried to shield them from seeing more, her slight frame not enough to block much of the mayhem. The little girl burst into tears and wrapped her arms around Sean's thighs. Karen dropped to her knees, hugged herself and rocked back and forth with her clucks trapped in the back of her throat.

"Jesus Christ!" Heinz yelled.

"No!" Alvarez yelled again, her right hand up in a warding off gesture.

It wasn't my weapon that had gone off.

Heinz finally reacted by pointing his rifle at Melissa's head, wisps of smoke still rising from the end of the Benelli's barrel. He stood between her and what used to be Damon and Lee. Not much remained of Damon's face, except where Lee's body had shielded it. Most of it was now permanently stained into the pillowcase and sheets. The back of Lee's head was also a mess of shards of bone and gray matter seeping out onto Damon's chest.

Alvarez opened her mouth, her jaw moving and her lips forming shapes without any sound coming out.

"Heinz," I said.

"Aye, mate," he replied as his training took over, his rifle locked in tight to his shoulder and his eye lining up the front sights with Melissa's forehead.

"Put the rifle down," I ordered him, keeping my voice even and calm. "There's been enough killing."

"Too much killing," Heinz said. "Especially from your angel of death here."

"They were both gone," Melissa said in defense of her actions. "Don't be an idiot."

"Enough, Melissa," I warned.

"Ok," Melissa amended. "Naïve, not an idiot. Better?"

"You're not making anything better right now," I said to her. "Show Heinz some faith and lower the Benelli."

"With him ready to pull the trigger? I don't think so."

"Heinz? You have any faith?"

"Not sure I got anything left in me."

"You knew Lee and Damon were gone, right?"

"Aye."

"Then it was a mercy," I told him.

Heinz sighed and slowly lowered his rifle. I don't think in his grandstanding he realized that the weapon was still empty. "Aye to that."

His shoulders slumped and he turned away from the bed full of death and blood, unable to look at his two teammates. He walked toward the other end of the ward. Jude and Sean were forced to pull the residents back against the beds so that he could stumble past.

"Fuck," Alvarez whispered, both hands to her chest. Her face had taken on a decidedly white pallor. Her cheeks glistened with a cascade of salty hot tears. She tried to form more words, but only succeeded in noiseless muscle movement. She stared at the carnage in front of her. When she could articulate something, her words were bristled with shock and blame. "What did your people do, John?"

The red, which had stood in stark contrast on the white sheets, was quickly fading as the blood began to oxidize into a darker rust color. Lee's arm was still draped over Damon's body in a protective gesture, her face resting on his chest and her dark eyes staring at me with what I could only assume was fear and contempt.

Why John? Her eyes pleaded. *Why couldn't you save us? Why didn't you do anything to save us?*

She didn't speak to me like Bob did, but I heard her voice whisper in my head all the same. I guess ghosts were ghosts, regardless of whether they were trapped in a lifeless corpse or a re-animated FRAC.

The door burst open behind us.

"What have you done?" Alisha asked, striding into the ward with two armed men alongside her. Their rifles were at a full, but awkward, draw.

The blame was definitely being laid at my feet.

Alvarez stared at the bed with her hands still over her heart. Melissa had returned to her bunk without another thought of what she had done. Jude and Sean continue to corral the residents several beds away, keeping their attentions elsewhere. Heinz was all but hidden at the other end of the ward, sitting on the edge of the farthest bed with his rifle across his lap and his head in his hands.

"Mr. Walken," Alisha said again. "I asked, 'what have you done?'"

Yes, Mr. Walken. What HAVE you done?

"Shut up, Bob," I muttered.

The two men fanned out, one covering me and the other moving toward Alvarez.

"Mr. Walk–"

"Damon turned," I explained in a monotone, careful to not let my derision at the situation come through. "He bit Lee in the neck.

Melissa put them both down."

Alisha pointed the end of her bo staff at Melissa. "You allowed her to do this in my house?"

It was all so quick, wasn't it?

"It happened quick," I agreed. "But it had to be done."

"It could have been handled in a much better fashion," Alisha advised. "We have our own methods for the termites... and those who become them."

Jude walked up, grabbed a sheet from the bed next to Damon and Lee, and swung it over the two of them. As the sheet settled over their cooling bodies, dots of red blotted through the linens.

"The kids are traumatized enough," she reminded Alisha and the rest of us. "Damon attacked Lee. If Melissa hadn't done what she did, it could have been much worse in here, Alisha."

The ward administrator shifted her gaze from the lounging Melissa to the dutiful Jude. The guard covering me moved a step closer. The one guarding the wide-eyed Alvarez fidgeted from one foot to the other, the barrel of his weapon dropping a few inches.

"I'll need to discuss this with the council," Alisha told us. "I understand the necessity of your actions, but your methods are not in keeping with how we do things."

"I'm sorry," I offered.

"We should have kept him away from your people," Jude said. "Kept him quarantined."

"I blame myself," Alisha admitted. "I allowed you access to the ward. I should have kept you separated."

Got to keep it separated! Remember... the song?

"Not now," I warned Bob.

"Excuse me?" Alisha asked.

I shook my head. "Where do we go from here?"

"My staff has found your man," Alisha replied. "Take care of this mess. Go get who you came for... and hope that the council is in a good mood."

35

Laundry Day

+80 Days – 1549 hours
25:24:59

Sean wheeled the remains of Damon and Lee down a dank, dark corridor in the building's basement in what seemed like an ancient laundry cart. He had put his tactical light into a loop on the shoulder of his vest. The light beam bounced off the walls and Heinz's tense back and shoulders.

"Thank God for the cart," Sean complained. "Bad enough that we had to drag them down two flights."

Sean and I had carried them down the stairs using the bloody bed sheets as slings. Heinz had not wanted to touch the bodies. Instead, Alvarez's last soldier scouted and cleared the way.

"Sure there isn't an incinerator?" Sean asked in a low voice.

"Don't let Heinz hear you talk like that."

"Like what?"

"With disrespect for the dead. Heinz said they were both against cremation."

"Damon turned." Sean reminded me. "Lee wasn't far behind. Do they still get a say in how they are disposed of?"

"Heinz still gets a say."

"Well," Sean started with hesitation, "maybe you should get your head out of your ass and lead this team. Maybe if you were in charge, we wouldn't have to bury anyone. Christ, you haven't been right since the museum." He leaned forward to muscle the laundry cart up a slight incline, the front left caster squeaking loudly while its partner spun in every direction except forward.

I had healed up from the battles at the museum. I was already healing from the bullet graze, knife wound, and the rip in my gut.

Sean wasn't disputing my physical condition. He was, however, telling me that I wasn't right in the head, wasn't he? I was a badass Marine Corps sniper, able to mete out death from up close and from a distance. Why was it so easy for me to sit back and watch as Alvarez—and now Alisha—call the shots? Why couldn't I step up and take control?

Bring out your dead!

Bob stood at the landing above the ramp, his hands clasped behind his back. He nodded to the unaware Sean as he passed by with the cart. Obviously, Sean didn't react.

How rude.

I gave him a stern look as I followed Sean.

That other mercenary is not very good, John. Very distracted. He didn't even notice me.

I ignored Bob's comment and left him behind on the landing. He shrugged and looked after me without another word.

Do not ignore me, John.

Why not?

Because Dick has neutered you.

What are my options, Bob? You want me to rock the boat in the middle of the operation?

You had done so while you were in the Corps.

This is different.

No. It is not.

I don't want to lose anyone else.

You standing aside has cost us four people.

Sean steered the cart toward Heinz's flickering light, swinging it wide to avoid scraping against the wall. I glanced back at the dim corridor behind us, parallel lines of pipes and conduits chasing each other into the blackness. I caught the faintest of sounds under the heavy silence. A random drip. A cricket in the far distance. A constant, almost sub-audible hum—more of a feeling than a sound—reverberated through the heavy cool air.

Step up, John.

"Mates!" Heinz's voice was like a bomb detonation, even at a whisper. "You're not going to believe this."

"What the hell?" Sean asked. Heinz held the front of the cart to keep him from pushing it forward. "We got a job to do. These are your teammates."

"I haven't forgotten," Heinz confirmed. "But you chaps need to hear this before we get on with our business. I'm certainly not doing anything else before we deal with it."

"Alright," I said. "Lead the way."

"John…" Sean started.

"Leave the cart," I ordered. "Let's see what has Heinz's hackles up."

"It won't be just me once you hear it." Heinz turned back to the corridor and walked away, his tactical light steady on the epoxy concrete floor a couple meters in front of him.

I tapped Sean on the shoulder. He let go of the laundry cart, unslung his M4, and followed Heinz. I brought up the rear with a slight pang of concern that we were leaving Damon and Lee behind unattended.

Leaving the dead behind. I am losing respect for you, John.

"They'll be fine." I whispered.

Oh, sure. They are in just peachy condition. Bob bent at the waist to take a closer look at the mercenaries under the sheets. He stood up again with a disgusted look, a grimace on his lips and a wrinkle in his nose. *Not fit for the living or the dead. You have definitely failed these people, John.*

"Fuck you." I hissed out the words, turning about to follow Sean with the slim hope that I wouldn't continue to see Bob's pale face or hear his hurtful words.

36

The Sound of Silence

+80 Days – 1604 hours
25:09:02

Heinz stopped after thirty meters, raising his fist for us to do the same. He blacked out his tactical light against his pant leg. We were plunged into a dim remainder of light as our eyes adjusted.

"Can you hear it?" Heinz's voice floated to us.

"I don't hear anything," Sean replied.

"Quiet a minute," I said.

The three of us stood there, our senses straining to hear what Heinz had heard. A cool dampness puffed against my skin. The distant crickets and drips had been replaced with something more rhythmic. The sound wasn't a mechanical hum, but something more melodic and organic.

"Singing?" I pondered.

"More like chanting," Heinz amended.

"I hear something," Sean added, "but I can't place it."

"Where's it coming from?" I asked.

"It's coming from up ahead," Heinz told us, "but I wasn't going to check it out without backup. All I do know is that when I hear something hinky, I'm not going to ignore it."

"Smart man," Sean agreed. "So, what's the plan?"

Both he and Sean looked at me.

"You are the senior in rank, Walken," Heinz reminded me.

Yes, John, you are the man in charge. As it should be, in my humble opinion.

My mind went blank for a moment. It seemed that all of my experience and training had been erased out of my head. What was the proper course of action when confronted with strange melodies in the heart of an undead FRAC apocalypse? I couldn't recall a single briefing or exercise from the Marine Corps that covered this situation.

The end of the world certainly wasn't in your USMC training manuals.

"No, it wasn't" I said.

"What wasn't, mate?" Heinz asked.

Shit.

I waved his comment away, hoping to distract him with another objective. "We follow the sounds. It's close. Either in a room or piped through the air ducts."

Brilliant, John. You really have all the angles covered. Feels like we are the Hardy Boys again. Just like we were at the museum. Remember the museum? You were so commanding back then. So handsome. So powerful. So decisive.

Bob made his points with a sarcastic tone. I was no better than Alvarez. This *was* a shit plan. "We aren't going to have any better plan before we know more," I said in defense of my own orders.

"It's a start, John," Sean said, nodding his support.

I wasn't sure if he truly agreed with me or was just supporting me out of a sense of loyalty and pity.

Does it matter? At least he has your back. Can you say the same?

"Yes," I replied to the question that Bob posed, answering both him and Sean at the same time. At least I wasn't making them wonder who I was talking to. "Let's isolate that sound before we lose it altogether."

37

Ships, Rivers and Things Dreamt

+80 Days – 1612 hours
25:01:37

We followed the humming voices. It seemed to come from everywhere at once before it suddenly faded back into silence. We found ourselves in front of a large metal grate at the end of a corridor, waiting for the melody to return.

Sean leaned his ear against the pipe cover.

"Definitely something," he confirmed. "Sounds familiar."

"That it does," Heinz added.

Sean and Heinz were right. The chant was familiar, something I knew from long ago. I just couldn't put my finger on it. Whatever it was, the rhythm folded over itself with each iteration.

"What's next?" Sean asked.

The grate was bolted onto the end of a rusted square duct, jutting out a few inches from the concrete wall. I shined my tactical light between the thick wires of the grate. Beyond the cover, the duct opened up to a two-meter diameter concrete pipe, less an air duct and more a service tunnel. Examining the bolts, I tested one with my fingers. The bolt squeaked, the thin coat of rust flaking off with my disturbance. After a few seconds, I had the three-inch bolt in the palm of my hand.

"Well done, mate." Heinz said. "You're just as juiced up as Alvarez, I take it."

"You'll have to take that up with your bosses," I replied.

"It's pretty bloody well evident," Heinz said, "since you're up and around after the crash."

"Don't remind me," I replied, touching my hand to my wound. The pain was manageable, sometimes so dull an ache that I forgot about the wound altogether. I moved around with enough flexibility that I didn't worry about tearing my side open again.

"Hey," Sean repeated, ignoring Heinz's comparison of me to Alvarez, "what's next? We going in?"

I worried that Sean was compartmentalizing every reference to me being something different than normal. Even as far back as Rainier Island, he must have noticed that the FRACs had reacted differently around me. Of course, we were in the firefight of our lives against a flood of the undead on that day. But, later on the road, it was just us at the construction site when we destroyed the walkers in the pit. I knew something had changed between us that night.

"John," Heinz coaxed. "You bloody finished with mulling over the question?"

I thought back to the Museum and how Bob and I shadowed Roy to see what was in the labyrinths under the galleries. All that came out of that was death and pain.

Do not forget your lovely companions still in the ward.

Melissa, Alvarez and Jude were still upstairs. Our women were armed and capable. Alvarez was armed, sure, but she seemed out of her depth since our arrival in Alisha's territory. Jude would protect the patients above herself. Melissa would take on all comers with her Benelli.

What a cadre you have assembled.

Selflessness, unbridled anger, and uncertainty.

All highly dangerous and effective.

"John," Sean urged again, Heinz looking on expectantly as he hiked up his weapon.

"Alisha says that the others will be cared after," I said. "We have another few minutes before we will need to get back to Damon and Lee. But only a few minutes."

"So, we're going in?" he asked.

"We are," I replied, breaking loose the rusted bolts enough to let Sean and Heinz finish unscrewing them. All the while the chant continued. When all of the bolts were removed, I grabbed the grate with my fingers and jerked it away from the frame. A shearing squeak and more flecks of oxidized metal flaked off. I set it against the cinder block wall while Sean and Heinz shined their lights inside the tunnel.

"Looks pretty clean," Sean admitted. "Dry. No excrement."

And the chanting continued.

"Let's go," I ordered, slipping past them and leading the way into the tunnel.

I hunched over and went to the first T-intersection five meters in. A slight puff of fresh air hit my face from the left-side corridor. A slight smell of rot came from the right. Unfortunately, the chanting also came from the right.

Can't catch a break, can we?

Bob sat cross-legged in the middle of the right-side corridor, staring at me with his hands in his lap and a grin on his face.

"Pressing on," I said, stepping around him. I couldn't bring myself to simply walk through him.

"Something to avoid up there?" Sean asked.

"Thought so," I replied, looking into the glare of Sean's beam. Bob had disappeared yet again. "But it's nothing."

At the next intersection was a large electrical junction box mounted on the opposite wall. A series of steel conduit pipes branched off from it in both directions. Sean shined his light to the left while Heinz did the same to the right. Both darted their light around for several seconds before joining me at the right corridor.

"It's close," Heinz announced in a low voice. "Has to be close."

"Agreed," Sean said.

"It is," I added.

The chanting was more distinct now. It was not singing, but more of a low humming. I could hear a basic rhythm with the same rhythm repeated on top of it. Then it was repeated again at a different point of the sequence. The smell was worse here, too. I don't think Heinz or Sean smelled it. I would imagine they would have made a comment about it by now if they did. Maybe satisfying their curiosity was more important than their delicate olfactory palettes.

The hairs stood up on the back of my neck. Heightened senses. Sucks to be me.

Heinz took point down the left-hand tunnel where the odor and sound was emanating from. Sean followed and I brought up the rear. It wasn't more than few meters before we came to a dead end. To the right was another electrical panel receiving the conduit from the box we just walked from. Conduit coming out of the top of the panel disappeared into the concrete behind it. To the left was a closed register cover high on the wall. The opening was smaller than the one we came through by half, this one more for ventilation than for service access. The humming was loud beyond the louvered slants. Heinz went to the register and forced the slants open enough to look through. A bit of light flooded into the tunnel; the humming became the loudest it had been.

"Row… row… row your boat…" a chorus hummed.

"Bloody Christ on the cross," Heinz muttered.

"… Gently down the stream…" The rhythm continued, then it overlapped on top of it. "Row… row… row your boat…"

Sean and I went to the louvre.

"…Merrily, merrily, merrily…" came from beyond the vent, while overlapping hums about streams and third renditions that started the whole thing from the beginning. "Row… row… row your boat…"

"…Life is but a dream."

"Jesus H. Christ," Sean said in amazement.

"…Merrily, merrily, merrily… Life is but a dream."

I looked through the louvers, trying to rationalize what I was witnessing. My shoulders ached. A buzzing crept into the base of my skull.

"...Gently down the stream... Merrily, merrily, merrily... Life is but a dream."

"...Life is but a dream."

38

Three Part Harmony

+80 Days – 1621 hours
24:52:41

The humming persisted. I stepped away from the register, leaving Heinz and Sean to gawk through the slats.

Row, row, row your boat...

The children's song reverberated inside my head.

Gently down the stream...

Bob stood with his back against the electrical panel, tapping his foot and singing the lyric softly.

"What the hell is this?" Sean whispered.

Merrily, merrily, merrily...

"Shut up and let me think," I spat out at Bob.

Life is but a dream... Sorry, John. It is quite the catchy tune.

"Sorry, Sean," I apologized, noticing Sean's cringe away from me. "I'm having a hard time with this."

"A hard time with this?" Sean asked, a finger pointing at the louvers. "I think it's safe to say that we are all having a hard time with this. Right, Heinz?"

"Aye, mate," Heinz confirmed. "I wasn't expecting this. I would have kept to my own business, had I known. You can bloody bank on that."

I went back to the register, hoping that what I had seen had been just been a trick of the light or a reaction to my blood loss... or that maybe one of those expanding pellets that stopped up my gaping wounds had found its way into my brain like a blood clot ready to cause an aneurysm. I widened the louvers and looked between them. The light streaming through blinded me for a moment before my pupils adjusted to actual light.

The humming had lessened, not in scope but in volume. The space beyond the register was a drastic juxtaposition to our concrete service tunnel. It was an auditorium with an angled floor with over twenty rows of cushioned seats with center and side aisles. At the front of the space, a raised platform was set into the wall with banks of speakers on each side and an array of lights mounted on a girder system above it. Flowing, but slightly frayed, blood red stage curtains were drawn back to reveal a deep hardwood stage with a second drawn curtain.

It wasn't the architecture that was the problem.

It wasn't the source of our dread and discomfort, although a murmur continued to come from the center of the auditorium stage. The chorus being hummed in a three voice round ended. It was replaced with a more disquieting silence.

"I'm freaking out a bit," Sean admitted.

"Right there with you," Heinz added.

"Something's happening," I observed, my eyes glued to the scene below and my right hand massaging my aching and buzzing neck.

The interior stage curtain moved, billowing out in a wave as something moved along it on the other side. Once the wave hit the center, it broke at the seam where the two curtains met. A hand slipped between the two sheets of heavy fabric. A second delicate hand sliced through the gap. After what seemed to be a dramatic pause, the two arms spread open to part the curtain wide enough to allow their owner access to the main stage.

A robed figure stepped forward.

"Is that Alisha?" Heinz asked. "Looks like her clothes."

"Does it?" Sean asked.

"Quiet," I ordered.

The hooded figure raised their hands wide in a welcoming gesture, the head bowed with the hood pulled forward enough to leave the face obscured in shadows. The robed figure nodded and swept their arms out to the empty auditorium. Their hands extended out in front of their chest with the palms out, pushing downward in a calming, hushing gesture.

The humming had stopped before the curtains had parted.

Now, no words were spoken.

Like a ringmaster, the robed leader turned sideways back to the second curtain, gesturing toward the crushed velvety red fabric. We waited to see what lie within the depths of the stage.

"Get on with it, already," Heinz muttered, beads of sweat on his neck. "Christ."

The ringmaster drifted to the left side of the stage and reached behind the curtain. With their arms hidden by the edge of the stage, the curtains suddenly swept apart, the squeak of pulleys being worked backstage filling our ears. The curtains were drawn fully open and slowed back to a resting state.

Surrounded by a circle of fat, dwindling lit candles were three wooden chairs. The hooded figure circled silently around them, the bottom of their robe coming dangerous close to a few of the candle flames. One of the candles extinguished altogether from the draft of the movements. They paused, only for a moment, with the dousing of the light before continuing around the chairs again.

"This is some fucked up occult shit," Sean commented. Even with wide eyes, he couldn't look away from the spectacle.

Heinz had been able to look away. He fidgeted with his M4's strap, readjusting the nylon band to a more comfortable position on his shoulder. When that was immediately less tolerable, he moved the strap back to its original position. Eventually, he pulled the strap off his shoulder altogether and held the weapon by its handle.

Down on the auditorium stage, the hooded figure was directly behind the center chair. They raised their arms high and wide. "We are in the presence of those wiser than ourselves," the hooded figure proclaimed in a low booming voice.

I don't think it was Alisha. The voice was decidedly

masculine. It commanded attention with its bravado and a heavy measure of bass, but it revealed little else.

"We require wisdom," the hooded figure continued, "as we are plagued by those who trample through our house, bringing disruption and death with them in their search for the Jesus Man. The question is… what do we do?"

The Ringmaster moved to center stage and faced the seats of the auditorium. A new rendition of the *Row, Row, Row Your Boat* hum started with a deep throaty voice. A higher octave and lighter version overlapped the first.

The three of us looked around the auditorium for a second person, not finding the source of the second hum. As soon as the bass voice started the third line of the song and the alto voice started the second line, another baritone began humming the song from the start. The three hums ran through the song twice before ending their iterations. Silence fell over the room again.

"Maybe the others are out of sight," Heinz whispered. "Is there a mezzanine under us?"

"Don't know," I admitted.

"Someone behind the curtains?" Sean offered.

"We have received our wisdom," the hooded figure proclaimed in a deep booming voice, catching our rapt attention. "The strangers in our midst must be purged."

39

Bring Out Your Dead

+80 Days – 1642 hours
24:31:59

We double-timed our way back to the service tunnel access panel. The others climbed through and took up defensive positions as I returned the grate cover to its frame and spun the bolts loosely into place.

"Come on," Sean said nervously.

"What the fuck, gents?" Heinz asked. "Should have left well enough alone, that." He moved his M4 around sporadically, the tactical light's beam bouncing off the walls and ceiling of the basement corridor. His strap was forgotten as it slapped against his thigh. His focus was now on something a bit more elusive and sinister.

"Ok," I said, the grate secured enough for casual inspection. "Let's move out." I wasn't sure what we had seen. It wasn't the most disturbing thing I had witnessed in my life, but the combination of the blanket of death and being in the catacombs under a crazy house didn't do anything to lessen the surreal experience we had just shared.

Heinz took point as we made our way quickly back down the corridors. After two rights and a left we found ourselves back at the laundry cart. The white sheet was dotted with crimson blossoms, ironically denoting life as it marked so much death.

"We gotta get them buried quick," Heinz surmised.

"You bloody high?" Sean spat out. "We ain't got time for that."

Ain't nobody got time for that!

I ignored Bob as best as I could, only wondering for a moment how a fragment of my broken psyche knew so much about fleeting pop cultural references.

"Can't leave them here," Heinz insisted. "We aren't animals."

"Mate," Sean shot back, using Heinz's vernacular with sarcasm, "that's exactly what we are. Maybe not an animal like that psycho on stage back there, but animals nonetheless."

"John?" Heinz looked to me to break the tie.

"Don't look to him," Sean argued. "We still got people to look after. You should realize that."

"What about these people?" Heinz asked. "Is it so easy to throw them away? Would you be okay with us just tossing your body aside if you died?"

"When it comes to choosing between them and the living?" Sean said. "Yeah... yeah, I would be."

What say you, Johnny?

I looked at the sheet, the red stains larger than before. The linen shaped a vague outline of Lee's face, tracing her forehead and tenting at the tip of her petite nose. Suddenly, the area under the tip of her nose billowed.

She's alive?

I snapped back the sheet to reveal her glassy and accusing stare. She was still dead, the ooze from the back of her gaping head wound becoming tacky on Damon's chest. Lee was not breathing.

"You crazy, John?" Sean blurted out.

You may be indeed a bit off your rocker, dear John.

"Maybe," I replied to whoever wanted my assessment.

"So," Heinz asked, using my actions as a teaching moment, "you're okay with leaving friends and teammates behind? Leave 'em here in this corridor to rot?"

"Can't leave them here anyway," I said. "We're in deep enough without anyone coming across a full cart. So, either we go on the way we had originally intended or we need to find another dumping ground."

Heinz's face cringed and his shoulders slumped at the bluntness of my words. "Some respect, at least?"

"Sean is right," I said. "We protect the ones still alive."

"See that?" Sean replied.

"But," I amended, "we need to give Lee and Damon something close to a proper burial. We definitely can't leave them here."

"Agreed," Heinz said.

"The time we've burned bitching about what to do hasn't helped, either." I pointed out. "Let's get this done and double-time it back to the ward."

"And what do we do when we get there?" Sean asked.

"What we have to," I answered.

40

Dirty Laundry

+80 Days – 1651 hours
24:22:19

Back the way we had come, a narrow cross-corridor led to a vast sunken room with a series of large water heaters. In the center of the floor, I took up two long rectangular iron grates that covered a drainage trough for water run-off while Heinz and Sean lowered Lee and Damon's bodies down the steel stairs. Heinz said a whispered prayer for Lee, placing two fingers on her linen-covered cheek. He repeated the same for Damon.

I laid to rest each of their lifeless sheet wrapped bodies under the floor in the trough. As Heinz offer a brief murmured eulogy, I realized that blood had found its way out through the expanding foam and waist compression girdle on my abdomen. My palm came away dark with blood, even though the wound didn't hurt.

Sean covered our flank above us, tensing more with every moment that passed. Heinz and I slid the heavy grate over the bodies, standing vigil for a moment before returning to Sean and the laundry cart.

"Thank you, mate," Heinz said with as much gratitude as the old warrior could muster.

We backtracked our way through the corridor with the cart. The remaining linen sheets—dotted with dark blood—lay unceremoniously in a wad in the bottom of it.

Could have used the rest of the linens to better wrap the bodies.

"Too late now," I said aloud, thinking the same thing.

Sean caught my comment as I stared at the contents of the cart. "We did the best we could for them, under the circumstances."

Sean misunderstood my utterance, but I did nothing to correct him. I appreciated that, in spite of his objections, he thought of others before himself. He thought highly of both the living and the dead, but would always put the living first. Not the best military strategist, as proven by his rescue attempt at the Worcester Art Museum, but a good man with the best of intentions.

Are you lamenting, again?

Maybe. Why don't I feel the same way Sean does? I don't seem to feel anything anymore. I feel mechanical. I don't know, like–

Like you're dead inside? Bob's bodiless words oozed through the pores of my skin, slipping through my scalp, finding their way through any fissure of my skull in their efforts to fill in the deep folds of my brain. The knowledge made me numb. Or maybe I had been numb all this time and just hadn't realized it.

Ever since losing Lucy and being injected by Diggs with his undead blood concoction, I had lost much of the hope and confidence I had clung to after returning Stateside from the Middle East. I thought leaving the island was proactive, but everything I had done since seemed to be reactionary. I had been highly trained to be a warrior once. A sharpened spear that the Brass could point their fingers at and say, fetch, or more to the point, kill. A precise weapon. Now I was just aimless and adrift, trying desperately to understand what the next right move was.

Maybe you don't understand how to feel. Maybe that was why you were such a good and faithful killing machine.

I searched my mind. My father was a hard man who worked tirelessly to provide a roof over our heads and hot meals in our bellies. He showed love in his own way. My momma was more affectionate, but was preoccupied with raising us.

How would you even recognize love if you aren't sure you know what it feels like?

Lucy's face bubbled up to the surface of my mind. Not the

diminished and matted version from a dark and foul barn, but the warm and smiling face of a woman who couldn't reach the paprika while trying to make a fish dinner. The face of a woman who slumped down a wall to the floor after bandaging the stump of what remained of a man's arm in order to save him.

Yes. There is no doubt that Lucy knew how to love. But her love and your attraction to her does not mean that you have the capability to love.

What about Jude? I fought an entire legion to save her.

Was that love? Or guilt for the sacrifice and suffering trying to save you? You are a driven man, John. You have a sense of duty... and your mind and body scream out against all injustice to those around you.

What about Garrett and everyone else on Rainier Island?

What about them?

I cared about them.

Did you? If so, I would imagine you would be there still.

I need to get home, I thought.

Home to what? To your family?

Yes.

You mean the family that you did not bother to contact when you returned Stateside? That family?

I wasn't in the right frame of mind when I had returned. I had needed to clear my head before I tried to talk to them. I was a shame to the family.

And now you may never get that chance.

The Gaunt Man stood at the end of the corridor, a faint flicker of amber candlelight backlighting his silhouette. His hands were clasped behind his back, a grim look on his face. His eyes glistened, reflecting back pinpoints of the tactical light beams.

I stopped short.

The laundry cart bumped into my thigh.

"Shit, John," Sean said. "Sorry."

Heinz looked back from his forward position. "What's up? You being squirrelly again?"

"Pain," I lied, putting a palm to the side of my torso for effect.

"I imagine so," Heinz agreed. "I'm surprised you're up and about at all."

Bob had gone quiet, but his eyes still appraised me. Heinz was close enough to touch to him with the barrel of his rifle. Bob looked at him, sidestepping to the wall as to not disturb the illusion that he was actually there. Nothing ruins the fantasy that Bob was real more than having someone walk through him.

Heinz cleared the dead-end hallway to the left and the stairwell to his right. "Let's move, gentlemen."

Sean pushed the cart past Bob and parked it in the hallway opposite the stairs. He went to grab the ball of linens before thinking better of it, following Heinz up the steps empty-handed. The linens stayed wadded up at the bottom of the cart, serving as an analogy of life. White with the virgin hope of a bright future, dotted with the bloodstains of sacrifice and loss, and eventually cast away after death. I tapped the edge of the cart with my fingers, lingering for a moment before silently renewing my vow to protect the living still around me.

41

Under New Management

+80 Days – 1710 hours

24:03:46

Two of Alisha's guards met us in the stairwell when we returned to the main corridor connecting the wings. They escorted us back to the ward, standing inside the door once we arrived.

Contrary to our paranoia, Melissa and Jude were oblivious to the strange facts of our situation. Melissa sat on her bed and watched the others in the ward, more out of curiosity then fear. Jude played Patty Cake with Sean's little pigtailed girl in his absence. When the little girl heard the door to the ward close, she looked up and smiled at the sight of her lost friend.

"Awn!" she exclaimed, butchering Sean's name in a truly elated and endearing way. She hopped off the bed and raced down the center aisle, tackling Sean at mid-thigh. She wrapped her arms around his legs and squeezed them tight.

"Hey, kiddo." He stroked her hair and gently yanked one of her pigtails.

"Stop," she squealed. "Stop it, Awn!"

"Go see what Ritchie's doing, sweetie," Sean requested. "I'll come play with you in a minute. Ok?"

"Kay!" The little girl bounded away in search of the boy who would undoubtedly tell Maria of any unusual situations he found himself in the midst of.

"Jude, Melissa," I said.

Jude's face fell as she read my expression. Melissa returned to her default defensive glare. We met in the aisle. Alvarez, who had been staring at the white board when we came in, joined us, too.

"What's up?" Jude asked. "Did it go okay?"

"It went, alright," Heinz muttered.

"What happened?" Jude pressed, more on edge now.

"I don't even know how to explain it," Sean answered.

"Christ." Melissa words coming out in a hiss. "Just spit out the goddamn words."

"We have more problems," I said. "We did the best we could with Damon and Lee. But Heinz found something else in the basement."

"Bloody crazy," Heinz elaborated. "Should have left well enough alone."

"Status report, soldier," Alvarez ordered. "Spit it out, like Melissa told you."

"Alright." Heinz took in a deep breath through his nose and expelled it out through his mouth. "We heard humming."

"Humming?" Alvarez repeated.

"Aye. Humming. We followed it into a service tunnel until we found a register overlooking an auditorium…"

At that point, Heinz lost a bit of momentum.

"There were three chairs on the stage with candles around them." I continued for him. "A person wearing a hooded robe came out and addressed them about us."

"Addressed who?" Jude asked.

"The fucking bloody empty chairs," Heinz muttered.

"Why is everyone in fucking robes around here?" Melissa muttered. "It's a goddamn commune."

"Whoever it was," Sean added, "was asking about what to do with us."

"And," I cut in, "apparently they want us out of here in a serious way."

"What about Westsmith?" Alvarez finally spoke up.

"What about him?" Sean replied with a question of his own. "Westsmith won't be the issue if we're all dead."

"Agreed," I said. "We cut our losses and regroup or go get

Westsmith."

"We're not leaving without Westsmith," Alvarez warned me. One hand went to the butt of her sidearm while the other went back to the front of her tactical vest. "We have orders."

"And if we're all killed," I submitted, "it won't really matter if we find him or not. He hasn't been too cooperative up to this point, has he? Two dead pilots–"

"–and don't forget our people." Heinz finished for me.

But yet he could not pull the trigger before Damon bit Lee.

"We're all under unbearable pressure," I answered Bob. Shit. "You got Westsmith in the wind. We have two of our own held as collateral. Jude has that blasted micro-charge in her neck—"

"I fucking know all that," Alvarez growled.

"And we need a plan of attack." I finished, in spite of her flaring anger. Or, maybe, to fuel it.

"It's all shitty." Melissa summed up our situation.

"We can't fight on multiple fronts," I advised. "Westsmith on the grounds... FRACs outside the property... People talking to chairs about what to do with us... we don't have the manpower or the firepower for all of it. You have to realize that, Rosalita."

Alvarez opened her mouth to argue my points, but stopped when I called her by first name. She shook her head in an attempt to shake the furrows from her brow. At least her hand had drifted away from the Beretta at her right hip.

While the others couldn't hear it, I could make out that Dwayne and Harry were outside the ward arguing about whether Wile E. Coyote could ever best the Road Runner, and whether he deserved to be able to. The two riflemen at the door rolled their eyes at what they felt was inane conversation.

"We can't return to Roanoke & Raleigh without Westsmith," Alvarez advised, speaking slowly and choosing just the right words before they leaped off the tip of her tongue. "That's the simple truth. We would never get back into R&R without him."

"So, we bring back Westsmith alive," Sean deciphered, "or we lose everyone we care about?"

"And, then I'm fucked, too." Jude added.

"Alvarez said she could disable the capsule," I reminded her.

"So," Jude replied. "Disable it now."

"I can't," Alvarez said with a shake of her head.

"I knew you were a piece of shit," Jude said with a glare and a hand drifting to her own sidearm.

"You said you—" I said

"I can," she cut in, bringing her hand up to ward off my rising anger. "But if I do, Dick would know and most likely remote detonate the charge himself."

"Now you tell us." Jude's shoulders slumped. She sat down on the nearest bed. She hugged a pillow and sunk her face into the end of it.

"If I disarm it now, R&R will be alerted that we're off mission," Alvarez explained. "If I do it at the last moment, we have the best chance at the element of surprise."

"Surprise for what?" Sean asked. "If the only way to get back into R&R is to bring in Westsmith, what's the point of the element of surprise?"

"Once we have Westsmith inbound, Dick will be too preoccupied with preparing for our arrival to notice that the capsule is off-line," Alvarez said. "Trust me that I won't let R&R do anything to Jude."

"If having Westsmith is paramount to our success, then we start doing things my way," I told her, looking at everyone to let them know that I was including them, too. "Enough snafus for one deployment."

"Ooh-rah," Sean said with conviction. "Now we're talking."

"About fuckin' time, Marine," Melissa added for good measure. "I'm tired of carrying you."

42

This Way, If You Please

+80 Days – 1724 hours
23:49:12

Dwayne and Harry came inside the ward and stood by the riflemen. They had finished their hallway conversation about the merits of Looney Tunes characters and had started up their ward argument about which captain of the USS Enterprise was the most capable.

We approached them as a group.

"Whoa there," Dwayne said, throwing an open hand up at us. "Where you all goin' in such a hurry?"

"We have a man to catch," I answered.

"Who?" Harry asked. "That Xavier fella?"

"That's him." Alvarez verified.

"Well," Dwayne said, "we know where he is. Ms. Alisha told us to tell you."

"So," Jude demanded, "tell us."

"Sorry," Dwayne apologized. "We didn't want to bother you while you all was talking."

"Very serious." Dwayne added. "Ms. Alisha said no interrupting when people talk."

"No harm," Jude said. "No foul"

Harry chuckled and started shifting his weight from foot to foot. "I like how ducks talk. They're funny."

"Where is Westsmith?" I asked, not finding it within me to be amused at his word association.

"Who?" Harry answered with a frown.

"The Xavier fella," Jude replied.

"Oh!" Harry's eyes lit up with the burst of understanding, the slow neurons firing all at once.

Reminds me of Joey. Remember Joey, John?

"Ms. Alisha told us to tell you when we saw you." Harry said, remembering his orders.

"So, where is he?" Sean asked, taking his turn to ask the same question we were all waiting for the answer to.

"Ms. Alisha said to meet her in the auditorium," Dwayne said simply. "She said she would have someone show you where that guy is."

"In the auditorium?" Sean asked.

"Of course, it has to be in the auditorium," Heinz said. "Just our luck."

"I love the auditorium," Harry said to nobody in particular.

"We're capable… and armed," Alvarez said. "I can't imagine dealing with the situation should be too difficult, whatever you think the circumstances are."

We all heard the nuances in her voice when she said *capable* and *situation*. Dwayne and Harry were none the wiser to Alvarez's meaning, Harry still rocking from foot to foot. Dwayne looked at us with longer eye contact, but even he seemed oblivious to what was really being said inside our group.

"So, can we go now?" I asked.

"Hmm?" Harry replied.

"We should go see Ms. Alisha," I clarified.

"Oh, definitely," Dwayne answered. "We should definitely go see her."

Dwayne abruptly spun around and walked out of the ward. Harry stood by the slowly closing door, watching his friend disappear through the lobby.

"We should go," Harry advised.

"Lead the way, hun," Jude said.

Harry went to follow Dwayne, trying to keep Jude from seeing the blush on his cheeks. He crashed his shoulder into the doorframe, his hands remembering too slowly to reach out to the door lever. The door had latched and didn't move with Harry's weight. His blush went from shyness to embarrassment. He stepped back, turned the knob and opened the door in the appropriate order. He smiled at us, happy with his success.

"We should go," he repeated. "Ms. Alisha don't like to be kept waiting."

43

All the World is a Stage

+80 Days – 1749 hours
23:24:43

Dwayne and Harry led us through a series of lobbies and adjoining vestibules. They hadn't returned to the conversation of Star Trek captains, instead gravitating toward a series of hypothetical scenarios of fictional characters. The riflemen on our rear flank kept us in a tight processional.

"Who would win?" Dwayne asked his partner. "Batman versus Darth Vader?"

"That's easy," Harry answered. "Batman."

"You kidding me?" Dwayne said. "What about the Force? Batman couldn't win against that!"

"Sure, he could," Harry insisted. "Batman always comes prepared. Throw a couple sonic grenades at him. Scramble Vader's brain. Use his awesome fighting skills. Boom! Done!"

"Okay," Dwayne conceded, leading us down two flights in a closed stairwell. "Superman versus Thor?"

"Superman," Harry said excitedly. "No question."

"No way," Sean whispered to me. "Thor would win."

Dwayne and Harry both cocked their heads to us.

"Bullshit, man," Dwayne said. "I'm with Harry on this one."

"Doesn't matter," Sean insisted. "Superman is susceptible to magic. Not sure Supes would be a match for the magic of Mjolnir."

"What's that?" Harry asked.

"Thor's hammer," Melissa answered for Sean. "Everyone knows that."

Dwayne opened his mouth to debate us, but left his mouth open without saying anything. Eventually, his jaw snapped closed with a click of his teeth.

"Right turn." Dwayne smacked his partner on the arm.

"Yep." Harry nodded. "Got it."

Dwayne stepped to our left while Harry opened a set of double doors to our right. He locked them in the open position and walked inside, disappearing into the cavern's darkness. Dwayne gave us a slight bow and swept a hand toward the auditorium.

"After you," he said.

Above the doors was a bronze placard designating this chamber as the Morningstar Theater. We filed in under the sign into the dark space. The center aisle ramped down to the vague shape of the raised main stage.

The flash of a match was followed by the whoosh of a candlewick catching fire. A fat white candle glowed under the light. It floated a meter above the stage, held in the hands of a familiar robed figure.

"Ease up," I told them. I felt anxiousness from Sean and Heinz as their hands tightened on the grips of their weapons. My words were easier said than done, my stomach turning into a sour churning pit, as well.

"Fucking robes," Melissa muttered.

The representative walked to center stage and place the candle on the top of a podium. The three empty wooden chairs were still positioned in a row across the stage. There was no question that we were in the same auditorium. The robed figure placed a hand on either side of the podium and leaned forward toward the light.

Harry waved us down to the third row and pointed to the seats on the left side of the aisle. As we sat down, Dwayne moved to the opposite end of the row at the side aisle.

The hooded figure rapped knuckles on the wood in front of them. Even with the candlelight so close, the face behind the folds of the hood was obscured from view. Assured that we were paying attention, the figure raided raised both hands from the podium. The figure bowed before dramatically sweeping the hood back to reveal familiar long hair. Alisha had revealed herself again in grand fashion.

"Welcome." Alisha greeted us with open arms.

Jude exhaled audibly, a slight wash of relief sweeping through her and some of the others. Sean and Heinz were still on high alert. Heinz kept glancing at Harry, sizing him up in case things went sideways. Sean did the same toward Dwayne.

"Thank you for joining me," Alisha said. "I understand we have had a difficult time, you and I. Circumstances have brought us together, for good or ill. That being said, we have found Alexander Westsmith."

"Thank you, Alisha," I said, standing up to show our gratitude with a slight bow. "We appreciate the efforts and consideration that you and your people have shown us."

"It is the least we can do for our fellow man."

"Can I ask?" I inquired. "Why the theatrics?"

Alisha gave us a slight smile, not of happiness but of something closer to resignation. "Routine and structure are of the utmost importance, especially in times like these."

"What's up with the chairs?" Heinz asked with a hint of venom.

"I don't know." Alisha shrugged. "They've been here for some time."

"How is it you don't know everything that happens here?" Sean asked. "You're the administrator, right?"

"You have so many questions," Alisha replied. "This part of the building wasn't part of my responsibilities before things… happened. But I do the best I can for my people."

"We see that," I answered, trying to soften the waves of tension coming off of Sean and Heinz. "So, to the main question at hand."

"Yes?" Alisha asked.

"Where is Westsmith?" I reminded her.

"Ah, yes. Your friend has taken up residence in Building #25."

"Shit," Sean muttered.

"What's the problem?" Alvarez asked.

"Exactly what I just said," Sean replied, shaking his head. "It's one of the condemned buildings on the property. The place is literally full of shit."

"Your friend is correct," Alisha confirmed. "No one goes in there. There were a few break-ins from squatters and from urban explorers, but I guess that's irrelevant at this point."

"So, we're cleared to go?" I asked.

"That is what the council has decided," Alisha said with a nod of her head.

"And the council," I asked, "isn't going to penalize us for what happened in the ward?"

"Correct," Alisha replied without pause. "They were in complete agreement about you. It helps that the residents of Ward 4 have taken a shine to you."

Harry rocked back and forth again, scratching at his bicep absently. Dwayne's eyes darted between each of us, his own tension rising.

"There is one other thing," Alisha warned. "Building 25 is close to Hillside Avenue. The fence is starting to buckle under the weight of the termites. It's only a matter of time before the fence comes down and the termites set up a new breeding colony. I ask that you do not disturb them any more than you have to."

"Wonderful," Melissa commented. "This day is just getting better and better."

"That was expected," Alvarez whispered. "If we keep it quiet, it shouldn't be a problem."

But it was a problem. While all of the buildings on the property were solidly constructed and designed to keep the patients inside and all others outside, the idea of FRACs streaming onto the grounds to overrun the entire compound sent a shiver up my spine.

"You'll have plenty of cover between here and there," Alisha advised.

"Easy peasy," Melissa complained.

44

A Numbers Game

+80 Days – 1803 hours
23:10:51

"I'm confused," Sean said, running his hands through his hair as Dwayne and Harry led us out of the auditorium.

"That's nothing new," Melissa replied. "What are you on about now?"

"I'm not shitting you," Sean said in a low voice, stopping to tie his left boot. "There's some serious fuckery going on here. It's like a cult or something. People in hooded robes. Councils we never seen. I don't like all this misdirection."

"We *are* in a mental institution," Melissa offered, as if that would explain every strange occurrence that had happened to us since coming to Creedmoor.

I stepped into the conversation. "Couldn't be sure if it was Alisha under the robes."

Heinz offered his opinion. "Looked like the same robes to me, mate. Just no bo staff."

"Voice wasn't the same," I assessed. "Not sure why they would decree to kill us, then point us in the direction of Westsmith."

"Trap?" Jude asked.

"Too convoluted," I answered. "Dwayne and Harry would have had an easier time mowing us down in the third row while we waited for Alisha."

"And it's too complicated to send us out on another chase," Alvarez said.

"Exactly. We have more tactical options out in the field," I added. "Room to maneuver."

Dwayne and Harry, realizing we weren't directly behind them, hustled back with their sidearms drawn. The others tightened their grips on their own weapons while Jude and I waited to see what would develop.

"Come on, guys," Dwayne insisted. "Can't guarantee how long this guy of yours is going to stay in 25."

"I don't want to be there at all," Harry added. "That place creeps me out. Bad enough Alisha picked us to take you there."

"I'm sure it's not that bad," Dwayne countered.

"Winston threatened that he was gonna lock me in there overnight." Harry looked at his shifting feet. "You know, after I had that accident."

We all looked on, not sure of the details of their conversation.

"Winston was a trustee," he explained, taking notice of our stares. "He'd been around back in Creedmoor's heyday. Back in the Fifties and Sixties when this place was booming."

"Uh huh," Harry added. "Before everything went into the crapper."

"Agreed," Sean said. "The apocalypse has been a bitch for institutional facilities."

"Not really," Dwayne corrected. "Creedmoor's been going to shit for years before the termites came around."

"True." Sean's sarcasm faded. "Couldn't even keep the Police task forces as renters."

"Ha," Dwayne snorted. "Had a big operation over in Building 70. Think it was NYPD Narco."

"NYPD was in Building 70 across the courtyard from the wards," Sean explained.

"Good to know," I said. I noticed that Judy, Melissa and Alvarez were starting to fidget—all for different reasons. Heinz stood stoically at the back of the group, his eyes scanning the corridor. "Let's get going."

Harry opened his mouth and let out a strange little squeak. He swallowed hard before he spoke again. "I was... I mean, we were wait– "

"It's okay, Harry." Dwayne waved us forward. "Let's show these nice people the way to 25 so we can be done with this. I want my gold star so I can go back to my room."

He stomped off in the direction of the stairwell.

"I guess we should follow him, too," Melissa speculated.

"You think?" I commented. "Let's follow the man."

45

Lock and Load

+80 Days – 1819 hours
22:54:28

Dwayne and the still flustered Harry led us through a long corridor and up a flight of stairs to an alcove. The batteries in the exit sign over the fire door had died way before our arrival. Our escorts slapped their hands against the latch bar and disappeared into the night. A warm flowery scented breeze buffeted my face as we found ourselves under a small portico. It faced the same courtyard where Harry had taken his break on the bench, only farther along the building toward its southeastern end.

"Wanted to tell Ritchie we were going," Jude said with a tinge of sadness.

"I was thinking the same about Agatha," Sean said in agreement.

"Agatha?" Melissa asked.

"You know," Sean reminded her. "Little blond girl. Pigtails. Enjoys tackling me around the legs."

"Oh, her." Melissa checked the breach of her Benelli and tightened its strap on her shoulder. "Agatha. Gotcha."

"Once we get Westsmith," I told them, "we still need to rally to figure out way a back to the city. I'm sure you'll get a chance to say your goodbyes."

Dwayne and Harry argued quietly several meters ahead of us. I couldn't quite make out their conversation, but Harry was flailing his arms wildly to drive home his side of the debate.

"Alvarez," I called out.

"Yes, Sergeant," she replied, the crispness back in her voice.

"Weapons check," I ordered. "Moving out in two minutes."

"Yes, Sergeant." Alvarez went to Heinz first, taking his M4 and checking the breach and magazine. She handed back the rifle and stepped over to Sean to repeat the process. When she approached Melissa, she was met with the barrel end of the Benelli.

"Your weapon," Alvarez ordered.

"Don't think so," Melissa replied.

"Leave her be, Alvarez," I said. "She's checked her weapon three times since we left the auditorium."

"Yeah, Alvarez," Melissa added. "Fuck off."

"Have it your way," Alvarez said with a shrug. "Ms. Sawyer?"

"Sure," Jude answered, pulling her sidearm. Jude pulled back the slide, tilted the sidearm, and released the magazine and showed that it was full. She slapped the magazine home and holstered her weapon before Alvarez could acknowledge her approval with a nod.

Yeah. Jude was definitely a badass.

I checked my M4 before inspecting my Glock. It had delivered more death since returning Stateside than in any military hotspot around the globe. The magazine was full and my pockets were filled with reloads but our ammo was down to a third. While my group hadn't fired any rounds, Alvarez's crew had nearly emptied their ammo reserves during their second run-in with Westsmith. The duffle was nearly empty, its nylon construction now sagging on Alvarez's back.

Dwayne and Harry came back, as if on cue. Harry looked at his feet, his weight rocking between them after he stopped walking. His brow was furrowed and his bottom lip was sticking out farther than usual.

"You ready?" Dwayne asked.

"Don't we look ready?" Melissa said sarcastically. "Christ! Let's move, already."

"Okay," he apologized. "Okay. We're going."

Harry sighed, still looking at his feet.

"Lead the way, brothers," I said. "Let's get you those gold stars."

That perked both of them up.

46

Building Blocks

+80 Days – 1837 hours
22:36:10

We moved through the center of the courtyard, Harry slowing as we passed the bench that faced the raised grassy area. He didn't look any farther than a meter in front of his feet as we made our way to the deep shadows of Building 70.

His hand went for another baby wipe.

"Stop," Dwayne warned his friend. "You don't have many left and I don't know if I can get you more."

The architecture of Building #70 was the same as the Wellness Center, only in a further state of disrepair. Strangely enough, we were near the recesses of its wards as we crossed the courtyard. instead of its main entries. Both buildings were built with their main entries facing south. My mind rejected the fact that its front door did not face the courtyard.

Seems crazy.

The buildings were built to face the same direction. Wasn't the diminished mind more appreciative of order in design? The fact that Buildings 70 and 73 didn't both have their frontage facing the courtyard certainly bothered me for some reason.

You and your infernal need for mirrored symmetry. Maybe the architects had a better plan in mind? Something beyond what you can comprehend?

Maybe. It still gnawed at the folds of my brain, though.

Get over it. Focus.

Bob, you're at the center of what keeps me unfocused.

Well, then… focus, Marine!

I pushed the echoes of Bob's words into the darker corners of my mind and followed our guides around the eastern corner of Building 70. Beyond it was a large flat lawn with yet another building of the same design.

"That's Building 71," Dwayne said, sounding like we had stumbled into the 3pm Creedmoor Psychiatric Center historic tour. "70 and 71 were built and opened at the same time."

"1929," Harry commented.

"Damn," Dwayne agreed. "That's ages ago."

"I hear that was when the hospital really started gaining momentum," Sean added.

"That's what Winston said, too," Harry said in a low voice.

We moved in formation toward the eastern corner of Building 71, using a series of covered walkways that directly connected the buildings. We passed another fenced-in basketball court, an asphalt oval walking track and a random copse of mature trees.

When we were twenty meters away from the corner of the yard, I had a clear sightline to where Hillside Avenue started a slow curve to the east. The eight-foot wrought iron fence looked like a solid wall in spots, except for the fact that the wall squirmed and wavered. It wasn't a wall. A massive group of FRACs pressed against the fence. They thrashed slowly about, moaning and chomping at the air. Their weight bowed the wrought iron between the posts, the bolts doing all they could to keep the sections of fence from snapping off.

Alisha had been right. The perimeter would fall eventually. But as long as the FRACs weren't provoked, the fence should hold for as long as we needed it to. Extract Westsmith and find a way back to Manhattan. That was the plan.

"Move easy," I ordered.

The rest of the group had already slowed their pace to a walk, careful to stay hidden in the shadows of the building. We took shelter under a portico.

"Must be twenty deep out there," Sean whispered.

Ahead of us stood the dark and dreaded Building 25.

An empty parking lot stretched out between us and the barbed-wire fence that had been erected around the abandoned structure to keep out vandals and adventurers. The lower windows were boarded up while the upper floors had a mish-mash of broken-out windows, boarded over frames, and a surprising number of still-intact panes of glass. The trees had grown close to the walls, their shade allowing for vines and moss to aggressively work their way up the brickwork and inside the hospital where the glass was missing. Where the glass was still resisting the urge to fall out of the mullions, the vines worked their way over it in search for higher elevation and other windows to explore.

"Dwayne," I said. "Where is Westsmith supposed to be holed up?"

"Third floor," Dwayne recited. "Western end."

"We have some cover with those generators," I said, pointing to the center of the parking lot ahead of us. "Then over the fence and onto the property. We have the trees and the other wings for cover.

"Anybody else with Westsmith, Dwayne?"

"No," he said with a shake of his head. "Just him as far as I know. He went in alone."

"Why does he even stick around?" Jude asked the group. "He had plenty of time to bail."

"Maybe he'd rather stay where things are familiar?" Sean speculated. "He's apparently been here for a long time."

"The walkers are definitely a deterrent," Heinz muttered.

"Better the devil you know." I started the familiar Irish proverb.

"He is the devil," Harry mumbled.

"Maybe," Jude replied. "Just doesn't feel right."

"None of this feels right," Melissa grumbled, always the voice of pragmatic reason.

47

Joe Cocker Songs

+80 Days – 1845 hours
22:28:39

We didn't need to go over the fence after all. Twenty meters from the cover of the generators was a slash in the chain links. Beer bottles were scattered in the high yellow grass and the still thriving weeds. Alvarez and Heinz slowly peeled back the edges of the chain links as quietly as they could. The metal tinkled softly like rusty sleigh bells.

Sean went through the gash first, fanning out left to the eastern corner of the wing closest to us. He disappeared into the building's shadows, covered by the canopy of the grove of trees growing unchallenged along the wall. Melissa stepped through and made her way cautiously to Sean. Jude quickly followed after her.

"Ok," I whispered. "Harry goes next."

"Nah." He shook his head. "Nah."

"Alisha said to bring you here." Dwayne pointed to his feet. "We brung you. That's it."

"No way I'm goin' in." Harry expanded. His dancing from foot to foot had gone into full swing.

"Burning time here," Alvarez noted.

"Ok," I said to Dwayne and Harry. "Tell Alisha thank you. Thank you for bringing us. Get back and be safe."

I shot out my hand.

Dwayne looked at it with a head tilt like a dog cocks his ears to a new noise. He slowly moved his hand out, finally locking his into mine. Once he committed, I found that he had a surprisingly firm grip. We pumped hands twice before he withdrew his hand and put it into his front pocket.

Harry was hugging himself and looking at the ground under his shifting weight with too much intensity to realize that my hand was still out to thank him, too. Instead, I put my hand on his shoulder and squeezed it for a moment. His swaying slowed and he nodded to himself with the tiniest of an upturn on one side of his mouth.

So sentimental.

"Walken," Heinz said. "Let's go, mate."

"Good luck," Harry mumbled, turning away with a jerk and trotting down the paved road that ran along the parking lot. Dwayne nodded and trotted after his friend.

Turning to Heinz and Alvarez, I went through the hole. I laced my fingers through the chain link that Heinz had peeled back. He let go and was the next through the fence. Alvarez, the last one on the other side, shook her head at Heinz who was reaching out to hold that side of the fence for her. She stepped to the center of the opening, letting the fence fall back into its normal hanging position behind her. I guided my side of the chain link back into place once she was through.

More beer bottles, discarded fast food burger wrappers, and a conspicuous used condom hanging on a dried-out bush from a long-ago thrill ride littered the grounds. There was no light or movement from inside. Most of the openings were overgrown with creeping vines. Wherever there was a crack or a sliver of an opening, vines were drawn to it and ventured through to explore the interiors. It reminded me of the kudzu vine that had been so destructive in the American south.

I am sure it will only get worse now that there is no one to tend to them.

An ache started to throb between my shoulders as a mewing sound rose up on the slight breeze. It came from our south.

From the fence at Hillside Avenue would be my guess.

With luck the perimeter would hold. We needed something to

go our way for once on this op. As quickly as the sound and the ache had started, it dissipated. I shook off the tension in my muscles with a roll of the shoulders. We moved in a tight single file formation from the fence to where the others were waiting.

"This place is disgusting," Melissa announced in a low voice as we huddled up next to a clear section of brick, surprisingly free of graffiti and vines

"You ain't seen nothing yet," Sean warned.

"Alright." I corralled the conversation back on task. "Dwayne and Harry went back to Alisha. We're on our own."

"Great," Melissa muttered, her words laced with the sarcasm that we had come to expect.

"They wouldn't have been effective," I advised. "Neither wanted to set foot inside."

"You mean," Sean added, "I had a choice?"

"You?" I countered. "No."

"How we getting in?" Jude asked.

I spied an open window frame on the second story. One of the branches from a gnarly tree had grown far enough over the sill to provide a perfect ramp up to the window. I pointed behind and above Sean's head. "There."

"Easier than jumping out of a perfectly sound helicopter, I guess," Melissa said, sarcasm indeed intact.

48

The Mouth of Madness

+80 Days – 1921 hours
21:52:46

We all stood inside the door trying to get our bearings as Heinz and Sean helped Alvarez—the last up the tree—through the second-floor window. Smaller branches from the tree limb had jutted their way through the opening with parasitic vines spreading out onto the surrounding walls. With the sun setting on the other end of the building, this former dormitory bedroom had taken on a decidedly dark green hue.

The air was stale and sour, in spite of the open window. It was as if the breezes knew to leave this place alone. The paint was peeling off the walls in narrow strips, several layers thick. We left a zigzagging series of boot prints in the layers of dust and powdered decay on the floors. There was no way we would not be discovered if someone came across our tracks.

There was a metal pipe headboard leaning against the wall next to an open closet with no doors. Hanging on one of several long-forgotten rusting metal hangers was a long line bullet cup bra. It was yellow and grimy, with red from the metal oxidation bleeding onto the wide shoulder straps. It served as a strange reminder that there had once been life in this place long ago.

I cleared the hallway. It was cast in darker shadows with long streams of vague light coming in from the other dorm rooms, each with its own degree of cast and color. More metal headboards were stacked up against the wall opposite our room. A few metal chairs, direct from the early 20th Century Institutional Décor catalog, were lined up under a mural of a peeling mountain rising out of an ocean of gentle waves with the single word *Wellness* written in block letters above the faded mountain peaks.

I guess some graffiti should be admired.

The hall ended in a yellowing and water damaged wall with a single window at its center. To our left, the corridor was lined with more rooms on each side, leading to a nurses' station. We filed toward the round desk in two columns led by Heinz and me, both of us clearing each room as we passed it.

The only sounds in the air were the quiet tapping and rubbing of our gear and the whisper of branches grinding against the openings of this abandoned dust-filled institution.

The nurses' station had not escaped neglect. Charts were strewn across the counter. Papers that had formerly been important in tracking the health and progress of its patients were scattered across the desk and on the floor under the office chairs. A lone half-empty cardboard dispenser of latex examination gloves sat on the floor against the wall.

Sean stared at the ivory colored rotary phone sitting on the cracked Formica countertop, controlling himself enough to not pick the phone receiver off the cradle in search for a dial tone.

"OCD much?" Melissa whispered.

"A little." Sean flexed his fingers on his left hand.

I snapped my fingers one time.

They stopped talking and looked at me.

I pointed at the adjoining corridor that ran through the center of the building. Ahead was a large lobby and the facility's main stairwell, separated by a set of heavy double doors. In their heyday, they would have kept us locked in this ward but, now, one of the doors leaned against the wall while the other hung at an obscene angle from one bent hinge pin.

Before we walked through, I turned back to the group. "Dwayne said that Westsmith is on the third floor on the other end of the building. With the stairwells centrally located, we don't need to split up."

"How good is this intel?" Alvarez asked. "We are dealing with crazy people."

"No guarantees he's still here at all," I replied. "But I can't imagine he's moving around too much if he decided to hole up here."

"Better to lay low," Heinz added.

"Up the stairs," I advised, pointing to our left. "Alvarez, Sean and Melissa will clear the left side of the wing. The rest of us will handle the right. Take turns clearing rooms."

"Typical sweep and clear," Alvarez ordered.

"Keep your tactical lights covered until you clear the room," I continued. "This place is going to get dark fast, but we don't need our lights tipping us off. We clear?"

"Easy peasy, right?" Jude said with her own tint of sarcasm.

"It better be," Sean said what I was thinking. "We need a win."

49

Climbing the Stairway to Heaven
+80 Days – 1931 hours
21:42:11

The central stairway was located at the back of the facility, opposite of a large common area. We paused at the first cut-back landing before splitting up into two groups, each taking one of the two narrower stairways leading the third floor. I cast a light down along the mahogany railing. The intricate wood engravings, porcelain reliefs, moldings, and tile work were a sad reminder of how fine craftsmanship would be forever lost to the world.

Looks like that attention to detail had been lost in here for many years before we found ourselves in this situation.

Sean tapped me on the shoulder.

Alvarez stood with one foot on the first riser of the other stairway, with Melissa and Sean in line behind her. All had their M4s up in a half-draw. Alvarez nodded to me as I took point on the other stairway with Jude directly behind me and Heinz covering our rear.

The chalky dust was a quarter inch deep on the steps, quick to give up any trespass. Spiders had taken advantage of the vacancy to weave their own intricate designs between the rails. Dozens of flies and moths had become entangled in the silky threads. A black fat-bodied spider stepped delicately on the results of its handiwork, carefully making its way to a still fluttering morsel.

We went up.

The tall windows revealed the buildings on the rest of the property in the darkening day, providing that strange momentary sensation of floating as we were seeing them for the first time at this perspective. The feeling flitted away as we set foot on the next level. The third floor was silent, only dimly lit by the faintest of light, taking away any hope to admire the peeling murals painted on the stairwell walls. Their faded pigments wrapped into the corridor where they had lost all definition against the darkened surfaces.

Alvarez and her group took up formation on the left side of the central gathering area, while Heinz took point on the near wall with Jude and me behind him. Another set of double doors separated us from the next wards. This time the doors were intact and closed, behind an even more ancient laundry cart filled with terry cloth robes.

Heinz walked over to the doors in a low crouch. He reached out to the doorknob to test it. He gave us a thumb's up. Before he tried to physically open the door, he stopped and turned on his tactical light to run the beam along the doorframe.

He shot his fist up in the air before derailing the tactical light from his rifle and taking a closer look through the wire-mesh glass. He shook his head and returned to where we waited. Alvarez, Melissa and Sean came over to our position.

"Westsmith is here, alright," Heinz confirmed. "The bugger's got the door trip-wired to alarm if we open it. Has beer cans strung up, if you believe that shite."

"Great," Melissa complained. "Now what?"

"Can you disarm it?" Alvarez asked.

"Of course," Heinz replied. "It's low-tech, but there is going to be noise regardless of how good I am."

"He can't get off the wing, right?" Jude asked. "Let's go in hard and flush him out."

"He's still armed," Alvarez reminded us. "I wouldn't advise a hard breach."

"My kingdom for a flash-bang," Sean commented. "There's a better way but you're not going to like it, John. None of you are."

50

Deep Guano

+80 Days – 1942 hours
21:32:37

Sean was right. None of us liked his plan. But we were quickly running out of time and options. Alvarez, Melissa and Heinz had stayed behind at the rigged double doors while Sean led the rest of us up to the fourth floor using the central stairway. Sean switched on his tactical light. I could see in the dark just fine.

If that capsule detonates, she may find herself just like you.

I wasn't going to let that happen. Alvarez assured me that she could disarm it if all else failed.

And do not forget the girls.

We'll get them back, too.

Your track record has spoken much to the contrary since this operation commenced, Sergeant.

As much as I hate your commentary, Bob, you're right.

I am very witty. And intelligent. Did I mention witty?

Let's focus.

Sean led Jude and me straight to a set of double doors like the rigged doors on the third floor. We approached with caution, looking for any sign of tampering while Jude covered our rear. The door was unlocked and trap-free. I turned the doorknob and started to pull it open.

"Hold on," Jude whispered to me. She leaned into Sean's ear and pointed at the door. Sean nodded and they covered the hinges and pins with their hands. Jude nodded to me. "Okay."

I slowly swung the door open, any squeak of the hinges muffled to the point of inaudibility. With the door open, a waft of dry rot assaulted our senses.

"Yep," Sean said, pulling the collar of his compression shirt up over his nose before moving forward. "This place is still disgusting."

"Christ," Jude said, doing the same. "What is that smell?"

"Better to show you," Sean replied.

The smell was awful. Whatever it was drifted heavy in the air. It was both an old and new scent, aged and decaying with a poignant sharp freshness over it. The hallway, luckily, was clear of furniture and debris. There was nothing to account for the foul odor. Sean pivoted his M4 into a commons area. Jude moved forward to the first of a series of large metal doors. I did a sweep of the left side of the corridor. Sean emerged from the commons room and moved to Jude's position outside a closed door.

Jude looked into the room and stopped. "Shit."

Sean and I filled the doorway, taking up a position on either side of her. The room was filled with it.

Shit.

Inside the room were a metal headboard and bed frame, a metal desk chair, and an overturned bureau of drawers. At least that was what I thought the shapes were. Each piece of furniture and the floor was completely covered in a foot-thick layer of bird shit.

Pigeon shit, to be precise.

The finished ceiling had been destroyed by water damage, the plaster and lathing crumbling. A large ragged bed sheet hung from the top of the outer wall, pinned in between the wall lathing and the rotting joists above. Pigeons slept with their heads under their wings on the joists, a random coo voicing their general contentment.

"Most of this floor is like this," Sean explained from behind his makeshift mask. "Been a nesting ground for birds for years."

"Should demolish this place," Jude said.

"Where's the spot?" I asked, steering the conversation away

from this distraction—disgusting and fascinating as it was.

"Kitchen is past the next cross hall," Sean replied.

"Okay, then," I ordered. "Let's move."

We backed out of the room and headed down the corridor. I kept my mouth closed and pulled up my collar like Sean and Jude had done, now knowing just what those particles in the air really were.

Being full of crap takes on a whole new meaning.

Each open door revealed more decay and more layers of foot-deep guano as a coating on whatever destruction, debris and furniture that was unfortunate enough to be left behind. The doors at the cross hall were wide open. We slipped through to another commons area with a relatively clear reception desk. The only thin coating on its surfaces was that of dust.

"Kitchen." Sean pointed to our left.

As if a health inspector was expected, the space was almost immaculate in comparison to the rooms we had seen. Steel prep tables and cabinets were bolted to the floor in the far corner. Other lighter tables had been flipped over and left on top of the prep tables like they were being put away for the evening. The space was clear of utensils and any other small appliances, but an oversized exhaust hood still clung to the rafters amid peeling paint and pocked plaster.

Sean led us to the other side of the room. He slung his rifle and pulled back an oversized refrigerated unit. It slid easily on its casters, in spite of the dereliction around it. Sean stepped back. In the wall, formerly hidden by the unit, was an opening behind the torn away plaster and lathing.

Reminds me of the hospital you were held in after you died. Remember the 'in-between' space?

Yes.

I switched on my tactical light and peered into the wall. The space was deeper than expected, enough so to fit the biggest of us—me. To the left, a series of vertical standpipes rose up from the floors below.

Sean tapped me on the arm and pointed down to the right.

There was a lighter section of the crawlspace below us. Not because it was painted a lighter color, but because the last wisps of daylight were streaming in from beyond the wall where it had been broken through from vandalism.

"It's another kitchen," Sean whispered to us. "Kids thought it would be fun to have a secret way up and down."

"Stairs too much trouble?" Jude asked in a low voice.

I swung the light left and right. The standpipes and the lathing would provide good handholds for shimmying down to the lower floor. Sean put his arm into the plumb wall and reached up the interior of the wall until the plaster was rubbing against his shoulder.

"Come on," he muttered.

He smiled at us and yanked down. Sean retracted his now dusty arm and brought with it what looked like a coiled snake. Jude stepped back. By reflex, my hand went for my knife handle. It paused once my brain processed that what Sean was holding was a frayed length of knotted rope.

"Like magic," Jude finally said to break the silence.

"Made the climbs easier," Sean advised.

I took the coil of rope from his hand and let it fall down the shaft. It slapped against the sidewalls until it became taut. I grabbed the rope above the closest knot and pulled it down with most of my weight. It strained in protest but held.

"Good to go," Sean said. "I'll take point."

He grabbed the rope from my hand and slipped into the shaft with one foot on the deck and the other pressing a knot into the back wall for leverage. He tested his grip for a moment before starting his descent. He made quick work dropping to the next floor, using some joist work as a ledge to get turned around. He wedged his torso against the rear wall of the shaft and let go of the rope. Sean pulled his sidearm and scanned the opening, looking left and right. He slipped through the gash and disappeared into the kitchen on the floor below. After ten seconds, his arm shot through the opening to give us a thumb's up signal.

Jude joined me at the opening, poking her head into the shaft. "See ya, sucker." She slapped me on the arm before grabbing the rope for herself. Jude kissed my cheek through the material of her compression shirt still over her mouth and nose, and then expertly climbed down the rope to the floor below. She disappeared through the opening, leaving the rope slack again.

I took one more look around the kitchen. The day was all but gone, with just the faintest glow clinging to it. The shadows had lost their definition, blending into the monochrome of the rest of the abandoned space.

A pigeon cooed somewhere close.

The shaft was a black pit of shadows.

I shouldered my weapon, checked the security of my knife and Glock, took the rope in my hands and made my own descent into the darkness.

51

Great Unwashed

+80 Days – 1951 hours
21:23:01

I stepped out into the empty third-floor kitchen, the rope slapping against the wall after I let go of it in favor of my Glock. The dust was disturbed with dozens of vague shoe prints like dance instruction patterns. Fresh shoe prints. Not just the treads of R&R combat boots. Someone—apparently a bunch of someones—must have caught Jude and Sean unaware. Apparently, Westsmith wasn't the only one holed up in Building #25. Whoever they were, they had better not have hurt my people—or there would be a fury to pay.

A flash of white flitted from the far end of the kitchen.

I'm late.

I chased after the white. By the time I reached the corridor it was empty. Sean and Jude were nowhere to be seen.

Late for an important date.

I didn't bother with my tach light. Enhanced vision and Marine training did the tracking for me. Of course, the distinct trail of fresh footprints was easy to follow. Even though the tracks were new, a thin film of dust had already collected over them. The hall narrowed. Three gurneys had been abandoned in a haphazard fashion, strewn at odd angles across the corridor. Their leather padded mattresses, also covered in dust, were worn but not cracked. The steel frames and the oversized wheels gave away their vintage heritage. Movement came from beyond the barricade, disappearing through to a dorm room on the left side of the hallway. A low throaty hum began, a single monotone noise that seemed to come from everywhere at once. Pulling one of the gurneys out of the way, I slipped between them and hugged the wall until I was outside the last door. A large faded mural on the plaster beside me exclaimed, 'Be Well!'. Little wide-eyed terrified children held hands and danced around a pile of burnt dead rat carcasses.

You sure about that?

I looked again. The little children were holding hands, but they were smiling and dancing around a clump of daisies. They hadn't been screaming. They were unified and stronger by joining hands and keeping close to one another.

Unlike you.

"Shut up, Bob," I said in a hiss.

All alone again.

"Shut the fuck up," I said louder.

Another hum joined the first. It wasn't the same as the first. But it was. They covered over each other, indistinguishable from each other. The same low tone, but warbling like two waves slowly syncing up.

I pulled the door open. Stepping inside, I cleared the corner to my three o'clock then pivoted to clear the rest of the room. The room was empty. The two tall windows were intact, their glass having escaped both poorly aimed stones and the rigors of the advancing vegetation.

I stepped to the middle of the room. The hum persisted and intensified. That same monotone note assaulted me, churning my stomach and giving me a headache. I swallowed bile back in my throat. My balance faltered and I staggered a step before regaining my footing.

The hum grew louder.

My forehead pounded.

White blurred across the doorframe.

A furry white figure lunged into the room.

I grabbed the terrycloth robe—and the person in it—and flung him into the wall behind me. Plaster cracked and fell on top of him where he fell in a heap on the tiled floor.

I doubled over and retched.

Another white robed figure ran into the room, thrusting something sharp at me. What the fuck? I side-stepped, jamming my knee into his bicep above the elbow as I drove down my fist in to his forearm. The elbow snapped. A knife dropped to the floor with a clink.

I'm late.

A third terry-robed man jumped onto my back, wrapping his legs around my waist in a vise-like grip.

Late for a very important date.

"Shut up, Bo–"

The new assailant hooked dirty putrid fingers into my mouth. He pulled my head to the right and roared a guttural scream into my ear, his breath a terrible hot stench.

My vision went red.

I grabbed him around the back of his neck and used his weight and momentum to flip him over, letting out a warrior yell. There was a wet shredding sound as I pulled his head clean away from his robed body.

What the fuck?

I dropped the head and watched it bounce off the floor and roll away. The body's legs clamped tighter around my waist in a death-grip. The hood fell over the empty neck, the material starting to soak through with blood. I frantically peeled its thighs away, breaking the left femur in the process. The headless body dropped to the floor.

My vision was still crimson, the pulse of my heart loud in my ears. Did I just do that to a man? Was this the same shit as when I killed that man in the catacombs of the museum? Panting, I stepped away from it and spat out the rotten taste from my mouth.

Two more robed figures filled the doorway.

I raised the Glock and double tapped them in the chest. They looked down at their ribcages and put their hands over their hearts. When they pulled them away—in perfect unison—there was no blood on their robes.

Tactical vests, no doubt. Where did they get body armor?

The same place where Alisha and her men got all their weapons?

With scarfs covering their faces, they charged at me. I shot one in the forehead through his drooping hood. The hood billowed a little bit as it caught the blood and gore escaping through the back of his head. He tripped and skidded to the dirty floor at my feet.

The other assailant dipped under my next shot, which ricocheted into the steel door with a spark. He tackled me at the waist, driving me off my feet. My spine crashed into the edge of the windowsill.

I put the Glock against his hood and pulled the trigger. The muzzle flash was muffled, but the material started to singe around the entry point. As I twisted the body off my legs, I felt a tear in my abdomen.

The hum continued, even louder than before. This time I threw up uncontrollably. After several seconds of my body convulsing against my will, I wiped my mouth of the spittle on my lips and sat up again against the wall under the window.

I looked up to see a wall of white robes. Six white robed figures stood in a semi-circle around me in the small room. I raised the Glock, my other arm across my midsection with my hand pressing on my seeping wound.

"I would advise against that, Sgt. Walken," a voice called out, louder than the hum rising from under the hoods.

The men parted, three to each side. Filling in the gap was the hooded figure wearing the same robes from the auditorium. I focused the sights of my weapon at the center of the dark shadows under Alisha's hood. It looked like she had plenty of men to follow her orders. I couldn't figure out why she would send us here just to be recaptured. It would have been easier to confine us at the Wellness Center.

Divide and conquer?

She pushed her hands out from under the sleeves of the robe with her palms up. Slowly, she raised her hands and pulled back her hood. Like Jesus of Nazareth revealing himself to his flock, her long hair flowed past her shoulders, framing her bearded face.

Bearded face? What the fuck?

"Westsmith," I said with a sigh, the Glock centered directly on his forehead. "You're coming with me."

"Not likely," he said confidently. He slowly sidestepped, his robes flowing around him. "Do you like the robes? Ms. Alisha shouldn't be the only one who gets to drape herself in theatrics, wouldn't you agree?"

I could only glare at him as four more hooded men dragged forward the now disarmed Sean and Jude. Sean's eye was swelling and his lower lip was bleeding—again. Jude was in better shape, but her eyes were wide and her skin had taken on a waxy sheen.

She may be in shock.

Shit.

"What do you want, Westsmith?" I asked.

"Really?" he replied in genuine surprise. "No one has ever asked me what I wanted."

"First time for everything." I shrugged, using a moment to figure out how best to get Jude and Sean out of this new situation. Westsmith was chummy or charming enough with the residents on the property to get them to follow him. Desperation breeds servitude and compliance. I'd seen it all around the world.

"I just want to be left alone," he finally said with a measure of sincerity.

"Just you and your friends here?" I needed him to keep talking, giving me time to regain my strength and stop my brain from swimming inside my skull. I spat out more of the taste of bile and rot from my mouth.

"Friends?" He laughed good-naturedly. "They aren't friends. But they do as I ask. I have that effect on some people."

"Even when they end up dead?" I asked, my eyes drifting to the decapitated head in the corner. Westsmith glanced at it as well. Sean and Jude also darted their eyes from the captors at their sides to the bodies around the room. "They can't be that desperate."

"It's hard to say what drives an individual," he dismissed my comment with a shrug. "I'm sure you–"

Jude yelped as one of Westsmith's men bumped into her. Sean tried to get between them to shield Jude but his own escorts held him back with a grunt.

"You are outnumbered," Westsmith reminded me.

I responded by shooting Jude's aggressor in the side of the head. He slumped to the tile floor, his gloved hands dragging down Jude's arm. The second guard restrained her with a hand on both shoulders.

Several of Westsmith's men rushed past him toward me. I shot the two quickest and closest before the others piled on me. They pinned me down by their sheer weight, making it impossible to move or dispatch any more of them.

The Glock was swiped from my grip.

"Don't worry about the men you killed," I heard Westsmith say. "There's an endless supply of people lining up to be my friend these days."

52

Who Let The Dogs Out?

+80 Days – 2032 hours
20:40:54

Westsmith's acolytes were strong. Their fingers were vice-like grips on my arms. They half-walked, half-dragged me along the dank, dark corridor, with Sean and Jude close behind me. Our weapons had all been taken, rattling around in a burlap bag held by one of the hooded men at the back of our processional. Bag Boy would be the first target when an opportunity presented itself.

Westsmith led the way. He seemed to glide along the cracked and broken tile floor. The robes that he had stolen from Alisha swept half an inch off the floor, not disturbing any of the dust that had collected there over god know how many years.

I believe Sgt. Bowers had mentioned that Building 25 closed in the 1970s. Simple math like that shouldn't be a problem for a stout Marine such as you, should it?

Bob, my own personal Man in the Black Suit and Creedmoor historian, walked alongside me, careful not to get in the way of my handlers.

He is a little ripe, this one.

I smelled him, too. Both of them smelled of rot and a pungent dampness. The robes smelled of mildew and mothballs, serving to mix with the stench instead of covering it up. My escorts both wore gloves, the latex sticky against my skin. While their grips were firm, the meat of their hands was uneven and clumpy. Maybe these patients had been in a ward for disfigured people.

"If you want to be left alone," I said to Westsmith, "why are you hauling us around?"

Westsmith raised a hand that halted the processional. He spun around and approached me, his robes whipping around his legs with the momentum. He came within inches of my face, his sour breath assaulting my nostrils.

"You can't be let off without punishment," he whispered. "You came after me. Your master needs to know that I won't tolerate his dogs nipping at my heels every time I turn around."

"You can't have that," I mused.

"I'm glad we're in agreement."

Jude spoke up, "What did you do with–"

"The tracking device. How did you know about the tracking device?" Sean redirected Jude's question. Good. He and I were on the same page, worried that Westsmith would realize that Alvarez, Melissa and the others were still out there.

"Oh. That?" Westsmith raised his left arm from the folds of his robes. He revealed a forearm bandaged close to the elbow, the gauze stained through with a four-inch straight line of dark red. "I left it with a friend, as you must know. You did find me in his office."

"He must have been a good friend," Sean commented.

"One of the best, in my professional opinion," Westsmith agreed. "He really helped me to work through some of my daddy issues over the years." He smiled at that last comment, looking to each of us in turn. Maybe he thought we were already on the inside of the joke about his relationship with the now dead doctor.

"Well," Sean said, "he didn't seem to be in good spirits when we found him."

"Even the best of friends is allowed to have a difference of opinion," Westsmith admitted. "Sometimes it can put a strain on a relationship. But I left him in good hands."

Or between good teeth. Teeth with ravenous appetites.

"So," I said, redirecting the conversation back to my original question, "why punish us? Why not just kill us?"

"Oh, Mr. Walken," Westsmith said, laughing out loud. "I'm

sure you would continue to pursue me, even after death."

"And how do you know that?" I asked, feeling my escorts loosen their grips and start to sway side to side.

"Because I am you," Westsmith said earnestly. "And you are me."

"I highly doubt that you're like me."

"Really?" Westsmith's eyebrow rose up. "Do you really think your master wouldn't send someone after me who understood me? Who feels how I feel?" He searched my face but didn't find what he was looking for. His eyebrows dropped and his faced smoothed out. "No matter," he finally said. "Time is a wasting."

He turned away and waved us on to follow him. My captors tightened their spongy grips again. They pushed us along past Westsmith's disengaged early alarm system and now open double doors, steering us through the ruined and empty corridor.

54

When the Bough Breaks

+80 Days – 2037 hours
20:22:19

We went down the way we came up, except this time we got to see the more ornate first floor lobby and entry. At the large set of steel six-panel double doors Westsmith pulled a twisted length of copper pipe up from the handles. He put the metal around the back of his neck like a scarf and pushed open the doors. He strode through like a gunslinger swinging through the batwing doors of a Wild West Arizona desert saloon.

He is very confident.

Bob smiled at me from the other side of my right-side escort.

Mucho machismo.

We stopped before crossing the threshold. Westsmith was already on the sidewalk. When he reached the fenceline built to keep intruders out, he turned back to us. He stared at me and I met his gaze, defiantly standing my ground at the doorway.

A light warm breeze puffed at the side of my face.

A solitary crow cawed from the stonework arch over my head.

Suddenly, the guards' grips tightened to a painful degree, forcing me onto the stoop. Westsmith waited at the chain link, his hands hidden in the folds of the robe. Sean was two meters behind me. Jude was escorted out of the building last, closest to the guns but farthest away from our assistance.

You figuring to make a move, cowboy?

I'm thinking about it.

"Mr. Walken," Westsmith called out. "You can step over here, if you please."

I was shifted toward him by my hooded escorts. I tried to pull an arm away with a little bit of extra strength but their grips were like concrete wrapped around my arms. Their latex fingers dug into my muscles like steel talons.

We were lined up like school children at afternoon recess, each of us with our pair of escorts sandwiching us in on both sides. Westsmith, smiling at us, waved us on to follow him along the sidewalk between Building 25 and the more elaborately designed building adjacent to it. At the corner of the fenceline, Westsmith turned and spread out his arms as if to start a sermon. "Young lady and gentlemen, welcome to the new world. As you can see, we do things differently now."

He's definitely preaching.

We were all manhandled to face east.

From the boughs of one of the gnarled trees growing at the edge of the fenceline, hanging from frayed ropes between several large branches, was the rest of our team.

Well... mostly.

The bodies of a man and woman in black tactical gear swung through the loop of an expertly knotted noose. It was hard to see who was missing with the heads wrapped in strips of old towels. Maybe Melissa was still alive somewhere and hiding.

"As you can see," Westsmith said, "you cannot hide anything from us."

"What's your point?" I asked, swallowing hard and trying to keep my voice steady.

"Christ," Sean croaked.

"Macabre." Jude muttered to herself for good measure.

"I would have thought," Westsmith explained, "that you would have appreciated my efforts."

"Looks like a warning to me," I said, my stomach churning as I looked at the bodies swaying in the branches. "Just a cliché version of stuff I've seen in a dozen spaghetti westerns. Nothing forward thinking about it, as far as I can tell."

"Agreed," Sean said, following my line of conversation.

I appreciated that Sean was following my lead. Westsmith, on the other hand, did not seem to like our commentary. His brow furrowed again and his jaws clenched.

"A warning?" he blurted out. "You think this is a warning? I have no need to ward people away with human runes. As you can see, I can handle anyone and anything that comes my way."

"If it isn't a warning," I asked, distracted for moment when I thought I saw movement from the corner of my eyes, "what is it?"

"A statement."

"Of what?" Sean spat out. "Maybe something is getting lost in translation."

"Maybe," Jude chimed in, her voice straining through the quip. "But I'm not a marketing exec."

"Enough!" Westsmith's voice boomed.

The grips on my arm loosened and the acolytes bowed their heads and hunched their backs.

Cowering fools.

"This," Westsmith said, pointing at the bodies, "is for your master as a message that he will always fail against me. He doesn't control me like he always thought he could. I am free of him. When his little mechanical drones make their sweeps around Creedmoor, I am certain that one of his little video analysts will find the gifts that I have left hanging for him. Low hanging fruit, if you will."

"So, he knows that you can take care of yourself?" I asked.

"Exactly," Westsmith said with pride. "I have bested him at every turn, and will continue to do so."

"Why do you hate him so much," I asked.

"That is an obvious question with just as obvious an answer," Westsmith answered. "Especially for you, Mr. Walken."

"Sorry," I said. "Again, it seems I'm missing the point."

"Oh?" Westsmith asked with slight surprise. "Then let me

enlighten you."

The acolytes straightened up. Their grips tightened and their free gloved hands came up in an almost synchronistic motion. They grabbed at their hoods and pulled them down to their shoulders. The stench was now free to catch in the slight warm breezes. I crinkled up my nose.

I met the gaze of the man gripping my right arm. A pus-filled scar ran diagonally from his forehead through the bridge of his nose to the bottom of his jaw. The golden flecks around the outside of the irises were only partially hidden by the milky cataracts. The scarred FRAC snarled at me but made no move to bite me. The same was true for the undead acolytes holding the others.

"Shit, shit, shit," Sean muttered, trying to twist out of his captors' grip.

Jude tried to make herself as small as possible, shrinking away from the FRACS holding her at arm's length. She made a desperate mewing sound as the FRACs moaned at her.

"So, do you see?" Westsmith said. "We are living in a brave new world… with me at the head of the table."

Aldus Huxley's work is referenced far too often, I think.

I slammed my head into my scarred captor. Chunks of brittle skull shot into his brain matter as his forehead caved in. His grip tightened for a moment before going slack as he dropped to the sidewalk.

I punched the other guard through the face. My fist buried to the thumb, blood spurting down my arm. It pulled free with a sucking sound as the walker's undead life flickered and finally went out for the last time.

"Stop," Westsmith said.

I did not stop.

Sean tried to wrestle away from his escorts, grabbing both by the robes around their throats to keep them from biting him. His muscles strained against their strength.

You know all about that strength, don't you?

I threw a roundhouse kick to the temple of the closest of Sean's captors. The head severed away from the spinal cord, lopping over to one side. Only the rotting skin and a few strains of muscles kept it from decapitating completely from the body. The condition of the head didn't matter as the entire body collapsed to the yellow grass.

Sean grabbed his other guard with a handful of musty robes in both hands. It snapped at him. He dropped to the ground, planted both feet into its chest and flipped the FRAC over him and into the chain link fence. It landed on its head with an audible squish-laced crack. Its body slid down the fence, finally silent.

"Stop!" Westsmith yelled this time.

"John!" Jude screamed.

One of her undead captors gripped her at the shoulder and wrist, leaving her sleeved arm exposed to its open mouth of rotten and black teeth. The FRAC was perfectly still, waiting.

He's like one of those Central Park performers who paint themselves silver and only move once every ten minutes.

"I would advise you stand down, Mr. Walken," Westsmith warned. "I wouldn't want your pretty little girlfriend to be a victim beyond what she already is."

"John," Jude pleaded. "Please."

I put my hands up in surrender. Sean gave me a searching look. I shook my head. He relented and put his own hands on his head. I wasn't sure if the R&R-issued compression shirt would withstand a full bite.

Westsmith walked toward us.

The FRAC stretched its neck, opening its rotting mouth wider and closer to Jude's exposed flesh. A dollop of dark saliva fell from its lips onto her sleeve.

"John," Jude said with a cry, her muscles straining against both her captors.

I tensed.

"Your choice," Westsmith said as he approached us.

From the distance, a low murmur carried itself on the slight breezes that puffed around us.

"I guess we are not as alike as I thought. A pity." Westsmith stopped in front of me. He looked at Jude and made a slight nod to his remaining acolytes. "I would have imagined that you were the tip of the spear, but you seem too dull for that. You are sadly only a blunt instrument."

All of the acolytes stretched their jaws.

The FRAC holding Jude plunged his head down at her arm.

Blood splattered all over Jude's face and neck.

The crack from the gunshot came a millisecond later.

She screamed.

Westsmith spun toward the sound, its report echoing off the hard angles of the buildings.

The walker crumbled to the sidewalk. Its grip remained on Jude's arm, dragging her down with it. Her remaining captor held her firm. Jude's pupils were wide, the blood covering her face in stark contrast to the whites of her eyes. Her jaw moved but no sound came out.

"Show yourself!" Westsmith yelled.

Who was out there? Who escaped capture?

Westsmith's request was answered.

Jude's second captor's head erupted like a rotten melon dropped on a rock. The skull split apart as the bullet ripped through it. There may have been an audible grunt from the walker before it slipped against the fence post, but I couldn't be completely sure whether I heard it out loud or in my head.

The bag holding our weapons clanked against the sidewalk.

Bag Boy FRAC charged at Jude.

With her dead captor's fingers still digging into her muscles, Jude could only put one fist up in defense. Sean and Westsmith blocked my way to her.

She flick-kicked Bag Boy under the jaw.

Its head snapped up, but it still knocked into her.

Jude fell back into the fence on top of Bag Boy FRAC and her now-dead Strong Arm FRAC escort.

"Goddamnit!" Jude yelled.

I grabbed Westsmith under the arm, spun him off his feet and hurled him toward Jude. He crashed into Bag Boy FRAC, the two of them tumbling to the ground next to Jude. She punched at the fingers of the destroyed FRAC, finally cracking them back enough to peel herself free. Westsmith hopped to his feet, pulling Bag Boy FRAC up and pushing him toward Jude. Now free, she grabbed a stray 2x4 and bashed it into the side of walker's head. He crashed again into the chain links.

"No," Westsmith whispered in frustration.

"Yes," Alvarez said, the barrel of her sidearm pressed against his ear. "You're coming with me."

Melissa pumped the Benelli and shot Bag Boy almost point-blank in the face. What was left was viscera dripping off the lattice of the fence where its head used to be.

Heinz retrieved the burlap bag of weapons and took a peek inside. "Jackpot, mates."

"Dead or alive?" Westsmith asked Alvarez.

"Preferably alive," Alvarez confirmed. "But the prospect of dead is looking more and more attractive, so don't fucking test me."

54

Fork In The Road

+80 Days – 2230 hours
20:32:19

With the help from some stray plastic caught on a bush, we fashioned a tight binding around Westsmith's wrists. It took Sean a few minutes to gather the asshole's arms from under the sleeves of the robes. Afterward, Sean dragged him forcibly to his feet while Heinz kept his rifle trained on him.

"I would ask what happened to you," Alvarez said sarcastically, standing next to me, "but I guess I already have my answer."

"Where did you go?" I asked defensively, pissed that they hadn't come to help us sooner.

Alvarez heard my tone, but chose to ignore it. "We heard the shots. Saw Westsmith and his robed weirdos manhandling all of you."

"They were waiting for us," Jude answered. "We stepped out and there they were."

Alvarez nodded. "We fell back and followed."

"Thank you," Jude said. She had forgotten that there was blood on her face. I didn't have the heart to remind her of it, especially with nothing to clean it off with.

"Lovely. What's the new plan, mate?" Heinz asked impatiently to whoever was leading this team—either me or Alvarez. "I've had enough of this place."

"And we need a ride back to Manhattan, too." Jude added, holding the comfortable weight of her Beretta against her chest with both hands.

"Are we going to gloss over the fact that he was commanding

a platoon of deadheads?" Sean asked with exasperation. "I mean, what the fuck?"

I caught a stray look from Alvarez. She looked like she knew something more than the others. Maybe something that even Heinz hadn't been briefed on back at the R&R command center. Jude was trying to shake off what had happened. She had not been that close to being bit by a FRAC since she had joined up with me and Sean. Melissa examined her shotgun, her jaw flexing as she worked extra hard to keep her mouth closed and mind occupied.

"They acted like they were alive," Sean continued to rant.

"I could explain," Westsmith offered.

Melissa put the end of the barrel as close to his face as the FRAC's teeth had been to Jude's arm. "Don't open your goddamn mouth."

"As you wish," Westsmith said in a smaller voice.

Sean walked around Westsmith to talk to me in a more hushed tone. "This is freaky shit, John. He skeeves me out. What the fuck is going on?"

"Noted," I said, tossing a glance at our now quiet prisoner. "I don't have any answers for you. Let's just get him back to the city asap."

"Seriously?" he asked. "You don't have a clue about this clown? The way he commanded the walkers was like the kids at–" He stopped himself from finishing the sentence out loud, as if stopping the words from being heard would erase what he had already formulated in his head.

Yes. I had a clue about what was happening. I was the one who freed a horde of FRAC children and asked them to go against Roy, and then R&R's mercenaries outside the museum. The little pigtailed girl with the strobing boots had accepted my plea for help. But that seemed more a suggestion than an order and the hold I had on the children had been tenuous at best. We had lost Victoria because the undead bully of the group had veered off to bite her. While I barely understood my rudimentary, and mostly inconsistent, control over the FRACs, I couldn't comprehend Westsmith's level of dominance over them. I shook my head. "I don't know how he's doing it."

Sean must have seen something in my eyes because he snapped his mouth closed with a click of his teeth, deciding against raising another question. He slid the M4 off his shoulder and, with a shake of his head, went back to where Heinz and Melissa were guarding the prisoner.

"I don't want to hear about it," Jude said, her eyes a bit too wide for my comfort. That was what shock did to a person. The others were tightlipped, unwilling to speak up about what had just happened to us. In spite of how drained she was looking, Jude did speak up about another matter. "What about Lee and Damon?"

Now that we knew that Alvarez, Melissa and Heinz were alive and well, it seemed obvious that the bodies in the tree were Lee and Damon. I guess our impromptu burial was a wasted effort. Watching their bodies sway at the end of the lengths of ropes hurt my heart. There was something unusually brutal about hangings in the modern world.

The world is not modern anymore.

I took my tactical knife and took a swing at the taut rope.

"Wait!" Alvarez held out her hand in an attempt to stay my hand.

I pulled my swing, missing the rope before turning toward her.

"Westsmith is right," Alvarez said. "When the drones do their fly-bys, they will record the hanging bodies. R&R will analyze it and send us re-enforcements. Or take some sort of action, I'm sure."

"That's a big assumption," I advised. "We can't hold out hope for that to happen. Have you gotten through to them through your scrambled comm?"

"Nothing yet," Alvarez replied with a shake of her head.

Melissa jabbed Westsmith between the shoulder blades with the Benelli. "We better not have to walk to the city because of you."

I sheathed the tactical knife.

The ropes rubbing and creaking against tree bark unnerved me. The others did not seem to be affected by it, but my teeth clenched every time one of the bodies completed a slow swing.

"Let's move," I ordered.

We left through the same tear in the fence we had used to get into Building #25, not bothering with stealth anymore. We didn't get more than twenty meters before we encountered our first herd of predators. Green Eyes and her posse of cats ran across our path in full force, anxious to get to wherever they were going.

"Great," Sean observed. "There had to be a black one."

"Superstitious, much?" Melissa asked. "Quit being such a bitch."

Once the cats disappeared around the corner of one of the dorm buildings, we backtracked the route that Dwayne and Harry had used when serving as our guides. Once we were at the Wellness and Recovery Center, we stopped under the awning of the main entrance.

Heinz and Sean grabbed Westsmith by the shoulders and forced him to his knees. He looked back defiantly but kept his mouth shut. That was a blessing, at least. Sean placed the barrel of his M4 to the back of Westsmith's head as insurance of compliance. Westsmith bowed his head and remained still.

The rest of us huddled a few meters away to assess our mission status. Melissa, while listening in with our group, stared at Westsmith with a tight grip on the stock of her Benelli.

"You with us, Melissa?" I asked.

"Yep," she replied, not averting her gaze.

Alvarez and Jude looked to me for the next words.

"We have him," I said, pointing out the obvious. "And, as Jude said, we need a lift out. Alvarez, what's the likelihood we can get another Chinook inbound?"

"Hard to say," she replied. "R&R has their resources spread out thin these days. There isn't supposed to be any air support within five hundred miles of Manhattan at the moment."

"Great," Jude shot back. "This asshole took down our only means of getting the fuck out of here?"

"And nothing on the comms?" I asked Alvarez.

"I already told you no, didn't I?" she said with a glare. "The only other radio back to base is the one in the Chinook. The trees took out that antennae."

"So, we're on foot?" Melissa asked.

"Looks that way," Alvarez agreed.

"Going to be a tough hump," I said. "Especially with Westsmith."

"That won't be a problem," someone said from the doorway.

Harry and Dwayne walked over cautiously, stealing glances at our bound prisoner.

"Is he praying?" Dwayne asked of the knelling Westsmith.

"He better be," Heinz answered. "We've lost enough because of this bastard."

"Sticks and stones," Westsmith commented. "Your attitude is unbecoming. It's not the way a soldier should conduct himself."

"Keep your mouth shut." Heinz poked him with his rifle barrel. "You still need to explain how you managed to get those walkers to follow you around."

"Charm and charisma," Westsmith offered before Heinz slapped him in the back of the neck with his rifle butt.

"Still with the jokes?" Heinz spat out. "We lost four good people because of you."

"I'm pretty sure Ms. Lee and Mr. Damon were entirely your fault," Westsmith reminded him.

"Sonofabitch." Heinz raised his rifle to give Westsmith another shot.

"Stop," Alvarez and I said almost in unison.

Heinz lowered his weapon back to his chest.

I approached Westsmith and crouched down in front of him. His head was still bowed, likely more from the blow to the back of the neck than from any sense of prayer to a long-dead god. I lifted his chin so that I could look him in the eye.

"How did you control them?" I asked.

"Do you really believe that you and I are so dissimilar, Mr. Walken?" he asked.

"That's not an answer," I replied.

"No," Westsmith agreed, "but that's all the answer you are going to receive this evening. Ask me tomorrow... maybe my answer will be different."

"You may not make it to tomorrow," Melissa added.

"Full of venom, aren't you? You must have suffered some terrible loss."

"Your limbs are going to suffer a terrible loss if you don't shut the hell up," Melissa warned.

"I am sure that will be the case in any event." Westsmith chuckled. "But I doubt that my demise will come from you. Or any of you for that matter."

"You're a cocky lot, aren't ya?" Heinz asked rhetorically.

"Some may say that," Westsmith answered anyway.

"Enough," Alvarez said. "Let's stay on mission."

Stay on mission?

Bob stood near Harry and Dwayne, almost touching them. He looked between Westsmith and me, shrugging his bony shoulders at our predicament.

What are you going to do about Westsmith controlling FRACs?

I don't know.

I remember a group of children who seemed very keen to listen to you.

The children at the Worcester Art Museum had seemed almost joyous exacting their revenge on the man who had locked them away, tearing the flesh from Roy's body. Hundreds of kids chained behind the doors of a learning annex to die. It only took a few infected children to turn and ravage the others. I could only imagine the terror those last surviving children felt in those moments. But they had satisfied their revenge, and had helped me out in the process.

I thought FRACs were just 'things'?

They aren't people anymore.

Aren't they? You are talking like you think they are.

"John?" Alvarez asked, pulling me out of my conversation with Bob.

"What?" I asked, Bob having disappeared back into the night.

"Can we get your head back into the game, please?" she pleaded. "We need to get back on track and find a way out."

"Oh, I forgot to tell you," Dwayne said. "Alisha has your ride all taken care of."

55

He Who Laughs Last
+80 Days – 2221 hours
19:01:22

Sean and Melissa held Westsmith in the corner of the underground garage. Melissa seemed happy to have her Benelli pointed at the back of his head. Westsmith continued to bow his head with his hands bound in front of him, his lips moving as if in prayer. He looked a bit underdressed without Alisha's robes draped across his shoulders.

"Is this it?" Alvarez asked.

"I don't know, mate," Heinz commented, with his rifle cradled in his arms. "I like it."

Alisha, with Dwayne and Harry following at her heels like puppies, walked over to us from her inspection of the far side of the shuttle bus. She handed me the keys. "All seems to be in order."

"You sure you can spare it?" I asked.

"We have a bunch of shuttles fully gassed up and operational," Alisha assured me. "If this gift can help to conclude our business together, I would say that is a small price to pay. Wouldn't you agree?"

"I would," I replied, extending my hand. "We thank you."

"You are welcome, John," Alisha admitted, slowly extending her own hand from under her recovered robes. "Plus, I have several people and the council members being quite vocal about wanting to help you."

Dwayne and Harry averted their gazes to their feet, smiling.

Alisha put her hand in mine with a light squeeze and held my wrist with the other. "We wish you well."

"And you? Will you and your people be well?"

"We have done okay against the termites so far," Alisha answered, taking a step back. "I think we'll make a go of it for a while longer." Alisha nodded toward our guarded prisoner. "I'll be happy to be rid of him. He's as disruptive as any of the termites. The only difference is that he had free reign of the tunnels. And stole my robes from my quarters." She swished the robes, pivoting her hips to flare the hemline around her. After a few seconds, she let the material come to rest and looked up with a beaming smile.

"Any clues about the termites that followed him around?" Jude asked once Alisha was finished with reacquainting herself with her cloak.

"Of that I have no answers," Alisha said with a shake of her head. "It's a strange thing to believe. Very strange."

Dwayne and Harry both nodded in agreement.

I couldn't help but smirk at the irony of them mimicking what Alisha was doing. It was like she was controlling them, as well.

"These two will show you out onto Hillside Avenue," Alisha advised. "Once out the gate, head west."

"Thank you again, Alisha." I said, moving over to the shuttle for my own inspection.

She gave me a thin smile and nodded, her eyes holding back something. Sadness, maybe? It was difficult to know for sure.

Probably sad to see you go. You are very charismatic and handsome.

I gave him a stern look. He shrugged and put his hands up in the air while I kneeled by the front tire.

Any insight on Westsmith?

I always have insight, John. You know that.

Well?

It seems obvious, as we spoke about before.

Telepathic link to the walkers?

Just like you.

273

I'm not sure that's the same thing.

You are very dense sometimes.

"Walken," Jude called.

"Ms. Sawyer," I called back. I walked back to her and Alvarez, who was pacing as she attempted to raise command on her comm.

"What's up?" I asked.

"What's up with you?" Jude answered with her own question. I suddenly wondered if she caught me *talking* to Bob.

"Nothing," I replied cautiously. "How long is she going to keep trying?"

"Can't fault her for her persistence, I guess."

"She was always like a dog with a bone."

"Probably not the best analogy to share with her. Women don't like to be compared to dogs, even with the best of intentions."

"You're probably right."

"You kidding me?" Jude asked, planting one hand on a thrust-out hip. "I'm always right. You'd do best to remember that."

"Yes, ma'am. I'll try."

"Try harder." She smiled, but the smile was laced with a sadness—and a little fear. Her hand absently rubbed the sleeve where Westsmith's undead acolyte had drooled on her. I wasn't sure if this was better than her preoccupation with the capsule in her neck.

"We'll get you there, Jude," I promised, answering the question I assumed was on her mind. "I don't think Dick would leave us stranded after all of the resources he burned through to get us here."

"Maybe he'll cut us loose," Jude said with worry. "Maybe he doesn't want any blow-back."

"That might matter if anyone was still around at R&R to care," I surmised. "I'm sure, though, he still doesn't want to get his hands bloody. He's got us attack dogs to do that for him."

"Oh," Alvarez cut in with her forefinger pressed against her earbud, "he's got plenty of blood on his hands, I assure you."

"Why? What did he d– "

Alvarez raised her free hand, cutting off my question.

"Yes," Alvarez said into her throat mic. "Alvarez-one-niner-alpha-alpha-tango-niner."

She waited several seconds, not moving. Sean and Melissa looked on with expectant looks. Heinz moved in closer. Alisha and her men kept their distance, standing by the shuttle. Dwayne ran a finger around the casement of the rear driver's side taillight. Harry stared at the concrete joist work in the low ceiling.

"Yes!" Alvarez said in relief. "Copy."

It was then that I realized I should exhale.

"We need a clear route," Alvarez said, then waited several more seconds. "Roger that."

She pulled out a device similar to a smart phone, six inches long by three inches wide and a half-inch thick. She pressed a button on the lower face, the screen lighting up with a surface street map.

"Ready," Alvarez said. "Repeating... Zulu-Alpha-zero-zero-seven-three-X-ray-Lima." She pressed the corresponding key on the touch-screen device with each digit she spoke. The QWERTY keyboard suddenly disappeared to black. A moment later, a surface street map flickered across the screen.

"Got it," Alvarez confirmed. "Waiting for aerial overlay."

The street map minimized into the upper corner of the screen, replaced with a live aerial feed of the area.

"Received." Alvarez said. Four directional arrows displayed in the lower corner of the screen. She used her thumb to reposition the aerial feed from the drone's camera. "Understood. Alvarez out."

"Status?" I asked. "Chinook inbound?"

"Shit," She shook her head. "It's going to be a mine field maze out there. No Chinook. Looks like we are making due with the shuttle. It may be a bitch, but we should be able to thread the needle. Don't expect any armored or air support, though."

"How in the blazes did that just happen?" Heinz asked. "I thought you couldn't use your comm?"

"Apparently," Alvarez said with a shrug, "someone at R&R patched us through using the drone antennae array to bump the signal."

"Lee would've known that," Heinz replied. "Knew way more about R&R's tech shite than the rest of us."

"Yes, she did," Alvarez agreed with a twinge of sadness lining her voice.

It was at that moment that Westsmith broke his silence to let out a bellowing laugh. Its sudden eruption was disconcerting and ran a chill up my arms. Melissa spun the shotgun around in her hands and rammed the tailstock into the base of Westsmith's neck. He pitched forward with his mouth still open, the laugh cut short as he crashed into the epoxied concrete floor. Even with Westsmith unconscious, the remnants of his laugh echoed throughout the garage for a few more strange and uncomfortable seconds.

We needed to figure out a better way of shutting him up. Cracking him in the back of the neck all the time would end up cracking his skull or give him a concussion. Who knew what Dick would say to being delivered damaged property.

At least he was quiet... for the moment.

56

Pearly Gates
+80 Days – 2254 hours
18:28:37

Melissa sat in the captain's chair behind the wheel of the shuttle bus. Her foot pressed lightly on the accelerator to keep an even pace behind Harry and Dwayne. They walked on the main road that cut through the facility property, leading us toward the Hillside Avenue exit. Two more of Alisha's men had joined the front of the column serving as armed escorts.

Quite the arsenal for a bunch of orderlies. Bob sat on the last bench, his legs crossed and stretched out on the cushions. *I am like Rosa Parks before she sat at the front of the bus.*

Aren't you the trendsetter.

Heinz sat in the seat directly in front of Bob, his back against the window. The barrel of his rifle rested on the top of the seat back facing our unusual guest. Westsmith's head was bowed in semi-consciousness thanks to where Melissa had hit him. Flanking Westsmith across the center aisle was Sean with his own weapon resting against his chest with the business end angled toward our prize. The rest of the team had taken up residence at the front of the bus. Jude stared out the window to the darkness behind the driver's chair while Alvarez sat across the aisle clutching the breast pocket of her tactical vest and staring absently at her lap.

Oh, how the mighty have fallen. Bob laced his fingers behind his head. *This is a far cry from that lovely helicopter we enjoyed on the way in.*

Don't remind me.

"John," Melissa said.

On our right was Westsmith's Building 25 and the larger

outdated admin building that cast a looming presence over it. Our four foot soldiers closed in on the wrought iron fence and Hillside Avenue beyond.

"Shit," Melissa muttered to herself.

Outside the fence were hundreds of FRACs. They crowded together five to ten deep in spots, the stragglers that couldn't get to the gate wandering in the street.

"Shut off the engine," I ordered. "Douse the lights."

I pulled the lever next to the driver's chair, opening the bi-fold doors. Stepping down to the asphalt, I patted my Glock and tactical knife without even thinking about it. Dwayne, Harry and the others huddled together between the bus and the swaying, but eerily silent, walkers pressed against the fence.

"They usually like this?" I asked, knowing that this herd of undead was the same as from the drone's live feed.

"They're usually more spread out along the fence," Dwayne said. "They ain't typically bunched up like they are now."

One of the other armed men nodded his head in agreement. "Ain't never been this deep."

"What do you usually do about it?" I asked.

"About what?" Harry replied.

"About dispersing them?"

"Nothing. They get bored and wander off," the fourth man confirmed. "We haven't tried to get through them before."

"Any other ways out?" I asked.

"Of course," Harry offered. "The Winchester gates."

"There's two buses jammed into the gatehouse at Winchester," Dwayne said. "Remember?"

"Oh, yeah," Harry said with a nod. "Sorry."

"These gates swing both ways?" I asked.

Harry snickered at my comment.

The fourth man answered for Harry. "They swing in and out."

A few of the FRACs started to moan and stir along the left side of the entrance. They tried to shift around, but were too tightly packed together. Suddenly, a black and white patched cat slipped through two of the iron bars and raced away down the road. The FRACs surged into the fence for a moment before quieting.

"Gotta love those critters," Dwayne said to no one in particular.

You do not 'gotta' love the vermin.

Be kind, Bob.

I left the shuttle and the Creedmoor men behind. The FRACs on the sidewalk made no noise, content to continue their smooth rocking motion as I approached them. They did not react to my presence.

Maybe things are returning to some semblance of normalcy.

I pulled at two of the vertical bars. They were solid.

The hinges were heavy. They would need to be in order to hold up the weight of the gate and handle the swinging forces for so many years. The bolts holding the hinges to the brick posts were in good repair. There were no cracks in the brickwork.

It should hold for what I had in mind.

57

Bus Stop

+80 Days – 2308 hours
18:14:51

"Is this going to work?" Melissa asked, her seatbelt fastened tight across her chest and lap.

"It's the only passable exit," I replied, standing in front of the yellow line with a basic disregard for all of the rules with this stunt. "Alisha's men will still be able to get the gates closed again behind us."

Dwayne, Harry and the others stood at the entrance, two on each side of the chain. While Harry held the key to the padlock, the others held their rifles at full draw toward the walkers. A couple FRACs reached at them, but the rest continued to stare at us through the iron bars, swaying from foot to foot like a flag in a slight breeze.

They remind me of Dwayne.

Who does?

The FRACs do. Their swaying back and forth.

They're all Tiny Dancer FRACs, I guess.

Well, they will not be dancing for much longer, will they?

That's the plan.

I tapped Melissa on the shoulder. She, in turn, tapped the gas pedal. The shuttle lumbered forward until it was half a meter from the gate. Harry, Dwayne and the other guards still stood between us and it.

I nodded to Harry.

He waved back, the keyring dangling off his middle finger. With a bit of a smile, and assistance from Dwayne and one of the others, Harry jammed the key into the padlock and turned it.

Or, at least, tried to.

The key wouldn't turn in the bottom of the lock. Harry wiggled it and tried again. The key wouldn't budge. The padlock wouldn't open. Rotting arms thrust between the bars and grabbed at Harry's shoulders. He yelped and dropped the keys to the asphalt. The undead arms still clung to his clothing with snagging fingers.

One of the riflemen pushed the barrel of his Winchester 30/30 through the gate and shot one of the walkers point blank in the forehead. Its grip loosened but it didn't fall to the pavement, the mass of living dead pressing it tighter into the iron.

The rifleman took three more FRACS out, doing his best to muffle the shots. Dwayne finally pulled Harry away from the grips of the walkers, even as FRACs were being pushed into the bars by those behind them—like a Play-Doh shape maker pressing out a long star tube. Harry reached for the keyring with his foot, only succeeding in kicking it farther away from his fingers.

"Come on," Melissa complained, unbuckling and standing from the driver's seat for a better view through the windshield. "You need to get out there?"

I looked at the more agitated walkers and how well the perimeter was holding. "Give him a minute."

Harry dropped to his knees and crawled after the keys. One of the FRACs took its cue from Harry and kicked the keyring out of reach. Harry scrambled after them, jutting his arm under the gate in an attempt to get his fingers around the metal.

"Christ!" Alvarez chimed in.

"Just wait," I ordered, hoping that our new friends wouldn't prove my faith in them misplaced.

Harry dropped to his belly and scooted his body closer to the undead herd. He yelled in pain as one of the walkers stepped on his hand. He quickly pulled his hand out and cupped it with the other, getting back up to his knees. He bumped into the front of the shuttle and rocked back and forth.

Dwayne huddled with him with his arms around him.

The riflemen were getting anxious. Their weapons darted back and forth where the walkers were pressed into the bars, raising their ruined voices into more aggressive and agitated snarls. They knew they needed to conserve their ammo, both from a supply point of view and to keep the FRACs from becoming more aggressive.

"They fuckin' lost the key?" Melissa slammed her palms on the steering wheel.

Dwayne stood up and slapped his hand against the windshield. Between his fingers dangled the keyring. I gave him a thumbs-up and pointed to the gate. He smiled in triumph and nodded before turning back to the padlock.

Suddenly, a third rifleman raced over to the others.

"What's this shit?" Alvarez asked.

The third man waved his hand around for a moment before all three sentries ran off down the road, leaving us behind. Harry had gotten to his feet Dwayne's help, both of them looking after the retreating men with confusion. The same could be said for the expressions on our faces.

I opened the bi-fold door. Once the lever squeaked open and the sections of door slapped together, the smell and sounds of the horde assaulted my senses. It was amazing how much the barrier of some plastic and metal helped to keep us from overloading with the rot and rage of the walkers.

Dwayne and Harry met me at the door.

"We're gonna have to bail." Dwayne held the keys out to me. "The termites took down the fence on the south side. We need to get back before we are trapped out here with you."

"Sorry," Harry said without looking me in the eyes.

Dwayne still held the keys out to me. I stepped up into the shuttle again without taking them, making both of them more anxious. Melissa tapped her fingers on the steering wheel. Everyone else except a sweating and murmuring Westsmith—with Heinz staying behind to guard him—crowded behind the yellow tape of the center aisle.

"What's happening?" Jude asked.

Alvarez and Sean nodded the same sentiment.

"The dead managed to tear down one of the fences on the other side of the compound," Melissa told them.

"We have to get Westsmith back to the city," I reminded them—as if any of us needed to be reminded of that fact. "That clock isn't going to stop. We either stay and help or use the distraction to get out. I can't make this decision for any of you. We need a majority."

Jude and Alvarez looked at each other. They locked eyes and something transferred between them that only they seemed to understand.

"We can't leave them to fend for themselves," Jude announced.

"Ms. Sawyer is right," Alvarez added, checking her watch. "We need to help them."

Heinz and Sean nodded their consent.

"Decision made," I said. "Change of plans."

58

Black Friday Rush

+80 Days – 2321 hours
18:01:22

We left the shuttle behind, Melissa having parked its grille against the bulging gate and the FRACs behind it. Halfway between us and the safety of the Wellness Center were several dozen walkers crowded into a horde. They undulated back and forth as a single mass, moving like a flock of sparrows or a school of fish. It was both fascinating and unnerving, thinking that the FRACs possibly had the ability to think in unison—to think as a single body.

"We don't got the firepower to get through that, mate," Heinz assessed.

"No, we don't," I agreed.

"Get up," Melissa snarled behind us.

We turned in time to see Westsmith fall on his hands and knees. His skin had turned an ashen color, beads of sweat on his forehead and blood seeping through his shirt. Sean dipped down and grabbed him under one armpit in an attempt to drag him back to his feet.

"Christ," Sean complained with a grunt, "he's dead weight."

While Heinz and Alvarez watched the walkers with their M4s at the ready, I went back to Westsmith. He stared at my boots, his head bowed and his breathing ragged. I grabbed a handful of the back of his shirt collar and muscled him up to his feet. Westsmith didn't look at me, his eyes still closed and his lips moving without making sound. A line of drool slipped from between his parted lips. Melissa and Sean hooked their elbows under Westsmith's armpits to prop him up.

"Still heavy as shit," Sean said.

"He's full of it, I'm sure," Melissa agreed.

Once Sean and Melissa had a good hold on him, I let go of Westsmith's collar and grabbed his face with both hands. Using my thumbs, I opened his eyelids. While mostly showing white, I did catch a sliver of iris. Both eyes had flecks of faint gold and red at the edges.

Looks to be the same as you, John.

Fucking wonderful. And he's catatonic. So, that's a bonus.

"Sorry, Mr. Walken," Dwayne said as Harry bumped into me. "Harry don't like being out here with the termites."

"Neither do we," Melissa chimed in.

"Need to move, mate," Heinz advised. "The crowd is growing a bit surly."

"Dwayne," I said.

"Uh huh?"

"We need a way back," I told him. "What about the tunnels?"

"No tunnels this far away from the buildings," Alvarez cut in from her position.

"What the lady said," Dwayne said, finding his voice again. "What you see is what we got to work with."

Heinz and Alvarez stepped back toward us, the throng of FRACs shambling across the lawn. A few of them had ventured away from the main group, but still orbited around the herd without completely breaking away from its gravity. None of them seemed too interested in us, only a few of them glancing our way as they wandered within reach.

The Wellness Center was less than a hundred meters from our position. The walkers were circling as a mass on the grounds and parking areas between us and safety.

They look like a stalled hurricane on Doppler radar.

Can we get past them?

Probably, Bob shrugged.

As an experiment, Bob walked toward the closer FRACs and waved his arms around at them. They paid him little attention. Bob turned back toward me and shrugged again. Several walkers stumbled through him, his ghostly state not solid enough to impede anything of mass.

You're useless.

Or, at the very least, ineffective.

With that, he shrugged and disappeared. I was sure he hadn't gone far as he always had the safety of my mind to escape to.

"We go around them," I decided.

I looked at our catatonic friend. "Jude and I will cover the flank. Alvarez and Heinz will drive us forward. Dwayne, you and Harry stay with Sean and Melissa."

"Roger," Alvarez said while Heinz nodded.

Like the walkers, we closed our ranks and started forward.

Immediately, one of the FRACs who had been exploring the world outside the main body of undead lumbered toward us.

"On it," Heinz said, shouldering his rifle.

He stalked the walker with his tactical knife. When the FRAC was close enough, Heinz switched the grip on the knife handle and drove the blade into its eye. The corpse snarled, its mouth agape. Then it suddenly dropped to the pavement. The rest of the undead didn't seem to notice or care. We moved slowly, giving them a wide berth.

"Why are we going toward the dead?" Melissa whispered to herself. "And why is this fucker so goddamn heavy?"

"Eyes up," I reminded her.

We approached the cover of the building. The FRACs were still milling around on the grass in front of the main entry.

"Will we be able to get in through any of the other doors?" I asked Dwayne.

He looked at me, scratching his chin for a few seconds. "We should."

Harry offered more concrete intel. "There is usually one person at a door. Like Sally was. Should be good."

"About time," Melissa said.

Westsmith was coming around from his strange coma. He stood up on his own, allowing Melissa and Sean to loosen their grips. "What happened?" he asked loudly, the expression on his face one of shock and confusion.

"Shut up," Melissa hissed at him in a low voice.

But it was too late. The moaning from the horde grew louder. Several FRACs peeled away from main pack, shambling straight at us. Knifes weren't going to get the job done now. Stealth was no longer on our side.

"Make every shot count," I ordered.

Like the experienced warrior that he was, Heinz dropped to one knee and opened fire. His M4 had been flipped to single shot mode. Every squeeze of the trigger resulted in a headshot and a dead walker. Alvarez stood behind him, proving that she was just as capable.

Sean pushed Westsmith down to his knees.

I pointed to the ground and told Dwayne and Harry, "Down."

They quickly complied, squeezing their eyelids shut and hugging each other as tightly as they could.

The rest of us were in an undermanned, bastardized defensive British Square. Harry, Dwayne and Westsmith were in the middle, close to the ground, as we fired at the onslaught charging at us.

Hope this does not end like the Four Feathers. Do you remember that movie?

Luckily, the undead were not master strategists. They simply charged at us from one direction. Not one word, Bob. While they weren't flanking us from the sides, they were threatening to overwhelm us with sheer numbers. We kept firing, every headshot adding to the rotting human body wall between us. The FRACs next in line tangled themselves in the torsos and limbs of those who fell before them, making them easier targets.

Suddenly, the sound of laughter made the hairs on my arms and neck stand at attention. Even though everyone kept firing, I sensed the hesitation with this new distraction. Having a better sense of what to do—or just out of spite—Melissa stepped out of line and punched Westsmith across the jaw. While she shook out her fingers from the punch, Westsmith tumbled face first into the grass.

The laughter died with him.

"We really need to get some duct tape," Sean muttered.

59

Remember the Alamo

+80 Days – 2346 hours
17:36:03

The onslaught continued.

Everyone had switched to their sidearm.

We were out of ammunition for the M4s.

Over two hundred FRACs lay dead—again—at our feet in a massive crescent moon shaped pattern. Most of them had tried to climb straight over their brethren to get at us, the FRAC-made berm thickest at the center.

More walkers were attracted to the weapons fire. I even recognized a few of the patients from the recreation yard that we had not put down during our botched Chinook exfil. I could only hope that the FRACs in the surrounding neighborhood weren't savvy enough to wander around the perimeter to the breach point these walkers had pushed through. Walkers tended to move in a straight line toward sights, sounds and smells, but I didn't want to rely on that assumption.

We had less than sixty rounds between us, including the 9mm rounds and the shells for the Benelli. The air was filled with spent gunpowder and a mixture of copper and rotting meat.

Do you smell that? Smells like… victory.

Great flick… but shut the hell up.

I fired three times at a trio of local kids to drown Bob's voice out. They collapsed into each other in front of me. One of them, an Asian girl, still had a torn and bloody Hello Kitty backpack strapped to her shoulders as she crashed face first into the grass.

A man in a fluorescent orange vest and concrete dusted blue jeans caught my attention. While the safety goggles covering his eyes were smeared and foggy, the FRAC still made a relative straight bee-line toward us from our left flank. He wasn't alone. A pack of walkers in varying degrees of decomposition followed him out of the darkness.

"Nine o'clock," I yelled.

Heinz and Melissa turned their attentions and weapons left. Melissa's Benelli boomed when Roadwork FRAC stepped to within a couple meters. His face disintegrated against the blast as did the left side of an elderly woman who had been trailing him. As the two bodies dropped to the edge of the pile forming around us, Heinz and I had clear sightlines to take down another pair each as Melissa pumped for her next shot. We continued to fire, blazing through the rest of our ammunition. A series of "outs" were shouted in quick succession and the sound of gunfire ceased.

During a lull in the attacks, we holstered our weapons and pulled our tactical knives in preparation of going hand to hand. Sean stepped in front of Jude and Melissa. Heinz attached his knife to the barrel of his M4, turning his rifle into a bayonet.

"What the hell?" Melissa growled.

"Jude, Melissa," I ordered. "Cover Westsmith and the others."

"Bullshit," Melissa continued.

"All of us have more hand-to-hand experience," I spoke over her. "You'll be the last line to keep them safe."

"If you guys go down," Jude said with practiced practicality, "we're dead, anyway."

"Speak for yourself, Sawyer," Melissa argued, wielding her shotgun like a ball bat. It was fast becoming her go-to move when she needed to work close-up.

More of the undead poured toward us from the darkness. The FRACs surged forward again, maybe sensing that we were more vulnerable. Heinz stepped forward and thrust his blade into the eye of the closest FRAC. The eyes were always great soft targets. He withdrew the blade, the eyeball skewered on the tip. A spurt of black goo escaped from the socket now that the eye and optic nerve had uncorked from the head. Heinz flicked off the eyeball with disgust.

A more energetic walker lunged at our position. I stepped forward and side kicked him in the nose. His face caved in and he fell backward into the oncoming dead behind him.

Thank god for rotting flesh and more brittle bone.

While the new FRACs were skirting around the left of the dead body barricade, a couple were still trying to climb over it. Alvarez jammed her blade into the back of one head, then the other. The blade bounced off the second walker's skull, forcing her to drive the knife in at a different angle to sever the brain from the spinal cord. Both bodies stretched over the top of the pile, their arms dangling down on our side.

Three overweight FRACs lumbered toward me. I started toward the female—the largest of the three—her morbid obesity not a hindrance to her pursuit of fresh meat. Instead of pitting my strength against her mass, I side-stepped Mama Cass FRAC and drove my elbow into the back of her neck. The Corps had taught us to use our opponents' mass and momentum against them. She stumbled to the grass.

The two other heavy walkers behind her attempted to walk through me. Their combined weight and tangle of arms drove me to the grass next to Mama Cass FRAC. She snapped her teeth at them while she tried to get her hands under her. The overweight FRACs reacted to my attempts to get them off me, snapping their jaws at my flailing arms. The shorter of the two tried to bite through the material of my shirt sleeve but found the Kevlar blend too durable to bother with.

"John!" Jude exclaimed.

Heinz used his bayonet to spear and thrust away yet another FRAC trying to pile on top of the two already on me. I grunted from the exertion of lifting them off. Mama Cass FRAC inched toward my face, spittle launching from her lips. The other two walkers fought each other, hindering themselves from getting to me first. It took all of my strength just to keep them away from anything vital. Smalls FRAC jabbed an elbow into my side, making me wince. Biggy FRAC growled at my discomfort.

I turned my head away from Biggy FRAC's snapping jaw, coming face to face with Mama Cass FRAC's craning neck and foul breath. Her black gums and crooked blood-stained teeth had chunks of dark meat trapped between them. I pulled back my face to keep her teeth out of reach of my neck. She jutted out her jaws again for a second bite attempt.

An R&R issued black boot slammed into her skull. It lifted and dropped again with extreme force. Mama Cass FRAC's eyes bulged. The face squeezed, making the lips look plumper. A third thrust of the heel made her head explode, spraying gore all over my face.

Smalls and Biggy FRAC howled as they smelled a different type of blood and meat on my skin. I got my forearms up under their jaws and lifted them away from my face. Cold saliva drooled from their gaping mouths. Their bony fingers raking against my sleeves.

You have to admit that Roanoke & Raleigh produces a good line of designer paramilitary wear.

Heinz's bayonet thrust into Biggy's mouth, inches from my forearm. The walker chewed on the metal for a few seconds until Heinz twisted the blade deeper into his mouth. When the blade finally poked out the back of Biggy's neck, he stopped moving.

Dead weight.

You are a strong man, John. Quit your bitching and start your lifting.

I dropped my forearm to bring Biggy closer before thrusting his body up. He lifted off my arm enough for me to snap my grip into his throat. I hurled him into Smalls, whose lighter frame was no match for Biggy's level of obesity. They collided and dumped onto the ground next to me, sandwiching me between them and the gory remains of Mama Cass.

I scrambled to my feet. Sean was there to get an elbow under my armpit to assist. I spun the tactical knife in my grip and sunk it to the hilt in Smalls neck above the Adam's Apple. He gurgled, spit out black blood and went still. I backed up into the others, all of us surrounding the shaking Dwayne, Harry and Westsmith. We were now surrounded.

Stop.

The FRACs continued to press forward.

My side was bleeding profusely.

Stop! Now!

They did pause, but only for a moment.

When one of them attacked, one of us would jab out a knife to take it out of the picture.

It. Him. Her. You need to get your pronouns figured out.

Really? You're worried that I am misidentifying the undead?

It is a controversial topic.

I slammed my blade into the ear of a young woman.

Another soft target.

Her baby bump was finally exposed when she crashed into the ground. Something moved under her skin. My stomach churned and my throat felt like burning acid. I swallowed hard to keep what scant food I had in my belly on the inside. Only the gods knew what was still growing in her belly.

The others chipped away at the walkers within reach.

I slammed the heads of two FRACs together. Their milky eyes rolled back as they dropped on the undead pile.

"Not gonna make it," Sean croaked his opinion of the situation. He took out another walker as it tried to claw its way into our dwindling perimeter.

Sean may be right.

"We fight to the last," I called out to both Sean and Bob.

"Roger," Alvarez acknowledged.

"Damn right, mate," Heinz shouted. "Take 'em all to hell with ya."

We were in a hopeless situation. There were too many. I would never be able to get all of them to safety, even with Alvarez at my side. The others were going to die. There was nothing I could do to change that. I tensed my muscles and coiled my legs in preparation to launch myself into the pack of FRACs collapsing our perimeter.

Like you did on the island. Just with less firepower.

There was a popping sound from the other side of the horde. More popping sounds erupted in the dark. We strained our necks to find the source. The FRACs around us did, too. They loosened up their advance on us to drift off toward the repeating noises.

The pops weren't military-issued rifles set to single fire.

It reminded me of my childhood.

I sat on a felled log with my back against a rotted tree trunk, tree branches piled up around me. I stared into the valley from the hunting blind, watching a doe and her two fawns work their way up the natural crease where my ridge and another joined at 90 degrees. After a few minutes, the family made its way up to the ridgeline above me.

They were magnificent creatures, both majestic and fragile, only five meters away. One of the fawns twitched its ears and wiggled its tail as it pushed aside snow foraging for food on this cold November midday. The mother was farther away, but more visible as she was higher on the ridge than her fawns. She looked around, wary of immediate danger. It was a shock to my adolescent mind when her neck ripped open in a spray of red. She squealed in pain and ran off, leaving blood on the snow and her two fawns to fend for themselves.

It took another second before the pop of my father's 30/30 hunting rifle reached my ears from the other side of the ridge.

I heard that same sound now.

The pops from several hunting rifles.

The sound of the cavalry saving us from the undead.

"Looks like we get to go on the offensive, mates," Heinz said, a smile curling up his lips.

We broke formation as the last of the FRACs turned away.

I coaxed the cowering Dwayne and Harry to their feet, while Sean did the same for Westsmith. He definitely looked worse for wear, his skin pale and his hair matted from sweat. We moved to our 2 o'clock around the body barricade, steering clear of the pack of walkers.

"We could drop them from behind," Sean offered.

"Not unless you want to get cut down by gunfire from the other side," I advised.

"Oh," was all Sean replied.

As we cleared the barricade, we could see the muzzle flashes coming from outside the main entrance. We climbed to the portico of the closest ward entrance. Dwayne rapped on the door with a series of knocks and leaned his cheek and hand against the peeling paint. A couple of the FRACs were attracted to us as he tried the knocks again.

Probably prefer a noise that does not put a bullet into their brains.

Alvarez and Heinz drove their blades deep into the soft palate under their jaws. The FRACs fell, making thumping noises in the grass. It reminded me of the sound that Charlie Brown made after missing the football that Lucy always pulled away at the last second.

Harry whined quietly. He wiped his blood-splattered hands against his pant legs. His eyes darted around as he slapped his cleaner hands against the door. It opened suddenly, pitching him forward onto the vintage mosaic tile floor of the lobby. He made that same Charlie Brown sound.

I don't know why pratfalls amused me, but I chuckled to myself as I ushered the others behind the relative security of the heavy door.

60

Rinse Cycle

+81 Days – 0017 hours
17:05:56

We found ourselves back in the ward. This time, the residents of the ward did not rush toward us with open arms. Besides the late hour, all of us were covered in blood and gore. Our previously clean black camos were nothing to want to hug. The others' faces and hands were sticky with sprays and streaks of bodily fluids not their own. I was sure I looked just as awful. Even our weapons were coated with a thin film of the cast offs from the undead.

Dwayne and Harry had fared much better, with only a few drops on their shoulders and arms. Harry whined uncontrollably under his breath as he stared at a particularly large droplet on his sleeve. He hadn't noticed all of the gore smeared on his pants. Dwayne patted him on his other shoulder, careful not to transfer any goo between them.

Westsmith was the only one of us without a drop of blood or gore on him. He looked like he had stepped straight out of a 9-to-5 job ready to take on all comers at the local pub. I think he knew well enough to keep his mouth shut and his eyes averted from any of our glares. He was preoccupied anyway with several flies buzzing around his head. It was satisfying to see him unable to swat them away, his wrists still bound behind his back. He didn't seem to mind, though, as his eyes darted after the pesky insects as they flew synchronistic patterns around his head—odd since I had always experienced flies to keep to their own flight plans.

Two of Alisha's people came in. One of them carried two buckets of steaming water. The other carried two empty buckets of the same type with white towels rolled up inside them. They set them on the tiles in front of us, water sloshing over the sides.

"Alisha says to clean up," the dark-haired bearded attendant told us. "Use the towels with the water and put the dirties in the empty buckets."

"Take the towels out of the buckets first," the other helper advised, not a drop of sarcasm in his voice. Neither waited for an acknowledgement before turning back to the doors.

Once the door closed and their footfalls were no longer audible, Dwayne spoke up. "What a bunch of yo-yos those two are. Right, Harry?"

"Umm hmm." Harry continued to stare at the blood drying on his sleeve.

I took a dry bucket in each hand and dumped the towels on the bed next to us. Without a word, everyone started to disarm and disrobe. Rifles were leaned against the wall, while sidearms in their holsters and knives in their scabbards were placed on the floor next to them. We shrugged out of our tactical vests and, without any modesty, the others took off their compression tops.

There we stood, the men bare-chested and the women in R&R issued sports bras. Each of us took a towel from the bed. I motioned for Jude and Melissa to go to the water buckets first. Melissa refused the special treatment, so Alvarez took her place to soak a clean towel in the steaming water. The two of them took the dripping towels and moved to the empty buckets to sponge off the viscera on their bare skin.

Jude wiped off the gore in deliberate, but fluid movements while Alvarez scrubbed her own skin until it replaced the red of the blood with that of irritation. Sean looked down to the other end of the corridor while Heinz watched over our spotless prisoner, both still men of honor and chivalry.

I assume chivalry is dead within you, Sergeant.

It wouldn't be the only thing that was dying inside me, would it?

So morbid in these early hours, you are.

That's my sparkling personality you're getting a glimpse at.

Oh? Is that what we are calling it these days?

Yep. Bob had kept me distracted enough to be caught completely unaware of the damp towel that slapped across my face.

"Your turn," Jude announced, her clean hands on her curvy hips and a bright smile on her washed face. The fact that she was jutting out her chest was almost lost on me—almost.

"Thanks," I replied, quickly taking the wet rag directly to my face and hair. It was near heavenly, as if hot water was a luxury I had only read about but had never experienced. I savored the moment as the film of the undead shed from my living skin. I ran the towel over the compression cincher and pulled away an ample amount of blossoming bright red to contrast starkly against the white.

"I'm surprised you're being so shy," Jude teased.

"That's me," I replied. "Mr. Shy."

I finally unbuckled the mostly cleaned cincher and let it fall to the tiles. With everyone looking on, I shrugged out of my compression shirt and dropped it into the murky water of the second bucket. After a few more dunks and wrings, I spread out the shirt on the metal footboard where Jude had laid out the others.

"You still look a wreck, John," Melissa commented. "And you're still bleeding out from that stomach wound."

I cleaned more blood from my exposed abdomen. The red on the bleached white towel made me realize that the smell of the blood from my wound must have made me visible to the non-patient walkers during the battle... not the viscera from Mama Cass.

I relieved Heinz from his guard duty. He joined Alvarez and Sean with their baths. Westsmith sat against the wall near the medical supply cabinet and the white dry-erase board. I cleaned my Glock with a dry towel while I watched the back of his nodding head.

"Am I worth it?" he asked suddenly.

"No," I replied without hesitation, continuing to clean the weapon I loved—and hated.

"At least you're an honest man." Westsmith chuckled. "There seems to be a short supply these days."

"There was a short supply before," I admitted. "I'm not sure I ever counted myself among one of the good men."

You want me on that wall. You need me on that wall.

"*A Few Good Men,*" Westsmith said. "I loved that movie. I'd watch the entire movie when it was on cable just to get to Nicholson's monologue at the end. Fantastic."

Bob, did he just hear you?

Maybe you said it, Bob spoke in a whisper.

I'll be glad when this shit is done, I thought back to him.

"It's okay if you don't care for the movie, John," Westsmith allowed. "Prefer a solitary life on the road?"

"I prefer to be able to make my own choices."

"Same here," he said. "Small world."

Alvarez, Heinz and Sean occupied their time with wiping down the weapons and tactical vests.

"You don't have to follow orders," Westsmith said in a low voice. "R&R is not the armed services. And it's not all powerful, either."

"And, yet, here we are."

"Yes." He nodded. "Here we are. But not for long, I suspect."

I decided to leave him to his own assessments. He wasn't going anywhere for the moment.

The others finished cleaning the tiles where the water and blood had splashed from the buckets and set all four buckets near the door. They had wiped down their cargo pants, but nobody was up for dropping their pants for the duration of waiting for them to dry. Luckily, the material that R&R used repelled the blood and gore easily without staining, because going topless was the limit for our group today.

Jude found a pair of robes from the closet next to the bed and offered one to Alvarez, who waved her off. Melissa took it, her modesty coming back in a big way now that there were other options. It was only then that we received visitors. Sean's little girl, Agatha, ventured over to where he was leaning against the second bed's footboard. She was tentative as she approached him, like a squirrel stalking a new and unusual food source.

"Hey there, little lady," Sean said softly.

"Termite?" she asked in a small voice.

"No, sweetie." Sean shook his head. "No termite."

She rushed into his arms, wrapping her own around his neck and burying her face into his still wet hair. She pulled back and rubbed his cheeks. "Scratchy."

"Just for you, kiddo." He rubbed his face against her cheek. She squealed and slapped his bare chest.

A pair of lanky legs and slippers shuffled up to Sean and Agatha. "I'm gonna tell Maria."

Sean looked up at the looming—although in no way imposing—Ritchie. "Okay."

Jude, now sporting her tightly tied robe, corralled Ritchie around the waist. He moaned playfully and slapped his arms together awkwardly, trying to walk away from her unwanted affections. Although he couldn't express it, I think he loved the attention. Jude gave him a kiss on the cheek—one of the loud sloppy varieties.

"Ewww," he said with a laugh, finally getting out of her embrace. "I'm telling Maria."

"I hope so!"

He giggled to the point of doubling over and racing away toward the other end of the ward. Jude turned back to us, a big smile lighting up her face. Sean put a palm up while Agatha continued to hug him. Jude slapped it in a loud clapping high-five.

"Thanks for not leaving me hanging," Sean said. "Especially after today."

"Never, soldier," Jude replied. "Never."

61

Simple Request

+81 Days – 0129 hours
15:53:29

I actually found myself drowsing off when the sound of the door clicking closed snapped me awake again. A moment later, Alisha loomed over me in her flowing robes. She was a much more imposing figure than Ritchie could ever hope to be. The others continued to sleep off their stress, exhaustion and the toll that bleeding off adrenaline caused.

"Sergeant Walken."

"Yes, Alisha?"

"I need your assistance."

I looked up through the folds of her hood, not wanting to get up so soon.

"Please," she asked, holding out a clean shirt.

"What do you need?" I took it in my fist.

"I told you. Your assistance."

"What about Westsmith?" I pointed at the curled up back of our acquired R&R property.

Alisha tapped her bo staff on the tiles lightly. Two of her riflemen came to her side from the doorway, armed and alert.

"They will watch your man."

"Fine." I pulled myself up away from the wall and shrugged into the T-shirt. It had a faded graphic of Mickey Mouse as Steamboat Willy on the front. It was tight, but comfortable.

"Follow me, please." She turned about and left the ward, fully expecting me to obediently tag along behind her.

We went out to the corridor and then into the vestibule with the series of locked doors. Once past the middle entry, Alisha led me to a stairwell that my group and I had not encountered before, pressing into the fire door lock bar and ascending up into the darkness.

A mystery's afoot!

I followed up two flights to a landing between the third floor and what looked like an access door to the roof. We didn't need to go to any higher for Alisha to show me what she wanted me to see. A broken window provided all the view I needed.

Hundreds of FRACs milled about between the wreck of the Chinook and the Wellness Center courtyard. The moon cast them in silvery monochromatic tones, lighting them in both a ghastly and mystical way. There were far more than what we had fought through earlier, with FRACs continuing to wander through the downed section of fence. They stumbled over the wrought iron, some getting their feet caught between the rails as they tried to walk over it. Once inside, the majority of them moved across the grounds to join up with the growing herd.

We were safe in the Wellness Center. The doors were heavy gauge institutional steel. The windows were high and narrow, with bars over the frames on the first floor. Alisha and her people would be able to hold out for the long term. We couldn't stay, though. We were still on the clock.

"As you can see, Sergeant, we have a problem that needs to be cleared up."

"This wasn't our doing, you know."

"That was not my inference. Said simply, I need a man of your caliber. The council agrees."

"You don't have men for this?"

"We have plenty of men," Alisha agreed. "It's not about the number of bodies, but of experience." She waved her hand over the landscape. "This is way beyond our expertise, and we need that fence mended."

I watched the walkers avoiding the abandoned cars in the

parking lots and wandering across the lawns. As I tried to formulate a plan for repairing the downed section of fence, I caught sight of the edge of an aluminum rectangular box, reminding me of something that Alisha had mentioned when we first met her. "I think I can help."

62

Put a Cork in It

+81 Days – 0200 hours
15:22:11

This is a bad idea.

"Another one of my bad decisions, huh?"

I did not say that. Maybe I am using the wrong term.

"I'm sure you are," I replied, free of the shirt that Alisha had given me to wear. After agreeing to help Alisha, I had quietly retrieved my now dry compression shirt, cincher and tactical gear from the ward. "That shirt was definitely a bad idea."

I stalked along the edge of the building away from where the FRACs were congregating. I could see the Faith Chapel that Sean had pointed out when we had been searching for Jude and Melissa.

It was over 24 hours ago. A lifetime.

Sarcasm noted, ghost.

Ghost? You do know I am not a ghost, correct?

"I try not to think about it."

I approached the edge of the Wellness Center, peeking around the rough brick corner while keeping most of my body concealed in shadows. A few of the walkers had separated from the main group. It wasn't typical for FRACs to go lone wolf when close to a larger group.

There are four of them.

I jammed my knife deep into the ear of the closest walker. The young black man dropped at my feet. His death was louder than his assassination.

Looks like you are back to being invisible.

"Good," I whispered aloud, hoping that the wound in my side didn't open up again. "That's why you and me are out here instead of the others."

You and I, you mean. That does not mean that they are not all capable men and women.

"That point has never been in doubt, Bob. But we're out of ammo. They're all exhausted. Christ, people shouldn't have to see what we've seen. Alvarez and Heinz have seen war... that's what they signed up for. Even Sean, having served stateside, probably thought that he was going to be heroic like an action mov–"

I buried the knife high in the throat of a second FRAC. She gurgled as she tried to make her mouth work. When I twisted the blade, she stopped making sounds and succumbed to gravity. She was a nurse in life, still wearing the baby blue scrubs that had been required at her job.

Actually, she was a dental hygienist.

"That's right, Bob," I said. "I forgot that you commune with the undead."

I have helped us out of a few scrapes.

I couldn't deny that he had been as much a resource as he had been an annoyance up to this point.

The other two FRACs kept to themselves around the crash site of the helicopter transport. The Chinook looked forlorn as its blades drooped to the ground, one of the tips buried in the grass. One of the walkers bumped into the dark carbon fiber blade, continuing to push against it in spite of the fact that the blade was digging into the flesh of his arm. The other one wandered away toward the downed section of fence. Some of the other walkers were still caught between the wrought iron rails, only succeeding in sliding their feet to its top edge. Outside the fence small groups of FRACs contemplated whether to wander the neighborhood or join with the growing undead mosh pit.

Back to business, I assume?

"Yes, sir."

Alisha had mentioned that the food and supplies delivery

driver had abandoned his truck after finding out the world had gone to shit. I imagined detaching the rig from the trailer would have required more time than the driver probably thought he could afford. A cursory look into the trailer revealed a haphazard stack of palettes, but not much else. I closed and latched the doors. The trailer sported the new low aerodynamic skirts that most CDL operators had started to add to their rides. It was amazing what inventions higher gas prices led to.

Necessity is the mother of invention.

"So I hear."

Those skirts were important. Otherwise, my plan wouldn't work. I pulled myself up to the rig's driver's door, half expecting to see Sebastian sitting there with his grimy Mack truck ball cap, his faded USMC bulldog tattoo and a welcoming smile.

That was not the case.

My spirits fell. I missed my friend.

Focus, Marine. I am sure he would tell you the same.

"Roger."

The leather and cloth captain's seat was well worn and smelled of sweat, cigars, and stale farts. The passenger footwell and seat were filled with discarded burger wrappers and bags from Wendy's, McDonald's, and Taco Bell. Apparently, the truck driver was not a snob when it came to fast food. My stomach growled a bit. My tour in the Middle East had kept me away from all the greasy processed American fast food chains. My first mission returning stateside should have been a sleeve of salty McDonald's french fries. I couldn't have known that the world was going to end.

As luck would have it, the keys were still in the ignition. We were on private property with gates. security personnel and a low chance that someone would be able to drive a multi-gear truck. Carjackers with a commercial driver license were few and far between.

I turned the key in the ignition. The dash displays glowed into life. The radio blared Spanish music. It took me a couple seconds to figure out how to shut it off. The song wasn't from any remaining operating local radio station, but from a CD in the disc player.

The battery charge was strong, even after so many weeks of being idle. I took a long exhale, pressed my foot onto the clutch pedal, and turned the key over all the way. The rig roared into life, its engine sputtering exhaust out through the vertical stacks behind the cab.

I tested the gas pedal, making the engine roar even louder. I put the rig into gear and pressed the accelerator. The engine strained to get itself and the off-loaded trailer up the incline of the loading dock. Slowly, we crested the ramp and gained speed as I steered the rig down the service road toward the main gates.

Bob appeared in the passenger's seat.

Road trip! We could just keep driving, John. God is my co-pilot.

"Bob is my co-pilot. What could possibly go wrong?"

Exactly.

I shook off the thoughts for escape and steered hard hand over hand toward the open section of fence. The rig bounced up over the curb as we gassed the truck onto the grass. The lack of rain this summer had kept the ground hard enough to take the weight of the truck and trailer. We went diagonally down an incline, the empty trailer threatening to tip. It wasn't top heavy so it eventually settled back down onto its axles.

The self-mutilating FRAC from the crash site shambled toward the truck, along with the one who had changed its mind about leaving the property, bringing several dozen of the undead along with it inside the perimeter.

The power of the people!

We slammed into the wishy-washy FRAC. He took the full

309

weight of the truck's grille, flying off the bumper and sailing several meters ahead into the grass. The tires on the passenger side bounced up and down as we drove over him. His numerous new friends and supporters converged around the front and passenger side of the cab.

The ground at the bottom of the hill—what looked like an almost dried out creek bed—was still spongy with softer earth, sucking at the tires. The rig started to slow as it was being mired in the swampy area of the lawn. I stomped on the gas pedal, churning up chunks of mud. The passenger side sunk deeper into the muck. I downshifted and gunned the engine. More mud flew from the spinning tires. The truck continued to tilt. I could feel the trailer starting to tip. The steering wheel fought me as it dragged counterclockwise. My foot jammed straight-legged onto the accelerator.

I muscled the steering wheel toward the open section of fence. FRACs rushed at us. They pushed their weight against it. More FRACs— attracted to the roar of the engine—were caught under its front axle. The bodies under the wheels were either helping or hindering our traction—it was difficult to tell. In the end, it didn't matter.

The trailer tipped first, dragging the cab along with it. Bob continued to sit calmly in the passenger seat, even as the food wrappers flew around him. The passenger window suddenly imploded as the night stars were replaced with grass, mud and metal. We slammed to a stop, my hands in a death-grip on the steering wheel to keep me from hurling through the cab.

Always buckle up for safety.

My leg was still jammed into the accelerator pedal, the tires spinning and the engine straining. I finally remembered how to bend my knee, taking my foot off the gas pedal. The engine instantly quieted. I released my grip off the steering wheel and fell against the center console.

I flexed my fingers.

My shoulders ached. My right leg throbbed from the impact. The angry bees were swarming at the base of my skull. I was experiencing a wonderfully grim trifecta of painful affliction.

Two walkers slapped against the front windshield.

I sighed, pushing myself off the center console and rolling down the driver's window. I lifted myself out of the cab—now the top—to assess how badly I had missed the opening in the fence. I grabbed the strut for the side mirror and got my boots under me.

Standing on the sidewall of the sleeper section of the cab, I could see the damage. A trail of deep parallel tire tracks marked my haphazard attempt to get the truck into position. FRACs swarmed the overturned rig. Bob and I had crashed into a brick and concrete support post on the left side of the downed fence. The trailer had wedged between the posts, leaving those FRACs caught in the fence crushed underneath.

I walked the length of the trailer's sidewall with the dead slapping against the chassis and roof. The roof may not hold as well as the wrought iron rails would have, but it would work for the interim.

"Shit, Bob," I said as I limped back to the rig. Yep, I had definitely fucked up my leg. It wasn't broken, but I had jammed up my knee and ankle. "It actually worked."

Did you have any doubt?

I had to laugh at that, knowing that I have had several conversations with him in our R&R concrete cell that centered on this topic. "I'm nothing but doubts."

Well... it was a job well executed.

I continued to laugh, only stopping when my stomach wound started to send daggers of pain back up to my brain. It was only then that I wiped the tears from my eyes.

The horde of FRACs had wandered away from the Wellness Center toward us, shifting their attentions to our exploits. They were now scattered across the lawn on this side of the entrance roads, working their way around the trees and the downed Chinook.

The cats had returned, too. Some of the FRACs peeled away from the herd to wander after the cats. They did nothing to attack the felines, just interested enough in their darting antics to distract them from us. It reminded me of the day that Holly had come to Rainier Island. Back then, the undead had no interest in the pack of rabid wild and domestic canines that had attacked them, even when the larger coyotes dragged a couple of the walker to the ground and ripped off their limbs. The green-eyed leader of this herd of cats looked at me, meowed, and dropped to her back to roll around in the grass—even as walkers stomped past her.

I envied that fucking cat.

I guess we should make our way back to the Center, huh?

"We will," I replied in agreement as he snapped me out of my revelry. "We have to make one stop before we do, though."

63

Taking Stock

+81 Days – 0215 hours
15:07:59

I scaled down the open door of the trailer to a spot where the walkers hadn't managed to converge yet and limped my way over to the helicopter crash site. The leg didn't slow my progress but my knee was painfully grinding bone against bone which couldn't be good.

Once at the fuselage, I pulled my way up into the open side door behind the cockpit. The metal echoed with my steps, the interior like the stomach of a dead relic. The slight tilt of the deck put extra pressure on my right leg, but I muscled my way to mid-cabin using the hand holds on the sidewall.

A heavy-duty nylon duffle poked out from a cubby under the row of benches where Alvarez's team had sat during the inbound flight. Half her team was now dead. Killed in a mission that was supposed to be "easy peasy", according to her. I patted the bench and grabbed the bag before moving farther down the cabin.

I flapped the duffle open when I got to a storage locker. The crash had warped the door enough for me to slide three fingers under one edge and give it a yank. I ripped the door off the hinges and tossed it across the cabin, a metallic thud resounding through the cabin as it slammed into the opposite wall.

Jackpot!

The ammunition locker was still full of all the magazines we needed for the M4s, Berettas, and my Glock. There were even several boxes of shells for Melissa's Benelli. I packed the duffle tight, not worrying about the weight. As long as the straps held— which they were designed and manufactured to do—I would be fine.

After straining to close the duffle's zipper, I reloaded my Glock and pocketed several magazines, slung the heavy load across my shoulders like a rucksack, and made my way to the rear deck. I slapped the red release plunger and listened as the Chinook's batteries buzzed the ramp's motors to life. The ramp extended and descended, stopping when it touched the ground. Easier to walk out than climbing back out from the side hatch.

Are we there yet?

"In a few minutes."

Not all of the stragglers of the herd had made their way to the truck at the fence line, close enough to be attracted instead to the whine of the hydraulics of the ramp. They snarled at the ramp, but took no notice of me. I pulled the Glock and tactical knife anyway.

With the closest of the walkers cocking their heads at the pale blinking amber and green lights of the ramp hydraulic controls and the rest of them spread out across the lawn, I walked past them into the night without incident. My knee struggled with the weight on my shoulders, making my limp more pronounced. The rattle of my cargo did make some necks turn in my direction, but they were quickly drowned out by the wind rustling through the trees. Suddenly, a human scream pierced the night. When another scream came, all the FRACs turned and staggered toward the rig like drunken marionettes.

"Help!" the voice yelled.

"Are you shitting me?" I asked myself. The Wellness Center was close. The helicopter crash, the overturned truck trailer and the growing throng of walkers was behind me.

"Help me!" the voice screamed again.

"Goddammit," I whispered. With a sigh and a hike of the duffle bag, I turned around and headed back toward the fenceline.

64

Every Tom, Dick, and Harry
+81 Days – 0241 hours
14:41:26

I chambered a round in the Glock before I moved toward the truck. The FRACs had moved toward the back of the open trailer where the screams were loudest. I flanked wide to the right for a better view of the rear deck. The right-side door had remained locked in place, serving as a pony wall for whoever was inside. Luckily, the rear of the trailer was not completely overrun yet. I limped closer, passing by the oblivious undead around me. Some reached out and scratched at my duffle, but most ignored me completely.

The wooden pallets had overturned when the trailer had gone over. They made a crisscross pile of jagged wood stakes and obstacles. It was difficult to see where anyone was hiding in there. I whistled in three sharp bursts, hoping the walkers weren't bothered by it.

Nothing.

I chanced whistling again, a pudgy FRAC next to me looking straight at me. I put the Glock against his throat and squeezed the trigger. Blood sprayed from the back of his head, his singed skin having muffled the report and muzzle flash.

A head popped up from behind the snarled pile of wood.

"Harry?" I said out loud without thinking.

"Nah?" he replied in a whisper, realizing a lower voice was more beneficial when hundreds of hungry undead were within earshot. I motioned for him to come toward me.

Another pair of walkers sniffed their way around the edge of the trailer. One of them bumped into me. It snarled at the space between us, annoyed at me for being a barrier it could not see. Once the second FRAC rounded the corner, they snarled at each other. My tactical knife slid easily into the first walker's ear. I pulled out the blade as he dropped, having ample time to drive it into the second walker's empty eye socket. He fell on top of the other.

Harry approached the doors.

Even with the FRACs milling around, I chanced speaking. "We have to go. Now."

Harry shook his head.

I grabbed him by the back of his neck and pulled him against the closed door. "We go now or I leave you. Your choice."

He continued to shake his head, but the rest of his body ignored his higher rational brain functions and found the courage to climb over the door. I lifted him over the rest of the way and we moved away from the doors. Unfortunately, more FRACs had arrived. They covered our left flank, lumbering after us—Harry, specifically—and cutting off the escape route back to the loading docks.

The FRACs were funneling us in on both sides, leaving only the corked-up section of fence at our backs. The Wellness Center loomed ahead of us a couple hundred meters away. In our way was the downed helicopter, a parking lot, the courtyard, and the hope that someone would hear us quickly enough to let us in before we were overwhelmed by the undead.

65

Floating in the Ocean

+81 Days – 0301 hours
14:21:00

It seemed like we were two bobs in a sea of rotting flesh and a terrifying murmur.

Don't forget about me. That would add up to three Bobs.

"Not that kind of bob, Bob," I said.

Harry looked at me with a crease in his brow.

I pointed him at a slot where the FRACs were thinnest. He hesitated, but I grabbed him by the bicep and ran him through alongside me. Two walkers moved to intercept us, but they each got a bullet in the face for their trouble.

The gunshots had attracted other FRACs. The closest ones were collapsing our clear tunnel to the Wellness Center. We were running—literally—out of options. With a terrified Harry in tow, the weight on my shoulders from the duffle, the shooting pain from my right knee, and only so many rounds for the Glock that would attract twice the number of FRACs for every one of them I killed, I could only see one recourse.

"There!" I pushed Harry to our 10 o'clock. He stumbled, but recovered quickly enough to keep from having his calves clawed at by a walker crawling along on its belly.

Harry practically fell up the ramp, his shoes slapping on the metal deck. I followed and slapped the glowing red button on the hydraulics console panel. The pistons whined and the ramp lifted up from the grass. Three walkers managed to get their arms through before the ramp lifted into the closed position. As a result, their severed arms slid down the ramp and bumped off my boots.

"Shit. Shit. Shit." Harry stumbled along the closed incline of the ramp, clawing at the slats in the metal to keep from sliding to the deck.

With only the blinking colors of the console panel beside me, and the intermittent moonlight coming in from the side hatch, my enhanced vision could only make out dark lumbering silhouettes. A moan rose from the moving shapes bunched up at the front of midship, more squeezing out of the cockpit. I had locked us in with a bunch of walkers. With only the hatch open for ventilation, the air quickly became stifling with the stench of the dead. Every snarl expelled rot from their lungs. Every movement puffed out the stink trapped inside their clothes.

"Stay still," I ordered.

It was unfortunate that Harry was the reason why the FRACs were so motivated to get to the rear of the Chinook.

"It's going to get loud," I warned him.

"Good," Harry whimpered. "Kill the termites!"

I attached the tactical light to the Glock and flicked the on-switch—lighting up the FRACs. There were seven walkers. Four men and three women.

Are you taking a consensus?

"Not now, Bob," I said, scanning the faces of the dead. Each growled more loudly as the beam flitted across their cloudy eyes. My heart sank. I couldn't explain why.

"Cover your ears."

"Nah."

I braced my senses as I squeezed off the first round. The retort boomed through the confines of the Chinook's fuselage. The first shot evaporated the face of a young woman in a dusty rose silk blouse and a black pencil skirt. Her heels were long gone from her ensemble and her nylons were in ruins. Her straggly and matted long auburn hair looked worse. She collapsed.

The others looked her way as her body thumped against the floor, but they continued toward us. I slipped off the duffle. It banged against the deck, the contents rattling as they shifted. The groans became growls as they reacted to the new sound, but they quickly dismissed the noise as decidedly nonhuman. They craved hot blood and flesh, not metallic mass.

Focus. They are like sharks smelling a drop of blood in the ocean.

"You want blood?" I asked, letting loose three more shots.

The echoes from the Glock were deafening, ringing in my ears. The three FRACs I shot fell to the deck. Harry screamed, covering his head with his biceps over his ears. The remaining ones rushed at the sound of Harry's voice. They closed the distance at a surprisingly quick shamble, taking me off-guard.

My next shot went wide and sparked off the fuselage.

The lead walker reacted to it and launched himself straight at me—actually at the source of the last muzzle flash. I brought up my knee and I drove the heel of my sidearm down, catching his head between them and crushing it with a sickening crack.

Sharp pain stabbed out like hot daggers from my knee into the surrounding muscles. I lost my balance and fell against the ramp. As my back slammed against metal, I fired again.

The next dead FRAC's head and shoulders landed between my legs. His fingers instinctually curled up in the fabric of my cargos before the light went out altogether in the base of his brain.

Harry screamed again. Hands slapped against metal. My neck ached, a collective of revving buzz saws to match the hundreds of FRACs swarming around the outside of the transport. I may have let out a yelp of pain.

The last female, a small statured woman of Asian descent, crawled across the calves of the dead walker between my legs. She reached out at Harry, her lips peeled back showing a black mouth with only a few teeth left. She still had her incisors.

That is all you need for rending muscles.

I kicked her.

"Fuck!" My knee erupted in new agony. Spittle flew from my lips.

She righted herself and continued stalking Harry.

Harry pistoned his legs wildly at Tokyo Rose FRAC. In his effort to ward her off, his kicks only served to make him lose his footing on the ramp. He slid closer to her fingers and gaping mouth.

"Ahh," he cried, desperately thrusting his sneakers against Tokyo Rose's face.

Her remaining teeth were not faring well against Harry's foot attacks. The canines that were so important for biting into living flesh were suddenly gone, kicked down her throat by Harry's adrenaline-filled thrusts.

I twisted my body and drove the butt of my Glock into the back of Tokyo Rose's skull. I pistol whipped her until I heard a crack and the heel of the Glock disappeared into her brain.

"Nah. Nah. Nah." Harry pulled himself as far up the ramp as he could. He tucked his feet under him and wrapped his arms around his knees. He cried softly, cringing whenever a slap sounded from the other side of the metal.

"It's okay, Harry," I said to soothe him. "You got her."

"Termite," Harry mumbled.

"Yes," I amended my statement. "You killed the termite."

I squeezed his forearm, feeling his trembling body. Some of that was adrenaline, but the majority of it was the sheer fear of death and the animated dead. Fear of becoming food for ghouls. Or worse, becoming one of the termites.

"You did great, Harry," I said. "Let me check the rest of the cabin, okay?"

He whimpered, not wanting to be left alone.

"Let me make sure we are safe." That seemed a strange thing to say as hundreds of bloody and deteriorating palms slammed against the Chinook's metal skin. "Ok?"

Harry nodded quickly, before he lost the nerve to offer his agreement at all.

I checked the Glock's magazine. Only three rounds left, plus one round in the breach. My right knee throbbed, but seemed okay. Of course, that would only remain true if I didn't continue to brutalize it by thrashing against the undead while shouldering a hundred pounds of ammunition.

Making my way past the dead walkers with the use of the hand bars on the fuselage, I limped toward the forward cabin. It was brighter here, with the moonlight streaming through the open hatch. Luckily, even though it was a good-sized opening, the hatch was high enough off the ground to keep the FRACs from climbing aboard.

Outside, it seemed that every FRAC on the grounds had decided to set up camp around the helicopter. They swayed twenty deep on the port side of the transport around the hatch. I imagined the starboard side was the same.

A low growl came from the cockpit. Something small scrambled into the shadows. I shined my tactical light into the crushed forward compartment, but the shape scurried away under the instrument console. I worked my way inside and leaned against the back of the pilot's seat.

The dead FRACs in the back of the aircraft had taken some flesh off of the dead pilots—surprising since they had been cooling in their harnesses for over a day. The shape growled again from the footwell. It was small.

A child FRAC?

The beam of my light eventually found the culprit. It even had a mask on in an effort to hide its identity. The raccoon put its tiny black hands up in surrender, and then scampered away without giving itself up for further interrogation. Smart animal. Maybe it could go hang out with the herd of cats.

The white metal first aid box was still on the floor. I flapped open the lid and grabbed a roll of athletic tape. Continuing to lean against the back of the pilot's seat, I untied and removed my boot, pulled up my pant leg to my thigh, and used half of the roll of tape to wrap my knee. It reminded me of the pre-game rituals of high school varsity in the locker room before hitting the gridiron at the games under the Friday night lights.

Ah... glory days.

"Not going to be any more of those." I dropped my pant leg and pulled on the boot. I pocketed the athletic tape. Flexing the leg, I still had limited range of motion but had added some much-needed support. I reached up and pulled myself out of the cockpit, trying to use my right leg as little as possible.

The FRACs still milled around outside. They were quieter now since there was no gunfire or screaming to agitate them. The moonlight was waning, replaced with the slimmest of pre-dawn amber blossoming to the east.

An arm wrapped around my chest.

Rot expelled from her lips as she stared at Harry. Her hospital-issued sleeping gown had degraded to sticky soiled shreds. My Glock was pinned in its holster as the former inpatient pressed against me trying to get to Harry.

I spun left as another FRAC managed to hoist itself up through the open hatch. I smashed its fingers into the opening's metal edges with my boot. The skin burst and the muscles oozed out. It fell back into the throng of FRACs outside. I didn't think the walkers were that agile.

My spin caused Hospital FRAC to lose her footing. With my arms free, I straight-armed her in the chest. She slammed into the same jumpseat that Westsmith had been strapped into. Her moans escalated as she tried to get up again. Another institution resident able to see me and keep off my undead radar. Being me wasn't winning any advantages these days.

I unsheathed the knife.

322

"Make it stop!" Harry cried, causing the already moaning FRACs around the hatch to raise their voices in unison.

I plunged the blade into the hollow of the former Creedmoor resident's neck and twisted the handle. She slumped forward in the jumpseat. Pulling the blade and moving quickly to Harry, I clasped my hand across his mouth and gestured for him to be quiet with a finger to my lips. His eyes were wide with panic. It probably didn't help that black goop covered my face or that the hand that held the shushing finger also held the still dripping tactical knife.

After a minute of keeping my hand over his mouth, he slowly nodded. I released him and stepped back. Harry started to speak, but I gave him a stern look and a shake of my head. He clamped his hands over his mouth to keep in the mewing sounds his throat was making, but did nothing to keep the tears from streaming down his cheeks. He had also wet himself, his pajama bottoms dark.

I offered my hand. After a moment, he freed one hand from across his mouth and took it. I pulled him up and led him to mid-cabin where I motioned him to sit down on one of the port side benches. "You okay?" I whispered.

Harry gazed up at me for several seconds. His face went from a scrunched up pensive look to, finally, a slack look of simple exhaustion. His hands dropped to his lap. He nodded his chin to look at his slowly wiggling fingers, which seemed to calm him. When his breathing had returned to a normal cadence and his pounding heartbeat slowed, he whispered, "I peed myself."

"We all do," I replied softly, sitting on the bench beside him

"Nah," Harry scoffed. "Not you."

"How do you know I didn't?"

Harry shrugged.

"Me and a bunch of guys were on a cross-country ski trip in the U.P.," I explained. "Junior year, I think. I was driving because I had the only four-wheeler. Didn't drink coffee back then, and my mom forced me to promise to not let anyone else drive."

"Really?"

"Really. And when I fell asleep at the wheel, we almost went into a two-hundred-foot ravine." I fell silent for a moment, the telling of the tale bringing back a flood of unwanted memories and emotions. I choked them all down. "I was responsible for those guys. I was almost responsible for getting them killed."

"What happened?"

I looked at the bloody stump of the tree branch that had impaled itself through the cockpit's instrument panel and then through my midsection. "We were saved by a tree limb. It wedged into our bumper before we went over. After that, we managed to get everyone out of the Jeep and wench it back on the road. My buddy Louis drove the rest of the way, even though I was too wired to sleep after that. When I went to change, I realized that I had pissed all over myself."

"Really?"

I nodded. "We never talked about it after that."

The slapping on the hull had diminished. Harry had calmed down. I could only hope that I had a better chance that he wouldn't lose his shit out there when we made our last dash to the Wellness Center. Even so, I wouldn't be able to fight my way through the undead with him in tow. He was going to be useless with a weapon, more prone to shooting himself in the foot or me in the back. I couldn't carry him and the duffle, plus take on all comers.

The odds were not in our favor. It was just the two of us, a fairly stripped-down Chinook, and two pristine M240 7.62mm fully-automatic machine guns. Both with a shit load of belt-fed ammunition.

Sometimes I wondered just how stupid I was truly getting.

66

Two Men, A Duffle and a Machine Gun
+81 Days – 0429 hours
12:53:39

I stood at the open hatch. "We need to move, Harry. We can't stay here forever."

Putting the stock to my shoulder, I flexed my finger before pressing it to the trigger. Squeezing the curved thin metal, the barrel erupted in a stream of gunfire. Rounds shattered bone and pulverized rotten flesh, ripping through torsos and heads before the shrapnel chewed up the walkers or grass behind them. Others shambled into the kill zone, stumbling through the twisted limbs of their compatriots and headlong into a strafe of bullets as they tried to get to the source of the noise and flashing lights.

When the weapon emptied, I lifted it from its mounts. The weight was hefty but comforting. My knee, though, was not as on board with my plan as I had hoped. The added weight of the ammunition wasn't going to win me any more support, but that couldn't be helped at this point.

I swapped out the weapon's belt feed with a full one, giving us a hundred more rounds to rip through any undead obstacles. Two other full ammo boxes sat at my feet. I nodded to Harry. "Hit it."

He nodded and tapped the amber plunger, making the ramp descend once again. As soon as the hydraulics hissed to life, he retreated to mid-cabin with his forearms over his ears.

A wave of FRACs lumbered aboard. They were the first to be cut down by a strafe of bullets. The interior of the cabin lit up yellow and orange with the muzzle flashes. Mists of blood and gore splattered onto the ceiling and walls, painting the gunmetal gray with black and maroon. The smell of burnt gun powder filled

325

the cabin, watering my eyes and making it hard to breath.

When the gun stopped firing and the belt exited the right side of the weapon, I quickly fed a fresh one through. While I worked, a hulking Hispanic man in a blue Polo shirt rushed straight at the barrel of the gun. When I pulled the trigger, a flash of yellow evaporated what had been his face a moment before. What remained of his body crashed into the spent brass and the ammo boxes, scattering it all across the deck.

More walkers rushed up the ramp.

Heads exploded. Chests ripped open. Arms were severed from torsos at the socket. Even using controlled bursts, me and the machine gun ate through the rounds too quickly. I backed up to where Harry was curled up against the bulkhead. He had his thumb in his mouth and his other arm doing its best to keep his ear covered. He rocked back and forth, his eyes squeezed shut.

The empty belt thumped onto the deck. I felt around for the last full one that had slid out of reach. Grabbing it and snapping it into place, I fired into the mass of FRACs that were bottlenecked at the ramp. They quickly piled up, creating an obstacle that the other walkers were forced to climb over.

Dead bodies are a great way to build a wall.

I kept firing until all I heard were clicking noises coming from the machine gun. Dumping the weapon to the deck, I shouldered the still full duffle and pulled Harry up to his feet by the arm. "We move! Now!"

I pushed him to the forward hatch. Realizing I was forgetting something, I went back to the ammo locker and stuffed my pockets with more full magazines for the Glock.

The FRACs had flanked to the rear of the craft, all trying to get inside the Chinook through the ramp. Their curiosity allowed us a momentary corridor to escape.

Harry had the sense to climb down. I followed after, the weight of the duffle making me buckle to my knees. Once I got back to my feet, I followed Harry by stepping through the putrid pile of bodies. We made our way around the copse of trees at the front of the helicopter. My Glock and knife were quickly put into service as we encountered straggling FRACs who had honed in on Harry's acrid scent and movement. Once the rest of the undead realized that their prey was outside the helicopter, they gave up on trying to get inside the cabin in favor of slowing chasing after us across the grounds.

Harry was surprisingly quick as he sprinted ahead of me. My legs failed the challenge of keeping up with his panicked pace, but did allow me to target and put down the FRACs angling to intercept Harry. I reloaded the Glock, stopped and shot three of the ones gaining on him. One fell at the back of Harry's feet, making him yelp and run that much faster to get away.

He is the bait? You know what happens to bait?

After emptying the magazine, I reloaded the Glock again and limped after the deserting Harry. "Not if I can help it."

What ever happened to, 'Leave no man behind?'

"Harry's just scared, Bob," I said. "Leave him alone."

As you wish... deserter.

"You're testing my patience." I fired four times at Harry's back, three FRACs losing their footing and skidding to the pavement with another hole in their heads. One of them hit the curb hard enough to snap the jaw off from the rest of his face. The last round fired went wide right and cracked the bark of a tree next to Harry.

Shit.

He cringed and veered away from the splintered tree trunk, zigzagging his way through the courtyard. As Harry moved left I shot the walkers—now more like joggers—to his right. I was trained to use deflection when firing at a moving object. Leading the undead targets, I fired ahead of the walkers so they would shamble into the path of the bullets. Most fell like slow-moving

327

steel ducks on a conveyor at a carnival midway game of chance. Like that game, more walkers seemed to joined the pursuit of the scared Creedmoor resident.

Several FRACs veered toward me, attracted to the Glock's multiple muzzle flashes. In between bursts, they would slow down to wait for more stimuli in order to hone in on their target.

Good to be invisible again.

A boy, complete with the patchy scrub of early adolescent facial hair, got in the way of my sightline of the walkers chasing after Harry. His lips peeled back as he looked directly at me. A gurgling growl erupted from his torn throat, more vibration than voice.

Behind him, Harry had tripped and fallen.

A woman, rollers in her hair and a kerchief dragging behind her by one hairpin, dropped to her hands and knees in order to crawl over to the floundering Harry. His legs pistoned behind him, but his feet couldn't find purchase in the grass and gravel. Hairdresser FRAC grabbed at his ankle with bone-exposed fingers. He screamed, slapping his hand across his mouth a moment later.

Shaggy FRAC lunged at me, his fingers out like talons. I kicked him with my left foot. His face caved in. My right knee collapsed. I fell to the ground, the duffle now under me. The boy still had life in him as he grabbed at my foot. He quickly pulled himself over my calf, his rot carrying to my nostrils from the breeze that was washing over me.

Angling the Glock, I shot the kid in the side of the head. He slumped down on my leg, giving me clear sightlines to Harry's attacker. Using my left forearm as a stabilizer, I lined up a shot that could send shrapnel high into Harry's thigh if I wasn't careful.

Click. Nothing.

I reloaded quickly with a red-striped magazine.

Harry slapped at his attacker, his fingertips getting awfully close to Hairdresser FRAC's open mouth and snapping teeth. I took a deep breath in through my nose and let out a long, controlled exhale through my lips as I squeezed the trigger.

Her mouth was still agape with the hope of biting down on hot human flesh. But, the rest of her head was gone. Her skull, from the ear canal up, was simply gone. The 9mm round shouldn't have done that much damage to a body, even if its balance was off and caused it to tumble before impact.

Hairdresser slumped her dead weight on Harry's legs. He kept one hand over his mouth and tried to push her off him with the other. His hand sunk into the gray matter of her open skull. He recoiled, looking at the ooze on his fingers with wide-eyed revulsion.

I rolled onto my side and got to my feet, the duffle still strapped to my back. The limp wasn't worse, but the pain was. I gritted my teeth, set my jaw, and lumbered forward. Had anyone been looking at me from up-range they would have thought I was just another one of the dead. Especially with the real living dead shambling alongside me.

Another walker in the scattering herd advanced on the prone Harry and his shuddering, twitchy movements. I stopped, lined up my sights, and squeezed the trigger. The walker's head vaporized, the rest of his body crashing to the concrete path. Christ! That is some advanced ballistic tech.

Thirty seconds later, I came upon the cowering Harry. He was curled up in a fetal position, his hand still clamped over his mouth and his eyes squeezed shut against the horrors around him. He kept raising his other hand—still covered in black oozing gore—to his mouth as if to suck his thumb, but pushed it away each time the putrid smell reached his wrinkling nose.

"Ready to go home?" I asked, a few dozen FRACs still making their way to our position. Harry nodded but didn't make an effort to move. I hooked my free elbow under his armpit and pulled him to his unsteady feet. Christ, now I had another hundred and sixty pounds to burden my knee with. I don't know why I was bitching—the strain of the duffle was nothing compared to the particles of glass, wood and metal that had rubbed into my muscles and bones during the museum fights.

Wrapping my arm around his middle, I grabbed Harry's belt and, mostly, dragged him toward the Wellness Center. He didn't look up at the raised center terrace in the middle of the courtyard as we passed it, concentrating on wiping his gooey hand on his shirt. I pulled him up the steps to the portico and pressed him against the left-side door. I knocked the same knock that Dwayne had used earlier. From inside, I could hear yelling and the faint scuffling of a commotion.

I repeated the coded knock.

More yelling came from the other side of the door.

Moans grew louder from behind us.

Harry started to cry, his body trembling. "...termites... termites..."

With my hand still pressed into Harry's chest, I swung around with the Glock. The FRACs crowded around the steps like parishioners waiting to be let in for Sunday Mass. They didn't try to come up to the porch, keeping to the pathway like puppies that didn't know they could climb yet. Suddenly, an aggressive walker in a business suit took a tentative step toward us.

"...termites... termites..." Harry repeated.

I shot CEO FRAC in the mouth, his Type-A personality brains splattering all other the FRACs directly behind him. A woman—also dressed for success—got the tumbling bullet directly to the bridge of the nose. The back of her head opened up as well, sending bone fragments and the last pieces of the metal round into the walker next in line.

The gunshot riled up the crowd of undead, making them realize that steps should hardly be a deterrent to getting to the pops, flashes, and fresh meat under the portico. They pressed onto the lower steps, bumping and snapping at each other.

"...termites...termites!" Harry started banging on the doors in earnest, completely forgetting about codes or protocol.

I holstered the Glock in favor of the tactical knife.

A FRAC ventured to the second step. He received a blade under the jaw for his ambitions. He fell backward into the herd. I half-expected the walkers to lift him up like a lead singer surfing on the raised hands of mosh pit fans, but he quickly disappeared to the pavement to be trampled underfoot.

A seemingly frail old woman in a floral housecoat muscled her way to the third step. She growled at Harry. He responded by pressing himself flatter against the door and slapping his hand against it. The FRACs pressed into her, pushing her to her hands and knees on the edge of the porch.

She crawled across the porch at Harry with surprising speed.

I dropped a knee—the wrong knee—into the back of her neck, driving her face to the concrete. My blade went deep into the base of her skull, severing her spinal cord and shutting down her brain. I grabbed her body and flung her back into the crowd, slamming all of the advancing FRACs off the steps and back onto the pathway. They snapped at what was rammed into them, turning on the body of the old woman and on each other. It was a mindless aggressiveness, each FRAC reacting to the new stimuli. When the body finally fell to the walkway, the frontline of FRACs pressed forward up the steps. They fell forward more than climbed, but four of them now found themselves on the porch.

I put myself in front of them, serving as a barricade between Harry and the undead. I switched the grip on my tactical knife and swung it into the first walker trying to regain its feet. My blade went deep into its brain through the back of the neck.

I drew the Glock again. Sights and sounds were the enemy, but, caution and stealth were no longer a luxury we could enjoy. The barrel of the Glock went against the ear of the second FRAC trying to get off its knees. I squeezed the trigger and watched as its head erupted like a bullet through a balloon. The third FRAC was not afforded any protection as metal, skull fragments and gore entered its brain, extinguishing the undead life out of its body.

Slaps from behind me. Growling in front of me.

Caught in the middle... with you.

"I'm a little busy at the moment, Bob," I advised.

Stealers Wheel reference.

"Well done. Kudos to you."

"Termites!" Harry yelled behind me.

I punched the last portico FRAC in the face as he started to get his feet under him. His features caved in with the imprint of my fist, leaving a crater where the bones around the cheek and nasal cavity had embedded into its brain. He regained his feet for a moment before I punched him in the chest. He sailed into the FRACs still trying to get up to us, halting their progress again.

A squeaking noise came from behind me, followed by a loud slam and the click of deadbolts. I glanced back the door... and an empty portico. What the fuck? Harry was gone from the porch, as if he had never existed at all.

I surely hope that is not the case. The lack of Harry's existence would not bode well for the state of your mental health.

That sonofabitch had just abandoned me.

I turned back to the diminished, but still intimidating, herd of walkers in front of me. Without Harry as the mechanical rabbit to propel them forward, these undead greyhounds had lost their reason to give chase. Instead, they started to wander off to the more open grounds of the courtyard.

Once the FRACs had dispersed, I pushed the bodies littering the portico out of the way in order to sit down on the top step. The shuffling of the contents of the duffle served as a sudden reminder that I had carried over a hundred pounds the length of a couple football fields. I would gladly allow someone else to take the weight off my shoulders.

I flexed my knee as I watched the dawn breaking over the eastern sky. I couldn't see the sunrise, but it was evident as the color started to bleed back into the world. The bodies of hundreds of walkers littered the grass and asphalt like the aftermath of a forgotten Civil War battle.

The Battle of Creedmoor.

The door did not open behind me. There was no rattle of chains or the clicks of unlocking deadbolts. There were still unintelligible raised voices on the other side of the metal, but, for the moment, I was content to sit and watch the world wake up for another day. There was no guarantee as to how many daybreaks I had left in me. For all I knew, this would be my last. So, I intended to enjoy it.

The bodies around me continued to hold a buzzing electricity, even after final death. I held out my hand, almost able to feel the vibrations humming through the air between us.

You are getting too nostalgic in your old age.

"Maybe."

Or, maybe, you are getting metaphysical.

"That must be it, Bob," I said in agreement. "Death tends to do that to a person."

As long as you do not dwell too long in it. The fascination of death is a sucking philosophical black hole.

"Even if it's all around me?"

Especially then.

I sat in silence for a few minutes, watching the clouds burn with purples, pinks, reds, and oranges. "It looks like Harry is not that interested in letting me back in," I said once the sun fully erupted into the morning sky, finally getting to my aching legs and glancing once more at the door.

That was a dick move.

I let out a tired laugh at Bob's uncharacteristic vulgarity. "You said it."

I could force open the door, but that would just mean another compromised entry point. Whatever Harry's problem or motivation for locking me out, I couldn't sit on the steps and dwell on it forever.

"Oh, well," I finally announced. "I guess we go back the way we came."

67

In Through the Out Door

+81 Days – 0530 hours
11:52:59

The return to the rear of the Wellness Center was uneventful. Without Harry around to attract the undead, none of the remaining walkers were interested in my movements. I rounded the brick corner at the loading dock. A walker in a puffy vest and an oily ball cap bumped into me. He snarled at the interruption. My knife went into the soft palette under his jaw, the blade visible in the back of his throat.

Three more FRACs wandered around on the platform by the delivery bay roll-up doors, apparently much more coordinated and adept at climbing steps than most of the others in the herd. I pulled my tactical knife from Puff Daddy FRAC's neck, letting him fall between a bush and the brick wall. I whistled loudly twice to bring the others toward me. They couldn't *see* me, thankfully.

I walked toward them as they awkwardly shambled down the steps. The closest one, a male, tripped on the last step and easily fell onto my knife blade. His forward momentum dragged his head off the blade and slammed his face into the concrete walkway. Behind him, a small Asian woman with a smiley face surgical mask hanging off of one ear teetered at the top step. I thrust the knife upward under her chin. The smiley face didn't frown, but her cloudy eyes rolled back to white as she tumbled down the stairs. The last walker was a girl who was still young enough to have her baby teeth. Her neck was torn open, deep enough to see a white sliver of her clavicle. She limped along the walk, bumping into my thigh. She looked up at me, her eyes lacking the typical cataracts. Her irises sparkled as the morning light reflected off the gold and

335

silver embedded within the hazel green.

I returned the knife to its scabbard as she snapped her attention to the sound of the far-off bark of a dog. Holly would be happy to know there were still more of her kind out there. I watched her walk away until she disappeared around the corner of the building before I made my way to the heavy door. Pressing my ear against the metal where the door met the frame, I could hear the faintest of voices on the other side. My guess was that the voices were not in the delivery area.

The question was whether I should damage the door to get in. Or, maybe pull the roll-up door off the tracks to be able to crawl under it. I looked around, the loading bay looking different now that the truck and trailer had been moved. At the far corner, almost out of sight under a snarl of vines, was a caged access ladder bolted to the brick wall. The cage was not big enough to allow me to keep the duffle on my shoulders, but it would be easier than jimmying the doors open. The ascent was cumbersome as I was only able to use one arm and one good leg to hoist up the duffle after me. After a couple minutes, I was at the parapet, dragging the duffle up onto the roof with me.

The delivery area was a single story, flat-roofed addition to the Wellness Center building complex. From here, I could see Ward #4 lined up in parallel with the other dormitories. Were there other residents in those wards, too? There were more people in the Wellness Center than we had seen so far.

Abutted to the receiving bay was a bank of windows overlooking the roof. These windows led into a public corridor in a converted admin wing of the main building. They were not barred with metal like the first floor of the wards. Using my tactical knife, I had an easy enough time slipping one of the window's slide lock. What was more difficult was separating the upper and lower pane due to layers of paint sealing them together. Once opened, I listened for voices or movement. All seemed quiet in this section of the building, even the muffled voices heard from the outside of the delivery door had disappeared. I slipped inside and pulled the duffle in after me. With the light streaming in, it was easy to find my way to the stairwell that led me down to the lobby cross-corridors. I shouldered the duffle and gripped the knife tight as I descended to the first floor. The corridor was empty, but new intermittent voices came from the direction I was trying to get to— Ward #4. Luckily for me, Alisha's men were sloppy with locking doors behind them and I had easy access through the empty wards.

It wasn't until I reached the hallway that led to Ward #4 that I could make out actual conversation. Heinz and Alvarez were shouting at someone. Dwayne screamed. What sounded like one of Alisha's riflemen—Darwin, maybe—countered my team's threats. I counted my pockets for spare magazines before sloughing off the duffle and hiding it under the ward's reception desk.

Approaching the door with caution, I repeatedly heard the demands of "put your weapons down" from both sides. It was when Jude screamed, "No!" did I kick the door in, my Glock drawn.

Heinz and Alvarez snapped their M4s up against the six riflemen training their weapons on them. Peter and Darwin were among them. Melissa and Sean were on their knees with their legs crossed at the ankles and their fingers interlaced on the top of their heads. Westsmith was gone.

"Stop!" Jude yelled again, her arm around Ritchie and the other palm out toward me. Another of the staff held a Beretta aimed at the back of her head.

Dwayne and Harry hugged each other on Melissa's bed, crying.

I felt a sting in the side of my neck.

Exhaustion quickly came over me. The pain in my leg, side and shoulders drifted away. My knee didn't hurt as much, anymore. I dropped to my hands and knees, the Glock skittering away across the tiles.

There it goes...

"We need to hold you for evaluation."

I didn't understand what Alisha meant, but her strange words were the last things I heard before the morning light streaming through the windows turned back to night.

68

Rubber Fetish

+81 Days – unknown

::**

My throat felt like sand had been poured down it through a funnel. There was no saliva in my mouth to swallow the grittiness away. I coughed, but that didn't help matters.

A warm constricting darkness enveloped me, my arms hugging tightly around my chest. The pain in my shoulders—not only from the duffle but from the proximity of walkers—was a constant buzz. I tried to roll my shoulders and flex my arms, only able to twist my torso at the waist. The rest of my upper body was wrapped up tight with heavy bands. My arms weren't just hugging my chest, but pulled across each other and tied behind my back as far as they could be pulled.

I was in a fuck–

...*ing straightjacket.*

"You kidding me with this bullshit?" I yelled into the empty room. The frustration in my voice was quickly swallowed by the padding on the walls, the idea that an echo could survive at all inside this rubber room would be mental fodder for a crazy person.

Apparently, someone considered you to be certifiable.

I twisted my body, slamming both sides against the cushioned wall. Then I jammed my back and head against it. I might as well since I wasn't going to be able to hurt myself. That was the whole point of the room, wasn't it?

"Those ungrateful assholes," I spewed. "Should just kill them all."

That idea would haunt you if you succeeded in carrying it out.

"Mowing down some self-righteous pricks would make me

feel better."

Would it?

"Yes."

Or you would buckle under the weight of an albatross of your own design?

I sighed and slumped my aching shoulders. "Probably."

"Probably, what?" a voice drifted out of the darkness.

With no windows or any source of light except a sliver from a crack under the door, I could only make out the vaguest of forms in the darkness of the opposite corner of the room.

"Do you always talk to imaginary friends when you think you're by yourself?" the voice asked in a humming low tone. "Maybe that's why you were thrown in with me."

"Why are you in here?" I asked, unable to place the voice as anyone I had met while in Creedmoor. My head was still groggy from whatever I had been injected with.

"Me?" he replied with a chuckle. "I may have brought harm to myself and others." He paused for several seconds before he added, "Definitely harm to others."

"Why?" I asked, still trying to place the voice.

"Oh, they all deserved it," he said in a pleasant conversational way, as if we were exchanging baking recipes or comparing the size of the motors under the hoods of our cars, "if that's what you were worried about. Just like you were saying earlier about the folks who stuck you in the neck and stuck you in here." He chuckled again, apparently tickled with his use of repetitive words.

I pulled my arms again. There was no leverage to be had. Arm muscles weren't designed to pull with any pressure from the position they were in. I felt like an alligator.

An alligator?

While I couldn't make out my fellow inmate, Bob's illuminated form stood out in stark contrast with the room around him. He sat cross-legged against the door, his head cocked to one side.

Reminds me of all of the locked rooms we have shared, he ruminated. *So, what is this silliness about alligators?*

"Alligators," I said aloud.

"Crocodiles" the voice asked. "Are we playing word association?"

"No," I replied with a shake of my head that he couldn't see. "I feel like an alligator."

"That's an odd choice. I would rather be a panther."

"I was thinking that I feel like an alligator, is all. I can't move in this straightjacket."

"Aha," he commiserated. "Understood. Go on."

"Alligators have a massive bite force. Over 3,500 psi, if I'm remembering right."

"So... you have a mean bite. I'll be sure to steer clear of you."

"The problem is," I clarified, a smile creeping to my lips, "for as much strength as I have, this contraption easily holds me. Just like the fact that an alligator wrangler can hold the reptile's jaws closed with their bare hands."

"Can they?"

"Sure. Alligators have massive muscles to chomp down with, but the ones that open the mouth are fairly weak."

"Didn't know that. You're a walking encyclopedia." He laughed good-naturedly. "Well, a sitting encyclopedia, I guess."

Yes. John is a fount of knowledge. Bob gestured to the other inmate as if my flesh and blood companion would be able to see and hear him. When the other patient didn't answer him right away, Bob folded his arms. *How rude.*

"You have a name?" I asked the only other real person in the cell.

"Yes," he replied simply.

He fell silent, without offering any more details.

See? Rude.

Maybe, Bob. Maybe.

I took a different tactic.

"Did you actually harm anyone?" I asked.

He remained silent.

"I bet you didn't," I goaded. "Probably all in your head."

Probably. Rude people are a bit full of themselves.

"Hush," I whispered to Bob, then to my new friend. "Just as I thought. You're all talk."

A sudden scraping of woven nylon against another material.

Out of the darkness, a black and white shape appeared.

He lunged at me, his arms as pinned as mine.

I brought my legs up to catch him in the chest.

Wide-eyed, with a scraggily beard with drool matting it down, the man pressed into my legs in an effort to get closer to my face. My back was wedged against the corner where the wall and floor met. My legs bent under his weight, the right knee holding up.

"Ask them," he demanded, more spittle spraying from his lips. "Just ask them. You'll see!"

I bent my knees a few more degrees, like I was using his body as weights for a set of inverted leg presses. His features lit up as he found his face a few inches from mine. The beard smelled musky, reeking of stale soup and a lack of a personal grooming regiment.

He smiled with his proximity to me.

I gazed at his darting eyes, returning his maniacal smile with a pleasant one in return. I shot him a wink.

His exuberance froze as I pistoned my legs out, my unnamed friend's face contorting as he sailed through the room. He hit the middle of the opposite wall. He bounced off with a soft thump and dropped to the less padded floor with a louder thud.

He groaned and rolled onto his side. "You wait and see."

"I'll be right here."

"Done!" he yelled. "Done! Done!"

What is he going on about now?

"I have no idea."

"Done!" he yelled again, with even more fervor.

A loud click.

Blinding light exploded from the quickly opened door. Bob, who had been sitting in front of the door, disappeared as if he had been burned away. My sight was compromised into a gash of white even as I rolled up on my feet. Something or someone knocked me back onto my ass. My shoulder banged against the wall. There were the scurried hissing sounds of canvas on canvas.

The door swished closed and the loud click denoted that it had locked again. The room went back to blessed darkness, even though a tall rectangular blob of white continued to burn into the center of my vision. I blinked it away, the shape retreating from a stark white to softer fuzzy amber. When the blinking shape was only a hazy dot, I opened my eyes fully again.

Bob had returned, still sitting against the door.

Well... that was interesting.

"Interesting wouldn't be the word I would use to describe the shit happening around us."

It has been entertaining. There is no doubt about that.

"That's a better choice of words." I twisted my shoulders and pulled my arms in a renewed attempt to get myself out of the straightjacket. "But we don't have time for this bullshit."

I agree, Sergeant.

No more words were spoken as a wash of blinding white enveloped the room again. I squeezed my eyes shut against it, feeling two bodies slam me against the wall. Hands gripped around loops on my chest and back, dragging me forward into the center of the room.

A third man covered my head with a canvas hood. The darkness returned, without my eyes needing to accomplish it on their own.

Small favors, I guess.

Another shot in the neck.

Goddammit!

As my worldview narrowed, I was lifted off my feet and carried out of the room to whatever new madcap awaited me.

69

Sitting in Judgement

+81 Days – unknown

..**

There was a strange, but familiar murmur coming from all around me. I was still being carried by two large men, their fists wrapped around the loops in the straightjacket that made directing unruly patients easier. I had no idea how far I had been carried.

At least it didn't seem like I was out as long as the first time. And my throat wasn't an arid desert. I continued to be dead weight, the toes of my boots bumping off the floor once in a while. Getting a solid purchase was not in the cards until they walked me up a series of steps. At the top, their footfalls echoed off a hollow platform—wood, from the sound of it. I was dropped into a hardback chair, its legs skidding back a few inches with a screech. The men quickly strapped me to the chair back with a rope or cord across my chest and through the loop straps.

The murmuring ceased as soon as the chair legs came to their shrieking stop. I could feel the presence of many eyes, not just my two looming muscular escorts. Through the hood, I could make out a large shadow flitting across a raised platform, its form flowing and floating back and forth. A deeper silence came over the crowd.

"We are gathered to determine the course of justice in the matter of this man before you," the voice boomed throughout the room.

I had heard that voice before, but my mind was having trouble cooperating due to the aftereffects of the second dose of sedatives. Something was placed around my neck, twine digging into my skin as a placard settled on my chest. A loud murmur rose from the congregation.

I guess you have been labeled as something controversial.

"I'm sure I have," I muttered.

"You see?" the voice proclaimed. "He is disturbed and needs to be committed!"

The hood was snapped from my head.

I blinked the world back into focus and color, the floating pinpoints of light receding quickly. The fuzzy figure stepped back, handing my hood to one of four armed men standing on the stage. The figure took a moment to pull back his own hood. I guess we were both being unmasked today.

Alisha gazed at me. Her slight smile and warm eyes denoted a look of earnest compassion. There was no malice to be found there. She took the bo staff from the same man she had given the hood to. "Hello, John," Alisha said in her soft voice.

Behind her, several dozen men and women looked on from the seats in the familiar auditorium. Four more sentries stood two on each side aisle, their weapons at a half-draw. This facility was, indeed, a madhouse. Or, at the very least, a prison.

"Sergeant John Walken," Alisha spoke in her deeper base voice as she turned and addressed the audience, "stands accused of several crimes. He is a danger to himself, a danger to others, and on the verge of lunacy."

"This is such bullshit," I whispered to myself.

No one is more lucid than you, sir. I will stand as a character witness.

"Thanks," I said.

"As you can see," Alisha's voice boomed as she spun around to me with an accusing finger, "he speaks to the dead as if they are his companions. He communes with the termites that threaten our very borders."

"I plugged up where all your termites were streaming in," I reminded her. "Or have you forgotten?"

Alisha's face softened. "We do remember. And we thank you

for your service."

"So, how about we dispense with the ties?"

Alisha's eyes narrowed and the corners of her lips dropped. "You are unable to understand the concept of what's real and what is not." Her voice had deepened again to address the crowd.

"How do you figure?" I asked.

"It is not for me to figure, as you say," she answered, climbing the steps to the stage. "We have others to bear witness."

"Jesus Christ." I rolled my eyes.

Harry was escorted down the center aisle and approached the stage. He stood at the front of the center aisle in front of Alisha, staring at his wringing hands.

"What say you?" Alisha demanded, banging her staff on the stage's lacquered wood planks. The thud resounded throughout the auditorium.

Her voice sent chills up my arms.

The sharp bang made Harry wince.

"He talks to the air like somebody is there," Harry recited. "Then he left me to be eaten by termites."

"Are you fucking kidding me!" I cursed.

Harry looked away with tense muscles.

A sudden sharp pain erupted at the base of my neck.

"You will remain silent," Alisha warned me as the rifleman on my left returned to his station and gripped his weapon in a half-draw.

All I could do was glare at her. She met my gaze and held it, showing no distress in what she was doing to me.

It's a kangaroo court.

Damn right, it is.

Without looking away, she spoke up. "Thank you, Harry. You are dismissed."

Harry slumped his shoulders. He hurried up the aisle with the armed escorts in tow. He pushed the doors open and exited quickly. Before the doors could close, the bearded man from the padded room entered. He didn't require an armed escort to stalk toward the stage. When he moved to end of the aisle, Alisha put up a hand in a gesture for him to stop. She continued to stare at me, her face contorting into different looks—anger, interest, compassion, duty—taking on several distinct emotions in turn.

"Tell us your tale, Jack," the soft-spoken Alisha asked. "If you please."

"It's just like that nitwit Harry said," Jack started.

"Do not speak ill of your family," Alisha barked in a booming voice, never breaking eye contact with me.

Jack took a step back and started pulling at his beard. "Sorry, Ms. Alisha."

"Then continue."

"He was talking to himself, just like Harry told ya," Jack started again. "Then he demeaned me and my character."

"And?"

"And," Jack finished, "he attacked me."

"How?"

Jack pulled up his T-shirt, showing the angry purple and yellow boot-shaped bruises on his chest. I think I even saw a bit of the tread impression on his skin. Jack turned around for all to see before he dropped his shirt and addressed Alisha. "He kicked me against the wall, then stomped up and down on me before your men came in, Alisha."

A new round of whispers and muttering accusations rumbled through the crowd. One of the riflemen shook his head with a look of disgust. Two of the others tightened their grips on their weapons. One of the guards flanking me moved a step closer.

Alisha's face fell with sadness, her eyes dropping from my face to the floor. "It is unfortunate, but with the evidence that we have heard, we must render the verdict of commitment."

The staff struck the floor.

Alisha glared at me with piercing eyes. "Guilty."

Her bo staff struck the floor, more loudly.

Her left cheek twitched and a deep furrow appeared between her raised eyebrows. "Guilty."

The staff banged against the planks. She spun away from me to address the audience again, but not before I caught the white of her wide darting eyes and her peeled back lips that revealed a wide grin. "The verdict is guilty!"

Jack screamed in agreement, his fists shaking violently toward the stage. Drool dripped from his gaping roaring mouth, several teeth not in attendance along his lower jawline.

Apparently, he is one of Ms. Alisha's staunchest supporters.

As the fervor of the room heightened, many of the onlookers had gotten to their feet, slamming their hands into the seatbacks in front of them. Three of them erupted into a fistfight, unable to process their glee concerning my upcoming commitment. The riflemen on the left aisle had to descend into the rows to pull two of the men off the third.

The bo staff slammed onto the floorboards continually for several seconds until the commotion died down.

"Take your seats," Alisha demanded. "Now!"

The crowd muttered and found their seats. Two of them almost got into an altercation about wanting the same seat, but one sideways glance at Alisha's glares made them forget their quarrel and sit one seat apart from each other. They both put a hand on the armrest of the seat between them, still laying claim to it in a very passive aggressive way.

The staff slammed against the floor four times like a gavel in an unruly court. All eyes met Alisha's, although I could only stare at the back of her head.

"The verdict has been reached," Alisha said with authority. "And with it the sentence is death!"

Shit.

"Shit."

70

Going to the Chapel

+81 Days – unknown

::**

The hood had been pulled back over my head before I was dragged from the auditorium. My Cobra watch was still attached to my wrist, but my wrist was twisted behind my body in the sleeves of the straightjacket... so knowing the time was a moot point.

I hated not knowing the time.

During this transfer, my feet were being dragged across the tiles and down stairwell steps. Either my escorts were shorter or not as strong as the previous pair.

I do not think they realize that you are awake.

They sedated me again?

Yes, John. Please pay better attention.

Sorry.

I accept your apology.

"Don't know why Ms. Alisha needs to make such a spectacle about killing this guy," the pallbearer to my left complained.

"Keep you voice down, bro," the other replied with a whispered hiss. "You wanna end up like him?"

"He did take care of the termites."

"So what? Ms. Alisha says he's unstable. You want him turning on you?"

"What? Turning into a termite?"

"No, idiot!"

"Don't call me an idiot." The reply was somewhat teary and whiny.

"Toughen up, dude," the other one said. "I'm talking about this guy one day flipping his lid. Going on a rampage and killing one of us. Do you want to be responsible for a dead kid?"

"No," came back as almost a whisper.

"Alright, then. Enough chatter about it. Let's get our job done."

"Just happy that we don't have to be the ones."

"To do him in? I'm okay with that, too."

As long as I was in the not-quite-steady hands of these men, I wasn't yet a dead man, yet. There was a strange irony that I had to *play dead* in order to figure out a way to keep from ending up dead. What had they done with the others? I could only hope that they hadn't already been sentenced to death.

They wouldn't have gone quietly. Alisha and her people must have come to the ward with the proverbial olive branch. There was no way that Heinz and Melissa would have been taken so easily— especially if they were still armed. They were always on high alert, especially now. Sean and Jude, on the other hand, trusted the people in this place, having made emotional connections with kids like Agatha and Ritchie. I wasn't opposed to grabbing tight to whatever shred of humanity the world still had to offer, but unfortunately this new world was not ripe for unconditional love.

Those kids... Ritchie... are nothing but unconditional love. They are like FRACs in that way.

What the fuck does that mean, Bob?

They both operate on a very simple level. They are driven by primary motivations.

FRACs stalk the living and feed on them.

Yes, Bob replied simply. *Ritchie and the others are the same, both operating at a blissfully unaware state where the dramas of the world are lost on them. They are the true innocents.*

Probably why Jude and Sean were so drawn to them. The kids, that is. Not the FRACs.

And, maybe reminders of the people they have lost since the fall.

Maybe.

Heinz didn't seem like one who dwelled too much on familial obligations. He probably dreamed of being a mercenary as soon as the first plastic toy gun was placed into his hands. Melissa, while she had lost all of her nuclear family, continued to boil over with so much rage that she couldn't feel any other emotion underneath it all.

Alvarez was somewhere in the middle. She had grown up an orphan, looking to the Corps as a place to belong. She used the Marines to build a surrogate family to replace the one she never knew. Of course, she was happy to have been able to point her angst toward an enemy and squeeze the trigger. She had been the point of the spear. She was typically clinical and cautious, but the months spent under Roanoke & Raleigh's boot dulled the fine sharp edge that the Corps had spent tax dollars to produce.

A door opened and a cool breeze hit my body. Unfortunately, the hood and straightjacket dampened my enjoyment of it.

"Damn," the more dominant escort exclaimed. "It reeks out here."

At least the hood did have one advantage

"Told you before that he took care of all the termites," the more submissive guard replied about my recent exploits. "There shouldn't be more than a couple of them skittering around the grounds now."

"Small favors, I guess. Even the worst of them can do good if pointed in the right direction."

"See? There's one."

We stopped.

I was sandwiched between the two of them as the right guard adjusted his grip.

The familiar retort of a beloved sidearm.

It was followed by a second pop.

At least I knew where my Glock was.

"Jesus! Got it in two," the right guard said. "Right in the noggin. Did you see that little girl's chest blow out?"

"Awesome. Now can we get him to the church on time, please?"

Was that the same little girl I had let go?

My heart sank with the thought of it.

71

Short Staffed

+81 Days – unknown
::**

Another door opened.

This time, the breeze was not of the cool variety. It was damp and hot, smelling of old wood and paper. Paint and lacquer had been used sometime in the distant past to hold the smells together, losing out to the evidential decay that came with neglect and the slow permeation of the elements.

My escorts' feet thudded softly on a carpeted wood floor. Hushed whispers surrounded me. After being half-dragged a dozen or so meters, I was dropped into another chair. These people loved their hard, wooden chairs. This time, with my chin still drooped to my chest, I saw a sliver of the world beyond the black hood. My escorts bound me to the seat with two bungee cords through the jacket's loops. Once they hooked them to the chair back, they stepped away and sat down on benches on either side of me.

"We are assembled," a deep voice boomed throughout the space. It was the same voice as from the auditorium; the same voice that had sentenced me to death.

Alisha.

She continued. "Sergeant John Walken has been sentenced to death for the crimes of neglect, of assault against a trustee of this facility, and for future crimes of insubordination and murder."

"This is bullshit," Jude's voice declared before a clicking of an AK-47 silenced her.

"How do you plead?" Alisha asked.

Did she know I was awake? Or was she simply playacting for her own fantasy fulfillment?

Someone stepped toward me from the front of the aisle. The form blotted out the light. The hood was ripped from my head. I closed my eyes before anyone noticed I was awake, keeping my chin down to my chest. Murmurs rose from those who were assembled. The shadow swished away, allowing me to peek around. Luckily, all eyes were on Alisha's theatrics. Several dozen spectators were assembled in the pews. Jude and my people were seated in the second row to the right side of the aisle, several riflemen training their weapons on them. Their clothes were dry, minus the tactical gear which I assumed Alisha and her men had confiscated.

Alisha dropped the hood onto the first pew and spun around.

I continued to look down with only the top of my head for her to look at—although she seemed too wrapped up in her sermon to notice.

"We have been infested," she said, pointing the end of her bo staff at me. "A single termite that seemed to be of no consequence. Easily destroyed under a heel at any time... now is the time for us to carry out that task... before the one termite turns into many." Each time she paused, her voice changed. It went from that deep masculine gravelly commanding rasp to a high-pitched whine. Then it changed to the soft earnest tone of the Alisha we first met—the woman who had bandaged up my arm with duct tape. "Bring out his accomplice," the masculine voiced Alisha ordered.

I cautioned a look around. From the back of the altar—more like a stage—two of Alisha's men brought out Westsmith. He looked worse for wear, sporting a split lip and blood on his shirt. Jack, my former padded cellmate, jammed a leg into the back of Westsmith's calves to force him to his knees. With a huge grin on his face, Jack pressed a Beretta to the back of Westsmith's skull, forcing his head forward.

"Both need to be eradicated," the softer Alisha said with regret.

Three members of the gallery stood up and stepped into the aisle.

"Come forth," Alisha addressed the three, a look of surprise on her face.

Two of the three stood in front of me, cutting off my view of Alisha. The third stood behind me and the chair I was bound to.

"We plead for leniency for John Walken," Dwayne's voice said.

Dwayne? He was coming to my aid?

"And you all plead the same?" Alisha asked.

"Yes," Sally said, standing next to Dwayne.

"Nah," Harry said nervously from behind me.

I felt one of the bungees loosen from across my chest.

"Sorry, John," Harry whispered in my ear, his voice almost bodiless in my head.

The other bungee loosened.

Sally started her defense of my character. "John Walken could have killed us all when he arrived. He could have killed me instead of protecting me from harm from your riflemen. He put his own safety at risk by using his own body as a shield."

The bo staff banged once against the floor.

"And," Dwayne interjected, "he saved Harry from the back of the delivery truck. He didn't have to go back to get Harry... but he did."

The strap from the right sleeve of the straight jacket slipped a little.

The bo staff banged against the floorboards again.

"We plead for the council to show mercy," Sally said.

Another sharp thud from the bo staff.

I felt pins and needles in my right arm as circulation returned to it.

"Ya gotta understand that Harry can get his facts all twisted around when he's all excitable," Dwayne added. "You know how he is, Alisha."

"Enough!" the scowling Alisha yelled. "Guards, take these three away!"

My two guards stood up and put their hands under Sally and Dwayne's arms.

"Go," Harry whispered to me as the left sleeve fell loose. "Be free."

I rushed out of my chair and shouldered into Sally's assailant. He slammed his hip into the side of the pew, dragging Sally down with him. The other people started to yell, moving away from the melee. The riflemen guarding Jude and the others raised their weapons to full draw, keeping them in a seated position with their hands up as they looked on helplessly.

"Stop him!" Alisha demanded.

Dwayne showed backbone by shoving his guard away.

A gunshot.

Splinters appeared on the chair beside me.

I hiked up the extra-long sleeve and grabbed my Glock from Sally's guard, punching his lights out with my left hand. "Stay down, Sally."

She nodded, squeezed her eyes tight, and covered her head with her hands as I crouched over her. I swung up my Glock as more wood splintered on the end of the pew beside me.

I squeezed the trigger.

Jack's grin never faltered as he received a massive hole to the temple. He fell backward from the impact. Westsmith swiped his sidearm before it hit the ground. He drew the weapon on the other unprepared guard, who immediately dropped his weapon to the carpet and raised his hands in surrender.

"Stop!" Alisha pleaded in a high squeaky voice.

Dwayne slapped at his guard with both hands. The guard, in turn, mimicked Sally and covered his own head to protect himself from the onslaught. Harry hid behind the chair. Sally had crawled into the closest pew.

The sleeve threatened to slide over the barrel of the Glock as I grazed one of the riflemen in the arm. He spun toward me. One of the spectators lunged from the pew behind him and wrestled with the rifle barrel. A shot went off, embedding in one of the roof beams. Another onlooker punched the rifleman in the face as the first one took control of the weapon.

Heinz used the distraction to throw a hymnal at one of their guards. It clocked him in the nose, making him crumple inward from the sudden pain. He dropped his Winchester, the gun going off when it hit the floor. The closest of his compatriots howled in pain as the bullet from the discharge went into the side of his foot. As he fell, it was easy for Melissa to take his weapon from his loosened grip. The tide turned quickly as Jude, Sean and Alvarez sprang into action, disarming and subduing the others.

Sean stepped toward the altar, positioning himself in front of the pulpit. He trained his weapon on Westsmith, who slumped his shoulders and lowered his weapon once he realized Sean had him dead-to-rights.

"Stay down," Alvarez ordered.

Heinz quickly grabbed from the top of a stack of dusty linens he found in a corner, ripping them in strips in order to attend to the guard's bleeding foot. The others pushed the remaining riflemen to the ground.

"Enough!" Alisha roared. She stalked up the aisle and swung her bo staff at me just as I finally shrugged out of the straightjacket. Stepping out of its way, I tripped over the chair in the aisle. My ass ended up on its seat, my momentum tipping it backward to the carpet. I rolled out of it onto my feet, thankful that Harry had crawled into the same pew as Sally.

Alisha growled as she thrust the staff into the center of my chest. Pain exploded in my sternum, taking my breath away. She followed with a jab to the throat. I couldn't take a breath in now, either.

The Glock came up. Alisha batted it out of my hand, sending my sidearm into the pew.

"Enough!" Her face contorted in rage.

She slammed the staff into the side of my neck. I rolled down the aisle in defense, staying away from the reach of her weapon. She swung it in a wide arc. I arched my face away from its tip... barely. With the next swing, I grabbed the staff in my right fist. It stung with a shock of pain. We wrestled with her weapon, both trying to gain control of it.

Alisha swung the sleeve of her robe over my head, obscuring my vision. A fist found my face through the material. I fought against the pain of the punch and the blindness from the robe, losing my grip on the staff in the process. The staff found me again, this time across the bridge of the nose. Stars joined the material of the robe in front of my eyes. I tore at the robe. It came away easily in my hands. The staff slammed against the back of my head, pitching me to my knees.

"Enough!" Alisha yelled again.

She was now without her cloak, but no less intimidating in an all-black full-length sleeveless bodysuit. It had seen better days, torn in numerous places across her chest, abdomen and thighs.

Her body had seen better days, too. Across her left arm were series of three parallel slash marks. They were still bloody, just starting to clot up. Her skin had a crisscross of older scarification in the same series of three. Both arms had the same scars, probably going back several years. Her legs were not scarred from cuts. Instead, where the material had ripped away, her flesh was gnarled swirls of melted flesh. It was discolored to an almost white, shiny and slick.

"Termite!" she screamed.

She advanced up the aisle, bringing down the staff with both hands like an axe. I crossed my forearms and blocked the staff between them, absorbing the blow. It hurt like hell. I would be surprised if I hadn't fractured my radius bone

She swung it down again. I caught it with one hand and punched upward with the other, cracking it into two. We both had a half. With a scream, she thrust the jagged end down at me. I redirected it into the carpet beside me with my half of the staff. Alisha's momentum and a well-placed boot to the belly sent her flying over me. Alisha crashed into the aisle behind me. I rolled over and got my feet under me. She let out a guttural animal howl as she lunged at me with her jagged end of the staff.

A gunshot blasted.

Alisha's chest exploded. She and her wooden spear crashed to the carpet, a shattered spine and liquefied muscles oozing out of a massive exit wound in her back.

The chapel went quiet, the echo from the Glock's report finally quelled. Everyone inside the nave looked at who pulled the trigger, me included. Dwayne stood in the middle of the pew with the still-smoking barrel of the Glock. His jaws clenched and unclenched, but his hand didn't waver.

Sally stood behind him in the row, her hand on his shoulder. Harry knelt in front of Dwayne, looking up at his friend in disbelief. After several seconds—maybe a full minute—the others in the pews started talking about what Dwayne had done. They didn't speak to admonish him, but to admire him.

"... can't believe he did it..."

"... that was amazing..."

"... now Dwayne can take on the termites..."

"... I guess he ain't as crazy as Ms. Alisha is..."

"... was... as crazy as Ms. Alisha was..."

Dwayne side-stepped around the still kneeling Harry and approached me. He turned the gun in his hand and held the grip out to me. I took the weapon and returned it to its holster.

"Thanks, Dwayne."

With his hands now free, Dwayne slipped the placard from around my neck. He smirked as he read it before tossing it to the carpet next to the cooling Alisha. Dwayne swallowed hard as he gazed at her body. "You and me have stuff we need to talk about now that the council is dead."

The rest of the people in the church had started to crowd around us, all muttering and nodding their agreement. I looked at Alisha's glazed-over eyes and hoped that the voices in her head were finally silenced. The placard lay between her face and her broken staff, one word written in block letters on it…

TERMITE

72

Council Counsel

+81 Days – 0801 hours
09:21:19

It had been a long night and I still hadn't seen the inside of my eyelids. I couldn't even remember when I slept last. Two days ago? Three? Probably before I was escorted from my comfy concrete cell at the bottom of the R&R tower.

That was definitely the last time you slept. Unless you count all the times that Ms. Alisha sedated you. Those should count, right?

Dwayne waited, looking inquisitively at me with his head cocked to one side. "Do you always talk to yourself?"

"What do you mean?"

"I don't know," Dwayne said with a shrug. "You're moving your lips like you're talking to somebody."

Shit. "Nervous habit, I guess."

"Uh huh," Harry chimed in from one of the other chairs in what used to be an administration conference room. "Lots to be nervous about."

"Why were you in the trailer?" I asked him.

Harry's only answer was to shake his head and look at his arms. They were covered by long sleeve blue thermals. He rubbed them and examined the fabric, flicking away any foreign lint or dust.

"Harry has always been a bit flighty," Sally offered from her seat alongside him. "No offense, Harry."

Harry shrugged again. I imagine he wasn't offended by much, as was evident by his focus on the condition of his sleeves.

"Back to business," Dwayne said, hoping to get the conversation back on track.

"Yes," I agreed. The quicker we redirected the conversation back to whatever it was that Dwayne wanted to discuss, the quicker they would forget about my lip-syncing conversations with Bob. Plus, we needed to get on the road to Manhattan.

"We need you to stay, John," Dwayne explained.

"Yes," Sally concurred. "We need a man like you to keep the peace. Without Alisha and her council, it's going to be chaos around here."

Isn't that the status quo for a loony bin?

Quiet, Bob. "Will Alisha's riflemen try to take over?"

Dwayne and Sally looked at each other for a moment before Dwayne spoke up. "I don't think so. They had it just as bad as the rest of us. As you saw, Alisha could be a little scary and volatile."

"I don't think they liked being forced to do some of the things that Ms. Alisha and her damned council demanded them to be," Sally added.

"Where is the rest of the council now?" I asked.

All three of them, Harry included, looked at each other before returning their attentions to me. Harry quickly went back to his sleeve inspections, while Dwayne cleared his throat to speak. "The council is dead. I killed them."

"When did you do that?" I asked with surprise. "Was there a coup while I was unconscious?"

Sally chuckled. "Alisha *was* the council."

See? Loony bin.

"Ms. Alisha was the council all by herself, John," Dwayne explained.

"Crazy bitch," Harry muttered, now picking at the loose skin around his fingernails. "Split personalities."

"So," I asked the stupid question, already feeling stupid for not realizing that all of Alisha's voices and contorted faces were from a fractured pyche, "she wasn't part of the original administration?"

Dwayne grinned. Sally brayed outright. She slapped a cupped

hand over her mouth, embarrassed by her own laugh. Harry paid neither of them any mind.

"Ms. Alisha wasn't even a trustee," Dwayne said. "She just happened to be the first person the administrators saw to throw the keys at."

"So the crazies did run the asylum," I said, with a mix of sarcasm and mirth.

"Yes, we did," Dwayne agreed. "And, now we need a replacement to Alisha's crazy bulldog personality to keep the rest of us in line."

Is that not the pot calling the kettle black?

"No," I said quickly. Dwayne and Sally's faces fell. "You don't."

"'We don't' what?" Dwayne asked, his eyes narrowing.

"Dwayne," I told him, "you took decisive action against Alisha. I heard plenty of admiration through the chapel afterward. The people are hoping for your leadership, now."

"I was an MTA transit cop once. Took a bullet to the brain after chasing down a punk kid in the tunnels. I wasn't right in the head after that. Why do you think I'm in here?" He told me. "Lost my job. Lost my family. What if lose the people here?"

"The fear of failure will keep you questioning yourself. It will make you a better leader. And, now, you have a real council you can enlist," I said, nodding toward Harry and Sally.

"Nah," Harry countered. "Nah."

"Well," Dwayne said once Harry quieted down. "We'll see who's up for the challenge."

"You'll survive," I said, with some earnestness. "All of you have made it this far already. You don't need me to get the job done. Plus, I have someplace I really need to be, so…"

"Of course!" Sally exclaimed. "Let's get you back to your people."

"Appreciate that," I said, pushing my seat away from the table

365

and moving toward the door.

Sally and Dwayne followed quickly. Harry continued to sit at the oval table looking at his covered arms. Leaving his friend behind, Dwayne led the way through the corridors back to Ward #4.

73

Call to Arms

+81 Days – 0813 hours
09:09:45

At the reception desk, I pulled out the duffle with the ammunition and swung it up onto one shoulder. Once he unlocked the main doors, Dwayne stepped back and let me enter.

Jude and Ritchie sat cross-legged on the floor with their backs against a metal footboard. Melissa was posed the same way on the bed itself, her arms wrapped around her Benelli. Sean was studying the electronic tablet that Alvarez had unlocked earlier, with her looking over his shoulder and pointing at the screen. Heinz was the only one who sat on the edge of the bed across the aisle with his M4 pointed at the wall, away from the team and the other residents of the ward. He was not alone. Partially hidden by the medical supply cabinet, Westsmith lay on his back under the white dry erase board and the scrawls about the undead termites. His arms were over his eyes and his chest rose and fell in a steady rhythm.

"You all ready to move out?" I asked.

"What happened, Boss?" Sean asked instead of answering my semi-rhetorical question. When I answered his query with a stare, he quickly held up the tablet. "Looks like we have a clear corridor for getting ourselves back to the city in one piece."

"Good."

Melissa slid off the bed with her favorite toy. Alvarez and Sean fell in step beside her. Jude got to her feet, leaving Ritchie on the floor. Heinz listened in from his post guarding the prisoner.

"What did you find?" Alvarez asked when they all faced me. "That duffel is R&R property.

"I'm sure R&R has thousands of duffels just like this one back

367

home. I'm sure that Dick couldn't give two shits about this particular duffel. It's what's inside that matters these days."

I dropped the duffel on the floor with a clunk.

Ritchie got up on his lanky legs and waved his hands at me. "I'm gonna tell Maria." Once he made his proclamation, he hugged himself and trotted off to the other end of the ward with a giggle and the intent to tell Maria all about us and our exploits.

"You're in trouble now, John," Jude surmised.

"Guess so."

We could still hear Ritchie's voice from the other side of the ward. Karen replied with her own hen squawk, filling the room with her ode to barnyard poultry noises.

Alvarez unzipped the duffel.

"Christmas fucking morning," Sean exclaimed, his interest finally torn away from the tablet screen. "Where the hell did you get all that, John?"

"I took a detour to the Chinook when I was outside," I told him. My voice had an edge in it. Things had gotten hairy out there. I had been on my own getting Harry back to the Wellness Center. Going out there alone had been my own damn fault.

That was your choice.

I don't want any more deaths on my conscience.

Sometimes, that is not your choice to make. People have a right to make their own decisions.

Sean looked back at his tablet with his jaw clenched. I knew he wanted to say something on the matter, but he swallowed the words. He was probably feeling my humming low-grade wrath. The others felt it, too. Couldn't they understand that I did what I did to protect them?

"That was a bullshit move, Marine," Jude broke the silence as if she overheard my thoughts. "We would have been out there watching each other's backs, you know. Maybe, if we had been out there, Alisha wouldn't have gotten the drop on us."

"Alisha and her goons swept in and forced us to our knees, John," Sean finally added. "You know the feeling of being helpless?"

I remembered having my wrists bound to the posts of a gazebo and left to die. Yes, I knew the feeling of helplessness well. I think Sean recognized something in my eyes because he fell silent again.

"Took my baby," Melissa said, not letting the Benelli out of her hands.

"Took all our weapons," Alvarez confirmed.

"Sorry, John," Jude apologized, coming over to give me a hug and holding on tight. I expected her to pull back after a few seconds, but she held on until I relented enough to hug her back.

Suddenly, smaller arms wrapped themselves around my thighs. I peeked down through what little space Jude had left between us to see Sean's little blond girlfriend Agatha giving me as hard a hug as she could.

"Thanks," was all that I managed to croak out.

"No thanks necessary," Jude answered. She pulled back, moved her hands to my arms, and searched my face. "It's us who need to be thanking you. We were forced to sit here while you risked your life for all of us... and all of them."

The little blond girl didn't follow Jude's lead. She continued to hug me as hard as she could. Once my arms were free, I stroked her hair, and pressed my hand onto the middle of her back. It was massive on her torso, but she closed her eyes, squeezed me harder and smiled. Eventually, she turned her face up to me and gave me a wide-eyed grin filled with baby teeth. She suddenly flitted away to tug on Sean's pant leg. The soldier looked down from the tablet. She wiggled her index finger to get him to hunker down to her level. Taking his cheeks in her hands, she pressed them together. Sean's lips puckered and he started moving them like a largemouth bass out of water. The little girl squealed in delight, filling the space with genuine good cheer. She kissed Sean on his fat lips and bounded away with more laughter. It was infectious as the rest of us started to smile. Heinz and Sean had the biggest grins of all.

As the little girl disappeared among the other residents, Dwayne came in with Harry and two of Alisha's former riflemen. Their body language told me that they were fine following new direction.

Everyone needs someone to rally behind, Sergeant.

I guess the next thing you're going to tell me is that people want to be led.

Well... I was going to tell you that, Bob said with disappointment.

Tough. You'll get over it.

"Sergeant Walken," Dwayne said formally, standing up tall as he squared off in front of me.

"Yes, Dwayne?" I replied in kind.

"Are you ready to try your shuttle run again?"

"I believe we'll be ready in a few minutes," I advised. "We still have to stock up on ammo. Whatever is left is for you."

Dwayne looked at the duffel and then back at me.

"For us?"

"Yes, sir."

All formality went out the proverbial window as he tackled me in a bear hug. "Thanks."

There was way too much PDA going on around here.

74

Refills

+81 Days – 0821 hours
9:01:33

We were soon laden with all the ammunition we could carry, every pocket of our cargos and tactical vests filled with fresh magazines and our weapons reloaded. The comforting sounds of metal slapping against metal and breaches being checked filled the air.

The faces around me in the ward were grim. While there was something to be said for completing this objective of the mission, everyone realized that we still had uncertain miles to go before we got our prize back home—even with the shuttle waiting for us at the Hillside gate.

Dwayne, Harry, Sally and several others stood outside the ward door. I hefted the three quarters full duffel and walked it over to Dwayne. He wrapped his hands around the straps. As soon as I let go, the duffel plunged to the floor and took Dwayne's hands with it.

"Shit!" he exclaimed. "That's heavy."

"Or," Sally offered, "you're really weak."

Harry brayed loudly with Sally's comment, his laugh much more comical than hers. Dwayne gave them a sideways glance, but he had just as wide a smile as they did.

"We're ready to go," I told them. "If you need more ammunition, there is still a bit in the helicopter. Just make sure there aren't any termites nested inside before you go in."

"Ok," Dwayne replied with a nod.

"I would advise getting it inside and distributed sooner rather than later. Better to have it at the ready than having to fight through termites to get more."

The new council nodded their agreement.

I hope they follow through versus forgetting everything you just told them the second we are outside the gates.

"It'll be fine," I said, answering—and hopefully quelling—Bob's concerns and bolstering Dwayne's confidence in his new position as leader of Creedmoor. "Now, let's get back to the shuttle."

75

Exit, Stage Left

+81 Days – 0832 hours
08:50:48

"How did Alisha ever find herself in charge?" I asked Dwayne as we walked up the road toward Hillside Avenue.

Sally and Harry followed closely behind us. Jude and the others were spread out behind the couple, with Westsmith bound in the middle of them. Peter, Darwin and one of the riflemen who escorted me from the padded room to the auditorium closed our ranks and protected our rear. I had my reservations about them, but they had steeled themselves for the task that lay ahead.

It was Sally who answered my questions while Dwayne simply shrugged. "Like Dwayne said, Alisha was shoved the keys when the administrators bailed on us. She literally found herself standing there with the keys to the kingdom."

"Why would anyone follow her?" Sean asked seconds before he veered off to take out a shambling walker who had been bee-lining toward us on a gimpy bare-footed left leg.

"It's hard to say," Sally answered after watching Sean dispatch the FRAC. "She was well-liked by the patients. And the staffers that did stay on found her charismatic enough to follow her orders."

"And she beat that termite to death," Harry said.

"Hell, yeah," Dwayne agreed. "I think that cemented her position. No one knew what to do when it showed up in the ward… until Alisha took a broom handle and bashed the termite's head in."

"Epic," Harry added.

She probably let the walker in to prove herself.

Cynical much?

Me? Never. I just have my ear to the ground, so to speak.

"Why didn't you leave? Jude asked.

"And go where?" Sally answered pointedly before adding in a nervous laugh. "Most of us aren't from around here. I'm not sure where I would have run to."

"And the other staffers?" Alvarez interjected herself into the conversation. "They must be locals."

"Local enough to take two subways and a bus to get here," Sally said. "A lot more difficult when public transportation breaks down. The authorities said to stay put once things went to shit. By the time people started to seriously think about leaving, there was no good way to leave."

"Staffers care for us," Harry said.

"They do feel responsible for us," Sally added. "Some of the people here wouldn't be able to fend for themselves out there." She emphasized *out there* as if the rest of the world was a dark, mysterious and scary place.

She was right. The world *was* a scary and dark place.

Even before the end of the world.

Bob was right, too. Terrorism had grown to an all-time high with plaza and concert bombings around the world. America had continued to be embroiled in a decades-long war in the Middle East and Europe. Celebrities and A-list stars seemed to have been exposed for their predatory sexual natures by major news outlets all within the span of eighteen months. Hurricanes, earthquakes, wild fires and mudslides seemed proof that the earth was rebelling against humanity's atrocities. The dead coming back to hungry life seemed the natural next step for cleansing the world of the parasites that we humans were.

While Darwin moved ahead to clear our path and draw some of the herd away, I moved past Sally toward three walkers. They bumped into each other as they lumbered toward the group. The trio was comprised of two emaciated male walkers book-ending an obese woman of Latina heritage. The skinny walkers had been dark-skinned in life but now, in death, their skin was ashen almost to white.

Two Laurels and a Hardy.

I drew my tactical knife and threw myself like a spear straight into the woman. The blade went deep into her nasal cavity. Normally, the knife would have stopped up against the skull by the guard, but the bone shattered, sending the handle and my fist into her head.

The shock of having my hand wrist deep in her skull was secondary to the putrid smell that escaped from her crushed face. As she dropped to the pavement, my arm was pulled down with her from the suction against my hand.

The two Laurels pressed in on me from both sides, their claw-like hands scratching wildly against my sleeves. The compression shirt's material held up against their assault. They were in an agitated state, but not from my presence.

Maybe they do not appreciate the fat one's smell.

Maybe.

I wrenched back my hand. The knife caught on the edge of the skull as I tried to withdraw. Goddammit!

I head-butted the Laurel on my left, bashing in his head with a single blow. He fell on top of Hardy FRAC, adding more dead weight for me to lift against. It was enough to let me pull my hand back with a crack on bone and the suction sound of her greedy gooey innards. My other hand held the last FRAC at bay by the throat.

Dwayne's shadow fell across my back and the downed FRACs. He swung his hand down and pounded the butt of his handgun into the last Laurel's temple. He retracted and slammed the weapon down again. Then a third time. Laurel stopped struggling against my grip, instead losing the fight against gravity

375

as he fell in a heap next to his companions.

"That's the way to be a leader," I said with a nod.

"Hopefully not too often," Dwayne said with a triumphant smile.

I flicked my hand several times, trying to throw off the disgusting goo that was congealing on my skin.

Harry stepped up to me, careful not to get too close to the pile of bodies in front of me. He held out a pack of baby wipes. "Here."

I stared at the half-used pack. "Aren't those your last ones?"

"Nah." He shoved them against my clean hand until I took them.

"Thanks." It was a gesture of gratitude that only me and Dwayne truly comprehended. Giving me his last pack of wipes was a heroic sacrifice to him. I pulled one out of the pack and started wiping the gore off my arm.

Harry hurried back to the safety of the group and farther away from his decision. Sally hugged Harry as he walked back. He wrapped his arms around her and buried his face into her ample chest. She was obviously not oblivious to his sacrifice, either.

To the victor goes the spoils.

The group was a little scattered. Heinz held his weapon on the kneeling Westsmith. The riflemen continued to take on the larger herd, their inexperience in battle showing but their determination to protect the group evident as well. Alvarez and Melissa were slamming the tailstocks of their respective weapons against several walkers flanking the group. Jude and Sean were doing the same, one on each side of Heinz.

I whistled sharply, but softly. Twice.

Everyone collapsed back into a tight group formation. We moved as a unit toward the Hillside Avenue entrance. The white of the back of the shuttle glistened in the morning light, a stark contract to the older institutional brick columns and black-painted wrought iron fences.

In the light, it was easier to see the disrepair of the entire perimeter on this side of the property. It would hold against the FRACs who might press against it, but not indefinitely. Weeds, tall grass, and trellising vines wove their way around the posts and through the rails. Beer bottles, discarded fast food wrappers, newspaper pages and other debris littered the bottom of the fences on both sides. A single purple knit scarf hung from a low bare branch, its bright color and newer appearance looking out of place.

There were still over a hundred FRACs along the fenceline, crowded deepest around the entrance. The rest of the walkers were scattered more loosely as they spread out for several meters on either side of the main herd.

"Same plan as before," I told them.

The walkers' groans rose in volume as Melissa climbed aboard the shuttle. Sean followed and moved to the back, with Heinz pushing Westsmith inside at the end of his rifle. Heinz shoved our prisoner onto the bench over the wheelwell. Alvarez sat down in the second row opposite the driver's seat.

Jude stood in the doorway with one foot on the lowest step. She waved to Dwayne and the others. Sally waved back. Dwayne smiled and nodded. Even Peter gestured his goodbyes.

Harry, true to form, uttered simply, "Nah."

"Ready?" I asked Dwayne.

Dwayne looked at me, his eyes darting at the immensity of such a simple question. Was he ready to lead remaining people of Creedmoor? Was he ready to take on termites they found their way onto the grounds? Was he ready to see us go?

"You got the gate?" I clarified my question.

Dwayne's eyes locked onto mine, holding my gaze steadily. "Absolutely."

"One day at a time, Dwayne," I offered. "You got this."

"Thanks." He held out his hand and I took it with a firm grip. We shook on his new position at Creedmoor and on the hope for a brighter future beyond simple survival. "Get lost, huh?"

"Sure thing."

"You're welcome anytime. Keep that in your noggin, too."

"You're the boss." I gave him a wink and walked toward the shuttle. Green Eyes spied on me from the tall dry grass, sitting quietly between the separated yellowed shafts with a lazy flick of her tail. I gave her a parting nod. She blinked and started to clean her shoulder.

Fucking cats.

I climbed aboard the shuttle. Melissa turned over the ignition. The walkers snapped their attentions to revving motor and the steady beams of its running lights. She reversed the shuttle until there was a meter of space between the bumper and the gate

Moans became growls.

Swaying became shuffling.

Dwayne and the others on the road skirted the shuttle's front bumper. Dwayne pulled the keyring from his pocket and picked through them until he found the right key. He stooped over and grabbed the padlock.

Sally leaned in to assist.

The riflemen backed up a step, keeping their weapons aimed at the gate. The top of the gate was bowing in toward us from the undead weight. I hoped that it would hold after we were through it.

Harry stood directly behind Sally, his hand on the back of her shirt. He succeeded in pulling Sally away while Dwayne managed to get the chains unlocked on his own. Dwayne held up the chain in one hand and the padlock and keyring in the other for our approval before scooting out of reach of the walkers and the opening gates.

"Now," I ordered.

Melissa pressed on the accelerator, urging the shuttle forward. Harry, Sally and the others side-stepped to the curbs, Dwayne shuffling out from in front of the shuttle at the last second with a big smile on his face and the heavy chain and lock in his hands.

The throng of FRACs pushed the gates toward us as a single herd, the shuttle bumper halting their progress. Melissa revved the engine and forced the gates back out toward the service street. It was a tug-o-war as the weight of the shuttle and the mass of the undead cancelled each other out.

"Gun it," I ordered Melissa.

She slammed down the accelerator, the engine roaring in response. The shuttle crept steadily forward, forcing the FRACs back. The gates were opening, with us trapped between them and most of the FRACs reaching through the wrought iron. The rest of the undead filled in the void in front of us. They clawed and pounded the grille, one going as far as slapping his bloated hand hard enough on the windshield to split the skin and smear blood and pus across the glass.

Melissa reached for the wipers, but thought against it.

"Smart thinking," Alvarez commented from the second row.

The engine red-lined as the shuttle surged forward. The nose of the bus was even with the ends of the gates. Metal gouged against glass and fiberglass as the iron scraped against the sides of the bus.

The FRAC with the burst hand disappeared, quickly crushed under the front passenger-side tire. The ride got bumpier as more undead were ground down under the weight of the shuttle's tires.

"Almost through," Heinz called out from the rear bench. "The ends of the gates are almost at the back."

"We slow down and we get stuck," Melissa advised.

"I know," I replied. "Just keep at it."

The gates scraped along the back of the shuttle, snapping toward Dwayne and his men as the bus cleared the last of the gates. One of the taillight housings cracked. Peter and Darwin rushed toward the gates as the twisting metal swung together. The men braced against them while Dwayne worked to get the chain through the bars again.

The FRACs seeped in from the sides of the gate as the shuttle moved forward. As the weight of the dead filled in the void behind the bus and threatened to push the gates inward, Dwayne clicked the padlock closed and backed away. Sally brought up her rifle as one of the walkers reached through the bars at them.

I hoped she knew better than to discharge that weapon.

She did know better.

Sally and Dwayne stood at the gate for a moment, watching it flex toward them. After a few seconds of staring at the integrity of the gate and the walkers, they retreated quickly up the road back to the Wellness Center. They would still need to fight through a few FRACs to get safely back behind brick and steel doors, but I had hope that they were all capable of getting the job done. Harry may have raised a hand in a hasty goodbye, but I would never know for sure.

"Come on, muthafuckers," Melissa growled through gritted teeth. "Come on." The shuttle's RPMs were still red-lining as it—and Melissa—struggled to get through the rows of FRACs blocking our path to the relative freedom of Hillside Avenue. Melissa shifted to S1 for more torque. The shuttle lurched forward again, bouncing over more soft bodies. The shuttle rocked up, then quickly down as the weight of the tires crushed FRAC skulls like watermelons exploding under the swing of an oversized wooden mallet at a Gallagher comedy show.

A retching sound came from the back.

Heinz covered his mouth as he doubled over in his seat. Nothing came out but the gagging of more convulsive muscle spasms. He and Westsmith were sitting on the seats over the wheel wells. They were definitely getting the full effects of the FRACs flattening under the chassis.

Finally, only two rows of FRACs clung to the edges of the front grill. One of them grabbed at the windshield wiper blades and snapped one of them off.

Well... now you will never be able to get all that goo off the windshield.

I'm surprised the wiper blade lasted as long as it did, I thought back at him.

Melissa let out a war cry as she jammed her foot down on the gas pedal. The rear double tires spun on the viscera of the dead, shooting sprays of blood up the rear side windows behind the wheel wells. The tires finally burned through the bodies and caught traction on clear patches of asphalt. The shuttle shrieked over the last few walkers as rubber burned into the pavement, fishtailing as it surged forward. Melissa compensated, steering into the slide until the shuttle stabilized and sped off in a westerly direction.

"Take that," was all that Melissa gave herself as congratulations for a job well done. I patted her on the shoulder.

Jude was wide-eyed, bracing herself against the back of the seat in front of her. Alvarez sat against the window with her crossed legs hanging off the seat into the aisle. Heinz was doubled over with his head hanging between his knees. Sean held his gaze and his weapon on the now alert and smiling Westsmith.

"That was quite the little adventure, Mr. Walken," Westsmith announced. "I am sure we'll continue to have fun together. Of course, that is nothing compared to what the Creedmoor folks are in for now that you've taken me away from my home."

"You're full of shite," Heinz said, still looking a bit peaked.

"Am I?" Westsmith shrugged. "Maybe. Maybe not. But we all know what happens to termites."

Melissa glanced at me, taking her eyes from the road. "Change of plans?"

I looked between Westsmith's smirk and shining eyes to the others' blood caked faces and slumped shoulders. Jude realized she was rubbing the side of her neck and pulled her hand away. Alvarez tapped her fingers on the seat in front of her, no longer sprawled out on her cushioned bench. Sean continued to glare at the back of Westsmith's head.

"John?" Melissa asked, her grip on the steering wheel ready to turn us back around toward Creedmoor. "We staying or going?"

The gates were holding. Dwayne and the others had retreated to the safety and protection of the Wellness Center. They had plenty of ammunition and the manpower to use it against the undead. Dwayne would do right by the others.

Manhattan was in front of us.

I glanced at my Cobra. We had a little over ten hours to get Westsmith back to R&R, get the capsule defused in Jude's neck, and get the rest of our people back. "Keep going."

Coming in 2019

Sgt. John Walken and what remains of his team
will return to continue their mission in the upcoming

Day Zero: Bad Company

Available Spring 2019

CREEDMOOR

Other Books by Charles Ingersoll

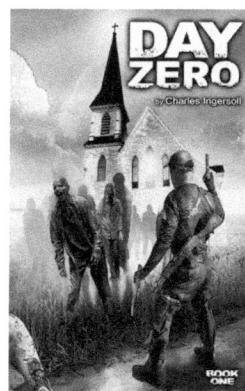  

Check out ***Day Zero*** and ***Day Zero: Gaunt Man*** to get caught up on the John Walken series, plus check out how the undead FRAC apocalypse began in the short story, *In the Beginning, God*, in the ***Reanimated Writers Anthology Undead Worlds***.

Now available in Amazon paperback and in most places where you enjoy downloading eBooks!

CREEDMOOR

About the Author

The love of zombies was in my blood immediately after watching George Romero's *Night of the Living Dead* at a far too young and inappropriate age. That feeling never faded, festering for forty years before that fever finally broke and beckoned me to write my own "Great American Zombie Novel". One story became a second. Two stories became an ongoing series.

I love comic cons, cosplay, movies and television, guns, the Marvel Cinematic Universe, and the supernatural. I currently reside in what the South Carolina locals call the Upstate with the two real loves of my life, my very own real-life Jude (Judy) and a certain fur baby canine named Holly—both straight off the pages of Day Zero universe.

A special *thank you* to my partner in crime, and to everyone who chooses to support my work to ensure that my zombie universe doesn't die a horrible death.

Learn more and be social

To find more information about Charles Ingersoll and the Day Zero zombie book series, please follow on:

Facebook @ https://www.facebook.com/dayzerozombies/

Twitter @ https://twitter.com/dayzerozombies/

Instagram @ https://www.instagram.com/dayzerozombies/

Website: http://www.dayzerozombies.com

bit.ly/dayzerozombies